PAYBACK

A Novel

David Nees

Copyright © 2016 David E. Nees

All rights reserved.

Payback is a work of fiction and should be construed as nothing but. All characters, locales, and incidents portrayed in the novel are products of the author's imagination or have been used fictitiously. Any resemblance to any person, living or dead, is entirely coincidental.

Please visit my website at www.davidnees.com

ISBN: 978-1975893293

Manufactured in the United States

For Carla

*Your support and faith in me makes
all this possible.*

My thanks go out to Eric who has been a source of encouragement and help. Thank you Diana, Ed, Chris for your insightful beta readings. Thanks go to another Ed for your Brooklyn insights. A special *thank you* to my son, David, for your insights in improving the front part of the story. Thank you, Lynnette Nees, for your great cover...as always. And, again thanks to all my family for putting up with my endless soliloquies about the story.

Switching genres (from post apocalyptic to thriller) is a bit unnerving. It's like starting over. But everyone's positive review of the story gives me courage. I hope you, the reader, will find this a good beginning and join me for the ride; many adventures to come.

PAYBACK

"There are two races of men in this world...the 'race' of the decent man and the 'race' of the indecent man." —
Victor Frankl

"Beware the fury of a patient man."—
John Dryden

For more information about my writing, please visit my website at http://www.davidnees.com

Chapter 1

Dan Stone lay on the rooftop under camouflage netting five stories up from a Brooklyn street. He looked through the scope of his rifle down the six blocks to the Sicilian Gardens restaurant. The restaurant didn't have a garden, but it was Sicilian. Owner Vincent Salvatore was a mob Capo and ran his crew out of it.

It was a good day, bright with no wind. In a corner of the rooftop, he could not be seen from the street, and from the air, with the netting, he would look like a pile of debris collected by the wind. Dan had been in position since early that morning. Ignoring the accumulated grime of decades that had collected on the roof and the parapet, he had settled down to wait. Dirt and grime didn't bother him, neither did the waiting. He would wait for as long as it took.

Below, the streets were busy. Store owners had rolled up their metal screens, unlocked their doors, and some had even swept the sidewalk in front of their establishments. From a nearby bakery Dan could smell the enticing aroma of fresh baked pastries. Trucks were pulling up to make their deliveries. People began their shopping. His Brooklyn had come to life.

He studied the restaurant through his scope. The few tables outside were not for customers, but for Vincent and his boys when they wanted to sit in the sun and enjoy the respect and deference they got from those in the neighborhood. Dan was waiting for someone special to show up. Someone he would send a deadly message to.

He had a Remington 700 SPS rifle set up with a bipod. It was one of the best shooting rifles one could buy on the civilian market. It was chambered for a .308 cartridge, almost identical to the 7.62 NATO round. The .308 was a good long distance cartridge capable of delivering a lethal hit out to a thousand yards. After acquiring the rifle, Dan had purchased a heavier match barrel which had been bedded in and floated during the installation. The trigger had been reworked to a light, two and a half pound pull. He had equipped the rifle with a Surefire muzzle break and suppressor. He was using a Leupold 3-20 power scope. The result of these modifications was a quiet and very accurate, lethal weapon. From six stories up, no one would hear a shot over the background street noise.

Now he lay and watched and waited. He had been a sniper in Iraq, so he knew about patience, about waiting. The day before, Dan had climbed to the rooftop and had lasered the distance to the restaurant. He had set the scope adjustments from his shooting notes and was confident in getting the shot right. It was what he had been trained for in the Army: one shot, one kill.

He stood six feet tall and weighed one hundred, eighty pounds. He had a youthful looking face with brown hair and hazel eyes that seemed to darken when he got angry or tense. He was lean and fit and could stand out or fade into the background depending on how he projected himself. His fingers were long and his hands strong and solid, making powerful fists when he balled them up. Growing up in Brooklyn, he had needed to use them many times.

Hours earlier he had gotten up in his Queens apartment, put on his Levi jeans, a black pullover shirt and running shoes. A blue windbreaker completed his outfit. He had a beard, fake glasses and his hair was colored much darker than normal.

He had packed his disassembled weapon and gear in a guitar case he carried on his shoulder. In addition, he had a book bag strapped to his back. To anyone noticing he looked like another marginally employed musician, heading off to try to find some work for the day.

With no direct route available, a circuitous subway ride, into and then out of Manhattan had brought him near to his old Brooklyn neighborhood. He had walked the last few blocks to the building he had chosen. He had let himself into the back stairs doorway at the rear where he had broken the lock the day before.

He moved with a cat-like grace that evidenced balance and power. He was not heavily muscled, rather had a body made strong through a balanced development of core muscles. He looked average, but was more powerful, than men much larger than himself.

Dan's thoughts wandered as he waited. This act was going to change his life. He had plotted revenge for months. The seeds of his decision had been formed after the fire. Now he was at the point of action. A line would be crossed. But, he thought with more than a trace of bitterness, a line had already been crossed when the mob killed his wife, Rita and their unborn child. Still, today would set him on a path of no return. Would he wind up dead or on the run for the rest of his life? In all the months leading up to this point, he hadn't been able to think through that question. Nothing seemed real beyond this act. He still couldn't imagine what might come next when he finished his mission.

What he was going to do was enough. Take the mob apart. *No one makes them pay for what they do. Now I'll bring a bill to them, and they'll pay it in full.*

A small group began to assemble outside the restaurant. Dan studied the men through his scope. With its magnifying power, he could easily see their gestures and smirks as if he was standing next to them. He settled on Joey Batone, one of Vincent's up and coming men. He was brash and aggressive, a soldier working part of Vincent's territory. Joey had directed the group that firebombed the restaurant Dan and Rita had opened.

Standing next to Joey was Angelo "Snake Eyes" Ricci. Balding, in his late thirties, he had the body of an athlete gone to seed—getting paunchy and out of shape but still wielding a lot of power. His squinty eyes gave him a permanently nasty look. The look told you much about his personality. Angelo worked directly for Vincent. He helped provide muscle with Joey. Whenever Joey had something serious to do, he took Angelo along. The word on the street was that Angelo was the one who threw the fire bomb into the restaurant that fatal night.

Dan suppressed the surge of anger that rose up in him. *You're the one. You threw the bomb.*

The group was enjoying the warm spring day sunshine. Through the scope, Dan could see Joey's darting eyes, always looking around to see if anyone was smirking at him—looking for any insults. There was Angelo, looking down at Joey. The others standing there were of no interest to Dan. His scope passed over them without stopping. Then he returned to Joey.

Time for you later. I want you to feel me coming for you.

The cross hairs slid over to Angelo. Dan's world closed in around him; there was nothing now but a tunnel, viewed through the scope. He and Angelo were now linked in a deadly connection. It was as if a thread was attached from his rifle to his target. That thread would be the path his bullet would take. Dan could visualize the track of the bullet from his muzzle to Angelo's head. The world around him faded. There was nothing but him, Angelo, and the deadly link between them.

With the suppressor, the loudest noise would be the sonic boom of the bullet traveling faster than the speed of sound. The bullet would arrive just before the crack of sound. That sharp report would not give any evidence of its source. He slowed his breathing along with his heart rate. He waited as his body settled down so nothing could disturb the rifle's deadly connection to the target. Then he exhaled part of his breath and in between the slowed beats of his heart, he gently stroked the trigger with his index finger. The rifle fired with a kick and a muffled pop. The back of Angelo's head exploded, splattering the pavement behind him with his brains and blood. His body collapsed, the legs going limp as he fell backwards.

Joey dropped to the ground, pulling out his .45. He looked down the long, straight street from side to side. The slight boom didn't register with the pedestrians. It was just one more generalized city noise assaulting their ears each day. But close to the restaurant, people screamed and ran across the street to get away from the body lying on the sidewalk. Fearful of another shot, Joey and the others ran inside. Someone apparently called the police and within two minutes a siren was heard coming toward them.

Dan picked up the spent casing, took his rifle apart and packed it up, along with his camouflage netting. He carefully made his way to the stair entrance, went down the back stairs to the rear door. Reaching the alley, he walked away from the direction of the restaurant with guitar case in hand, headed down a cross street, and in three blocks was down into the subway, catching the train to Manhattan. He looked like someone going about his business, just like thousands of other pedestrians in the city. From Manhattan he created a maze of stops and transfers, finally emerging in Queens, near the north part of Brooklyn. Quietly he let himself into his building and went up to his apartment.

He lay on his bed with his hands folded under his head, staring at the ceiling.

Now it begins. Stretching his arms over his head, he sighed. He didn't know where this path would finally end up, but he had started on it. There would be no turning back.

Chapter 2

Dan married Rita Colletti, his high school sweetheart, right after graduation. Her parents did not approve. They wanted her to marry an Italian boy, preferably from the neighborhood, live only a few blocks away, and provide them with lots of grand children. Marrying Dan changed those plans. Yes, Dan and Rita would live nearby and would have children, but to Rita's parents it was not quite the same.

Shortly after their wedding, Dan's parents were killed in an auto accident in Florida. His only sibling, Lisa, lived out west, having just married her college boyfriend. With his parents gone and his sister half a continent away, Dan felt a deep sense of isolation. His loneliness was softened by his marriage; it gave him a wife and a family. This sense of connection, to Rita and her parents, deepened his love for his wife. She was more than his sweetheart, since his parent's death she had become his lifeline.

He liked cooking and got work at a local restaurant. However, after a few years and feeling stuck with lousy job choices, he joined the army. He and Rita went where the army assigned him. During basic training, his talent with a rifle emerged and a sergeant encouraged him to try out for sniper school.

Dan took to the school and excelled. He mastered the art of camouflage and the intricacies of computing long range shots. The physical part, although challenging, did not slow him down. He had been an excellent high school football player and enjoyed the physical preparation for sport. He had played outside linebacker. He was small for the position, but played with a ferocity that gave him the impact of a much larger player. He had enjoyed the contact and relished taking down larger opponents on the field. During high school he worked tirelessly on his conditioning, forgoing the traditional strength training which focused on the large muscle groups. Instead he adopted a training regime which developed his secondary and tertiary muscles along with the larger ones. The result was a deceptively strong, agile body that resisted injury while being able to deliver devastating blows on the football field.

After graduation from sniper school, he was sent to Iraq. Rita, like many military wives, went back to live with her parents.

In Iraq, he came up against the hard reality of working amongst a population where it was nearly impossible to pick out the combatants from the civilians. Everyone blended in and only his own soldiers stood out, often lethally so. Dan quickly felt the pressure to keep the men on the street safe. Shooting from upper windows and rooftops, he felt responsible if any of the enemy in his field of action was able to strike the men below him.

This sense of responsibility gave him motivation to feel disengaged from his targets. They were the bad guys. They were trying to kill his buddies. They were responsible for the misery of the civilians.

There was a day, however, when a line was crossed.

He had been on a roof, setting up through a break in the parapet. His field of fire was the street ahead of him for six blocks. His team had cleared the street to the point where Dan was now positioned. His job was to look for bad guys as the men moved down the street. There was activity at the corners; people peeked around the buildings, but the street remained empty.

Suddenly a woman emerged from a doorway. She had a child by the hand, a girl about six. Through his scope, Dan saw a belt wrapped around her as the wind blew open her chador. She walked towards the men in the street.

Dan's spotter looked over at him. "You see what I just saw?"

"Some kind of belt?"

"What it looked like to me."

"Call it down to the lieutenant," Dan said. The radio crackled.

The men in the street started shouting at the woman, gesturing for her to stop. She kept coming, one hand up in a pleading gesture, one hand holding on to the child with her.

"She's gonna blow herself and the kid up," Ben declared.

Dan grabbed the radio. "Permission to take out the target."

"We can't tell if she's got a bomb strapped to her. You sure you saw it?" the lieutenant said.

"There's something under her cloak, we both saw it," Dan responded.

"You sure?"

"Christ! How can I be sure, we just got a glance, but we saw something."

"I don't know..."

"She ain't stopping is she? Something's not right."

"Yeah, but if you're wrong, we got a shit storm on our hands," the lieutenant replied.

"We got to do something, she's getting closer," Ben muttered.

"Call it up the line," Dan told the lieutenant.

"Got to get lawyer's permission, back in the states to fight this friggin' war," Ben muttered.

"Maybe they can decide here in HQ, before she blows anyone up." Dan watched through his scope. "Damn."

"What?"

"Someone's calling to her from the doorway she came from. See him? Looks like he's gesturing her to go forward."

He was right. The woman had stopped momentarily and looked around, as if confused. After she looked back at the man, who seemed to be shouting and gesturing her to go forward, she turned and shuffled towards the troops.

"She's using that kid to give her cover." Dan's voice was almost a grunt as he watched through his scope.

He reached for the radio again. "Lieutenant, permission to take this target out. She's going to kill that kid as well as blow some of you up."

"I called the shot back up to the Captain. I don't want to be hung out here."

"Fuck. You'll get everyone killed!"

"Just give it a minute," the lieutenant replied.

"She gets within fifty yards, we gotta do something. Doesn't matter if you get an answer or not."

She was a woman, a civilian. She looked to be under stress. Even as covered as she was, headscarf partly around her face, chador over her body, Dan could tell by the body language and what he could see of her face, she was terrified. She gripped the child tightly. Could he shoot her? And if she didn't have explosives on her, what would happen to him? How much should he risk for the men he felt duty-bound to protect?

"Oh, oh. We got trouble." Ben had turned his spotting scope back to the length of the street. "Three blocks down on the right, rooftop. We got three *ali babas* up there. Looks like they're waiting. Waiting for the woman to blow?"

Dan moved his rifle and found the men looking over the parapet of the roof. "Call it in."

"Three shooters, three blocks on the east-side roofs," Ben radioed.

"Taking the shot," Dan said. Everything went calm and quiet as he closed out the distractions and focused on the first shooter. *Take the one on the right, the next one will turn to run for cover, take him out next. The other one is close to the wall. He'll drop behind it.* He planned his sequence of shots.

Letting his breath halfway out in a gentle exhale, between beats of his heart, he stroked the trigger and the M110 barked and kicked. The first man's head exploded. The second man started to run, but a round slammed into his back throwing him flat to the roof. As Dan expected, the third man dropped behind the parapet.

The woman looked up as Dan's shots rang out. She let go of the child and began to run towards the men. Without a thought, Dan brought the rifle back to her and fired. He hit her center mass and flung her backward to the ground. Her body erupted with a loud explosion. The men had already hit the ground with Dan's first shots, so were partly protected, but the ones closest to the woman got hit hard. The child fell to the ground. Dan hoped she was not killed.

Who would do that to a child?

Back at the compound, Dan faced a dressing down from the Captain and Major. He was told a report was to be put in his file. He also realized that if he had been wrong, he would have wound up in the guardhouse facing significant time behind bars. His question to his superiors about whether he should have waited, even if that meant getting some troops killed, went unanswered. The officers knew they had to answer to those above them who did not take that consideration into account.

That night, Dan had sat in the compound alone with his thoughts. He didn't understand these people and how they could do what they did. He had never felt so alone, so foreign, and out of place in his life. He had also realized he could kill...anyone, even a woman, if he had to. He began to recognize something hard in himself that night, and a willingness to do anything that was needed for the right cause.

Chapter 3

Vincent owned the Sicilian Gardens located on 13th Avenue and Bayridge Parkway. He ran the mob's rackets out of the restaurant—loan sharking, numbers, protection, gas tax skimming, smuggling, hi-jacking, gambling, and prostitution—anything that could make him a quick buck. Vincent controlled fifteen made guys, who each had six to ten associates, not mob members, working for them. He answered to Carmine Gianelli, the underboss of the family Don, Silvio Palma. It was a rigid, hierarchical society with strict rules.

Vincent's crew had to deliver a certain amount of money to him and he had to pass a certain amount up to Silvio Palma. Carmine Gianelli received his cut from the Don. The made guys were the soldiers who ran the action on the street through their associates and were responsible for earning for Vincent. If they didn't bring in their share, they had to face Vincent and answer for it.

He ran a good crew, but life was harder after the Feds' crackdown on the mob. Much of the hierarchy was in jail and discipline had slipped. He was pragmatic and old school in his methods. He wielded a strong hand, keeping everyone in line, especially the young guns, who lacked the discipline of the older gangsters. He worked at keeping things peaceful which kept the money flowing. Vincent was not above violence; if anyone crossed him, he could be brutal and swift in his response. He had engaged in his share of beatings and murder coming up through the ranks, but always as a last resort. Violence was useful, but it also disturbed things and could interrupt cash flow. The threat of it was often just as effective.

Vincent was inside his restaurant when Angelo was shot. He heard the sonic crack of the shot, but it was the screams from the street that grabbed his attention—that and Joey running through the front door shouting about being attacked on the street.

"What the hell?" Vincent yelled as he came out of the back room.

"Someone shot Angelo. Right out front."

The rest of the men came through the doors. Vincent heard a siren approaching. "Hide the guns," he ordered.

The men handed their weapons to the bartender who put them in a bag which he dropped into a hiding place under the floor, behind the bar.

"Any of you see anything?" Vincent said as he headed for the door.

"Be careful, boss," Joey said. Vincent gave him a disdainful look and went out the door.

Angelo lay on his back, face up. There was a nickel-sized hole in his forehead. Vincent didn't need to look very close to know the back of his head was blown out. His skull lay too flat to the ground and all around it blood and bits of brain were splattered on the pavement.

"Jesus. How the hell did that happen?"

Joey came up beside him. "We were just standing around talking. I didn't see a thing. Then, wham. Angelo's head snaps back just as we heard the shot. I was standing right next to him. Shit it coulda' been me."

"You see where it came from?" Vincent asked looking around.

"He was facing down the street. It had to be from there." Joey pointed towards where Dan had positioned himself. "But we didn't see anyone. No one running or driving away. It just came out of nowhere."

Vincent looked at Joey. "Shots don't come out of nowhere. The shooter had to be somewhere, dumbass." He could hear the patrol car getting closer. "Take a couple of guys, go back inside and get your guns. Then go out the back, and get your ass up the block. See what you can find."

Joey disappeared back into the restaurant with two of his associates just as the cop car drove up. The officers got out. "Christ," one of the uniformed men said when he saw the body. "We better cordon this off." He told his partner to call it in to headquarters to get a detective out to the scene. The two began to hustle everyone back and string up some yellow tape.

"Who saw this happen?" he asked the group still outside.

No one spoke.

"Come on, I know some of you were out here with this poor SOB, anybody see anything?" Again, no one spoke. "Fuck it," his partner said. "Let the detective on call handle it."

Chapter 4

After two tours in Iraq, Dan mustered out and returned to Brooklyn. He and Rita decided to pursue their dream of opening a neighborhood restaurant and turn his interest in cooking into a business. With some money saved and a small insurance payoff from his parents' accident, they were able to embark on their dream. Rita would run the business end and Dan would run the kitchen end. They were good in their roles and looked forward to an enjoyable life together.

They would build a profitable business, raise kids, and be a positive part of their community. Their own restaurant. In their own neighborhood. Dan and Rita were thrilled over their creation. They floated through the final hectic days before going operational, running on adrenalin and enthusiasm.

After ironing out the bugs, the day of the grand opening arrived. Even Rita's parents came. Tommy Battaglia, Dan's best friend from high school, was there to celebrate with them. The only off note of the day was when Joey Batone showed up. He made a show of congratulating Dan.

"Hey, Danny, congratulations on your opening. You got a good looking place here. You should make a pile of money."

"Thanks, but what do you know about the restaurant business?"

"I know more than you think. I can tell a winner when I see one." He looked around the room. "You got a winner here."

"I hope so. All I know is it's a lot of hard work, but if I do it right it'll pay off."

"I bet it will." Joey and his boys moved off to sample the food laid out for everyone. Joey and his pals all wore expensive, dark dress slacks, tight silk shirts, and shiny black shoes. They walked around the room with an air of superiority, expecting other customers to get out of their way. Most of the patrons glanced at them and turned away. They didn't want any trouble.

Dan found Tommy near the back of the dining room, talking with Rita. "What the hell is Joey Batone doing here?" He pointed across the room. "He comes here, acting like he's got a special invitation, talking like he's an expert in the business."

Tommy stared across the room for a moment. "He works for Vincent Salvatore. He's a made man now."

"Vincent who?"

"Salvatore." He owns the Sicilian Gardens. He's a mob guy. Joey works for him."

"A wise guy, for real? He was such a punk in high school. But what's he doing here?" Dan turned to his wife. "Rita, did you invite him?"

"I didn't like him in school. Why would I invite him now?"

"It's an open house. He probably heard and came by just like everyone else. He is a part of the neighborhood," Tommy said.

Dan frowned. "I don't like it. We grew up with these guys around the neighborhood, but we never had anything to do with them. Never did." He had a bad feeling growing in his gut. "Now at our grand opening he shows up? What the fuck?"

"Shhh, don't talk like that," Rita said. "You run a classy restaurant now. You have to leave that street language behind."

Tommy grinned. "Maybe it'll add some color to the place, give it a real Brooklyn feel."

"Brooklyn feel, my ass." Rita shoved her husband. "Go mingle." Dan tried to grab her butt as he left. She deftly brushed his hand aside. "Too slow," she taunted.

Within months the restaurant was thriving. Everything was looking up for Dan and Rita, except for growing harassment from mob associates, generally led by Joey. They would come to the restaurant, order lunch, talk loud and act obnoxiously. The other customers would clearly be irritated but also intimidated.

Dan often complained to Tommy. "What do I have to do to get these guys to stop coming around or get them to behave? Do they bother you like this?"

"Nah. My place ain't for hanging out." Tommy owned a small auto repair shop in the neighborhood.

"Well they're having a bad effect on my customers. And now Joey's saying I've got to pay my share for protection of the neighborhood."

"Well..." Tommy paused. "I give them money every week. They keep an eye on things, no one steals or breaks in and no one causes problems for me. Maybe if you paid them something, they'd stay away or act right."

"Screw that. I work hard for my money and we're not exactly rolling in dough. I'm not giving these leaches my hard earned cash."

"I'm just saying it may be the price for peace."

"I know how the game works, but I'm not buying into it. They only get away with it 'cause you let them. They can run their rackets, but if they leave me alone I'll leave them alone. I just want to run the best restaurant in Brooklyn."

Tommy shrugged. "How does Rita feel about it?"

"She thinks they're a bunch of losers like I do, especially Joey. They were punks in high school and they're punks now."

"But now they work for the mob, so they can push more weight around."

"Maybe, but not with me; I'm going to kick them out for good the next time they start acting up."

"You're playing with fire, Dan."

"I'm not giving them my money for nothing. You can do that if you want, but that's not me."

Six months after opening, Joey and two of his guys were at the restaurant. He had been applying pressure on Dan and Rita for them to get in line and pay their share for protection. After lunch they became louder than ever, to the point of disturbing the other customers. Finally, Dan went over to talk with Joey.

"Joey, you got to hold it down. I can't have you coming in here and bothering the other customers like this."

"What're you saying?" Joey's voice rose. "I'm not good enough for your restaurant? Is that what you're saying?"

Dan tried to remain calm; he knew he was being baited. "Yeah, when you act like this."

Joey paused then swore. "What the fuck. Who do you fucking think you are? I come here and support your business. I offer you protection. Not only do you turn me down, you insult me by saying I ain't good enough to eat here. You think you're some kind of big shot? You're nothin'! You're lucky I haven't beat your ass already. I'm trying to be nice to you, to get you to come along, but you don't get it. You're nothing but a dumb jarhead. I'm only being reasonable out of respect for Rita...don't know what she sees in you."

Some of the customers started looking over at Joey's table. They began whispering to each other. Dan leaned over close to Joey. "Leave Rita out of this." He paused. "If you're going to beat my ass, let's go outside right now and see if you can do that. Tell you what." He straightened up. "You kick my ass, I'll pay your protection money. I kick your ass, you don't come back here...ever."

Dan stepped back as Joey sized him up. Dan knew his challenge in front of Joey's boys couldn't be ignored. Joey couldn't back down. He knew Joey didn't stand a chance in a one-on-one with him, but Dan also knew Joey's boys would join in and they would try to deliver a good beat down. He watched Joey begin to smile.

Just then Rita came over to the table. "Joey, just take your guys and leave us alone. We're not bothering you and we don't want you around talking like that. Go. Find someone else to hit up on, 'cause you aren't getting anything from us."

Joey looked at her.

Dan put his hand on Rita's arm. "It's okay, Joey was just leaving. We're going to talk about this outside."

"Yeah," Joey said, "we're going to talk about this outside. Don't worry your pretty head about it."

Rita glared back at him.

Dan expected Joey to jump him as soon as they were out of the door. He slid through the door in front of Joey without opening it much. Joey was slowed down, having to push the door farther open. Dan waited for a second after hearing him come through the door. There would be no further talk or squaring away. Joey would try to strike him from behind, and he expected the whole pack would descend on him, punching and kicking him when he fell.

Hearing Joey step forward, Dan ducked and swung his body, shoulders hunched, to the left. He felt a blow, something like a truncheon glancing off his right shoulder. It hurt but did little damage. He spun his body counterclockwise. As he came around, he slashed out his left foot aimed at Joey's knee. He hit just above the knee, caving in Joey's left leg. Joey cried out in pain, and Dan continued to spin again, this time leading with his left forearm. Knocking down Joey's arm, Dan's fist slammed into the side of his neck. Joey staggered back. Dan closed up and delivered a left underhand punch into Joey's solar plexus. He went down, gasping for breath.

It was over in three seconds. Dan turned to face the two guys who had come through the front door too late to help. Just then one of Dan's cooks, a large man, came rushing out brandishing a large kitchen knife and stepped towards Joey's boys. They hesitated, evaluating what they were up against. One of them pulled back his jacket to reveal a pistol in his belt.

"Go ahead and pull that. You gonna shoot both of us, here on the street, in front of all my customers? That'll get you twenty years to life, easy."

The thug hesitated.

"Go pick him up. He'll get his breath back soon, but his leg may be broken, better get it checked out. And don't ever come back to my restaurant."

The two lifted Joey to his feet and helped him stagger off to their car.

Rita came running out. Dan grabbed her as she was about to light into Joey and deliver her own version of an ass kicking on him. "Let them go, honey. We settled this. I told him if he kicked my ass, we'd pay his protection. If I kicked his ass, we don't and he doesn't come back."

"You sure?" Rita had a doubtful look in her face. "I don't trust Joey as far as I can throw him."

"I hope I'm sure. But now he knows I'm no one to mess with." He shook his head. "I'm not going to buy into that mob crap." Dan, Rita and the cook went back into the restaurant and were greeted by a standing ovation.

Chapter 5

Joey stood in front of Vincent Salvatore's desk in the back room of the Sicilian Gardens. From this desk—his throne—Vincent held court. His men came and went throughout the day, bringing him news of what was going on. Deals were made. Civilians also were ushered in to ask for favors or to correct a problem. Over the years, a web of indebtedness had developed with nearly everyone in the neighborhood owing some sort of favor to Vincent. Owing a favor meant going along with whatever Vincent wanted. His soldiers could beat up someone on the street and the cops would never have an eye witness. Even better for him, some of the cops owed Vincent and would help cover for him.

He was at a comfortable point in life. He had things under control. There were occasional periods of stress and some violence, but they always passed. He solved those problems and got back to business. That was his reputation and his value to Carmine Gianelli. Now Vincent was unhappy. There had been a scene, one which would cause him to have to react.

Joey had a full length cast covering his left leg. Vincent didn't invite him to sit or join him in lunch. He took his time, eating his pasta. Joey stood quietly, leaning on his crutches, not sure what would happen next.

Frank Varsa, a mob enforcer, stood to one side of Joey. The large man had a swarthy complexion with dark, humorless eyes that bored through you. He had black hair, combed straight back. He dressed in a dapper manner,

with carefully tailored, dark blue silk shirt and black, silk
dress pants. The elegance of his clothes did nothing to
soften the sense of danger from his presence. Nobody was
close to Frank. He rarely spoke to anyone other than
Vincent. Joey hoped Frank would not play a part in
whatever was going to happen.

Finally, Vincent looked at Joey. "So, you made a scene
and got yourself beat up outside Stone's restaurant, in
front of your guys. And they didn't finish what you started."
Disdain dripped from his voice.

"He surprised me. He moved so fast, my guys never had
a chance to react and then the cook came out with a knife."

"Shut up. You're supposed to be a tough guy. Frank, do
you think Joey's a tough guy?"

Frank looked at Joey who, after a moment, dropped his
eyes. There was no comfort in Frank's look.

"What do you think?" Vincent repeated to Frank.

"No, he's not a tough guy."

"That's what I think. We've made him, he's part of us,
but he doesn't seem to be a tough guy."

Joey started to respond, but checked himself.

"Here's the problem," Vincent continued, "You started
something you couldn't finish. Now I've got a situation to
deal with. I've got a punk out there who beat up a made
man, one of my men. You've put me into a situation where
I have to act and do something I don't wanna do, because I
can't let people go around disrespecting my guys. If it
weren't for that, I'd take you back there and have him beat
your ass some more."

"But I was doing what I'm supposed to do," Joey
protested.

At that moment Frank reached out, grabbed Joey by his
shirt and jerked him forward. He slapped him twice across
the face with his huge hand, so hard Joey almost lost
consciousness.

Joey's legs got wobbly; he struggled with his crutches and wiped blood from his lips and nose with his sleeve. He looked like a school boy who just got hit by the class bully.

"Joey," Vincent said, "don't become a liability for me. Your job is to bring in money, not create problems. If you can't get respect on the street, I got no use for you." Those words had an ominous ring to them.

"Now I have to discipline this guy; I have to knock him down a notch. What I want is for him to be making a lot of money. Money I can take a cut of, not getting his business interrupted because I have to teach him some respect, something you should have taught him."

Joey risked a question. "I'll take care of it. What do you want me to do?"

Vincent stared hard at him. "His restaurant has to have a little accident, something that will help him see the error of his ways. And then I expect you to become my top earner...or I'll let Frank teach you a little respect."

Frank grabbed Joey and escorted him to the door as Vincent turned back to his pasta.

Chapter 6

The call came in around 11:30 at night. Dan was asleep on the couch with the TV going, waiting up for Rita to return from her parents'. There was a fire at the restaurant; he should come down right away.

Dan hung up the phone and shouted, "Rita." He got up from the couch and ran into the bedroom. She wasn't there.

Where was she? He called his in-laws and woke them up.

"Dad," with his parents dead, Dan liked to call his in-laws "Mom and Dad", even though they had not fully warmed up to him after two years, "is Rita there?"

"Hell no. She left an hour ago. You woke us up. What's going on?"

"She's not home and I just got a call. There's a fire at the restaurant. I'm going there now."

Silence on the other end.

Finally, "I'll meet you there."

Rita was three months pregnant. Dan hadn't wanted her to be out late, but she often would stop by the restaurant to catch up on paperwork after visiting her parents', even if it meant getting home an hour later. Now in a panic, he raced to the restaurant.

It was engulfed in flames when he arrived. Fire trucks blocked the street; hoses were running everywhere, water spraying on the blaze and water running through the street. A fireman was up on a ladder manning a hose that pumped water on the roof. Dan could hear orders being shouted over the roar of the flames. Flashing lights created a sense of confusion as the firemen scrambled to save the building.

He was stopped at the police line. With the noise and confusion it was hard for Dan to be heard. It took a while for him to make them understand he was the owner of the restaurant. One of the cops led him to a fireman who took him to the captain in charge. He stood next to a pumper, alternately looking at the building and calling in directions through his radio.

The captain shouted at Dan. "Who are you?"

"I'm the owner of the restaurant. Was there a woman in the building?

The captain led him away from the roar of the pumper, over to his car. "Do you know of anyone staying late?"

"My wife may have stopped here on her way home tonight." Dan felt a cold chill flow over him.

"We recovered a woman from inside."

Dan sagged against the captain's command car. "Oh my God!"

"You know for sure she was here?"

Dan shook his head. "She sometimes comes back at night to do the books." He grabbed the captain and shouted into his face. "Where is she? I need to see who it is. Is she alive?"

The captain held him off, grabbing him by the shoulders. "I'm sorry. Whoever it is was badly burned. They've transported her to Lutheran Hospital ER."

Dan started to turn to run to the intersection and hail a cab but the captain grabbed him. "I'll get one of the officers to drive you to the hospital."

Dan raced into the emergency room and rushed up to the window. "Did you admit a woman who was burned? She was just transported here."

The woman behind the counter started looking at her records.

"Please, I need to see her." Dan was almost shouting now.

"It won't help to shout at me," she replied.

Dan turned to run towards the rooms.

"Stop!" the woman shouted. A cop standing near the desk grabbed him.

"Please, my wife may be in there. Let me go!"

The officer who drove Dan to the hospital came up and explained to the desk clerk what had happened.

"Wait here," the woman said, "I'll get the doctor." She ran down the hallway.

A moment later a doctor approached them. "Are you related to the woman that was brought in?" he asked.

"I don't know," said Dan. The anguish in his voice made the doctor wince. "My wife may have been at the restaurant. That's what I'm afraid of."

Dan let himself be guided to a bench along the wall. They sat down.

"The woman that was brought in was dead on arrival. There was nothing we could do, she was too badly burned. There was no chance to save her."

The breath went out of Dan. He bent over and put his head in his hands. "No, no, no," he whispered over and over.

"We need to identify her. I know this is hard, but it needs to be done," the doctor said. "Are you up to it?"

Dan nodded without speaking. *Maybe it's not Rita.*

The doctor motioned for the cop to come over. He helped Dan to his feet and escorted him down the hall to an elevator which took them to the morgue in the basement. Another doctor met them outside the room.

"Remember, she was badly burned," he warned. Dan just looked at him.

The doctor led him into the room. A body lay on the table, covered with a white plastic sheet. He took hold of the sheet and paused, looking at Dan. Dan nodded and he slowly pulled the sheet back. Her hair was burned off, her face locked in a scream of agony. She was hardly recognizable, but it was Rita. Dan cried out, a primal cry of anguish. He backed up. His chest heaved as he started to hyperventilate.

"Rita, Rita," he said over and over in a hoarse voice. Stumbling against another gurney, he almost fell to the floor, and crashed against the wall. He leaned against it for support. His legs felt like rubber. He put his face in his hands to try to slow down his breathing. His stomach heaved.

"Rita, Rita, what happened?"

The doctor helped get Dan outside and onto a bench in the hall. "I'll make sure you get any personal items we recovered." He spoke some more words that Dan didn't hear. Dan sat there, staring ahead with vacant eyes. Words meant nothing to him.

He had seen death and dealt death in Iraq, mostly at a distance but sometimes up close. He had grown a thick layer of protection against the shock of it. This was different; this was his wife, his life.

Suddenly his father-in-law came running down the hall. He looked at Dan and stopped. He could see the reality in Dan's face. "No, no, this can't be! No! No!" He started for the door but the doctor and cop stopped him. "Let me in! I'm her father!"

They looked at Dan.

"No, Pop, don't go in. She's badly burned."

The older man struggled for a moment longer then collapsed against the cop, sobbing.

The next few days went by in slow motion agony for Dan: visiting the hospital again to fill out forms, arranging for the body to be transported to a funeral home, filling out reports for the police, and going through the remains of the restaurant. He could barely focus on the tasks. It all seemed meaningless. Tommy was with him almost constantly, running interference for him, and helping with the details.

Finally Dan began to function and question how the fire started. The fire department hadn't completed their investigation and couldn't say. They had no hard evidence of arson, so they assumed a gas leak. Neighbors spoke of a loud bang and flash, and then the blaze growing rapidly. The theory was that there was an explosion which stunned Rita, keeping her from fleeing the blaze.

During this period, Dan visited his in-laws. There he received a cold reception from Rita's father.

"I don't think I want you around here anymore," the old man said at the door.

"What do you mean?"

"If it hadn't been for you and your tough guy attitude, Rita would still be alive."

"I don't understand, Pop."

"Don't call me Pop. You refused the offer of protection from Vincent Salvatore's men. Rita told me about it. Not only that, you insulted them. Beat one of 'em up. You wanted to be a tough guy, a big army hotshot. Well, you got my girl killed. This wouldn't of happened if you had gone along and played ball. They would have seen to it that no one messed with the restaurant and my girl wouldn't be dead now. And neither would my grandchild." He started to cry and slammed the door.

Dan stood on the stoop stunned. This was crazy. His heart was broken and now the only couple that remotely filled in as parents just shut him out of their lives. Dan turned to go. His world was crumbling; his wife was gone, and his in-laws blamed him for her death. He trudged down the street mindlessly, his thoughts all jumbled, and walked for blocks, finally ending up at Tommy's repair shop.

Dan walked into one of the bays. "Rita's parents won't talk to me. They think I caused Rita's death."

Tommy came out from under the hood of a car and wiped his hands. "How is that?" He grabbed Dan's arm and walked him outside.

"Her dad thinks the fire was because I didn't go along with Vincent's guys. You know, Joey. He thinks I pissed them off. If I'd have paid for protection, the fire wouldn't have happened." He shook his head.

Tommy put his arm around his friend. "That's hard. But you can't blame yourself. Her dad is grieving. He may not mean what he says."

"I've been thinking. It had to be the mob." Dan looked at Tommy.

"Why do you say that?"

"Add it up. I don't pay their protection money, I break Joey's leg, and our restaurant gets blown up." Dan looked away. "But who would have thought they'd go that far? Broken windows maybe, but blowing it up? Killing Rita?" He shook his head.

The official report that came out was that a gas leak caused the explosion, triggered by a vandal throwing a Molotov cocktail through the window. A fireman investigating the remains had quietly picked up all the remnants of the flash-bang grenade, which then disappeared. The police at various levels were not fully satisfied, but with new homicides occurring regularly, they soon had to move on to other crimes and this one, though tragic, had an explanation. They knew they would never track down the person who threw the bottle into the restaurant.

The funeral service didn't go well. Dan was a wreck, even with Tommy at his side. The service was too much for Rita's parents as well. After the service Rita's dad walked up to Dan. He had an angry look on his face, layered over his grief.

He poked his finger in Dan's chest. "You caused this. You acting like a big shot. We lost everything. We're done with you. Don't ever come around again." He turned to his wife. "Come on." His voice shook with rage and hurt as he pulled his wife away from Dan.

Tommy came up just as they were stalking off. "I'm sorry they have to act that way. Sorry you have to deal with their grief on top of your own."

"Maybe it is my fault."

"Bullshit. Rita wouldn't let you wimp out. She was against going along with Joey as much as you were."

Dan turned to his long time pal. "Seems like you're the only friend I've got. My parents are gone, Rita's gone, and my in-laws blame me for what's happened."

Tommy put his arm around his shoulder as they slowly walked away from the grave.

Chapter 7

A few days after the fire, Joey sat in the car next to Frank. Another of Vincent's men, Roy, was in the back seat behind him. No one had spoken since they had picked him up at his home in Brooklyn.

"Vincent wants to see you. I'll pick you up," was all Frank had said when he called. It was after midnight which did nothing to ease Joey's anxiety.

When Joey came out of the front door, Roy was standing by the front passenger door. He opened the door for Joey. After Joey got in, Roy opened the rear door and sat down directly behind him. Joey sat still; the hair on the back of his neck bristled. He felt exposed and tried not to fidget. Were they going to kill him? Roy could slip a blade in the back of his neck and he'd be dead in a second. He could fire a silenced .22 into the back of his head with the same results. He could slip a garrote around his neck and finish him slower but cleaner.

"Frank, what's up? I thought we were going to the Gardens." Joey's voice trembled as they headed southeast, away from the restaurant. Frank didn't answer.

"Frank, talk to me, what's going on? Am I in some sort of trouble?"

Without looking at him, Frank said, "The meeting's not at the restaurant."

Joey kept quiet, trying to remain composed. They could whack him just as easily at the Gardens as somewhere else. This had to be because of the mess at Dan's restaurant. How could he have known the flash-bang grenade would start such a fire? They had used one to ignite the five gallon jug of gasoline they had thrown in moments before. Maybe there really had been a gas leak. It wasn't his fault. He had been trying to do what Vincent had asked.

They drove in silence, finally getting on Brookville Boulevard and heading through the marshes towards Rockaway Boulevard. The mob owned a cement plant near the intersection. They pulled off and stopped at the plant making sure they couldn't be seen from the road. When they got out Roy yanked a hood over his head as Frank grabbed him. Joey tried to fight, but a sharp blow to his stomach bent him over. They weren't suffocating him, just blinding him. They tied his hands behind his back, led him across the road, and walked him stumbling and dragging into the marsh. Joey's feet squished in the soft ground. He could smell the pungent stink of the seaweed and mud; the smell of life and death and decay. Joey shivered as he shuffled along. Roy had a tight hold on his arm, leading him forward and holding him when he tripped. When they reached a slightly higher piece of ground, Frank took off his hood, untied his hands and thrust a shovel into them.

"Dig."

Joey just stood there staring at him. "Frank, don't do this. You don't have to do it. I'll do anything you ask."

"Dig, or I'll start beating you."

"I didn't know the place would blow up like that. I just wanted to be sure the fire would start. I didn't know she was in the restaurant. If I had known, I wouldn't have done it that night."

Frank punched Joey in the face, knocking him to the ground. "Dig."

Joey struggled to his feet and began digging.

An hour later Frank stopped him, took his shovel and told him to sit in the hole. Joey was whimpering, "No, no."

Frank took out an automatic and pointed it at Joey. "You want to say anything before I do this?"

Joey looked up at Frank's impassive face; there was no mercy, no compassion there. Just his cold, dark eyes that told Joey this was simply another chore. Joey was just a problem that needed to go away, and Frank would not think about it for an extra moment after he was dead. He would just go on to fix the next problem. Joey slumped against the wall of dirt. His bladder let loose and a wet stain spread over the front of his pants.

"Look at me," Frank commanded. "Look at me."

Joey barely raised his head. Frank pulled the trigger. The blast hit Joey at the top of his forehead and he fell to one side, screaming. As he screamed, he realized that he was still alive. His screams collapsed into sobbing. When he was able to, he opened his eyes.

Frank stared at Joey's tear-stained face, now covered with dirt, and his forehead, burned and bleeding from the wadding of the blank round fired at such close range. Finally he said, "You just witnessed what will happen if you fuck up one more time. No questions, no discussions, you get shot in your own grave and disappear. We cut off your hands and head; you'll never be found. No coffin or funeral. Got it?"

Joey nodded, unable to say anything.

"Now get out of there."

He climbed out of his grave and quietly walked back to the car with Frank and Roy.

Chapter 8

Two weeks after the funeral, Dan had settled the insurance claims. The money came to two hundred thousand dollars. At that point he was rudderless, without direction, ambition or energy. Tommy came to see him with a six pack of beer, a strong, amber ale. Tommy would not buy fancy beer for himself: Miller or Bud worked just fine, but he knew his friend. Dan always had good taste in beer. He opened two bottles and sat down in the kitchen across the table from Dan.

"So the insurance payments are settled?"

"Yeah."

"What're you going to do? Open another restaurant?"

"No. No appetite for that anymore. Don't know what I'll do. I can't think straight since that night." He took a long pull at his beer and got up to open two more.

"Don't start drinking heavily on me."

"Nah, don't worry about that. Rita'd be pissed if I became a drunk."

"It's going to be hard for some time, but you need to rebuild your life and get on with things at some point."

Dan stared at the floor and spoke as if not hearing Tommy. "I talk to her a lot. Don't hear her talking back to me. Maybe when I do they'll have to put me away." He tried to smile, but it was not convincing.

Tommy tried to smile as well. They drank in silence for a while.

"You find anything more about who set the fire?"

"Just rumors. Seems like things got fucked up. It was supposed to just be a small fire to teach you a lesson; get you on board."

"So who did it?"

"The word is Joey was involved...and someone named Angelo. He's a big guy, an enforcer. Works with Joey a lot. The whole thing came out worse than expected. I don't think anyone knew Rita was there. That's the rumor, but you know how it goes, no one will ever know for sure."

Dan looked at Tommy long and hard. "I know." Tommy looked at his friend. Dan's body was all tensed up. "It all fits as I said before." There was a hard tone in his voice that Tommy had not heard before. His eyes were dark, his face grim.

"Dan, I think you should go away for a while, get away from this place. There's too many open wounds here now. Don't you have a sister out west?"

"Yeah." Dan visibly relaxed. "Maybe I could go out to see her. We keep in touch a couple of times a year. I'm thinking of selling the house." Suddenly he got up and paced the kitchen. "Were you sent to get me out of town? Vincent send you?"

Tommy looked at Dan with a hurt expression on his face. "What do you think? I'm not their messenger boy, but if I hear things I'll tell you. You're my friend."

"I'm not going to let them get away with this."

Tommy gave Dan a cautious look. "What are you going to do?"

"I don't know, but this can't go unanswered."

"That doesn't sound like a good idea. If Vincent thinks you're a threat to him, he'll come after you and you don't want that. Not if he sends Frank Varsa."

"So who's Frank Varsa?"

"No one you want to mess with. I hear he's a dangerous guy."

"I'm a dangerous guy," Dan responded.

"Dan, this is the mob. We can co-exist with them, but you don't want to cross them. They can get to anyone. Don't think they can't get to you...and will, if they think you're a threat."

"So I should just go away?"

"Going away will be good for you; give you time to grieve, and if anyone here is worried about you, they'll relax. It's a good thing to do for a lot of reasons."

"Ever think about going into psychology? You could set up a neighborhood counseling service." Tommy smiled, and then Dan added, "You could help everyone feel better about the mob screwing them, and get paid from both sides."

Tommy's smile disappeared. He turned his head away.

"Sorry, Tommy, that was a low blow. I know you're trying to help."

He looked back at Dan, "You got too big a burden right now. Let your sister help."

Chapter 9

Dan's sister, Lisa Jackson, lived with her husband, Rob, in Montana. She was not someone that would be called pretty or considered glamorous, but a handsome woman, with a medium build. Her plain, strong looks seemed to fit with the life they lived in this big country. She and Rob had met in college at Iowa State. She was drawn to his practical sensibilities. He had studied agriculture and had wanted to start a ranch in Montana after college. After a year of dating, Lisa had decided to give up being an east coast girl and stake her future with Rob and the west. The open spaces of Iowa had gotten in her blood, and she no longer had a taste for what she thought of as the crowded east.

Their ranch was located north of Big Timber, Montana, up towards Lower Glaston Lake. It was northern prairie country with long views framed by mountains to the north, west, and south. To the east the view stretched out to the horizon in grassland. From their house they could see for miles in every direction and follow the dirt road to the horizon. All the local vehicles were painted with the same dusty, tan patina from those roads.

Lisa and Rob worked hard to keep a screen of evergreens alive on the northwest side of the house. They'd planted the trees to break the fearsome winds that swept through in the winter. This was a hard country, empty, with a spare beauty. Lisa and Rob liked it that way. She worked in the courthouse in Big Timber while Rob concentrated on the ranching. They had a hundred head of cattle and were steadily growing their herd.

A few days before he arrived, Dan called Lisa to let her know he was coming. This was the first she had heard from him since the fire. She hadn't been able to attend the funeral. In fact, Dan had insisted she not try to come. Now, Lisa was overjoyed to find her brother was near and coming to visit. While they had grown apart since she married Rob and moved out to this remote ranch in Montana, she loved Dan, and they both realized they were the only family left.

Dan had spent two weeks on the road, wandering aimlessly, but inexorably towards his sister in Montana. Finally he pulled in to the ranch, road-worn and weary from the miles he had driven. Lisa came out on her porch as Dan exited the car. Her two dogs scurried around him barking and wagging their tails, bumping his legs in their eagerness to greet him. Lisa had watched his dust trail coming from three miles out. Now, seeing her brother so beaten and worn, tore at her heart. She stepped off the porch and grabbed him as he closed his car door, wrapping her arms around him.

"Oh, Dan, Dan," she said softly, holding him tight.

Neither spoke for some time. Dan just soaked up his sister's hugs. They were fresh water to a drought stricken man.

"Come in, you look terrible."

Dan started to go back to his car for his bag.

"Leave it for now. Come inside and sit." Lisa wanted to soothe away the layers of fatigue that seemed to envelop her brother. The dogs cavorted around, almost tripping them in their eagerness to be a part of the welcoming.

"I've been driving for two weeks straight," Dan said.

"It shows. And you smell like it as well." Lisa was always blunt with her brother. She sat Dan down on a couch in the kitchen. The house had a large, country kitchen with a long table and chairs. Along one wall, across from the sink and counter was a couch. It was odd piece of furniture to put in a kitchen, but it somehow looked right in this setting. A window over the sink framed the farm yard with the barn to the right. Across the yard the view stretched out for miles ending in distant mountains to the south. Dan sank back and stretched out his legs as if unwinding from a cell after months of confinement. Lisa wet a large wash cloth and gave it to Dan to wipe his face and head. Then setting a large glass of lemonade in front of him, she sat down on a chair at the table and looked him over.

"I'm glad I came."

"I'm glad you did. I hope you will stay as long as you like. There's no time limit on family. Guests, yes, but family, no."

Dan smiled for the first time in a long time. "I don't think I'll stay when the snow starts. Your winters are too much for me."

"You're just a soft city boy," she replied with a gentle smile.

"Maybe I got too used to the heat in Iraq. That heat would bake you from the inside as well as the outside."

They talked, brother and sister, for some time with no mention of the tragedy. Dan gulped down his lemonade and Lisa got out two beers for them. Half way through his beer, Dan started to nod off, so Lisa sent him to the guest room.

"Take a long, hot shower and stretch out. You need to wash the road off of you before you get into my guest bed. I'll bring in your bag and wake you for dinner later. Rob will be back in about three hours."

Dan just smiled, too weary to reply. He went upstairs to the guest room and stripped off his clothes. Once in the shower, he sighed as his body began to relax for the first time in two weeks. After, he barely made it to the bed before falling asleep.

Three hours later, Lisa gently nudged him. "Time to wake up, if you want to eat. You can sleep later. Come on downstairs and join Rob and me."

Dinner was quiet. Dan still didn't seem to want to talk about Rita's death and neither Lisa nor Rob pursued the subject. After dinner Dan went back to bed and slept soundly through the night for the first time since the fire.

Lisa and Rob cleaned up the kitchen and then sat in the living room with a couple of beers.

"So how long do you think Dan will be staying with us?" Rob asked quietly.

"As long as he wants."

Rob was silent for a while. "I guess he has a lot of hurt to heal and you're his only family to help."

"*We're* his only family. Dan looks up to you as well as me. With his in-laws rejecting him, we're all he has left."

"But what can we do? I mean besides just letting him stay here?"

"I don't know right now. We just give him love and support. Time will show us what we need to do."

"I hope you're right," Rob said. "It's kind of intimidating thinking we might be his only chance to get his life back on track."

"Since when were you intimidated, Mr. Jackson? I didn't think you backed away from anything." Lisa grinned.

"Maybe not physical challenges, but psychology is a new area for me. After all you came pretty well packaged from a psychological point of view."

"I'm glad you approved. But how would you have known? I might have been hiding my neurotic past until I got you hooked." She winked at her husband.

"Well, it worked. The rest of your packaging was so enticing I never checked further."

"Just like a man." She punched him on the arm, "only interested in looks."

"Well you had them, so how could I not appreciate them? Plus, I got the bonus of a tough, smart woman to go with the looks, beats an airhead any day."

"Thank you, dear. Now tell me all about the airheads in your life. Did you have many?"

"You got me. I was speaking theoretically."

"Thought so." She took his hand and leaned close to him, "Let's go to bed. Seeing Dan makes me realize how lucky we are, how special it is to have someone who loves and understands you."

"I'm with you, babe." Rob stood and grabbed her by the waist.

Chapter 10

It was a month after Dan had left town. Tommy was in his shop under a car, positioning the supports for the lift, when he saw a nice looking pair of legs come into view.

"Anyone here?" came a voice that sounded familiar.

"Be right there." He slid out from under the car and wiped his hands. A well dressed, good looking woman stared at him with a smile on her face. She had light red hair down to her shoulders, full lips and sparkling eyes with a hint of green.

"Are you going to say hello, Tommy, or are you just going to stare?"

Suddenly recognition flashed in Tommy's brain. "Doreen. Wow. What the hell are you doing here?"

"Is that a 'wow' of surprise or admiration, Tommy Battaglia?" Doreen's smile grew larger.

"I don't know...maybe both?" Tommy said. "What brings you back to this old neighborhood?"

"So are you displeased to see me back?"

"No, but, this is a surprise, you got to admit. I thought you vowed never to come back to Brooklyn."

"I did. But I just landed a great job with a Manhattan law firm so I moved back from Boston. And you're right, without that job offer, I probably never would have come back. It's good to see you, too, Tommy."

Tommy blushed. "It's good to see you Doreen. Didn't mean to be rude."

Tommy had always been nice to Doreen in high school and they became friends. He had defended her against the male bullies. She had been the ugly duckling all through school: shy and awkward, not good at sports or flirting. It had made her the brunt of cruel jokes from both boys and girls when she was not being shunned or ignored. Her reaction to the bullying had been to withdraw, and Tommy was one of the few people she had opened up to. After high school she went off to college with a vow never to set foot again in Brooklyn. Now she was back and had turned into quite the swan.

"Wow, you really made it."

"Who would have thought it, eh?"

"I didn't mean it like that."

"I know. I shouldn't tease you. You were nearly my only friend. I grew quite fond of you over those years, but I was too shy to let you know."

Tommy shook his head. "I was sad when you left and said you weren't coming back. I thought you were writing me off along with all the other jerks in high school."

There was an awkward pause, and then Doreen said, "If you're not doing anything tonight...if you don't have a girlfriend or something like that, I'd like to take you to dinner to celebrate my new job."

Tommy smiled at her. "I'm not doing anything special. But are you sure you want to hang out with me? I'm just a mechanic." He took the opportunity to tease her back.

Doreen's smile brightened. "Well, you're a pretty good looking mechanic. And I bet you clean up pretty well." She took a deep breath. "When do you close the shop? I'll come by to pick you up."

"For you, I'll close early. Come by at six. How fancy do you want me to dress?"

"Just slacks and shirt. I assume you have a shirt without your name on it." She winked. "I'll see you at six." She turned and sauntered out.

Since Doreen's return, things had started getting interesting in Tommy's life. For some reason she seemed to like him and wanted to spend time with him. Why, he couldn't say. She was smart and good looking enough to attract more eligible men who worked at her law firm— lawyers and accountants who wore suits and had larger incomes than Tommy ever expected to have. Their time together was filled with outings, restaurants, museums, and visits to the little towns along Long Island Sound. Tommy enjoyed it all, even the museums, because he was with Doreen. They talked a lot about their lives since high school—Doreen's adventures in the world of law and Tommy's adventures trying to start and run a business in Brooklyn. While their relationship had grown more romantic, Doreen still held back from a deeper involvement. Tommy didn't mind, but sometimes he wondered what Doreen wanted and where she stood on that issue; it had never come up in high school.

After going to dinner one night, they were walking back to Doreen's apartment in Queens. She lived in a complex called Astoria, medium rise apartment buildings set on well-treed grounds. It was a short walk to the 31st and Broadway subway station from where she could get into her Manhattan office. The apartments were well above Tommy's budget, but Doreen didn't seem to be bothered by the cost. It was nice and a hell of a lot less expensive than living in Manhattan.

"So Doreen, I gotta ask, why do you want to hang out with me?"

"Why not? Don't you enjoy my company?"

"Cut the crap, you know I do, but you're in another league. I'm just a mechanic from Brooklyn."

"Maybe, but you own your own repair shop. That sets you apart. Not many are smart or brave enough to do that. Plus you're a no bullshit kind of guy. I like that."

"So are you...and I like that too."

"Tommy, I get enough bullshit every day at work. Those suits you think I should be hanging out with, the ones you think are above your station, well, they're pretty full of themselves and not all that interesting when you get below the surface."

They stopped at the entrance to her apartment building.

"You stood up for me in high school. I don't think you know how much that meant to me. I think I kind of fell in love with you then—high school love. But I was too shy to do anything and too scared that you would run away. I needed you as a friend."

"Then you ran away," Tommy replied. "You headed out after school and never looked back. Actually I was fond of you. I knew you'd be someone special. Not sure how, but I sensed it."

"And now I'm back." She leaned in close and gave Tommy a long and tender kiss.

"Can I come up?" he asked.

"No." She pushed him back just a little, "You think I'm that easy? I'm supposed to buy you dinner, and then take you up to my apartment and screw you? What's up with you Tommy?" Doreen jabbed him in the chest as she smiled at him.

Tommy smiled back at her jab. "Damn, Doreen, you sure have gotten pushy since you got that college degree."

"All good things come to those who wait, remember that, Mr. Hot Pants. Now good night." She smiled and disappeared into the apartment building, leaving Tommy on the steps. He turned and started back to the subway with a grin on his face.

Chapter 11

Dan stayed in Montana with Rob and Lisa for two months. For the first two weeks no one talked about the fire. They lived completely in the present in all their conversations. He helped Rob with the ranching and repairs around the house and barn. He also started a workout routine on top of the chores. He ran four miles a day, did calisthenics, practiced the hand-to-hand fighting he learned in the army, and when he had time, charged up and down the surrounding hills for some intense interval training. One day Lisa caught Dan leaning against the corral fence after a grueling half hour round of calisthenics and fight maneuvers, staring at the mountains off to the west.

"You seem to be getting ready for something. What's with all this working out?"

"Maybe I am."

"Want to talk about it?"

"No." Then after a pause, "But you do, don't you?"

"Only if you want to. Keep it a secret if you need to or confide in your older sister if you think that's a good idea."

Dan cracked a hint of a grin. "So if I don't, I'm a bad little brother? Since you put it that way, how can I refuse?"

"Well then?"

Dan was silent for a moment. "I'm going back to New York. I have some unfinished business to take care of."

"You want to elaborate?"

Dan sighed. "I've got some things in storage to sell...from the house." He paused, "and some other things to wrap up."

"Those 'other things' wouldn't include going after the people responsible for the fire would they?"

"Don't want to talk about it."

Lisa ignored the brush off. "Aren't the police going to get to the bottom of that?"

"No. The investigation is over and you know what they concluded. It was an act of vandalism gone wrong. With so many homicides, they're happy to put this aside. They don't seem to have much appetite for uncovering local mob crime."

"So you're going to uncover it?"

"Always direct and to the point."

"Anything else is a waste of time, so, are you?"

"I didn't say I was going to do that. Just wrapping up personal things."

"Which might include going after those you think are responsible."

Dan turned to Lisa. "So I shouldn't do anything? Just let it be swept under the rug? Give them a pass and move on?"

"Easy, Dan. I'm not saying all that. Whoever did this deserves to die for what they've done. And the mob, as far as I'm concerned, they're parasites on the rest of society. But going after justice on your own, and maybe more...will that make things right?"

"I don't know."

"But you're going to do something, right?

Dan looked at his sister. She wanted the best for him, he knew, but did she know what that was? Did she know who he was now, after Iraq, after the restaurant?

"Let me tell you an experience I had in Iraq. I've only told a few other people about it. When I was over there, I shot a woman."

"Oh my God!"

He went on to tell her about the suicide bomber.

"That must have been so traumatic for you."

"That's the point." Dan's eyes bore into his sister. "It wasn't."

She looked at him in confusion.

"It was my job, to protect the troops on the street. I couldn't *not* do it."

"What happened to the kid?"

"Don't know. After the blast, she got up and ran to a door and someone let her in. She disappeared." He paused to reflect. "At least she got to live to think about it."

"And afterwards?"

"Same. No regrets. I realized I could do something unthinkable for most people. It was about protecting my guys, my tribe." He looked at the ground and kicked the dirt with his boot toe. "I realized I had something in me that maybe most people don't have." He looked up at her. "You disapprove?"

Lisa looked at her brother. She put her hand on his arm. "That's a shocking story, but I think I understand it...and you. No, I don't disapprove. But I remember your bouts of anger and bravado growing up. I don't want to see that get you in trouble. The people who did that to Rita deserve to be brought to justice, but leave that to the authorities. You can't buck the system, be the Lone Ranger. You'll just wind up in trouble instead of the guys who deserve it." Dan started to speak, but she went on. "And I worry about what any revenge mission will do to you. I don't think there's any healing for you there."

"Lisa, I'm not looking for healing. I don't think there's healing from this tragedy." He turned and kicked a clod of dirt by the fence. "How do I heal that hole in my heart? My Rita's gone. My child is gone. They took my family away!" He startled himself with his outburst. A feeling of rage mixed with grief rose up in him. He grimaced and growled, "I think I'm just growing scar tissue around that hole, but it doesn't go away."

Lisa reached over and hugged him. Then whispered in his ear, "You do what you feel you have to do. But come back to me. We're all we have left."

"I'll try."

Two weeks later, Dan said goodbye and set off south, heading to Denver. There he purchased a make-up kit and various disguises along with instructions from a costume supplier he found in the phone book. He spent a week in a cheap hotel practicing with the kit. He had much to learn, but he was determined to be patient and become an expert in disguises.

From Denver he drove to Oklahoma City and purchased a false driver's license. While in town, he junked his car and purchased a used one. With a different car and the new license in hand, Dan then went to Dallas to get a complete set of ID cards: driver's license, passport, social security and library card. Then he was off to Houston to repeat the process. From Houston, Dan traveled to Los Angeles where he acquired his final set of identity documents. He now had three complete and different identities, none of which were acquired with his true name. Only one set showed Dan's true image, the others were made using disguises—a beard, wig, glasses, false teeth, and other facial changes. He was a different person in each set of documents.

Next he had to acquire weapons. Using one of his false identities he purchased the Remington 700 SPS. He added a .45, a 9mm, and a .22 semi-automatic pistol to his arsenal. The pistols were also equipped with suppressors.

The weapons and a used car were all purchased with the same disguise and fake ID. This look and ID would be discarded. It was a dead end for anyone trying to track him from these purchases. That person would never again show up. Dan's last purchase was a replacement set of ID documents for the one he had discarded. His original car had disappeared and, if traced, would only show it abandoned in Oklahoma City. Dan Stone had disappeared. It was time to head back to Montana.

Chapter 12

It was a Friday, Dan had not yet returned to Brooklyn. Joey stopped by Tommy's garage. Vincent wanted him to check up on the situation with Dan. Nothing had happened since he had left but Vincent thought it wise to keep a loose check on him through Tommy.

Two of his guys remained watching from his car as he walked up to the work bay. "Tommy, how you doing? What's up?"

"Doing all right, Joey. What's up with you? I already gave this week."

"I ain't here about that, you're regular and everything's cool with us. I just wanted to see how you are since I haven't talked with you for a while."

"Well, things are okay. Work could be a bit better, but there's enough to keep me and Emilio busy. I got room for another mechanic, so if worked picked up, I could bring one on."

"Maybe I can help, steer some business to you," Joey said.

"That'd be good...but what would it cost me?"

"Nothing. You're a good guy so I want to help. I help you, you help me if I need it."

"Joey, what kind of help do you want from me? Short of paying you guys each week."

"Well, for one thing, you hear any more from Danny? I know he left town three or four months ago. Have you heard from him since? Is he coming back?"

"No, haven't heard anything since he left. Don't know where he is. You worried he'll come back? He supposed to stay away from his home town forever?" Tommy put his tool down and turned to him.

Joey looked at Tommy. They were about the same size, both fit, but Tommy had more muscle, having been a high school athlete.

"Don't go getting all militant on me, Tommy. I was just curious. Of course he can come back, but he made some serious comments about Mr. Salvatore after Rita's death...about me as well. I'd hate to see him come back and stir up trouble."

"He said some things out of grief. Look, I don't have any pipeline to Dan, but if he gets in touch with me I'll pass on your concerns."

"Thanks Tommy. See, you're a regular guy. I told Mr. Salvatore you're all right."

"Joey, let's make sure we understand each other. I pay you regular, like you say, but that's all the involvement I want. I got my business to run and I got my own life to lead. Leave it at that."

"Sure, sure, Tommy. I just wanted you to know I'm looking out for you with Mr. Salvatore. So everything stays cool." Joey gave him a wink and turned to leave.

Just then Doreen walked up. Joey stopped to stare at her, checking her out.

"What're you looking at, Joey?" Doreen said.

Joey stared. He was trying to figure out who this was. She looked and sounded familiar, but nothing connected.

"Don't remember me? I'm surprised. You certainly had a lot to say about me in school."

"Doreen?" Joey finally asked.

Tommy spoke up. "You mean you don't recognize her?"

"Doreen. What're you doing here?" Joey asked.

"It's a free country, I could ask you the same thing? I mean, right here, at Tommy's garage?"

"Tommy and me was just talking...about old classmates."

"And my name didn't come up? I'm crushed."

Joey stared at her. This was not the Doreen he remembered from school. Finally he turned to Tommy. "Just remember, let me know if you hear anything." And he brushed past Doreen and got into the car.

"Joey Batone, what a scumbag. What's he doing here? You don't hang out with guys like that, do you?"

"No. Joey's a punk, but he's a made guy now, so he gets to push his weight around."

"And you have to let him. Is that it?"

"Doreen, did you forget how things work on the street? I got a business, I got to get along."

"Piss on that. What do you have to do to get along?"

Tommy could see Doreen's anger showing. "It's nothing to concern you. You're smart enough to figure it out."

"So, what is it Joey wants to hear about from you?"

"Nothing."

"Tommy, don't brush me off as some air head with big tits. I asked you a serious question. I'm not making casual conversation."

There was a serious tone in her voice. Tommy figured he'd better let her in on the full story.

"Do you remember Danny and Rita? They got married after you moved away. Danny went into the army and when he got out they started a restaurant back here in Brooklyn." Tommy related the events up to Dan's leaving town. "So Joey's nervous. If Dan comes back and starts trouble, starts talking about who might have killed Rita, Vincent Salvatore won't like it and that's going to be a problem."

"Christ! Just for some talking?" Doreen looked shocked.

"That kind of talk could lead to an unwelcome focus on Vincent's operations. He'll strike back at anyone who stirs up trouble."

"This is heavy, Tommy, and you're in the middle of it."

"Yeah. For better or worse, Joey's acting like I'm a go-between. And I don't even know where Dan is or how to contact him."

Doreen's face was pinched and serious. "Let's go have dinner, up near my place. I want to talk about this some more. Then I want to do some research."

"Don't you get involved with this crap. This could get bad if Dan shows up again with a vendetta in mind. Part of me wants to see him come back to his roots and part of me wants to never see him again...for his sake." Tommy had a knot in his stomach. Being in the middle was a dangerous place.

"I get it. Hurry up and change, Tommy. Let's get out of here."

Chapter 13

Three days after leaving L.A., Dan arrived at Rob and Lisa's farm, road weary and unkempt. It had been a month since he had left them.

"Don't you ever stop to clean up when you're on the road? You must scare everyone in the diners."

Dan didn't respond to her attempt at light conversation. Later that evening they talked.

"Dan, it's like you've got this black cloud hanging over your head. I don't like this. I think you're worse off now than when you left. What did you do while you were gone?"

"Can't talk about it. Just preparation for what I've got to do."

"So you still want to go through with this idea?" He was silent, staring at the floor.

"Talk to me," Lisa said, "are you still going back to New York?"

Dan nodded.

"I was hoping that you would decide to stay here with Rob and me. There's nothing healthy for you back there."

Dan looked at his sister. "I thought you said they deserved to die for what they did."

"Yeah, but that was an emotional reaction. It's not the best plan. My hope is that you don't go back, and that you move on and build a new life."

"Lisa, I have no life. They took that away. I can't just walk away from that."

"Do you think Rita would approve?" Lisa asked.

Dan looked at her sharply. Anyone but his sister invoking Rita would have been met with anger, or violence. "I don't know. I talk to her about it, but she isn't talking back to me."

"What does your heart say?" Lisa persisted.

"Nothing. If you mean my emotions, the anger at those who killed Rita is there. My heart seems to be shut down. I don't sleep well at night. I run through all sorts of scenarios where I can save Rita, or where Rita does something different and she doesn't go to the restaurant, or arrives a half hour later, or earlier. That somehow she isn't there when the restaurant is burned up and we go on with our lives." He rubbed his hands over his face.

"Now I don't know how to live. I can't see beyond bringing vengeance to them. It's like a huge wall in front of me that I can't see over. I don't know what's on the other side—what's next in my life. Maybe nothing, but I won't know until I finish this—until I break through that wall."

"I can't see how Rita would like what you're planning to do."

"Hell, Lisa, I don't know, but I do know she never wimped out at standing up to bullies. We were in this together, in spite of what her dad thinks. I don't think she would want me to back down now."

"This is going to damage you, Dan. You know that, don't you?"

"What happened damaged Rita and our baby more."

Lisa sighed. She got up to get beers for everyone.

"Could you hire a private detective to uncover who did this? I mean, if the cops are not enthused about investigating, maybe you can, and get enough evidence so they have to act." Rob drained his bottle.

"I don't know. I think I would come up with the kind of evidence that would convince most people, but not a prosecutor. Especially one that might be a bit crooked. No one would get arrested and then I'd be marked by the mob—a target. Even if I didn't get killed, there'd be too much focus on me for me to act on my own—bring about my own payback. I'd be in a box."

"So you want to act now, in secret," Lisa said as she came back in the room. "You think no one will connect whatever happens back to you?"

"Sure they will, but they'll never find Dan Stone when they go looking. He's disappeared."

"What the hell do you mean—disappeared?" She sat down to stare at her younger brother.

"Gone. No one knows where. Can't be traced. You and Rob are the only ones who know anything about me since I left New York."

"And all we know is that you came to visit and then left. Is that the story?" Rob asked.

"That's it. Full of the truth, but with a little misdirection included. That's if anyone takes the trouble to come all the way out here."

"I'm thinking that might happen, if you do what you intend to do," Rob said.

"And we won't talk about what I intend to do. That's for your protection."

"Dammit, Dan! Lisa glared at him. "None of this will bring back Rita. It will only damage you. Don't do this. This isn't going to be good for you."

As she looked at him, Dan could see the sorrow emerge in her eyes. He knew his face reflected his decision.

"You're set on this," Lisa said. "I won't try to talk you out of it anymore. But will you be able to end it? Will you come back here when it's over? We're all we have for family and I don't want to lose you."

"Lisa," Dan looked at her and his tone softened with affection, "I'm lost right now, no good to anyone, or myself. I've got no life now. I don't know where this will wind up, but if it's possible, I'll come back. You and Rob are the only solid piece of ground I have to stand on, but until I knock this wall down, I can't move on."

The three of them talked late into the night, turning their conversation to the ranch and life in Montana, avoiding discussion of the terrible path that Dan was set on.

On his way back to New York, Dan drove conservatively, slept in his car and washed up in truck stop rest rooms. There would be no motel receipts, no credit cards; no record of the trip. Along the way, he purchased three pairs of pre-paid cell phones in different stores in different cities. As he approached the city, his mood became darker. His mind went into battle mode. The mission consumed his thoughts.

He had spent two weeks practicing with the weapons he acquired on his loop through the west. Up in the hills, he had gone through hundreds of rounds of ammunition, sighting in and practicing with the Remington 700. He had also practiced close in, tactical shooting with the hand guns. After each session Dan collected all the spent brass and put them in plastic bags. No bullets or casings would ever be found at Lisa and Rob's farm. The brass would be discarded many states away from the ranch.

A list grew in Dan's mind of those who he would go after. That list included Joey and anyone else close to him that was involved. He wasn't naïve; there would be other casualties in Vincent's crew as well. They would pay the price for the path they took. Not many gangsters lived to a ripe old age. Dan would make sure that several of them didn't.

When he got to the city his first step was to stash the car. He rented a parking space in a garage in New Jersey, paying for six months rent in advance. Then he found a monthly apartment rental in Queens, in a run-down area where characters came and went and no one asked questions.

He hadn't made a thorough plan. In the military, battlefield actions always started out with a careful plan, but they rarely survived the first encounter with the enemy. He would have to improvise along the way.

Chapter 14

Dan lay on the bed in his apartment after shooting Angelo from the rooftop. It hadn't been the hardest shot he'd taken as a sniper. Everyone in the crew would wonder what was going on. Was this an attack by one of the Latino or Russian gangs? Was someone going after Joey and just missed? He knew Joey would be on the alert with death coming so close. He was a big man when he had muscle on his side. Now death had struck someone standing next to him, out of nowhere. Joey would now be looking over his shoulder.

After arriving back in New York, he had spent weeks studying the movements of the crew: where they hung out, where they picked up money and dropped it off, where the gambling took place, and who the bookies were. As the patterns took shape, the plan began to form in Dan's mind.

The mob was all about the money in the end so he would attack their cash flow. There would be retribution and death, but he was going to hit them economically first. His plan was to work his way up the hierarchy of the gang. He wanted them to know fear, fear like they struck in others.

He took a deep breath and got up, pulled his rifle out of the case, dismantled and cleaned it. When he was done, he collected all the cleaning materials and carefully packed them away in a plastic bag. This would be discarded in some trash can at some distant subway station. Then he

sprayed room deodorant around the room to take away
the distinctive smell of the Hoppes cleaning fluid. It was a
pungent, metallic smell almost like being in a
metalworking shop. The odor brought back so many
memories of his time as a sniper. They would all be back
safe from a mission with some downtime ahead, maybe
only eight hours, maybe twenty-four. One of the ritual
chores was cleaning his weapon. He always relished that
time before he had to shut down parts of his mind to go
hunting on the battlefield.

*Just like in Iraq, only now I'm hunting bad guys here
in my own neighborhood.*

Then Dan put on his old man's disguise: balding head,
gray hair, glasses, old, rumpled clothes, and broken down
shoes that had seen better days. After checking himself in
the mirror, he quietly went out the back stairs and into the
streets. He was headed to his old neighborhood. He
wanted to check out the reaction to the shooting and to do
some recon on the associates that collected the numbers
money each week. Knocking off the numbers runners
would be his first economic assault on the crew.

Chapter 15

Doreen was at Tommy's shop Friday afternoon. They planned to go away for the weekend, out on the Island. She had allowed Tommy into her life more and more. When she had returned to New York and reconnected, she hadn't known what to expect. It had been kind of like going to a high school reunion and looking up an old flame—it could result in a disaster. What she had discovered was that her interest in Tommy, which had remained with her after school, did not disappoint upon reengagement. He was a fresh alternative to the stuffed shirts she worked with. She was a blue collar girl at heart and Tommy fit her style. He was smart, if not well schooled, and didn't try to be a big shot. He was also a gentle man. She liked that.

"Come on Tommy," she said, "let Emilio finish and close the shop, I want to go."

"Give me a minute. I have to get to a stopping point. It's a good thing this guy doesn't expect his car back until later next week."

Just then Joey walked into the service bay. "Tommy, I gotta talk to you."

"In a minute." Tommy looked out from under the hood.

"Not in a minute. I need to talk to you now. I don't have time to waste."

Tommy closed the car hood and came over to Joey. "All right, what's so important it can't wait a minute?"

"You remember the shooting last week?"

"The one at the Gardens?"

"Yeah, that one."

"Isn't that between you and the other gangs? What the hell do I know about it?"

"I want to know if Danny's back in town."

"I told you before I haven't talked to him. You think Dan had something to do with that? That's nuts? No one's seen or heard from him for over six months."

"But you'd hear from him if he came back?"

"Maybe, but I haven't, so I don't know anything about where he is. You still worried about him?"

"It's the things he was saying before he left. Talk like that don't help."

Just then Doreen stepped out from behind a car. "Joey, what are you doing here?"

"None of your business, Doreen. Me and Tommy was just having a private talk."

"You're worried about Dan? Why? Did you have something to do with Rita's death?" Doreen looked at him sharply.

"I told you, this is between me and Tommy," Joey said.

"Yeah you told me, but that doesn't make it so."

"Just mind your own business," Joey said.

Doreen's eyes narrowed. "Maybe you don't get it that some people can't be pushed around."

"Doreen, take it easy," Tommy said.

"You should listen to Tommy." Joey took a step forward. "You don't want to stick your nose where it don't belong."

"Joey, don't threaten me. I'm not some neighborhood honey. I don't live in your world any more. I work for a large law firm in Manhattan. They take care of their own. They don't like their employees to be threatened—by cops or gangsters."

Joey just stared back at Doreen. She refused to flinch. He turned to Tommy. "You hear anything from Danny, you let me know, okay?"

"Yeah, you'll be first on my list to call if the mysterious Danny shows up," Tommy said.

"Don't be a smartass!" Joey snapped and turned to leave.

"Joey, go fuck yourself," Doreen called out after him.

After Joey left, Tommy turned to her. "Jesus, girl, did you have to poke him in the eye like that? He's a dangerous guy."

"Maybe only because you let him be."

"I think you've been gone from the neighborhood too long. It isn't that simple. He's a made guy and you know what that means."

"I know what it means, Tommy. And I also know that it makes him a bigger bully than before and if you don't stake out a position of respect, he'll walk all over you. Look, I was bullied all my life growing up." She took a deep breath. "Now I've decided to not let bullies get away with it anymore. Not even made guys like Joey. I don't mess with what they're doing, and I won't let them mess with me. I don't have to take it, and you shouldn't either. Come on, let's get out of here, I don't want him to spoil our weekend."

As they drove down the block, they didn't notice the old man shuffling along the sidewalk, stopping to inspect the trash cans along the way. He recognized Tommy, and after a moment, realized that the woman in the passenger seat was Doreen.

Wow, Doreen's back and she's with Tommy.

He also had seen Joey leave Tommy's garage. *Must be asking about me.*

Maybe Tommy could be helpful with communications when the time was right. Dan wasn't sure. Doreen though, she was a complication...maybe a danger. The gang used leverage everywhere it could, and if they went after Doreen, she could be leverage against Tommy.

They drove in silence until they reached I495, the Long Island Expressway. Finally Doreen asked, "What was Joey talking about?"

"There was a shooting out in front of the Sicilian Gardens. A mob guy was killed. Shot in the head. He was standing right next to Joey when it happened."

"So why does Joey think Dan had something to do with it?"

"It was a long range shot with a rifle."

Doreen was silent as she digested the news. "That's not a typical gang hit."

"That's what everyone thinks."

"And Joey thinks the shot might have been meant for him?"

"Yeah. But if it was Dan, he wouldn't miss. He's a trained sniper."

"So do you think it was Dan?" Doreen asked.

"It might be, I don't know. You remember in high school, how he got thrown out of some football games? All the hitting on the field, it sometimes triggered something in him and he'd go berserk, attack the other players, not stop at the whistle.

"What you're describing sounds planned. Not like someone going berserk."

"He told me once that he learned to control that tendency in Iraq. Turned it into becoming more lethal with his rifle. He was almost kicked out once for not following proper chain of command, shooting on his own." Tommy sighed. "All I know is I haven't heard from him since he left. That was more than nine months ago."

"But he's coming back sometime, isn't he?"

"How would I know? He sold the house and his in-laws have disowned him. They blame him for Rita's death."

"Jesus. If Dan has come back and this is his doing, all hell is going to break loose. Especially if he's gone off the deep end."

"He wasn't in good shape mentally when he left. I'm sure of that. Everything's gone. Building a life with Rita— a family, their business—was everything to him. Now that's gone and his in-laws reject him. Can't begin to imagine how that would feel."

"Tommy, we've got to look out for Dan. If he comes back, or if he's back, we need to help him. If he goes looking for revenge, he's going to get killed."

"I don't want you to get involved with this, Doreen. That's why I don't want you tweaking Joey, pissing him off."

"I told you, standing up to Joey is the only thing he understands. I want him to think twice about fucking with me, or you. Leverage is important with these punks, you know that. I'm doing this for a purpose. And, besides, I am involved...because you're involved." She reached over and kissed him on the cheek. He turned and she gave him a full, deep kiss. As she pulled him to her, he swerved violently across the road. Horns blared and cars hit the brakes.

"Look out where you're going," Doreen shouted and laughed as she sat back in her seat.

Tommy gasped for breath. "You got to give me some warning before you stick your tongue down my throat."

"So, you don't like my kisses?" She leaned over to him again with a mischievous look in her eyes.

"I love them. Let's figure out how we can do this while I stay on the road." He gave her a lecherous look. "There's other things we can try that let me keep driving."

"Later, big boy. I'm not that kind of girl." But she gave him a seductive look.

"Mmmm. I'm looking forward to that."

David Nees

Chapter 16

"So what'd you find out from this guy Tommy?" Vincent asked Joey.

"He says he hasn't heard from him since he left town."

"You think he's telling the truth?"

"Yeah. I didn't get a chance to press him, we got interrupted. Some chick, I think she's his girlfriend."

"So you let a skirt get in the way of doing what I sent you to do?" Vincent's question held a hint of danger.

"She works for a big-ass law firm in Manhattan. What the hell am I supposed to do, beat her up?"

"Don't get smart with me. You go from being out of control to being too easy. You need to find the middle ground. You get respect because of who you are, and if you don't, you make sure that person learns to respect you. And it doesn't take blowing up the fucking neighborhood to do it. You understand?"

"I'm trying, boss. I really am. Things have been going pretty good since Dan left, haven't they? I mean, everything's peaceful, like you want, and the money's flowing. Ain't I earning like you asked?"

"Yeah. But something's up. Angelo getting whacked, right outside my restaurant...that ain't right. I need to get to the bottom of it. People are asking me about it. The Latinos say they didn't have anything to do with it. The blacks, the Russians say the same. No one wants a war. You say no one had it in for Angelo so the trail leads to nowhere except to Dan, and you tell me that's a dead end. I can't live with that."

"So whaddaya want me to do? If Tommy doesn't know anything, what do I do?"

"Lean on him. Make sure he doesn't and make sure he respects you. He needs to let you know if he hears from Dan. If he's back, I'm guessing there'll be more trouble...and you'll be in his sights." Vincent knew that last comment would remain in Joey's head as he dismissed him.

Dan watched the runner going from business to business, stopping in restaurants, picking up the money and taking down the numbers. He would finish his route and then drop the numbers and money off with the bookie. Dan shuffled unnoticed along the route, sometimes ahead, most of the time behind the runner. He was just part of the background scene of the city, an old man checking out trash cans as he wandered the streets—probably homeless, certainly harmless and of no interest to those around him. Even though Dan was six feet tall and solidly built, he had perfected a stooped shuffle that disguised his height and strength when he walked. The key was to take on the role, the persona of the disguise—become the disguise.

The next week, Dan showed up on the street, slightly balding, with thin blond hair. He had a false nose and a chin extension that gave him a heavier jaw line. False teeth and glasses rounded out his disguise. It was a bland look with nothing memorable about it.

He carried his 9mm and .22, both with their suppressors, in holsters under his windbreaker. The 9mm shot a sub-sonic round which made the suppressor more effective. The .22 pistol had a short, three inch barrel which kept its round sub-sonic as well. It was almost as quiet as a finger snap. As the man left his last stop, Dan sidled up to his right side and grabbed his upper arm. The man jerked, trying to turn to Dan.

"Keep walking. I have a silenced pistol pointed at your ribs. I can put a bullet in you without anyone hearing and just walk away while you bleed out on the sidewalk."

The courier, still trying to look at Dan, started walking again. He gripped his bag tightly in his left hand.

"That's better. Now we're walking along like old friends and we're going to turn into that alley coming up." They headed into the alley. The man stiffened in fear. "Don't worry. I'm not going to shoot you unless you make me. Stay calm and you'll be fine."

Dan steered him behind a dumpster, and stopped. "Hand over the bag." The courier didn't move. "You got two choices. Hand me the bag and don't get shot, or try to keep it and I shoot you. Either way I get the bag." Dan's pistol was now leveled at his chest.

"I'll get in some deep shit if I lose the bag," he growled.

"You're already in deep shit, 'cause you already lost it. I'm not asking again." Dan's voice was flat and unemotional.

The courier seemed to evaluate the threat and apparently came to the conclusion that Dan would shoot him without a second thought. He offered up the bag.

"Put it on the ground and slide it towards me with your foot...slowly."

Dan reached out and put the bag behind him. "Now take off your shoes and socks."

"What the fuck?"

"I'm not going to keep asking you to do things twice. Take them off or I'll put a bullet in your foot. Do it now!"

The man quickly bent down and took his shoes and socks off.

"Slide them to me, like the bag...slowly. Now, take off your pants. And don't open your mouth."

The man slowly unbuckled his belt and took off his pants.

"Here's what's going to happen. I take the bag, your shoes and your clothes. I leave from the other end of the alley. A half a block down the street to the left, I'll stash your stuff. If I see your head poking out of the alley before I'm off the block, I'll keep the clothes. Got it?"

The man nodded.

"You don't want to get shot, you want your clothes, you wait five minutes before you step out from this alley and trot down the block to retrieve your clothes. Then you go report you've been robbed."

"What if someone steals my shoes and pants?"

"Better hope there aren't any thieves in the neighborhood. It'll be an embarrassing walk back to your boss half naked."

Dan made the man sit down and then stuffed his shoes and pants into a plastic bag. Grabbing both bags, he backed his way down the alley to the street and turned up the block. He dropped the plastic bag next to some stairs, crossed the street, and disappeared around the corner of the next block. From there he quickly walked three blocks, going through two alleys and dropped into a subway station. The train was not due for ten minutes. Cursing under his breath, he went back up to the street and looked around.

There didn't seem to be any abnormal activity, so Dan hailed a cab and had him drive ten blocks to the next station. When the train arrived, he rode into Manhattan. Getting off, he headed into a restaurant, ordered a coffee and went to the rest room. In the stall, he took out the money and put it in a folded shopping bag, and then stuffed everything back into the original bag. After sipping the coffee, he looked at his watch and muttering something about being late, left. Two blocks later he cut into another alley, took out the shopping bag with the money, dropped the courier bag in a dumpster, and headed to the subway. After two transfers, he arrived back at his apartment.

He stretched, and began taking off his disguise. Fifteen minutes later he looked like himself again. He went to the fridge and took out a carton of orange juice. After a long pull, he sighed and dumped the shopping bag onto his bed. He stared at the bills for a long moment; they made a pile three feet wide. Then he started counting. When he was done, Dan sat back, took another pull at the carton. There was twenty-two thousand in the bag.

He sat and stared out of his window, gazing at the nearly constant activity of the streets.

A decision made, he jumped up and put on another disguise. This one had long, dark hair tied in a pony tail and a mustache. He added brow ridges and the enlarged nose. The look was more threatening now. Dan knew of two other courier routes. He left the apartment and headed down to Brooklyn, without a detour into Manhattan.

Strike hard and fast, before they know what's going on.

He grabbed the next runner just as before. With his grip firmly on the man's right arm and his .22 hidden in his jacket pocket, pressed against the man's ribs, he steered him into the alley.

"Drop your bag and slowly slide it over to me," he directed.

The man leaned over and set down the bag. As he straightened up he pulled a pistol out of his jacket. Before he could raise it, Dan fired twice. The gun made a muffled cough. The man jerked back as the two rounds slammed into his chest. His 9mm went off as he fell backwards. The shot ricocheted off the alley wall.

"Damn!" Dan cursed. Now he had to move fast. Anyone could have heard the shot. He grabbed the bag and headed down the alley just as some people peered in from the other end. He walked as rapidly as he dared in a zigzag pattern across multiple blocks. Along the way he turned his jacket inside out, changing the color from black to tan.

After making sure he wasn't being followed, he headed for his next target. He caught the courier a half block from his drop-off point as he walked towards Dan. The block was empty on his side. A few people crossed at the intersection ahead, but no one was looking at him. Dan stopped at a car, bent down to tie his shoe. As the man approached he straightened up and, pretending to lose his balance, lurched into him. He jammed his .22 into the man's stomach.

"Give me your bag or I'll shoot."

The man started to struggle, trying to grab Dan's pistol. Dan held him close with his free hand. The man was strong. He tried to twist away as he grabbed the weapon stuck in his gut. The .22 popped once. The courier slumped and Dan caught him and lowered him gently to the ground in front of the parked car, shielding both of them from the intersection. He quickly took the bag, crossed the street and headed to the far intersection.

The man lay against the parked car gasping for breath. Someone came out from a brownstone and noticed him. "You all right?"

"Help, I've been shot," the courier said in a barely audible voice.

Two blocks away Dan heard the sirens as he entered the subway. An hour and a half later, without the two courier bags, he arrived back at his apartment. From his shopping bag he counted a little over thirty thousand. Over fifty-two thousand for one afternoon—like shooting fish in a barrel. This was going to shake Vincent up, and he was just getting started. Opening a beer, Dan sat back, his mind churning from the day's events.

Chapter 17

Thursday evening the week after Tommy and Doreen had gotten back from their trip, Tommy was locking up his shop when Joey and Frank Varsa came up beside him. Frank grabbed Tommy and Joey threw a hood over his head. They shoved him into a waiting car.

"What the fuck?" Tommy shouted.

No one spoke. Tommy was jammed between two other men, his arms now tied behind his back. They drove for some time before stopping and parked in an alley in a quiet section of Brooklyn. Tommy guessed it might be a warehouse district. After getting out, they led him into what seemed like a large space and then into a smaller inner room. They tied him to a chair and removed his hood. A single light overhead illuminated him. At the edge of the light stood Joey and a large man Tommy had never seen before.

"What's going on?" he said.

Frank stepped up and slapped him across the face, splitting his lip open.

"You don't ask questions. You're here to answer them. So shut up until I tell you," Joey said.

"Joey, what are you doing?" Tommy asked.

Frank stepped up again and whacked his head. Even with an open hand the blow almost knocked him out.

"Shit." Tommy winced as he expected another blow, but Joey held up his hand to stop the other man.

"Tommy, some of our guys was robbed yesterday and a lot of money was taken. People were shot, one was killed."

"What does that have to do with me? I was at the shop all day long. I got cars to repair."

Again the man stepped up and this time hit him in the rib cage with his fist. The air burst out of Tommy's lungs and he slumped over, gasping for breath.

Joey grabbed his hair and pulled his head up. "If you don't want your ribs broken, you better do what I told you. You don't talk. You just answer questions. No more smart mouth, understand?"

Tommy nodded.

"Now, like I said, some guys were robbed yesterday. We think Danny's back. We want to know if he's contacted you."

Tommy struggled to regain his breath.

"Has Dan talked to you? Answer me," Joey said.

Tommy shook his head no.

"I didn't hear you," Joey said.

"No, he hasn't," Tommy said, his voice barely audible.

"How can I be sure of that?" Joey asked.

"Joey, I don't know how to prove it to you. He hasn't called me. I told you I would let you know." Tommy's ribs hurt; it was hard to breathe, let alone talk.

"Yeah, but you were being a smart-ass when you said that, showing off in front of Dopey Dorey. No more smart-ass now, Tommy. You tell me the truth or I'll fuck you up."

"Joey, I'm telling the truth. I never bother you. I pay my money each week. I just want to run my business. I don't want any trouble."

"But now that Dopey's come back, maybe you got something to prove? Maybe you want to show her you're a tough guy? 'Cause she's sure got a smart mouth."

"No, no. I don't want trouble. Why pick on me?"

"'Cause you and Dan were buddies. I know he'll contact you if he's back."

"He hasn't called me. You think he's back, but I haven't heard from him. Did it occur to you that he might not have any reason to talk to me?"

Frank struck quick and hard, this time smashing his right fist into Tommy's left arm just below his shoulder. The blow knocked Tommy and the chair down. The big man reached over and with one arm picked him and the chair up.

"You got to watch that smart mouth. I'm not going to put up with it any more. I expect you to talk respectfully to me." Joey squinted at him, his face screwed up into an angry mask.

Tommy nodded. His arm felt like it was broken. If that blow had been higher his shoulder would have been dislocated.

"Tommy, I want you to meet Frank. You've probably heard about him." Joey grabbed Tommy's hair and jerked his head back so he was staring into Frank's face. "Look close. Frank doesn't care about you. You're nothin' to him but a piece of meat. If we get a reason to kill you, Frank will do it. But before he does, you know what he'll do?"

Tommy just stared at Frank. He was dressed in expensive clothes but his face stunned Tommy. There was nothing in his eyes. They were dark. No light, no hint of compassion or reason. He shuddered and felt his bladder begin to lose control.

"Before he kills you, he'll kill Dorey in front of you...slowly. Then he will kill you and both of you will never be found again. You got that?"

Tommy nodded yes.

"This ain't high school anymore. I'm not fucking around and you'll disappear, along with Dopey Dorey if you don't do what I say."

Tommy nodded again.

"Now we're gonna take you back to your shop. You don't talk to anyone about this and you call me the minute you hear from Tommy. If I find he's back and contacted you and you didn't let me know, I'll turn Frank loose on you."

Frank shoved the hood over Tommy's head and cut him loose from the chair. He half carried, half dragged Tommy to the car. His ribs and arm screamed in pain as he was stuffed into the back seat. When they got to the shop, Frank opened the door and threw Tommy to the ground. He yanked the hood off of him, untied him, and they drove off.

Tommy lay on the pavement for some time, groaning. Slowly he crawled to the wall of the building and propped himself up. He just sat there letting the pain subside, settling himself down. Then he eased his phone out of his pocket and called Doreen.

"Hey," Doreen answered. "What's up?"

"I need you to pick me up." Tommy's voice cracked with the effort to talk.

"Where are you? What's wrong?"

"I'm at the shop. I'm hurt. Hurry."

"Don't move I'll be there as quick as I can."

Fifteen minutes later, Doreen ran up to him. "Tommy, what happened?" He was still sitting on the ground, his back against the wall of the building.

"I'm hurt. Help me get into the car, and then we can talk."

As the two drove off down the street, a car parked down the street pulled out and followed them.

"Tommy, what happened? Were you in an accident? Did someone mug you?"

"I was hit by a car."

"Bullshit."

"I was."

"No you weren't. I've seen what happens when a car hits someone and that doesn't look like this. Were you mugged?"

"No."

"What was it then? Tell me what happened. Who did this? We'll get the son of a bitch and put him in jail and sue his ass off."

Tommy just leaned against the window and stared out at the traffic.

"Tommy, talk to me," Doreen said.

"Not now. It hurts. Can I stay at your place tonight?"

"Of course. I'll take care of you. Do you think you have any broken bones?"

"Maybe ribs."

They drove to the parking garage in silence. The car followed them at a discrete distance, unnoticed by Doreen and Tommy. The men in the car watched the two walk into the apartment complex. They drove by the car and wrote down the make and license number. Then they headed back to the Sicilian Gardens.

Chapter 18

Dan got into his car in the long-term parking garage in New Jersey. He turned the key and was relieved to hear the engine come to life. The new battery had been a good investment. He was headed to Pittsburgh. From there he would mail a prepaid cell phone to Tommy and use that to contact him. After seeing that Doreen was back, he had to figure a way to give Tommy some cover. Doreen could be vulnerable. If Vincent got to her he could use her to turn up the heat on his friend. That could drive Tommy to help Vincent and possibly get both of him and Doreen hurt, or worse.

As before, he drove carefully and slept in his car, washing up at truck stops and purchasing gas with cash. There would be no record of his trip. Tommy would see the package coming from Pittsburgh. Dan could call him from his apartment and pretend he was in the Midwest, or anywhere else; the call could not be traced. He set a limit of a dozen calls and then he would leave town and send Tommy another phone from another city. Dan needed to communicate with his friend, but he also needed to find a way to keep him out of danger. As he escalated his attacks, the threat to Tommy would grow.

Doreen got Tommy up to her apartment. He insisted on trying to take a shower so she helped him undress. She made no comment when she noticed his wet pants. The shower didn't go well. He nearly fell with the pain as he tried to step into the tub.

"Tommy, just let me get you to bed. You need rest more than a shower. I'll wash your clothes while you relax."

He didn't argue and she helped him back to the bed. After making sure he was breathing well, she gave him some left-over Percocet, and he lay back with a long sigh.

"Can you tell me what happened now?" she asked.

"I got beat up."

"I see that, but how did this happen?"

"I don't want to talk about it."

"Why? To protect me?"

Tommy just stared at her from the bed.

"If you think I'm not involved, you're wrong. I picked you up and took you here...to my apartment. I'm involved, Tommy, so you better tell me the whole story."

Tommy sighed. "It's the mob. They beat me up."

"Joey did this to you? I want the whole story." Her voice rose in anger.

Tommy looked at her for a long time. "I shouldn't have called you. I didn't know what to do. I could hardly move. I'm sorry."

"It's okay. Do you think I would just let you keep me out of this? Even if you didn't call me I'd know something was wrong. I was there when Joey was asking you about Dan. I'm no fool, Tommy Battaglia, and I care what happens to you. After all our time together, I think I deserve to know what happened."

Tommy smiled. His growing romance with Doreen never ceased to cause him to smile. And last weekend had been nice. He and Doreen had gone out to the Hamptons, stayed in a motel and spent the weekend either in bed, walking on the beach, or eating. He had never enjoyed doing so little so much. His affection for her now had grown into a passion. Whatever she saw in him, he was glad of it. She slipped back into his world so effortlessly from the high powered world she inhabited during the week. She seemed happy to be with Tommy, happy to be part of his life. One thing was certain, where Doreen was involved no one could ignore her presence.

"Tommy, I'm waiting, don't you dare drift off until you tell me what's going on."

"It's about Danny." His words were beginning to slur. Doreen waited. "Joey and this guy, Frank, grabbed me after I closed the shop. They put a hood over my head and took me to some warehouse, I don't know where." He went on to describe the interrogation. "I was scared. I'm still scared."

"Joey's such a damn punk," Doreen muttered almost to herself.

"Doreen, you keep saying that, but this is serious. Joey has friends...friends like this Frank. Joey didn't beat me up, this guy Frank did. Joey's a dangerous guy now."

Doreen didn't say anything.

"Frank, he scares the hell out of me. Doreen, I looked in his eyes, there was nothing there. Like I was staring at an executioner. There was a deadness in his eyes...not something dangerous, something missing. I can't quite describe it, but it scared me." Tommy shuddered. "If Joey or his boss gave the word, he'd come for me and kill me in a minute. Joey said as much." Tommy started to choke and caught himself. Pain exploded from his cracked ribs.

"Easy, Tommy, it's all right."

"No, it's not." Tommy fought to get himself under control. "Joey said if I fucked up they would come for you too. They'd kill you in front of me before killing me. I really fucked up, Doreen, and now you're in danger. Shit, how did this get so screwed?"

Doreen reached over and hugged him as best she could. "You didn't fuck up." She stroked his uninjured cheek. "They figured, right from the start, that Dan would reach out to you. Joey said that to you before. You didn't do anything. You're Dan's friend, so you're the target."

"I'm supposed to let them know if Dan contacts me, but I don't want to set him up. Jesus, I hope he doesn't come back, but I'm afraid he already has...those bag men robberies. The mob's pissed off and I'm stuck in the middle. And now you're involved."

"I'm involved because I want to be involved with you."

"Looks like you picked a bad time to hook up with me. I'm sorry, Doreen."

"Don't be. We'll figure this out and if Dan does get in touch with you, you've got to let him in on what's happening. If he's doing this he's got to know how dangerous it is for you. You two are good friends, he's got to protect you."

"I hope you're right." Tommy began to doze off.

Later, after Tommy had gone to sleep, Doreen made a call to Larry Moore. The firm used Larry when they needed hard-to-get information—information that you didn't find in the regular places.

"Larry, can you find out something for me? I need some info on a couple of mob-type guys in Brooklyn."

"You doing some work on the side, Doreen?" Larry responded.

"I've got a friend who may be in trouble. I need to know about some of the people giving him a hassle."

"What you got?"

"A Joey Batone, lives in Brooklyn. I need to know everything about him, especially who he works for. There's also a guy named Frank. I don't know his last name but he's a big, scary guy who hangs out with or works with Joey."

"That's a pretty tough order. Am I getting paid?"

"Larry, we pay you way more than we should, you know that. I also know you pass on insider trading info for some of our lawyers for some extra bucks. We turn a blind eye to that, so I think you can do me a small favor."

"Ah, Doreen, I can't get anything over on you, can I? This will take a little while, if I'm not getting paid."

"How long is a little while?"

"Give me a week or two."

"Do it in a week, and I'll put in a good word for you with Samantha, our receptionist."

"Oh, god, she's so hot. You'll you do that for me?"

"If I do, can you behave and not make me look bad? I have to work with her."

"If it results in a date, I'll be on my best behavior. Hell, I'll even shower and change my underwear."

"That's more than I want to know, Larry. Call me when you get something and I'll meet you somewhere away from the offices." She hung up.

Chapter 19

The next week Tommy was back in his own apartment, still sore, but functioning. He had gone back to work. He had to remind himself to just focus on his job, his business. Maybe nothing else would happen. Then he received Dan's phone in the mail. Two days later it rang.

"Dan, is that you?" Tommy asked when he answered.

"Yeah. How you doing?"

"I'm okay, where are you? Are you back in town?"

"No, I'm in the Midwest at the moment. "

"You sure? What are you up to?"

"I've been moving around. Sometimes I'll stop and work in a kitchen somewhere. Not sure what else to do at the moment."

"Maybe you should open a restaurant somewhere, get a new start. You know how the business works."

"I don't think I have the heart for it right now."

"You got to get on with your life. That may sound hard, but life goes on and you need to move on."

"So you think I shouldn't come back? The few friends I have are back in Brooklyn."

"There's some dangerous people here in Brooklyn as well. They're worried about you coming back. Some of them think you've already come back. There were some shootings and robberies "

"They think I did them? So now I'm supposed to hide from the guys who killed Rita?" Dan's voice cracked. Tommy could hear the anger, how raw his wounds still were.

"I don't mean it like that, but you have to move on sometime."

"Maybe I should come back and take care of that business before I move on."

"Dan, don't...please. There are some bad guys, dangerous guys who are on the alert. They think you're already back. Hell, from what I've heard happen, it sounds like you're back to me as well."

"So is Joey the one making threats?"

"Joey's dangerous now, don't think he isn't. He's got some dangerous people around him—more power, and it shows. You don't want to fuck with him or his associates, a lot of people could get killed."

"A lot being them. I don't plan on getting killed."

"Dan, you could get me killed...and Doreen. She's back and we're seeing each other."

"Doreen's back?" Dan feigned surprise. "And you're going out? I'm happy for you. Love blossoms from a high school friendship, like something out of a sappy movie."

"Don't joke. Joey had me beat up and threatened to kill me and Doreen if I don't let him know when you contact me. Dan, I'm stuck in the middle, and me and Doreen could get killed if you come back and start a war." He went on to describe his beating from Frank and Joey. "So I got to relay this conversation to Joey, if I want to protect myself and Doreen."

Dan was silent. His brain raced. Things had moved faster than he expected. *Now I have to figure out how to protect Tommy and Doreen.* He thought hard about his next move. *I have to cut him off...so completely that Joey thinks there's no leverage there.*

Finally he spoke. "Tommy, go fuck yourself. You pay your protection money like a good boy, you counsel me in my grief and convince me to leave town, all for your mob masters. You're nothing but a dog that comes when they call, just so they'll leave you alone to fix cars. And now you tell me I'm supposed to stay away from my home because you'll get hurt? To hell with you...and Doreen. I'm not responsible for your safety. Take this phone I sent you and throw it away. I won't be calling you anymore. I may come back and I may not, but that's my decision. I won't make it because Joey's got you scared shitless. And if I do, I won't be stopping in to visit."

With that he hung up. Dan turned aside, his face grimacing in an attempt to not cry. It was hard to cut off his best friend like that, but it was his only hope to protect him. *Still got to do what I came to do.* He hoped Tommy could navigate this mess because Dan was going to make one. He didn't throw the phone away and he hoped Tommy wouldn't either.

Later that day Tommy called Joey to let him know about the conversation.

"I don't believe him. These heists were his doing. None of the other gangs would invade our territory like that."

"Joey, I don't know what goes on in your world. I'm just passing on the info, like you asked. He told me to fuck off. He thinks I'm your errand boy, trying to get him to stay away and not cause trouble. Right now he doesn't give a shit about me...or anyone else."

"Maybe that's reason enough for him to move on, since he's broken with you," Joey said.

"Maybe...I hope so. I did what you asked. If he calls me again, I'll let you know, but he ain't listening to me. Now please leave me alone."

"I'll leave you alone when I want to. You still do what I tell you."

"I told you I will. I'm not being smart. I'll let you know, but I don't think I'm going to hear from him anytime soon."

"Long as you do what I tell you," Joey said, getting in the last word.

Larry called Doreen later that week. "Got some info for you."

"Let's meet at Serendipity. It's on 54th between Madison and Park, say 4 p.m.?"

"Pretty far from your offices, why so circumspect?"

"Just being careful. See you then."

When they got together, Larry handed Doreen a folder.

Joey worked for a company called Eastside Trucking, with offices in Brooklyn. He was a union manager and was paid a lot of money. The company was owned by another firm, Eastside Investments, which Larry traced back to Vincent Salvatore.

"Vincent's a Capo for Carmine Gianelli, Silvio Palma's underboss. This guy Joey is pretty far down the ladder, but he's fully connected. You mess with him and you get the whole Salvatore crew after you."

"What about this guy Frank? You find anything out about him?"

"Not much. There's word of a Frank who works directly for Vincent, but he's not involved in any of the connected businesses. If this guy is the Frank you're talking about, he's more of an enforcer, a killer. He's a big guy, physically powerful. He's a fancy dresser, but word is he makes people disappear. My contacts didn't want to talk about him at all."

"Larry, this helps."

"You in trouble? You don't want to mess with the mob at this level, Doreen. It's not good for your health or your career."

"Yeah, I know. I'm just trying to help someone navigate some dangerous waters without getting hurt."

"Well, keep yourself out of it. That's my advice. Use your research skills for nailing those corporate fucks. It's safer and there's more money in it."

"Thank you for that career advice. I don't know what I'd do without your counsel, Mr. Moore."

"Happy to help...now about Samantha—"

"I had to help her remember you. Apparently you haven't made much of an impression during your infrequent visits. But she thought you were pretty good looking...she has no taste. Anyway I think you're good to try for a date. Just remember to be a gentleman and don't make me regret helping you with your social life."

"You're a sweetheart. Let me know if I can help any more on this."

Chapter 20

"Doreen, I want you to keep this." Tommy handed her the cell phone Dan had sent him. They were at her apartment after dinner out together.

What's this?" she asked.

"It's a phone Dan sent me. He called me on it." Tommy related the conversation.

"I know he sounded like he was writing you off. Do you really think he meant what he said?" Doreen asked.

"I'm not sure. Sometimes I think he really does believe I'm a lap dog for Joey. Other times I think he said that to protect me. Not sure how much good that'll do, though."

"Well, I think he's trying to protect you. Don't you think you should keep the phone?"

"No. If you're right and Dan calls when Joey's around, the shit will really hit the fan. I don't want any part of that."

Doreen looked thoughtful. "I guess you're right. I'll take the phone and keep it in my apartment. No way Joey will find it here. I may even try to call him myself."

"Jesus, Doreen! Don't go getting things more screwed up than they are already. Just leave it alone. I've got you too far into this already."

"Don't go telling me what I can and can't do. I'm involved and want all the information possible to help us. Tommy, listen to me." She grabbed his face in her hands. "I want to help us out. You understand what I'm saying?"

Tommy looked at her and shook his head. "Don't go getting all mysterious on me. I'm not in the mood for guessing games."

Doreen smiled and put her arms around him. "What I mean, Sherlock, is that I love you and we're in this together. Is that clear enough for you?"

Tommy just stood there, his eyes opened wide, staring at her face up close to his.

"Well, cat got your tongue? A girl offers herself to you and you just stare at her?"

"Doreen, wow, I didn't expect that. I mean we've had a great time together. I know I've enjoyed it, but I thought this might be just a fling for you."

Now Doreen got a serious look in her eyes. "It's not a fling for me. I've thought about it for some time. I want to share more than just some sexy weekends together."

"But you belong to a different world than me," Tommy started to protest.

"I can move easily between those worlds...and my heart isn't in that world, just my head. I like it. I like the battles and the victories—fits my combative nature—but it isn't where I want to plant my heart." She paused. "So, what about you?"

"I don't know what to say—"

"Better say something, big boy."

Tommy simply grabbed her and gave her a long, deep kiss. "Is this a good answer? I think I love you. I know that sounds weird, but I've never been in love. Been in lust a bunch, but this feels different. I held off working this out because I thought you weren't going to stay around for long. You don't think you'll get bored?"

"Not if you play your cards right, I won't." Doreen put Dan's phone down as she and Tommy kissed their way into her bedroom.

The next day, after Tommy returned to his apartment, Doreen called Dan.

"I told you not to call me," Dan said when he picked up the phone.

"You didn't tell *me* that. Don't you hang up, Dan, I want to talk to you."

"Doreen? What are you doing with this phone? Did Tommy give it to you? That dumbass, he's going to get you hurt."

"Don't talk about Tommy that way, this is my call. The phone is safer with me than with Tommy, and right now I need some answers."

"No you don't. Why the hell are you involved anyway?"

"Are you stupid? Tommy and I are seeing one another."

"How the hell would I know?"

"Well, you know what Joey did to Tommy. I'm sure he told you about me, and Joey also knows about Tommy and me."

Silence.

"Yeah, Tommy told me," Dan finally said. "Things are going to get hotter. I'm sorry that you and Tommy are in the middle."

"So you've been back already? These robberies, this killing, it's your work?"

"Doreen, I've got nothing to say about anything that's going on there, so don't ask."

"But you're planning more things to happen—bad things."

Dan didn't answer.

"Dan, this isn't going to end well...for any of us."

"I'm not thinking about where it ends."

"But it's going to ruin our lives. Do you think Rita would want that?"

"Rita stood up to these thugs with me. She wasn't afraid of a fight, she wouldn't be intimidated."

"So you have to get revenge? Even at our expense?"

His anger now rising, Dan almost shouted, "What do you know about this? My world was taken away. You know what that's like? I've got no one now."

Doreen was silent for a while. "I can't know what you feel, but you're going to get us, your friends, killed."

Dan was now pacing his apartment. *If she only knew I'm here in Queens. Why the fuck did she have to pick now to come back?*

"Dan, I'm serious about Tommy. I'm going to marry him, but he doesn't know it yet…and don't you tell him."

Dan smiled in spite of himself. "Bad timing."

"Yeah, real bad timing. You get your revenge and Tommy and me get our lives blown up."

She sounded angry now. Dan could hear a toughness in her voice.

"You think this over carefully, Dan. You start down this path, you'll get us killed."

Dan stopped pacing at the anger in her voice. "You two need to get out of there right now."

"How do we do that? Just walk away from our jobs? Tommy can't close the repair shop just like that. We're supposed to tear up our lives so you can go on a killing spree?"

"I didn't say I was."

"You didn't have to."

"I'm not going to argue with you and I'm not promising anything. If I come back to my home town, which is something I think I should be able to do, things are gonna, get nasty and it may not be my fault. You better get away for a while."

"So you can start shooting people? You're thinking crazy."

"Damn it, Doreen. I didn't say that. Just my being back could put you in danger. That's how fucked this is. They kill my wife and child and then my friends could get killed just because I want to live back in my neighborhood? I can't live with that."

"So the answer is to kill them?"

"If I have to. You better get away before the shit hits the fan." With that Dan hung up.

Doreen sat there. He was not going to stop. Part of her understood it and part of her was in a rage about it. He was about to mess up both her and Tommy's lives.

Chapter 21

The firm where Doreen was employed specialized in corporate litigation. She worked in discovery as a researcher and legal aide, arranging and managing the information on lawsuits and preparing the background material for the attorneys. Much of the work was high profile, they were an expensive firm, and it was due in large part to her work behind the scenes that they enjoyed front page success. She was precise, tenacious and smart.

Within days of accepting the position, her boss said he had some work to do in the Atlanta office and suggested she might want to spend a month down there. Doreen initially begged off. She had just moved to New York City and needed to get settled in before running off around the country.

After Dan had hung up Doreen sat and stared at her phone. She finally picked it up and called her boss.

"Andy, Doreen. I want to ask you about that work in Atlanta. You still need someone to go down there?"

"As a matter of fact we do. You change your mind?"

"Yes. I've got things under control here at home—all moved in—and I could do that work for you."

"When do you want to leave?"

"Soon. I can let you know in two days, is that okay with you?"

"That's fine. Thanks. I won't forget this."

"I'm glad to help," Doreen said with a smile.

Next she called Tommy. "We need to get away."

"Yeah, I've been thinking the same thing, but how? I can't just shut the business down and expect to come back and pick it up with no problems."

"I talked to Dan. I think he's coming back, if he hasn't already. And he's going to go to war with Vincent's crew. We're going to be caught in the middle and we don't want to be there."

"Doreen, you should go away...or move into Manhattan for a while."

"And leave you here to get whacked by Joey and that Frank? We have to go away together. Dan isn't going to stop for us."

"I talked to Emilio about running the shop for a while if I took a vacation."

"What did he say?"

"I offered him twice his normal pay, so he'd like to do it, but he knows about Joey and all this crap going on and he's worried about his family. He doesn't want to catch Joey's attention."

"Tommy, how much do you take in a week at the shop?"

"What's that got to do with all of this?"

"I've got an idea. Just tell me."

"I'm not selling out if that's where you're going."

"Nothing like that. Just give me an estimate."

"I gross a little more than half a million a year, so that's about ten thousand a week. 'Course I net a lot less."

"How much do you think your net is?"

"It maybe averages out to around twelve hundred a week. Like I said, I ain't exactly rolling in the dough. What you see is what you get."

"I'll take it, Tommy. You have other qualities besides a fat paycheck."

"So what's your plan if it isn't me losing my business?"

"Let me make some calls and I'll get back to you."

Doreen set it up with Dan. He would put fifteen hundred a week into an account Doreen would set up, a grand for Tommy and five hundred for Emilio to keep him from going to another shop. Next she called Tommy and told him to shut down the shop, they were going to leave town in two days.

"What did you do? I told you that would ruin the business."

She explained the arrangements.

"Get Emilio to wrap up the current repairs. Make a sign and close the shop. Call it renovation or whatever. Let the customers know you'll re-open in a month."

"Joey will know something's up—"

"Yeah, but we'll be gone. He's going to have his hands full with Dan, if what we're thinking is correct. We'll be the least of his worries."

"You're something...you know that?"

"I get paid to solve problems. I find solutions."

"So where are we going?"

"I'll tell you when I pick you up. Can you close things down in two days?"

"I'll try."

Chapter 22

Two days later Tommy was hanging up a sign when Joey stopped by.

"I just wanted to talk about your conversation with Dan some more. In case I missed anything." He noticed the sign. "What's going on? You going somewhere?"

Tommy turned to him, "I'm taking a vacation. I don't like being in the middle of things. I got nothing to do with you or with Dan. If you guys have a beef, it's not my business."

"You getting smart with me again? Maybe I should get Frank back to give you another lesson."

Tommy looked at Joey. Joey's suspicious, darting eyes were settled firmly on him. He had muscle now and Tommy understood he wasn't to be messed with.

"Think you're a tough guy? Did you forget how you pissed your pants that night? You'd like to take a swing at me, but you don't dare, do you?"

Tommy sighed. "I don't want to take a swing at you, but I can't stay here. I'm a civilian and you should leave civilians alone."

"I leave them alone when they're not involved, but you are. You're not going anywhere. You're my connection to Dan. You stay in town, got it?"

"I'm closing the shop—"

"I don't give a fuck what you do with the shop, but you're staying in town...or I have Frank visit you." Joey stepped up close to Tommy. "Do you get what I'm telling you?"

"Yeah, I get it." Tommy headed back into the office. "I got to close the shop now."

"I know where you live. I expect to see you around."

Tommy closed the garage and headed to his apartment. Joey got back in his car and drove off. He headed down to the Gardens. He wanted to talk to Vincent. He didn't dare screw anything up with him again. He was let into the back room and Vincent looked up from his desk.

"What's up?"

"It's Tommy. He's closing his repair shop. He wants to leave town. Something's up. He knows more than he's telling."

"You think Dan's back?"

"I don't know. Tommy claims he don't know, but he's scared and wants to get away."

Vincent turned to Frank. "This is what I was worried about. Now we got to finish this. I'm not going to have him shooting up my crew and stealing from me. Those robberies must have been his doing. And his friend, Tommy, figures he's going to start in again."

Vincent's eyes narrowed. If threatened, he was a dangerous man. He turned to Frank Varsa who was sitting in a corner of the office.

"Frank, you and Joey go over to Tommy's place. You say he's closed his shop? That's fine. He'll be taking a trip, but it will be with us. I want him in our control, tonight."

"What do you want us to do with him?" Joey asked.

"Take him to the warehouse. Lock him up there, leave someone with him and then go get that girl. If this is war, I want hostages."

On his way back to his apartment, Tommy called Doreen. "I think we got a problem. Joey came around today and saw my sign. He told me not to leave town. I agreed, but I'm afraid he may bring that guy, Frank around. This could have tripped the switch."

"We better get out of here tonight," Doreen said.

"That's what I was thinking. I'll pack my bag. You gonna pick me up?"

"Yeah, I'll pack right away and head over to your place."

Tommy got to his apartment and began to sort through the clothes he wanted to take. They would be gone a month, but he wanted to pack only one suitcase. As he was coming from the bathroom with his toothbrush and shampoo, he glanced out of the window and saw Joey's car pull up at the end of the block. He could see two figures in the car. When they got out he recognized Joey and Frank. They stood staring up at his apartment window. Tommy stepped back, not sure if they saw him. His gut tightened. He sucked in a breath and his legs started to shake.

Oh shit! They're here! He was frozen, like a deer staring at a light. Were they coming to grab him? His sense of self preservation finally kicked into action. He grabbed a couple of things, threw them in his suitcase and shut it. He glanced out of the window again. They were not at the car; he couldn't see them. They had to be on their way up. He went to the door and listened. There was no sound. Taking a deep breath, he slowly opened it and looked out in the hall. It was empty. He quickly stepped out, closed his door and ran down the corridor to the stairs at the far end of the hall, hoping they were coming up in the elevator.

As Tommy disappeared down the back stairs, Joey and Frank arrived on his floor. They quietly walked to his apartment and knocked on the door. Frank stood against the wall, out of the view of the peephole. After several more knocks, Frank moved over and without a word, lunged against the door, breaking it open. They quickly checked the rooms and ran back out into the hall.

"He must have seen us. He's gone down the back stairs," Joey said.

"You follow him, I'll go down to the front. He can't be far."

Tommy hit the alley and ran full tilt to the next street over. He sprinted to the corner and turned it just as Joey came into view. Joey set off at a run, working his phone to tell Frank to bring the car around.

Tommy dropped his suitcase, better to survive without it than to be caught with it. He was in full sprint mode. He turned down another alley as Frank came around to pick up Joey. Tommy knew the neighborhood as well as anyone. The alley he ran down was closed off with a chain link fence. He leapt onto the fence at a full run, grunting at the impact and immediately clawed his way to the top and over. The car came screeching around the corner as Tommy hit the ground. The car stopped at the fence and both men jumped out. Joey fired a couple of shots as Tommy ducked around the corner and back out onto the next street.

Joey and Frank jumped in the car and backed up the alley, looking to intercept Tommy on the next street. While they were going around the half block, Tommy ran into a small restaurant, one of three on the street. Without breaking stride, he ran into the back room, through the kitchen and out into the alley.

Which way? I don't want to meet them coming out on the street. Panting, trying to catch his breath, he turned right and began to run again. If he could get one more street between him and the car, he would have a chance. He sprinted out into the street, slipping through the cars like a broken field runner. Without slowing down, he ran full speed down another alley on the other side of the road and down the block to another street. He was now two streets from where he entered the restaurant.

Joey and Frank came around the corner but there was no Tommy in sight.

"Maybe he went through one of these restaurants," Joey said.

Frank nodded and Joey jumped out at the first one and ran inside. "Anyone come running through here just now?" he shouted. Everyone looked up startled. "Answer me," Joey demanded.

"No one ran through here. We don't want any trouble," the manager said.

Joey didn't hear the rest. He was out the door to the next one. Here the manager simply pointed to the rear and nodded. Joey stepped back out of the front door and waved to Frank. "Drive around back, he went in here."

The car squealed away and around the corner. Back in the restaurant, Joey drew his pistol and headed for the kitchen. The patrons ducked for cover. The kitchen staff just pointed to the back door without saying a word.

Joey stepped out of the door as Frank drove up. "He's not here. He must have gone to the right or you would have run into him," Joey said.

They got in the car and cruised the neighboring streets. They stopped to check the nearest subway entrance. Joey went down but didn't see any sign of Tommy. Getting back in the car he said, "Let's go up to the girl's apartment. He may be headed there. We nab her and maybe get both of them."

Frank shot out into traffic. Driving fast they would only take ten minutes to reach Doreen.

Meanwhile, Tommy crouched in a basement doorway, sweating and panting from running. He watched as the car drove by, looking for him. They turned the corner. Tommy hesitated. Would they circle back? They knew he was somewhere near. If they saw him again, he might not have the advantage of a head start. Taking a deep breath, he stepped up to the street. His eyes darted up and down the block. If he could grab a cab, he could get away. But there were no cabs on this cross street. He needed to get to the next intersection, there was more traffic on 18th Avenue;

he could easily get a cab. He walked towards the intersection, hoping Frank and Joey wouldn't return.

When he reached the avenue, Tommy hailed a cab. He gave the driver Doreen's address and sank back in the seat, still sweating and panting. Suddenly he stiffened. Were they on their way to Doreen's? They might know where she lived. It wasn't impossible for them to find that out. If they got her...Tommy felt his stomach turn. He pulled his cell phone out and called.

"Tommy, I'm almost ready," Doreen said when she answered.

"Don't go to your car," Tommy shouted. "Joey and Frank came to my apartment. They were going to grab me but I got away. They chased me, they shot at me. I lost them but they may be headed to you."

"Oh my God!" Doreen said. "How would they know where I live?"

"They could find out. They could have followed you home one time. You got to get out of there now and don't go to your car. They may know which one it is. They may be only five minutes away."

"Where should I go?" Doreen asked.

"I don't know...Christ—"

"I know," she said. "We'll meet at my office, 111 East 59th, between Lexington and Park."

"Got it, now go. Take the stairs and watch when you exit the building." Tommy hung up. The driver looked warily at him in the mirror.

"No problems for you, just some people I don't want to run into, not cops." He gave him the address in Manhattan."

"I don't want no trouble. I don't like to go into Manhattan. Too much trouble and I don't have a fare for ride back."

"I'll double your fee, so you're covered for the ride back." Dan reached into his pocket and handed the cabby fifty dollars. "This should be a good down payment." The cab driver still looked at him. He was afraid. "All you got to do is drop me off. You'll be paid for the return trip. You do this or you have trouble with me, right here, right now." The driver looked away and turned to head into the city. Tommy leaned back with a big sigh. What he feared was happening. The shit had hit the fan and he didn't know how this would end.

Chapter 23

Dan was out on the streets of Brooklyn. He reveled in the clamor of the city: the mix of smells coming from restaurants; the odor of diesel exhaust from the delivery trucks plying the streets; the sounds of the traffic; people walking, waiting, or meeting one another, and others avoiding eye contact, trying to carve out a solitary space amidst the cacophony of the streets. The whole mélange assaulted the senses. He loved it and fed on its energy. Here lives were being lived in close contact, jostling and bumping into and around each other, feeding off of each other and earning a living from each other.

The mob was also part of the street with all their associates, some young teens eager to show their toughness and be a part of the money and action, others were older, tougher, not made guys but living off the organization. They were like an infection, feeding off the lives of honest people, and sucking up the energy of the city. They contributed nothing except possibly a misguided sense of cool—a patina layered over the true reality of their brutality.

Dan was energized by his mission. *I'm going to clean things up. He had begun to think of his actions as more than taking revenge. I'll take this crew down and free up my part of Brooklyn.* His excitement grew. He thought of saving his neighborhood, of being an avenger and hero for the public good, cleaning up the city. He felt a purpose beyond his personal one. *This is for Rita, for Tommy, for everyone in the neighborhood.*

A sense of satisfaction flowed over him as he considered the larger mission. Yet a small voice came into his head. A voice from his mother, "Vengence is mine, saith the Lord." Dan wanted to hide from the thought, but it persisted. When did his mother say that? He was about thirteen and was going to do battle with an older boy who had insulted his sister. Dan wanted to think of himself as the protector, the valiant knight, even though his older sister was not shy about defending herself. His mother warned him against the pride of such a stance.

He pushed back against the inconvenient thought, not wanting to offend his mother's memory, but also not wanting to face her admonishment, even coming from beyond the grave. *We never let go of our parents' lessons. Maybe they never let go of us.*

"This is different, Mom," he said out loud. But he didn't fully believe it.

The patterns of Vincent's crew were well known to Dan, Joey's group in particular. Joey had his own small crew of six guys. They all worked the scams and did the collecting for him. Things improved for his team when Joey was inducted in the mob. It elevated their status and offered them more opportunities. The point was to be a good earner; it was how you moved up. From all the sources there was up to fifty grand a week flowing through Joey's hands. If one added in the other made guys, Vincent was taking in a quarter million a week, easy. Dan's attack on Vincent's money would interrupt this cash flow and create problems for Joey and Vincent. Dan wanted to be sure Carmine got involved before he was done.

Friday was a big collection day for the protection racket. Dan put on a new disguise and headed out. His plan was to intercept each of the bag men near the end of their routes. It was time for all out economic war on Vincent's crew.

He had grey hair, long and scraggly, white beard with broken glasses that had been tapped together. He was a man who wandered the streets during the day, looking for little treasures or scraps of food and if he remembered, would spend the night in a homeless shelter, getting a simple meal, no one to pay attention to; no one to reckon with.

Dan walked up to the runner, mumbling something about some spare change for subway fare. The man tried to shove him away. "I ain't got nothing for you." Dan crowded him, persisting as the man walked along, trying to shake him. "Look, get out of the way, old man. Go bother someone else."

Dan was now next to him as they approached an alley. He stuck his .22 into the man's side. "This is a silenced gun. I can drop you right here and no one will hear. Want to live, just turn and walk into that alley, now."

The man looked hard at him. "What's going on?"

"A robbery, dumbass. If you don't want to get shot, move now." Dan pressed the gun further into the man's rib cage.

The man stumbled. Dan grabbed him by the arm and turned him towards the alley. The runner stiffened. He twisted his head to see who had grabbed him, apparently shocked by the strength of the old bum. In the alley, he followed Dan's directions. In quick succession, Dan hit the two other runners before disappearing into the subway and heading to his apartment via a circuitous route. Later that evening, in his apartment, he counted his take, thirty-five thousand from the three bags. He was sure he was making a large impression on Vincent and his crew.

Chapter 24

Gino Seppe worked the drug trade. He had a small crew that dealt the drugs directly, but he mostly concentrated on collecting the protection money from the other dealers out on the streets. He kept their corners free from the rival gangs. In return, the dealers sent him regular cash payments. It was a protection racket—protection from other gangs, and from the mob itself. Between the mob and the cops it was an expensive business to be in. But there was so much money in it that even with all the payoffs, the dealers made huge amounts of money. Vincent got involved because it was too lucrative to ignore. He left the dealers alone, kept the violence to a minimum, and the drugs flowed, along with the money

Gino worked out of an apartment building in the drug neighborhoods. This was well away from the Garden's and Vincent's home turf. His guys would make their rounds of the dealers, checking to see that everything stayed quiet. Late in the evening, the dealers would send someone around to drop off a payment. It was late night work and Gino would stash up to thirty grand a night in the apartment he set up in the seedier section of town.

That night Dan paid a visit to Gino. He was disguised as an old man; he had the grey beard and white hair. His nose was bulbous and scarred. He had added wrinkles to his cheeks. When he knocked, someone other than Gino called out through the door, "Whaddaya want?"

"Got a package for Gino. Luis said to bring it over," Dan said.

Someone looked through the peep hole. "Leave it outside and take off."

"No. Luis'll kill me. He told me, 'Don't leave it in the hall.'"

There was some muffled discussion which Dan couldn't hear.

"Why's Luis dropping off money this early?" the voice asked.

"He shut down. The corners got hot. He got a note in the package. There's trouble with the cops."

"Why didn't he call?"

"I don't know, man. He don't explain things to me. He just tell me what to do. Look, I got to give this to you and then I gotta go."

"Okay, stand back." The door unlocked. Dan had both hands on the bag, one partly inside with his .22 pistol at his finger tips.

The door opened and Dan sprang forward against Gino's guard. Pressing the .22 to his chest, he fired two muffled shots. The man fell back to the floor, and Dan immediately swung the pistol to Gino who was reaching for his .45 semi-automatic.

"Don't or you're dead. Get on the floor and slide the gun over to me."

Gino stopped.

"On the floor!" he commanded, "Or I'll drop you like I did him."

Gino did as he was told. Dan backed up and closed the door.

"You're in big trouble. Do you know who you're fucking with?" Gino growled.

"Gino Seppe. You work for Vincent."

"Yeah, and Vincent's not going to like you fucking with me—killing Sammy like that. What the fuck do you want?"

"To quote a line from an old western, 'Your money or your life.'"

"You're a dead man. You try to steal from Vincent, he'll find you and you'll die painfully. You better get out and run like hell while you can."

"I got a better idea. You give me the money already here in the apartment, we wait together for the rest of it to come in, I leave, and you get to live. Don't do what I say and you get killed like Sammy here." Without waiting for a reply, Dan continued, "Now I've got to tie you up while I put Sammy somewhere out of sight. You put your hands on the back of your head. Here's how this will work. I've got some handcuffs. You're going to lie down on the floor. I'm going to put my knee on your back, you're going to put each hand behind your back when I tell you. You try anything and I'll put a bullet through one of your butt cheeks. Try something again and I'll do the other cheek. Don't worry, you won't die, but you'll have a sore ass."

When Dan finished handcuffing Gino, he dragged the dead guard into the bedroom. Then he searched the apartment for weapons. He found a sawed-off twelve gauge, another .45 pistol and a Tec-9 machine pistol with two thirty round clips. Dan put the shotgun and Tec-9 in his bag.

He dragged Gino back up onto the couch. "Okay, Gino, where's the money hiding? I know it's somewhere here."

Gino didn't answer. He just glared at Dan.

"We can do this the hard way or the easy way. I'll start by putting a bullet in your right kneecap. No one will hear the shot, but you'll limp for the rest of your life. What'll it be?"

Gino just stared at Dan.

"Okay, tough guy." He pulled out the .22 and put it up against Gino's knee. "Last chance." He looked hard at Gino. "Think about what just happened to Sammy."

"All right. Don't shoot. The money's behind the side wall of the kitchen cabinet. The one under the sink."

"Wait right here. You leave this couch, even handcuffed, and I mess up your knee." Dan went into the kitchen and found the money in a large plastic bag. Coming back into the living room, he said, "Now we just wait for company. I'm going to take off those handcuffs, but the same rules apply. Move without my permission and I pop you in the ass or in the knee—my choice. Got it?"

Gino just glared at him but didn't move. Dan took off the cuffs and turned the TV back up so anyone coming to the door would hear it. He sat back on the other side of the room from Gino, cradling his silenced .22 in his lap, the barrel facing Gino.

"Why you want to do this? You know Vincent will come after you." Gino said after some silence.

"I'm not worried about the heat," Dan responded.

"Who are you?" Gino asked.

Dan smiled at him through his disguise. "Just an old man who wants to cash in on the action."

"Bullshit, you ain't no old man. You don't move like one."

"I stay in shape—no drinking or smoking. You should try it. I'm just out to get my share. Then maybe I just disappear."

"You better. Vincent will hunt you down and kill you."

"So maybe I should kill you? Leave no evidence behind? I've got nothing to lose."

Gino's eyes got larger. "I'm doing what you said. You got no reason to kill me, you said so yourself."

"Just remember if anyone asks about Sammy you don't explain yourself to these guys. You just want your money. Got it?"

Gino just glared back.

"I'll be standing near you with a weapon clearly in view, just so these guys know that I'm doing Sammy's job. I'll take you and the courier out if you force me to."

They settled back to wait. Around one a.m. the first guy came to the door. Dan opened it and stood next to Gino as he took the money. No questions asked, minimum fuss and time spent. This was just business and the quicker it was done the better. The couriers were clean after dropping off the cash.

At 3 a.m., the last runner arrived, and Dan stuffed the cash into his bag along with the shotgun and Tec-9. Grabbing both men's cell phones, he handcuffed Gino's hands behind his back and through the steam radiator piping. To get free, Gino would have to rip out the pipe with no leverage, something Dan figured he couldn't do. He would stay put until someone came looking for him.

"Don't go anywhere," he said. "This looks like a good haul."

"Enjoy it while you can, dead man," Gino shot back, glaring at him.

Dan let himself out and disappeared down the back stairs.

Chapter 25

Marty Singleton was a homicide detective in the 66th Precinct in Brooklyn. He was two years away from retirement. As much as he tried not to, he was starting to count down the days to when he could step away from his job. His boss, Ron Donovan, had stopped by his desk that morning. Now Marty had a headache. There seemed to be an increase in street robberies and some killings to go along with them. The odd thing was all the victims were connected to the underworld.

The last bit of information came through earlier in the week when someone responded to shouts for help in an apartment, called the police and they found one Gino Seppe handcuffed to a radiator, along with a dead man in the bedroom. Gino said he had been robbed, but was vague about the apartment and its uses. The dead man was a low level hood with a long rap sheet. After being freed, Gino went all coy and quiet. That was similar to the other victims; they didn't seem to want to talk to the police too much.

Gino, it turned out, was connected to a local crew under Vincent Salvatore's control. Donovan wanted to know what was going on. The last thing he wanted was a gang war in his precinct. That was exactly the last thing Marty wanted as well. People could get killed and he didn't want himself included in that group. Donovan however, was all about his clearance ratio and the killings were starting to make it look bad. With a sigh, Marty got out of his chair.

He called out to his partner, Jimmy McMurray, "We gotta go talk to Vincent Salvatore about all these robberies and shootings. Find out what he knows." They had worked together for the last ten years and got along well. Jimmy often said he didn't know what he'd do after Marty retired. Marty said that Jimmy should retire early and come along with him and his wife, Barbara, when they went traveling around in their RV. They could go to Florida and fish together.

"You think he knows something?" Jimmy responded as he grabbed his jacket.

"Vincent always knows something, you know that. All these guys were connected to him in some way. Now this Gino character...he was running some kind of scam from that apartment."

"Yeah, we checked it carefully. There was no evidence of gambling or drugs. We did find a .45, but Gino said it belonged to the dead guy, Sammy. He was vague about his relationship to him."

They headed to the garage. "Any prints come back from it?" Marty asked.

"Sammy's, so it's a dead end and supports Gino's story."

"What exactly is his story?"

"He and this Sammy were hanging out. A guy knocks on the door, jumps Sammy, shoots him, cuffs Gino to the radiator and proceeds to rob them."

"Why would someone go to that shit-bag apartment to rob someone?"

"They got something going on, a stash house for some mob money...drugs...who knows? All we know is that Gino said he had some savings hidden away under the sink and the guy found out about it and robbed him."

"That's convenient...some money saved. What, he didn't believe in banks?"

"Guess not."

"You find any drugs?"

"No, we looked hard for that, but the place was clean."

They drove the rest of the way to the Sicilian Gardens in silence. Entering the restaurant, Marty told the manager he wanted to see Vincent.

"You have an appointment?"

"No. Didn't know he took appointments, like a doctor or something. Don't be cute. Tell him Marty Singleton from the 66th Precinct is here. It's about the robberies and shootings. If he doesn't want to talk with me here, I can bring him down to the station to talk. I figure I'm doing him a favor."

The manager scowled.

"If it's not too much trouble for you, boss," Jimmy added.

He disappeared into the back room. A few minutes later he reappeared and motioned for Marty and Jimmy to come in.

"What can I do for you gentlemen?" Vincent asked, not rising from his desk.

Marty looked around the room. No one was there, but there was a back door. He'd bet a Benjamin that someone Vincent didn't want them to see had just exited through that door. No matter, he had a different agenda today.

"We want to talk about this rash of robberies and killings going on in the neighborhood. All the victims seem to be connected to you."

"I don't know what you mean," Vincent replied.

"Vincent, we're not stupid. These guys were runners delivering money to you. We even had some of them 'fess up about what they did."

Vincent just stared back at him.

"Look, I'm not here to try to bust you on some minor gambling or numbers charge, but I don't want a gang war in the neighborhood. My captain is serious about this. We need to cooperate to stop this before innocent people get hurt."

"Detective, I don't want innocent people getting hurt either. But I don't know how I can help."

"So you don't have any idea who it might be."

Vincent appeared to think about it for a moment then shook his head.

"You don't think another gang is raiding your territory?"

Vincent just looked at him.

"You know the Russians or some Latino gang? We're all friends here, we can talk off the record." Marty said with a smile.

After a long pause, Vincent looked directly at him. "There isn't a gang war going on. I'm just as mystified as you, but if I think of anything I'll let you know."

"Well that was helpful," Jimmy said sarcastically in the car. "At least we got out of the office on a sunny afternoon. If we keep this kind of detective work up, we're sure to win an award."

"Funny man. Had to try though. I don't think he knows what's up himself, although he's probably got some good ideas he isn't sharing."

"Same old crap. They'll take care of it themselves."

"And hopefully nobody gets caught in the crossfire."

After the cops left, Frank and Joey came back into the room. Joey sat at the desk and Frank stood in the corner.

"They don't know nothing," Joey said.

"Yeah, but now they're more focused on us, which isn't good." Vincent paused for a moment. "This has to be Dan. It's the only thing that makes sense."

"Yeah, but each person looks different. Do you think he's got help?" Joey asked.

"I doubt it. Gino said the guy looked like some kind of bum, an old guy, but he didn't move like one. It had to be a disguise. And all this starts just after Tommy and that girl get out of town. You two screwed up there." Vincent glared at Joey. They had reported back how Tommy must have seen them approaching the apartment building; one chance in a hundred he had looked out the window at just the right time. Their story related how they looked hard for him and then had staked out Doreen's car, but she had never shown.

Joey didn't say anything, but he was pretty sure Vincent wouldn't do anything about not getting Tommy or Doreen because Frank was involved. Without Frank, that mistake could have cost him his life.

"So he works in disguises, we still have to find him." Frank suddenly spoke up.

"It makes it harder to see him coming," Vincent said.

"So how many different looks has he given us?" Frank continued. "He's gotta have a limit. We look for all the people who fit the descriptions."

"So we just start shooting every bum we come across?" Joey asked.

Frank just looked at him with those eyes. Joey shivered, looking back at the gaze that told him, he was just a piece of meat. He turned away. Frank might just be that crazy. He just might shoot all the bums until he killed Dan.

"It's a start," said Vincent. "Get me a list of how each guy looked."

Chapter 26

The black Lincoln Town Car pulled up near the wall in the warehouse parking lot. It was in the shadows of the side of the building, shielded from the street, and had a view of anyone coming into the lot. A few minutes later a black S500 Mercedes pulled in, drove past the Lincoln, turned around and pulled up in the shadows behind it. Frank got out of the Town Car and opened the back door. Vincent stepped out and walked back to the Mercedes which had its back door open. He got in.

"How you doing?" Carmine Gianelli asked as Vincent shuffled himself into the seat. Carmine was only five years older than Vincent. Unlike Vincent, Carmine presented a dapper look to the world. His hair was dark and slicked back, his voice smooth and mellow. He had a powerful build, one that indicated he exercised and kept in shape. A hard energy slipped through his smooth looks and manners, letting you know that he would not let anything get in his way. Vincent knew his good relationship with Carmine depended on continued performance, and now things were getting problematic.

Vincent began to sweat. "Could be better."

"How's Sheila?" Carmine was aware of Vincent's sometimes tumultuous marriage, and he always worried about Sheila's stability. One thing he didn't need added to his problems was an unstable mob wife.

"She's fine," Vincent said. He didn't share business with her and she only shared things with him when she was discontented which, unfortunately, was often.

"What's going on with these robberies?" Carmine continued. "It's starting to get noticed and it's interrupting cash flow. I got the boss asking me questions. I need some answers."

"I'm getting it under control."

"How are you getting it under control?" Carmine asked.

"I think it's one guy who uses disguises. Even knowing that, we're still having trouble finding him."

"One fucking guy? One fucking guy is taking out your runners? Stealing your money? I'm supposed to believe that?"

"I know it looks bad, but we didn't see this coming, and it's taking time to figure it out. We'll get this guy. It's only a matter of time."

"So who is he anyway?"

"It's a long story—"

"I got time, tell it to me."

Vincent recounted the tale of Dan and how his wife got caught in a fire bombing and died. How it seemed to send Dan over the edge. He had disappeared but now seemed to be back, getting revenge by killing and robbing Vincent's crew. Carmine listened calmly. Vincent couldn't tell if the story was making him look better or worse. In any case, he had to tell it straight. Carmine could get the story from lots of sources, so better from Vincent than anyone else.

"He got family, friends in the area?" Carmine asked when Vincent was done.

"His best friend and the guy's girlfriend skipped out of town before we could nab them. I think they saw this coming."

"What about family?"

"Only the in-laws and they've disowned him. They blame him for their daughter's death. They won't talk to him anymore."

"What are you doing about them?"

"I was taking care of them since their daughter died. You know, sending them a little money now and then. They didn't blame me, they blamed their son-in-law."

"Maybe you should squeeze them?"

"They moved away a month ago. House is all closed up. Don't know where they've gone, but I got someone checking regularly to see if they come back. I still don't know if that would help since they shut him out of their lives." Vincent caught Carmine's frown in the glow of the parking lot lights. "The guy and girl left town, but they'll be back. He's got a repair shop in town and she's got a good job in Manhattan—they gotta be back soon. We'll nab them as soon as they show up."

Carmine turned to him, "You better not just wait for that to happen. If this gets worse the boss ain't gonna like it. We're not going have one local punk disrupt this family. You get this taken care of right away. You want any of my boys?"

"Not yet. I've got Frank Varsa. He's tough and smart. We know what his disguises are and we'll check out everyone who looks the part—"

"What about Joey? Seems he caused this problem."

"Joey's under control. Frank's staying close to him and he's scared shitless of Frank. Joey's working hard to stop this guy."

"Just so you know, I don't like loose cannons. You run a tight ship...keep it that way." Carmine reached up and tapped the driver, who got out and opened the door for Vincent. The meeting was over.

Later Vincent met with Frank. "You make a list of what each guy looked like in the robberies. Then we pick up anyone who looks like that. No violence, but we check to see they are not wearing a disguise. Be careful, this guy can handle himself. We got to find him and stop him quick or things are going to get hot for us."

Frank nodded. He would get Joey focused. Delicacy wasn't in Frank's repertoire, but he could improvise. Things getting hot meant things getting hot for Joey, if not Vincent. Frank didn't plan to be a part of that. He figured it wouldn't be long before Vincent would want him to take Joey out. That would be enjoyable.

Chapter 27

"Gas company." Dan held up an ID card. "We had a report on a gas leak so I've got to check with all the tenants to see if they've noticed anything."

Dan knew where the high stakes card games were held. It was pretty common knowledge in the neighborhood. What he didn't know was how much protection was assigned to the games. So far Dan had been focused on the street action. He guessed no one thought the games might be targeted. He needed to strike before anyone considered that possibility. But first there was some research to do.

He had been an old man and a musician, a vaguely threatening man with a big nose, and a blonde, long-haired surfer type. Now he needed another look. He would be a gas utility inspector. He had acquired the uniform some weeks earlier. It would give him entrance to the building and a reason to survey the tenants so he could find the right apartment. Along with the gas uniform, he would have a mustache and slicked back black hair and glasses.

Thursday afternoon Dan drove to the apartment building. He grabbed his clipboard and entered the apartment, stopping to knock at the first door. A woman from inside called out.

"No. We got no leaks. There's no smell."

"So I can complete my report, who am I talking to?" Dan asked. The woman gave him her name and he thanked her and moved down the hall. This would take some time.

Two hours later he had gone through the building. Now from the third floor he started back down, hitting all the doors where no one had answered. In the rear of the building, on the first floor, a man answered his knock.

"Who's there?"

"I'm from the gas company. We had a report of a gas leak and so I've got to talk to all the tenants to check if they've smelled anything unusual, either in their apartment or the hallways."

"You running a scam?" came the reply.

"No sir, just doing my job. Gas leaks can be dangerous. Can't be too safe."

The door opened and a thick, burly man stood there with a scowl on his face. "Lemme see your ID. This sounds like a scam."

Dan showed him his ID, still looped around his neck on its lanyard. The man scowled at it while Dan quickly scanned the room. He could just see the edge of a round table that was placed in the center of the living room.

Another man came around the corner. "What's up?"

Pulling the badge back Dan said, "So you haven't smelled any odd odors?"

"No. Just you." He laughed along with the man in the hall.

It was time to go. "Thanks for your trouble. I'm sorry I bothered you. You can't be too careful with gas leaks." And with that he turned and headed down the hall.

"Hey! What do we do if we smell something odd?" the man called out after him.

"Just call 9-1-1. They'll send us back out," Dan replied as he kept walking.

"If Smitty starts farting, we'll threaten to call 9-1-1 on him," the other guy said to his partner. They both laughed and closed the door.

Dan got in the van and drove off to a side street to get ready.

Two for protection. Another to tend bar and maybe a dealer unless one of those monkeys deals the cards. I got three or four to deal with, max.

His challenge was to not have everyone run for the door when he broke in. He had to quickly get control over the group. He put his 9mm with its suppressor in a shoulder holster. It was loaded with sub-sonic rounds. If he had to use it the shots would not be heard in the next apartment.

He kept the gas company uniform on, but attached a button camera attached to the front of his jacket. Later, in the early evening, he entered the apartment building and knocked on the door.

"Who's there?" came the response as someone looked through the peep hole.

"It's me, the guy from the gas company. I didn't get you to sign off on my inspection sheet. My supervisor said I have to come back and get a signature."

"Go away. I told you we didn't have a leak."

"I know, but my boss is all over me on this. Help me out. I just need you signature and then I can call it a day."

"I told you, go away."

"Come on. Help me out. I got a date tonight. It'll only take you a second and then I'm outta here. My boss wants to cover his ass and I gotta get this done before I can get off."

"Hold on," came the reply as the locks were released.

When the door opened, Dan lunged forward with his 9mm out. He shoved it in the man's chest and pushed him backwards into the hallway. As the man backed up, trying to get his balance, Dan tripped him and shoved him hard to the floor.

"What's going on?" called the dealer.

"Everyone freeze!" Dan shouted. "Get on the floor!" he yelled to the bartender. "No one move."

The men at the table were looking at him wide eyed. The dealer pushed back from the table and reached around to his back. As he pulled out his pistol, Dan shot him. The bullet hit him square in the chest.

He immediately turned his pistol to the doorman on the floor, who thought better than to try for his gun and spread out his hands out away from his body where he lay on the floor. Dan motioned to the bartender to crawl over into his line of sight.

"You," Dan shouted to the smallest guy at the table. "Come over here."

The man got up and nervously walked over to Dan. "Go grab the gym bag and bring it inside. Then close and lock the door. If you try to leave, I'll shoot you dead before you take two steps." He did as he was told.

"Now, get the plastic cuffs out." Dan instructed the man to cuff the doorman and bartender.

When they were secured, he directed the group, "Everyone, take out your cell phones. Don't pretend you don't have one. Hold out and I'll shoot you." All the phones came out.

Turning to the man who locked the door he said, "Collect those phones and bring them over here. I want to see them turned off in front of me." The man did as he was told.

"Now gentlemen, we're all players, I see. So you know that you win some, you lose some. This as your 'lose some' night. Here's what you're gonna do. Take out all your money and wallets and put them on the table. Little man here is going to collect it all and stuff it in the bag. I'm going to check for holdouts personally. If you've left something off the table, I'll put a bullet in your ass and you can explain that to your wife."

"You'll never get away with this," the doorman said from the floor.

"I'll take my chances," Dan replied.

"There's some important people here. You don't know what you're getting into," one of the players chimed in.

"Shut up," said another.

"Important people...like important enough to not want their name and picture broadcast to the public? That kind of important?"

"You dumbass," the other man said through clenched teeth.

"I have your IDs. I'll be able to figure out who all of you are. I think that maybe you don't want this incident publicized, so you should just behave and keep your mouths shut."

Everyone was glaring at Dan. They were over the shock and now getting furious at the prospects of damaging publicity. Next Dan frisked each player, turning their pockets inside out. Then he had each one remove their pants and shoes. The gym bag was now full of money, including the crew's "bank" money used to float players who had run out. Dan had one of the players stuff all the pants and shoes into a large garbage bag he had brought with him.

"Here's what's going to happen. I'm going to leave with the money and your clothes. I'll leave the clothes at the back of the alley. I think you should cut Mr. Doorman here loose and he can retrieve the bundle. The wallets will be sent to Mr. Salvatore at the Sicilian Gardens. I keep any cash I find. If you behave, no one gets hurt, and you can call it a bad night."

"And you won't publicize this?" one of the players asked.

"I'm not sure. Depends on how you behave and what might be in it for me."

"So you're blackmailing us? That's a federal crime."

"Just thinking about the possibilities, seeing as I'm probably dealing with some important people here."

"The Feds are going to get in on this," the same man continued.

"Only if you want them to. I'm going now. If anyone pops their head out or tries to follow me, they'll get shot. And no one gets their pants back. And I'll probably be pissed enough to send all your IDs to the press."

He checked the plastic cuffs on the two men and left the apartment. It would take at least five minutes to cut the men free with only a kitchen knife available. He would be long gone by then.

Later that night, back in his apartment, Dan went through the money—ninety-eight thousand dollars, counting Vincent's bank money. The wallets showed that he had hit the jackpot. They included a union boss, Brooklyn council member, a prominent businessman, someone from the state's attorney general office, the Director of Transportation, and a Housing Authority board member. This would create some serious trouble for Vincent.

The next day Dan packaged up the wallets, a DVD copy of the card game participants, one of his pre-paid cell phones and a note. "Call me on this phone. We can discuss how you get the original video."

Chapter 28

Vincent was fuming. Everyone was keeping clear. He had told Joey to get his ass down to the Gardens. Joey was worried. His only protection was that he and Frank were working together.

For two days Vincent had been fielding angry phone calls from the six men at the card game. The heat was on. Someone had even called Carmine Gianelli who was now not so polite, telling Vincent over the phone to take care of this problem in a hurry or face consequences.

"Who in my crew's gonna find this punk?" Vincent shouted. No one dared to answer. "Is he a ghost? He got some kinda supernatural powers that none of you can track him down? He can just make fools of us?" The questions flew in anger and no one answered.

As Vincent raged, one of his guys stepped up and handed him a package.

"What's this?"

"I dunno boss. It came in the mail and it's addressed to you. No return address."

"I can see that," Vincent growled. "Here," he handed the box to Joey. "Take it out back and open it. If it's a bomb I hope it blows your fucking head off."

Joey reluctantly took the package and stared at it, holding it gingerly away from his body. He started breathing hard and his hands began to shake.

"Stop looking at it and get your ass outside and open it," Vincent commanded.

Joey gently carried it out back. He kept staring at it for some time, not sure how to proceed. One of the men peeked out of the door and shouted at him, "Open the fucking box and bring it back in here, Vincent's waiting."

With a deep breath, Joey carefully sliced the tape on the edges and gently pried the lid open. He sighed as nothing exploded. Inside were wallets, a DVD, a note and a cell phone. He quickly brought the package back in to Vincent.

Vincent was slightly calmer, having scared the hell out of Joey. As he looked through the contents his face went from some relief to consternation and then to anger. After reading the note, he had everyone clear out except for Frank, Joey and three other crew bosses.

"Get me a DVD player," he ordered.

The DVD was edited. It showed someone entering the apartment and getting everyone under control. The scene of the dealer getting shot was deleted.

It focused on each of the players. They were clearly identifiable and there was no doubt that they were gambling; the money could be seen on the table. The doorman, handcuffed on the floor, was easily identifiable. He could tie Vincent to the players. That fact was not good for any of the parties.

Vincent looked at the phone then put it aside along with the note. He gave the box with the wallets in it to Joey. "Get on the phone and call these guys. Let them know we have their wallets. Don't go giving that message to any receptionist or secretary. You got to speak to each guy. You can't leave a message. Can you do that without fucking it up?"

Joey nodded and took the box. Everyone left the room. Vincent just stared at the phone for some moments before picking it up. On the speed dial there was one number. He pressed it.

A man answered on the third ring. "Nice of you to call."

"Who's this?" Vincent asked.

"I'm the guy you need to settle accounts with."

"You're the guy who knocked off my card game. You're the guy who's been knocking off my runners. I'm going to find you and kill you." Vincent was working himself into a rage.

"Stay calm, Vincent," the voice replied. "We have business to work out."

"We got nothing to work out except that I want my money back and I want you out of town."

"I can always call Carmine and do my business with him."

Vincent paused. He didn't need Carmine to get any further into this. Things were already looking bad for him. Plus, he had to figure out how to get this guy stopped.

"You're Dan, aren't you?" he finally asked.

"Doesn't matter who I am," came the reply.

"Yeah, but you're him, right? You're taking revenge for the fire in your restaurant. We can work this out. I didn't call for that and no one knew your wife was in there."

There was a long silence on the other end.

"We'll work this out, one way or another. Here's where we start. You've seen the video. It's not good news for anyone, you included, if it goes public. There's six of those guys there. I figure keeping them anonymous is worth about fifty grand a piece. That comes to three hundred grand for the original video, no copies kept by me."

"Three hundred grand? You fucking kidding me? You knock my guys off, steal my money, rob my game and then want me to pay you three hundred grand for a video? You're crazy."

"You don't want to pay, I'll check in with Carmine and then send it to the media if neither of you are smart enough to keep this under cover. I assume you cleaned up the apartment because you wouldn't want the cops looking too close into your games. All your scams are up for a close inspection if you're not careful."

"You punk," Vincent shouted, "you think you can come into my territory and shake me down? I'll find you and I'll kill you."

"You haven't yet, and this is about to get nastier. I don't think Carmine will like what's coming next. You've got an hour to think about it. I don't hear from you in an hour, I call Carmine." The phone went dead.

Dan's phone rang an hour later.

"What's the deal?" Vincent said when Dan answered.

"Three hundred grand in cash. Joey delivers the bag." Dan went on to describe how the delivery would take place.

"So you get the money and I have to wait for the video to come in the mail? That don't work for me." Vincent said. "We got to make an exchange, money for video."

"Yeah, and I get killed. No, we do it my way, I don't trust you. I'll be watching the drop. You don't call the shots, I do."

"How do I know you just won't rip me off for the money?"

"You don't. But I trust you less than you trust me. Ask your card buddies if they want to fuss about the details...or do they just want this to go away?"

Chapter 29

Two days later Dan was hiding on the second floor of an abandoned warehouse near the water front. He had positioned a table in the middle of the main floor and given instructions to Vincent to empty the bag of money on the table and leave. Dan figured there would be an attempt to take him out at some point in the exchange. He just had to make it happen so that he could control the outcome.

Joey entered at the appointed time and placed the bag on the table. After looking around and not seeing anyone, as instructed, he turned it over and dumped the bills on the table. Then he took the empty bag and left the warehouse.

Dan watched the car drive away. He sat at the window, watching. He could see no one on the street. *Where will they come after me?* He planned to leave from the back of the building but there was no assurance Vincent wouldn't have people waiting on all sides of the building. This time he was not in disguise. Underneath his jacket though, he wore a bullet proof vest. He carried a .223 Ruger Tactical carbine and his Colt 1911 .45 semi-automatic on his belt. He had a back pack for the money and extra magazines for both the Ruger and the Colt. If there was going to be a shootout, he would need a large amount of fire power and that meant enough ammo to beat back Vincent's men.

He watched the street. His sniper training took over. Even in this urban setting the rules still applied. Don't move until you are sure of remaining concealed. Locate your opponent. The one who locates the enemy first usually prevails in the fire fight. The trouble now was the enemy would know his position after he retrieved the money.

He crept to the rear of the warehouse and carefully looked out at the other buildings nearby. Most were abandoned. He studied them. *If I can locate them, I can even the odds.* Even nightfall would not hurt his situation.

Dan was facing south. The afternoon sun was now to the southwest. On the east side of the warehouse, he saw a flash of reflected light. Someone's in those windows. One shooter was placed to the east. He would be shooting into the sun and not be effective. *Where are the others? They must have other shooters and men at the street level.*

Then a thought occurred to Dan. The buildings were heated by steam. There must be steam tunnels connecting the buildings, servicing the different warehouses. *Why didn't I think of that before?* He quietly descended the stairs, stuffed the money in his back pack, he then explored the main floor, looking for stairs or a ladder going down to a basement. If he could find a tunnel and go through it to the next warehouse, he would emerge from the building with the advantage of surprise.

Got to be quick. These guys won't have much patience. If they came in, he could be trapped either on the main floor or in the basement. Dan shuddered at that thought.

His search revealed a trapdoor in the floor. He managed to pry it open. Below, as he hoped, was a tunnel lined with large pipes and electrical conduit. Dan quickly climbed down and set off to the west. *Wherever this winds up, it beats walking out into an ambush.*

After three minutes of running bent over through the tunnel, he came to a set of climbing rungs ending in a round cover. *Probably comes out in the alley between buildings.* Dan climbed up the shaft. He carefully lifted the cover just above its rim and slid it over. Taking a deep breath, he poked his head out. As he had hoped, he was in between the buildings. No one seemed to have spotted him. A dumpster sat next to the adjacent building. Dan slid his pack out of the hole and climbed out. He dashed to the cover of the dumpster just as the shooter from the south side building fired. The shots hit the ground just behind him.

After gaining the cover of the dumpster, Dan lay on his stomach and risked a glance at the shooter's position. He figured the man would be aiming higher, expecting him to be kneeling or crouching. Sure enough a shot rang out over his head. Dan was able to locate the position. He backed up and then turned to the side of the dumpster next to the building. There was space between the container and the wall. Dan slid his rifle through the gap and squeezed himself into the slot until he could target the shooter's position. It took a moment and he got the man in his sights.

His carbine didn't have a scope but the target was not far, about fifty yards away. He'd only get one clear shot. Others were probably already headed to his position and he needed to move. Slowing his breathing down, he steadied the rifle, and between breaths and heartbeats, his index finger stroked the trigger in a smooth motion, careful to not pull the rifle off the target. The carbine spat once and the target fell back from the window.

Dan jumped up and ran forward to crouch behind a set of concrete steps leading to a door in the building, near its corner. He saw two men coming forward along the wall of the warehouse he had just left, moving towards the alley. Dan fired rapidly and they both went down before they could return fire.

More would be coming. He ran back down the alley and scrambled through a broken window. Once inside he scanned the area. He was in a large, empty room, but not the main warehouse space. Dan headed towards the back of the building. The men would be coming along the back of the warehouse he had escaped to attack his position in the alley. He figured they had some coming from the other end of the alley as well to box him in.

He held his rifle shouldered and ready to shoot anyone looking in through the windows. Stepping carefully to not crunch any broken glass or debris, he moved forward. Suddenly a head appeared. The man let out a startled sound and started to bring his rifle up. Dan's shot hit him in the face and he fell backwards out of sight. Dan jumped behind a column and two other men fired blindly into the warehouse.

Crouching, he came around the column firing. He hit one of the men and the other dropped down below the window. Dan charged to the window and reached through it to shoot the guy crouching below.

Shots whistled through the warehouse from the windows on the alley. *Gotta go.* Dan sprinted through the warehouse away from the windows and through a door into the main section of the building. He ran full speed through the cavernous building to the far front corner. At another broken window he stopped and carefully peeked over the rim. No one in sight. He scanned in both directions. *I'm a step ahead now.* He had a chance. They would be coming into the warehouse. They would be slow and careful. Dan had killed too many for them to be careless.

He climbed out of the window and dropped to the pavement five feet below. After another look around he ran across the parking lot to some junked cars along the fence. He had to find a way through the fence. He couldn't go to the main gate which was back towards the building where the drop was made. The gang was concentrated there, in the alley, and now moving into the warehouse he had just left. *Got to get through the fence and disappear.*

He crouched and ran along the fence until he came to a broken section he could squeeze under. As he was going through the break he heard the shouts. They had spotted him. Dan fought to keep his panic down as his back pack snagged on the fence. Pulling harder only hooked him tighter. He forced his rising panic down and made himself back up, shift the pack sideways, and crawl forward again.

Finally through, he sprinted down the street as shots came his way. He turned the corner. A car squealed out of the parking lot, heading in his direction.

Dan ran down the street until he reached an inset doorway offering some protection. He turned to wait for the car to come around the corner fifty yards back. *Think I'm just going to run down the street so you can shoot me down? Idiots.*

As the car started around the corner, Dan opened up with his carbine, pumping round after round into the windshield. The car careened wide to the left and ran up on the sidewalk to slam into a building on the other side of the street. He continued to fire into the front, and then the back seats.

When he changed magazines someone opened the back door on the far side of the car. The man fired a couple of shots—pistol shots Dan guessed from the sound. They would not be that effective at over fifty yards. Dan sent multiple rounds into the back of the car, pinning the shooter down. Then he jumped out and ran away from the car, to the next doorway. The shooter poked his head up to fire again and Dan sent him hiding with another multiple round burst from his carbine. Then he ran, turning the corner at the end of the block.

He was still in the old warehouse area. He ran full speed down the block and through another alley, which brought him out to a street of row houses. He stopped before entering the street to disassemble his carbine and stuff it in his back pack. He kept his pistol in its holster under his jacket. Then he emerged on the street and started running again.

His lungs were on fire and legs giving out when he heard the sirens. The arrival of the cops meant Vincent's guys would have to disappear. They couldn't pursue him. But he could also be stopped by the police, and with the money and weapons in his backpack, it would be all over for him. Like Vincent's crew, Dan couldn't get caught. He had to put more distance between himself and the car he shot up.

After five more blocks, now more walking than running and being careful to not to draw the attention of any cruiser going past, Dan arrived at a subway entrance. This was always a dilemma. Going down into the station meant putting himself into a box with only one exit. If any cop patrolling the station received an alert about the shooting, he might stop a male with a back pack. There were certainly enough bodies to be found some eleven blocks away to make this a major incident. But if there weren't a cop, he could quickly disappear. Staying on the streets and walking posed a greater risk of being stopped, and getting a cab would leave a record of his presence. He was not in disguise; bad choices all around. He slowed his breathing, wiped the sweat from his face, and started down the steps.

Chapter 30

Marty Singleton and Jimmy McMurray sat in their captain's office. Ron Donovan was not happy. There had been a robbery at a local card game and some prominent citizens were involved. He had been advised to keep a lid on it, but the attendees were worried about a shake-down. One said the dealer had been shot, but the cops had found no evidence.

"You telling me that you didn't find any signs of a shooting?"

"Nothing yet," Marty said. "I'm sending a forensics team over with high intensity lights and luminol. If there's blood there, we'll find it."

"Someone gets shot at close range and there's no bullet hole...anywhere?" Donovan continued.

"Could have been a small caliber or a sub-sonic round. It may not have gone through the body. Right now we can't even establish that someone was shot in that apartment," Marty responded.

"What can you establish?" Donovan asked.

"We got fingerprints. We're running them now. We know who was there. But do you want me to get prints from all the people at the game? To match them up with what's in the apartment?"

"We've got to be careful here," Donovan replied. "We've got one hand tied behind our backs because of who was there. No one wants the publicity, but they want us to find this thief."

"And we're getting no help from Salvatore," Marty added.

"Both hands tied behind our backs," Jimmy chimed in.

Donovan just gave him a sour look.

"I got one lead. It's a long shot."

Donovan looked over at Marty. "Well, what is it?"

"There's word on the street that a guy, Dan Stone, is behind the robberies and shootings. He's got a grudge against Vincent. It's from that restaurant explosion last year. It was his restaurant and the guy's pregnant wife was killed in it. Maybe he's getting revenge."

"So, you going to pick him up? This is good. Maybe we can put this to rest after all."

"Problem is, he left town over six months ago and no one's seen him since."

"Then why do people think he's behind all this?"

"He's got the motive...and I did some checking. He was a sniper in the army before getting out. He did two tours in Iraq. He would know what he's doing."

"So you got a ghost, someone no one's seen in six months, who might have a motive and who's an Iraqi vet? What the hell do I do with that?"

"Like I said, he's got the connection because of the fire. Apparently he made some threats towards Vincent before he left."

"Okay, follow it up. He got any friends from the neighborhood?"

"Already working on it, Captain. I'm trying to get on top of this for you."

"For all of us. Last thing I need is to have city hall pissed and the commissioner on our ass."

Two days later Mike Warner, an FBI agent, sat in Ron Donovan's office.

"Captain Donovan, I've been tasked to take charge of an investigation into Vincent Salvatore. We know about the recent spate of robberies and shootings with his gang.

The Agency feels we have an opportunity here that we need to exploit."

"What is the opportunity that's so important you can come in here and get in the way of my on-going investigation?" Ron asked.

"I'm not at liberty to say, but we have determined that there has been an attempt to blackmail some public officials, so if I need to, I can use that to make this a federal matter."

"Where'd you get that information? I certainly haven't come to that conclusion." His face grew red; Ron was beginning to let his anger show.

"Again, I can't divulge that information at this time, but I can assure you that we've been given the go from my boss, Hank Wilson, the Special Agent in Charge for New York...in cooperation with your commissioner. You can make the calls to confirm this." Mike was polite but cold. "I'd rather have your cooperation without making this a larger issue." He had his job to do and didn't enjoy insulting local police departments. But over the years he had found that they could also muck up his work. He had learned to establish his authority and position early on so he could do his work without interference. "I'd like to be able to call on the detective working the case. It'll make my work more efficient and I can be out of your hair sooner."

"So you come in and take over the investigation and want to use my detective to pursue it. Are you gonna pay him as well? Seems like I'm providing the manpower and you're taking the credit."

"Captain, you know who's involved. We've got something unique going on here. Something that we've not seen outside of a mob turf war and this doesn't seem to be one of those, it's different. In addition, there's also these prominent citizens...this could turn into a pile of shit for everyone. If you want your fingerprints on it, I'll be happy to oblige. I'm not out to nail some public officials for illegal gambling, I can save that for another day. I'm after larger game. But this could get ugly before it's over."

Ron Donovan just scowled, but he didn't have an answer. He had already received the phone calls from multiple sources after the card game was robbed. Things were delicate. Maybe it was for the best that it was now going to be out of his hands. Still, he didn't like the feds intruding on his turf. They always acted like they were better than everyone else.

Mike gave the captain some time to digest what he had said, suggested a meeting with Detective Singleton, and then asked for a room his team could use on a regular basis. After going through Singleton's information, Mike had Tommy's name and address. Two days later they had Emilio in the precinct office. The most Emilio would claim to know was the name of the woman who came around to see Dan, either Darlene or Doreen.

A search of the high school records for Tommy's class turned up three Darlene's and one Doreen. One was deceased, two were married, one lived in California, which left a Doreen in Boston. Following up on her, they discovered her new position with the Manhattan law firm. A phone call to her firm yielded her location in Atlanta. Mike called the FBI office down there and had an agent find her and arrange a visit.

Chapter 31

A week after the warehouse shootout, Dan walked down the street where Joey lived. It was lined with brownstones, solid construction but undistinguished in their sameness. The area had not yet experienced the yuppie renovation that was occurring elsewhere in Brooklyn. It was two in the morning and the street was empty, all the houses dark. He walked up to Joey's car parked in front of his house. Quietly he bent down and punctured the street-side tires, and then the ones on the curb-side. He then walked away into the shadows. Two blocks later, he slipped into a cluttered alley and curled up next to a dumpster. He wrapped his coat around himself, set his watch to buzz his wrist with a silent alarm and tried to go to sleep. With him he had his guitar case holding his Remington rifle.

At nine a.m. Joey stepped out of his front door, glanced up and down the street and walked to his car. He knew Vincent was on a tear and he needed to be at the Gardens early. If shit was flying, Joey wanted to make sure it didn't fly his way.

The robberies and the shootout at the warehouse had resulted in seven of Vincent's men—some members of the crew, some associates—getting killed or wounded. This was a major screw up. Now the police were hot on this. It made the papers and was being written up as a major gang war. The reporters were unaware of Dan's connection to the shootings. Meanwhile no one in the mob could lay a hand on him. He frustrated every move they made. Joey knew this problem was attached to him. Yeah, he had handled the firebombing of the restaurant badly, but it was an easy mistake to make. Who knew this guy would come back like some comic book avenger and start robbing and killing the crew? If things got worse, if Vincent needed a fall guy, Joey knew he would be it. They needed to get Dan out of action. His face twisted into a scowl as he pondered how that could be done.

When he got to his car, he saw the flat tires. "Shit!" He walked around to the street side and saw the other two flat as well. "What the fuck?" As he started to the driver's door, pulling out his phone, the windshield exploded in a thousand shards. Joey just stared at it for a moment. He hadn't heard a sound. Suddenly he realized someone had shot out the windshield.

He twisted around to the rear of the car and crouched down. Pulling out his phone, he hit speed dial. "Frank, someone's shooting at me in front of my house. They slashed my tires and now they're shooting at me. Get over here quick."

"You see where they are?"

"No, but they shot the windshield, which means they're east of me. Come in from the east end, down 83rd Street. You may be able to see them. I can't see nothing from here. Hurry."

"Don't panic." Frank said.

Joey figured Frank would connect this to Dan. He hoped Frank would intercept him as he came down the street. Dan might be getting over confident. After the call, Joey made a dash for his front door. There were no more shots.

Joey watched from a window in his apartment as Frank drove slowly down his street, obviously looking carefully around. When Frank got to the car, Joey stepped out of the house. He was just angry now, his fear having subsided since nothing else had happened. To the neighbors it probably looked like a serious vandal attack on the car. He now felt silly which only increased his anger.

"I'll bet Dan's behind this." He got in the car with Frank. "I didn't hear a fucking sound when the windshield shattered."

"If he was far enough away, shooting a sub-sonic round with a suppressor, you wouldn't hear it," Frank replied. "He's pretty damn professional."

Joey just shook his head; he didn't understand the finer points of shooting. But it seemed to him Frank was starting to develop a perverse admiration for Dan.

Joey suppressed his anger; Frank never failed to make him uneasy. Darkness hovered around him, as if light just disappeared when it hit him. Joey didn't want to let his emotions show in front of him.

"Better call the garage to pick up your car with a tilt bed. You don't want the police to start asking more questions."

The gang had a favorite garage they controlled which did business without asking questions. At times they helped to make cars disappear and fixed bullet holes that could prove embarrassing.

"What's next? Is he going to start shooting at everyone or just me?" Joey knew Dan was targeting him. It was only a matter of time before he'd get killed like Angelo. The thought made him shudder.

"Maybe he wants to make you sweat for a while before he takes you out," Frank said without humor.

Joey looked over at him. "Why the fuck you say that?"

"He shot Angelo in the head in front of the restaurant. Angelo was standing right next to you. Now he shoots out your windshield. You think he's that bad a shot, he missed you twice?"

Joey sensed Frank enjoyed twisting a knife in his ribs.

He turned to look ahead. "I don't know what to think. All I know is I'm the only one getting targeted." He paused. "You really think he's playing with me?"

"Question is, when is your number up?"

"Maybe we should give the police more help?"

Frank looked over at Joey with those dead eyes. "You think Vincent'll go for that?"

"So I just wait around to get shot? That's fucked up."

Frank shrugged and drove on in silence. Joey got on his nerves. Frank knew killing...close up. It didn't bother him. He knew he was different but he didn't care. He'd rather be a cold son-of-a-bitch than a punk like Joey. Joey was all bluster and toughness when the deck was stacked in his favor. Now he was beginning to wilt under the pressure.

A smile almost cracked open on his face as he thought about how Dan was messing with Joey before he killed him. Frank was sure that was the end game. In a way it was a shame that he couldn't do it, but he didn't doubt Dan could...and would.

When they arrived at the Gardens, Detective Marty Singleton was there talking with Vincent.

"Joey, come in, you're one of the people I want to talk to," Marty called out.

Joey walked into the back room looking at Vincent. His boss's expression gave no clue as to what was going on.

"Where were you this past Tuesday?" Marty asked before Joey could ask Vincent anything.

"Why you want to know? Who cares where I was?" Joey was buying time until he could figure out what to say.

"I care, answer the question," Marty replied, now less friendly.

"And if I don't? What are you charging me with here? I do something wrong?"

"Joey, just answer the question. I can take all of you down to the station for questioning, get your lawyer involved, maybe get other people involved. I'm sure Vincent here doesn't want to go to the station and I'm sure he doesn't want some other people brought into the act."

Vincent nodded to Joey, who stood for a moment, still not knowing what to say.

"We were all hanging around here at the restaurant," Frank said.

"Who the fuck asked you? And who are you?" Marty shot back.

"That's Frank Varsa," Vincent said. "He works for me, keeping an eye on the restaurant, especially with what's been going on lately."

"That's convenient," Marty replied. "Vincent, we have some of your guys in the morgue from that shootout at the warehouses. This is getting out of hand. I've got five people killed and two wounded."

"I know. I visited those guys yesterday. It's a shame. Someone seems to be attacking my business. Did you check on my competitors?"

"You're the only one I know who competes this way in business."

Vincent pointed a finger at Marty. "You may not think that could happen, but you should still check them out. We need the police to protect us from attacks like this."

"I'm touched. So all of you were here minding your own business when this shootout occurred?" Everyone nodded. "If that's so, what were those guys of yours doing at the warehouse?"

"They were keeping an eye on things...you know, since all this started." Vincent spread his hands in an expansive gesture.

"What about the weapons I found on them? They're not registered."

"Lieutenant, I don't know anything about them. I hire the guys to watch out for my business, I don't supply them with weapons. If they get them without licenses, I don't have anything to do with that. You have to ask them."

"You mean the ones that are still alive. I plan on doing that as soon as they're able to talk. In the meantime, if I find any of your finger prints on the weapons or car, I'll have you arrested for supplying false testimony."

"We ain't under oath," Joey finally spoke up.

"I can arrange that real quick if you want. Now, you want to change your story?"

Joey shook his head.

Marty turned to Vincent. "Vincent, get these guys out of here, I need to talk to you alone."

After the others left the room, Marty continued, "Look, we know what's going on. We don't have to be coy with each other. We're aware of this guy Dan and how he might be connected to these shootings. The question is whether or not you'll help me get to him and put a stop to this. Captain Donovan is very nervous and so are a few politicians, some of whom are regulars at your card game."

Vincent stared straight back at Marty. He wasn't all that bad and brighter than most. "You must be getting near to retirement. I'm sure this isn't what you wanted."

"Don't worry about my retirement, but you can be sure, this isn't what I want to spend time on—one criminal going around killing other criminals. It's starting to look like a gang war. And the next thing you know, civilians are going to get killed. That's what I really don't want to happen. So help me out."

"I'd like to, really. But you know it don't work that way—"

"You take care of your own dirty laundry, right?"

Vincent nodded.

"Well, he's not part of your dirty laundry, so this is different. And, another thing, the FBI is involved now."

Vincent looked at him with sharper interest.

"Yeah, they came in after the card game holdup. What they're after I don't know, but it isn't the players. There could be a lot of heat coming your way. Now what can you give me? Help me shut this down."

Vincent thought for a moment. He figured it could be a dangerous move, but he needed something to change the balance, something to start putting Dan on the defense. "Lieutenant, you've interviewed my guys who were ripped off, did anything stand out?"

"Like what?"

"They all gave different descriptions. Yet we both figure it was one guy, Dan Stone. He's using disguises."

"Really?"

"Seems obvious to me. Check with the victims, get their descriptions and start looking for those people. It might help."

"Why wouldn't he just change disguises?"

"He probably does, but I'm thinking he has a limit." Vincent shrugged. "You asked me to help. This is what I got. What else you gonna do?"

Late Friday night, Dan slipped up to Joey's front door. In a plastic bag he had a dead cat—road kill he found on the street. He took it out and fastened it onto Joey's front door with a large wood screw. Joey would find it in the morning. On the cat, he pinned a note saying, "I'm coming for you." Dan figured the gesture might help spook Joey further.

That same night, Dan drove out to Vincent's house. He lived in a newer suburban neighborhood, large homes with large lots. Some of the homes, like Vincent's, had walls and a gated driveway mimicking a more palatial estate, but the effect didn't quite work out on the lots. Instead of an impressive statement, it looked contrived.

Weeks before, Dan had followed Vincent home. Vincent had gotten lazy over the years—lazy or careless. He drove home by the same route every day. Dan just followed him part of the way and then dropped off. The next day he waited near where he dropped off and, sure enough, Vincent's town car would come along. In a matter of four days, he managed to track him all the way to his house.

It was three in the morning. Everything was dark and quiet. Being Saturday morning, the whole neighborhood would be sleeping in. Instead of everyone rising around six to head off to work, people would be getting up around eight to enjoy a moment of relaxation before the family weekend activities began. He parked a block away from the house and carefully approached it on foot, keeping to the shadows. He was dressed in black jeans and a black hoodie covering his face. Vincent's gate was strong and locked—not there just for decorative effect. He scanned the house with his night vision scope. There were motion sensors mounted high on the walls, aiming at the yard. From what Dan could tell they had overlapping fields of cover. *Probably go around the whole house. Detectors and flood lights. Trip the sensors and the lights go on, along with an alarm inside.*

There would be no outside alarm to wake the neighbors. If Vincent was smart there would also be cameras which would provide live video record of the intruder.

Looks like I leave my calling card on the front gate for now. He took out a dead skunk he had collected days earlier and put in his freezer. It had a note pinned to it which read, "Are you next?" Dan hung the skunk on the gate and quietly retreated back to his car.

He drove over to New Jersey and parked in the rented garage space. It would be 7 a.m. before he got back to his apartment. Fatigue pressed heavily on him, dragging him down emotionally as well as physically. He was wreaking havoc on Vincent's crew, disrupting their cash flow, killing or wounding their soldiers and making life unpleasant for everyone around Vincent. And he guessed he was beginning to terrorize Joey. The game had to end in Joey's death. Yet, as he moved closer to that moment, he felt no rush, no sense of anticipation. Killing Joey had begun to lose its emotional energy. It now seemed to be something he had to do, a task to complete. What lay beyond, he couldn't tell and didn't want to think about. There was no "beyond" for him...not yet.

Chapter 32

It was a small, cramped office in a corner with no view, but it was better than a cube. Jane Tanner smiled at the thought that this tiny space measured her ascendance in the world of the CIA. *Small indicators, small victories. We take joy in them when we can.* She had worked for the agency for almost ten years now.

Jane had grown up looking for excitement. After college she tried some teaching jobs, but got bored with them. Always a good researcher, when she saw an ad for Internet research, she answered it and found herself working for the CIA. Of course her family and friends couldn't know. As far as they were concerned, Jane worked as a network administrator in some consulting firm. Something boring and, if questioned, it had the cover of a government contract complete with security demands so she could not really talk about it.

When she had tired of reading wire reports, looking for kernels of information, threads that could lead to something important, she lobbied to move over from the DI, Directorate of Intelligence to the Natioanll Clandestine Service, formerly the Directorate of Operations. She was elated at being accepted, but wondered three months later during her training at the Farm whether or not she had bit off more than she could chew. She relished the excitement of field work and was good at collecting assets. There was something about being a woman that made it easy for her to connect with the strange misfits she handled in the spy business. The informants were a mixed bag and often needed a delicate, even empathetic hand. Good, bad, or mediocre, they were out there alone and she was sensitive to that isolation and danger. Many opened their hearts to her and became more effective under her guidance. Now after six years overseas, Jane was back at Langley.

The modern CIA was less and less involved in gathering human intelligence, HUMINT it's called. Assets were not as carefully selected and they often were unreliable. Worse, there were incidents of double agents penetrating the system and compromising operations. The culture at the agency evolved more towards trolling the internet and sending out drones to do the dirty work—wet work. But drones were not always the best solution, in spite of their ability to strike from a distance. They sometimes created collateral damage. And now Congress was beginning to get all righteous about their ever-increasing use. The program was getting its teeth pulled and the bad guys were not being taken down.

Jane's new boss, Henry Mason, had read a research paper about using unorthodox methods—some would say old fashioned—to do some of the dirty work that had to be done. The service could call on the guys in the SOG, Special Operations Group. They were mostly ex-military people and their operations were done following those protocols. They did fantastic work but they were not the type of operators that could mingle in the streets of different countries, locating and removing targets. That was assassin work and it needed a special kind of operator.

So now Jane was back in Langley trying to start a new program, one involving great risk to her and her boss in this new politically correct climate. Henry didn't seem to care. He was old school and would be out in five years. He worked in the NCS. Henry was under the Special Activities Division (SAD). He directed black operations under the Psychological Operations sub-section. Black ops were operations that could not be attributed to the CIA or the

US. Sometimes they were aimed to mislead and point to a different organization or country.

Henry had decided to start a new deep cover operation under his section, one that had a specific purpose and one that no one but he and the person he would put in charge to run the op would know about. He wanted to strike back at the enemy before he was put out to pasture. What Henry was going to try to implement was a program to take the fight to the terrorists. To eliminate dangerous operators that SAD identified. There would be no attempt to turn them, or even spy on them. He was going to take them out: terrorists, gun runners, and the people who financed those operations. It was to be a disruptive program, eliminating key people that allowed the terrorist networks to operate.

Henry was deep enough in the CIA structure that his work would not involve the Deputy Director of the NCS or others at even higher levels. The program was small enough to avoid their oversight. The compartmentalization also gave them cover which suited Henry's purpose. With his long tenure and good record he was able to get the head of SAD, an old colleague, to approve a modest budget for a "research" program in black field operations that could be buried within the larger field ops budget.

Henry had come to know Jane from her days running assets overseas. He had liked how well she supported them and how well they had performed under her care. He had sensed in Jane a similar desire to take the fight to the bad guys, so he had pulled some strings to get her back to headquarters to put her in charge of this new operation.

After some discussion, Jane signed on. It may have been career suicide, but Henry had guessed right; she was frustrated and wanted to strike the enemy. Now for the past two months, Jane's challenge had been to find capable assassins who were not so amoral that they would turn on her or the agency when a better offer came along. It had been a difficult search so far; she needed something more than just mercenaries.

She stared at the file on her desk, thinking it might be the key to moving this new operation forward. Maybe the answer was in here, however unlikely that seemed. It was a stretch, but Jane was frustrated and ready to try stretch options.

Someone was taking out members of the mob in Brooklyn. The press kept talking about multiple people, but the file indicated that others thought it was the work of one person. Whoever was involved was very good at what they were doing. There were sniper level shots and a gun battle that had left five mobsters dead and two badly wounded. The file even had a name for the probable shooter, Dan Stone. He was an Iraqi veteran and had been a trained sniper. The problem for the police was that no one could find him. He had to be good to do what she read in the report, and he had to be good at avoiding detection and capture with both the mob and the police looking for him. But she wondered what his motivation was for what he was doing? The answer to that question would go a long way in determining if he was the right guy.

Just then her phone rang.

"Tanner, here."

"It's me, Fred," said the young man who had given her the file. "I just wanted to update you on the file I dropped off. It seems the FBI is now working on the case. Not sure what their interest is at the moment, but I thought you should know."

"Thanks, Fred." Jane hung up and went back to the file. After some minutes, she made a decision. She needed to find this guy before the cops did.

Chapter 33

Vincent's wife, Sheila, opened the front door to see her girls off to school. She had turned off the security system and unlocked the gate. The security rituals were something Vincent insisted on. Sheila thought they were excessive, but had acquiesced years ago.

She had met Vincent sixteen earlier, when he was a street hood looking to join the mob. Becoming a "made man" —a wise guy—was the only goal Vincent ever had. They always got the best tables at restaurants and didn't wait in line at the clubs. Even the hoods who weren't made men enjoyed some of the privileges if they were connected to a known mobster. In fact, that was how Vincent met her.

Sheila and some girlfriends were standing in a line on the sidewalk one night, waiting to get into one of Brooklyn's hot clubs when Vincent and his buddies walked right past them to the front of the line. After a few words with the doorman he let them in like they were VIPs.

Two nights later, Vincent and two other guys had walked up, while Sheila and her girlfriends were again standing in the same line. Sheila smiled at the recollection. She had called out to him, "Hey, big guy, how about gettin' us in?"

Vincent had turned to look at her. She knew what he was seeing—a well built, dark haired beauty smiling at him with a bold, saucy look in her eyes. She was with three other girls, all bleached blondes with big hair. Sheila stood out with her dark, curly hair in proud contrast to the dime-a-dozen, fake blondes in the line. Vincent had been intrigued by her looks and attitude so he went over and within a minute, Sheila and her girlfriends had been escorted into the club.

One thing had led to another and Sheila had found herself thinking about Vincent more and more. She had found out from some friends that he had been thinking about her the same way. She was different, he told her later. She wouldn't let him get her in bed. She would say, "My momma told me a man won't buy the cow if you give him the milk for free." She smiled at the memory. What she said might have confused Vincent, but the practical effect was that he wasn't getting laid.

Still, Vincent had kept going out with her. Sheila had guessed it might have been the challenge. She had made herself different from the others. While she was impressed with his money, his street stature and the respect he got, she didn't fall all over him. She had more self respect and she had understood that it gave her more class. Things progressed and they finally had gotten married after he was "made" and formally joined the mob. The mob liked their members having wives; it created a sense of stability. They didn't care about mistresses, sleeping around, but expected the men to keep the two worlds apart.

Sheila knew Vincent was a mob member but she had turned a blind eye to what that fully meant. She put up with the late hours, the dangerous men, the times away that might have been with another woman. She enjoyed the luxuries membership brought and had gotten used to shopping with cash. There was always cash and guns around the house. But when her first daughter, Tiffany, had been born, she had begun to change, grow more conservative. She didn't party anymore and worried more about little things going wrong. After her second daughter, Amber, Sheila had become more introspective, focusing on her girls, and not being so much a part of Vincent's mob life. The change didn't seem to bother Vincent who spent a lot of time at the restaurant. He seemed to be more comfortable there than at home, Sheila thought sadly.

She said goodbye to the girls as they started down the driveway to wait for the school bus. When they got closer to the gate, they saw the skunk hanging there. It looked like a note was attached to the animal. The girls didn't attempt to go closer, but turned and yelled to their mother as they ran back to the house.

"There's a dead animal on our gate," Tiffany said.

"It's a skunk," Amber added.

"Vincent!" Sheila shouted as she went in the front door. "There's a dead animal on our gate. What's going on?" There was a distinct tone of alarm in her voice.

Vincent came lumbering down the stairs in his bathrobe. "What the hell are you yelling about?"

"Someone's hung a dead animal on our front gate. There's a note or something stuck to it." She pointed towards the street. "Go out and take that horrible thing down! And be careful," she added as Vincent opened the front door.

He shuffled down the driveway in his robe and slippers. The skunk made a terrible smell, but Vincent got close enough to read the note. He looked around and quickly turned and hurried back in the house.

"Why didn't you take it down? Is there a note? Vincent, what's it say? What's going on?"

"I didn't take it down because it stinks. Now shut up for a moment." Vincent picked up his phone to call the Garden.

"Don't tell me to shut up." Sheila put her hands on her hips. "I want to know what's going on. You never tell me anything."

"That's because you don't want to know. And right now I don't know what's going on so shut up and let me make a phone call."

Just then the door bell rang. Sheila opened the door. "What do you want?" she said to the officer standing there.

"Ma'am, we received a call about that dead skunk hung on your gate," the officer replied. "Do you want to make a complaint?"

"We don't want to report nothing." Vincent stepped forward. "It's probably just some kids, so you can leave now."

"Well, it is an act of vandalism. And someone already did report it, so I have to take some information down. And there was this note attached. Did you read it?"

"Yes, you don't have to read it to me," Vincent replied.

"What's it say?" Sheila asked the cop.

Vincent shook his head at the cop. "I read it. I'll deal with this."

"It could be construed as a threat," the cop said.

"A threat? What the hell does it say?" Sheila's voice rose.

"I'll tell you later. I don't want to worry the girls," Vincent replied.

"They're already worried, not to mention grossed out. Vincent, maybe the cops should investigate this? Someone may be trying to harass us. Maybe this wasn't just some kids."

"Leave it alone. It's nothing."

"Don't tell me it's nothing." Sheila was yelling now. "It's a disgusting thing to do. It shouldn't be happening here, in this neighborhood."

"If it's vandalism, ma'am, it can happen anywhere, even in the best of neighborhoods."

"You see?" Vincent said. "We'll just give him the info for the report, and then we can go have our breakfast and forget about this."

Sheila shook her head and went to get her keys. "I'll drive the girls to school. They've missed the bus. But I want you to tell me what's going on when I get back."

That same morning Joey opened his door. As it swung in the dead cat almost smacked him in the head. He jumped back. "What the...?" He read the note and slammed the door shut. He backed against the wall, his breath coming in ragged pants. Then he turned and ran down the hall to the rear of the townhouse. He stopped at the door, took a deep breath and slowly opened it. He glanced out at the alley in the back in both directions. No one in sight. He let himself out and ran down the alley to the side street. From there Joey ran two more blocks before flagging down a cab and heading to the Gardens.

When Joey arrived, most of Vincent's lieutenants were there including Gino Seppe.

"Where's Vincent?"

"He's on his way," someone said. "Someone hung a skunk on his front gate. He said something about a note as well."

"Shit. Someone screwed a dead cat to my door along with a note."

Now everyone turned to Joey.

"I wonder if they're related," one of the guys said.

"Dumbass, of course they're related," Joey responded. "And who the fuck do you think did this? Dan. That fucker's everywhere. Don't he ever sleep?"

Just then Vincent stormed into the back room. "I want that Dan guy found. I want him found right away," he yelled. "Now he's targeting my house and freaking my wife out. That's the last thing I need."

"He hung a dead cat on my door last night too," Joey said.

Vincent turned to him. "The fucking guy gets around. Doesn't he sleep?"

"Just what I was wondering." Joey started to pace around the room. "Look boss, he said I'm next on a note stuck to the cat. I got to disappear for a while. Who knows where or when he'll take a shot at me." Joey was sweating.

He wanted to hide out but needed to get Vincent's permission.

"Frank, why don't you put Joey up at your apartment, for a while?" Vincent suggested.

Frank shook his head. "You want me out tracking this guy down, not babysitting Joey."

Joey was relieved. He didn't like spending much time around Frank. "How about me staying with Gino? He's not married and he's got an extra bed." Gino Seppe was the soldier who collected the drug payoffs for Vincent. They had to set up at a different location after Dan robbed him.

Vincent nodded. "All right. Both of you get out of here, before this guy starts shooting at the restaurant again. I'll call you when you can come out."

"How long should we stay inside?" Gino asked.

"Joey doesn't go out for a week at least. You can go out and get food, but make sure you're not followed. The last thing you want to do is to lead this guy to your apartment."

Vincent didn't know what he would do about his situation at home. Sheila was pissed. He had left for the restaurant before she got back from school. Now this problem had intruded on her personal life. She didn't know and didn't want to know about the seamy side of Vincent's work. But that side was now showing up at his house. He was boiling inside about this punk guy who they couldn't track down and who had the nerve to target his home.

The report of the skunk incident had found its way to Detective Marty Singleton's desk, since it had Vincent's name on it. Marty looked through it and then dutifully passed a copy to the FBI agent, Mike Warner. Mike smiled when he read the report. Dan was doing just what he'd hoped for. Now he just needed to let the pressure build.

The next week, at three a.m., Dan drove past Vincent's home. He slowed down and stuck the Tec-9 out of the driver's window and let it loose. Thirty 9mm rounds slammed into the front of house. The purpose was not to hit anyone, but to shoot up the front of the place. It was over in less than ten seconds and Dan quietly drove down the street and around the corner.

Sheila started screaming and turned on a light. Vincent grabbed his pants and jammed his legs into them, falling back on the bed in his haste.

"Vincent, what's happening?" Sheila shrieked. "Was someone shooting at us?"

"Stay away from the windows. I'll check things out."

"Be careful."

Tiffany and Amber came running into the bedroom, both yelling, asking what was happening.

"Everyone stay here!" Vincent yelled. "Stay away from the window and keep the lights off." He grabbed a .45 from the drawer in his night table and pounded downstairs.

The front windows were shattered, and there were bullet holes in the front door. Going into the study, he turned on the monitor, flipped on the outside flood lights and checked all the screens. Nothing out there. No movement, no motion. He got on the phone and called one of his lieutenants.

"Get over here. I've got a problem at my house." Vincent was careful about what he said on his cell phone. "Bring a couple of guys with you and call Tony. I need him to help calm things down." Vincent often used Tony to calm Sheila down when she got worked up. He would patiently listen to her, letting her get all her anxiety out, not contradicting her, not telling her she was wrong. Then in calm, smooth tones, he would talk her down from her hysteria. Vincent didn't have the patience and was glad he could send Tony around to do this job for him.

After hanging up, he looked out and saw a police cruiser drive up to the gate and stop. They shined their spotlight over the gate and up the driveway. When they lit up the front door and living room windows, Vincent realized they could see the damage. They would be coming up to the house and now he'd have to deal with them.

The officers got out and tried the gate. It remained locked. They went back to the cruiser, probably to call it into the precinct. Vincent went back upstairs.

"There's no one out there now, but keep the lights off."

Sheila was peeking through the window. "That's the police out there. Are you going to let them in?"

"No. I've got some of the guys coming over to stay outside the rest of the night. I don't want the fucking police in my house at three in the morning."

"Well, they need to know. I can't go back to sleep, I may as well get up—"

"Don't turn on the light," Vincent said sharply. "If you do, we won't get them out of here for hours."

"Someone's trying to kill us. The police need to get to the bottom of this," Sheila responded. The girls nodded, their eyes wide in fear.

"I told you. No cops! I've got some of the crew coming. They'll watch the place for me. No one's trying to kill us. Someone just wants to scare us, but I'll find him...and when I do—"

"Well, he's successful. I'm scared. This isn't right. We live in a nice neighborhood, this shouldn't happen here. You got to make this stop."

"I'm trying. But you gotta stay calm."

"Are you going to call Carmine? Maybe he can help."

"No, I'm not going to call Carmine. He can't do any more than I can. And don't you go calling him."

"Well, I'm supposed to have lunch with Gina this week. What do I say when she asks how things are? Do I just tell her, 'Oh fine, we're doing great, someone's just leaving dead animals on our gate and shooting up our house.' Tell me, what do I say? Because I don't know what to say or what to think."

Vincent sat down and rubbed his head. "Look, Sheila, I'll get this under control. Just don't start mouthing off to Gina. You know she'll just take all that back to Carmine and get him upset. Please, let me handle this."

The girls were crying now, both holding on to their mom. "All right, I'll keep this quiet, but how long do think it will be before Carmine hears about this? This harassment has got to stop. We can't live like this. How does someone just go around doing things like this and no one can stop him? That's why I think the cops should get involved—"

"Jesus, no. I told you, no cops!"

Now Sheila started crying along with the girls.

Chapter 34

When the report of the shooting came across Marty's desk he showed it to Mike.

"You going out to the house?" Mike asked.

"Yeah, this is more serious than a dead skunk. I'll have to get a full statement from everyone in the house."

"I want to talk to Vincent, alone," Mike said.

"Pick your time, but I've got to go to the house first."

Mike nodded. "I'll leave the house visit to you for now." After Marty left Mike drove down to the Sicilian Gardens. Vincent had arrived after dropping the girls off at school with strict instructions to not talk about the shooting. He didn't expect them to obey which did nothing to improve his mood.

"What the hell do you want?" Vincent said after Mike introduced himself. "I got nothing to say to you. I'm sure I'll be giving Detective Singleton a statement later today. That's all I've got to say."

"I'm not interested in a statement about the shooting. I want to talk to you about your safety."

"I can take care of myself. Since when is the FBI worried about someone like me?"

"Since you might become a target of your boss." Mike glanced around the room. "Look, we're alone so I'll speak freely. This trouble you're having is getting noticed. We know that Carmine is worried about it and so is his boss, Silvio. Now you don't want Silvio worried about you. That ain't healthy."

"What the fuck do you know about things? You don't know what you're talking about."

"I do know what I'm talking about. I've seen it happen, you've seen it happen. The boss loses confidence in you and you know too much. You become a liability. And you know the easiest way to eliminate a liability."

Vincent just glared at Mike but didn't say anything.

Mike continued, "I want to let you know, if things get hot, I'm authorized to provide protection for you and your family. A complete, new identity."

"The protection program? And all I have to do is rat everyone out. Get the fuck out of here. I don't need your help and nothing's going to happen to me or my family."

Mike got up to go. "Just keep the offer in mind. You owe it to your wife and daughters. If something happened to you, they would be in a difficult place with no one to help them." He handed Vincent his card.

"Get out," growled Vincent.

Later that same day Mike went out to Vincent's home. He introduced himself to Sheila and left his card with her after telling her that the FBI was interested in protecting the family if they were threatened by anyone. Sheila knew enough to not respond and told Mike they didn't need his help and she didn't appreciate his coming around when Vincent was not at home. Still, she kept his card when he left.

That evening Mike flew to Atlanta. He had arranged to talk with Tommy and Doreen the next morning. He met them at a Caribou Coffee shop near the Perimeter Shopping Mall.

After arriving in Atlanta, Tommy and Doreen had rented a car and drove to a Super 8 motel north of town where Doreen had rented a room under a fake name. It was not very super but they had wanted to stay anonymous. Tommy spent most of his time in the room, only going out occasionally to a movie or to eat nearby.

Doreen went into her firm's Atlanta office to spend her days sitting at a desk, combing through records in file cabinets to assemble the background documents her boss needed.

Neither knew how far the mob could reach but they didn't want to underestimate its abilities. Doreen figured men were looking for them and would find out they went to Atlanta. That fact would trigger enlisting local hoods to try to find them. She took a variety of routes on her return trips to the motel. She had work to do, but they had to remain in hiding.

"How'd you find us?" Tommy asked after they sat down. A local agent had visited them to tell them Mike was coming down."

"Airline tickets. Then combing through the cabbies with pictures of the two of you. That took some time, but we finally found one driver who remembered you." Mike smiled at Doreen. "Seems like being a good looking woman makes it harder to hide out. People take note, especially men."

She scowled back at him. "So why'd you track us down?"

"I need your help. I'm trying to get in touch with Dan Stone and both of you know him. I understand you're his best friend." He turned to Tommy.

"First of all, we should be clear that we don't have to talk to you," Doreen declared. "We're doing this only as a courtesy."

"And I appreciate that," Mike replied.

Tommy jumped in. "You want me to help you contact Dan, the mob wants me to help them contact Dan, but I can't contact him." He and Doreen had already decided that the cell phone was to remain a secret. "We left New York because we figured we'd become targets if Dan came back and started something."

"So you think he's back?" Mike asked.

Tommy shook his head. "I didn't say that."

"We left as a protective measure. If Dan came back, and I emphasize the word 'if', we didn't want to be caught in the middle." Doreen frowned and took a sip of her coffee.

"But it seems as though Dan has come back," Mike said.

"What makes you say that?" Tommy asked.

Mike recited the events that took place over the three weeks that they had been in Atlanta.

"So, you don't have any hard evidence, but you think it's Dan because of some things he said six months ago while grieving for his wife?" Doreen said.

Mike sighed and hunched over the table. "Look, we all know what's going on here. Dan vowed revenge and now we have someone shooting a guy in front of Vincent's restaurant, this string of robberies with shootings involved, a hold up of a card game, a shootout at a warehouse owned by Vincent that no one can explain, a dead animal left at Vincent's home and a drive-by shoot up of his house. It's pretty clear someone is after Vincent and his crew. It's also pretty clear that someone is probably Dan."

"That's a nice recitation, but you're repeating yourself. It still starts with a suspect premise," Doreen said.

"The bottom line is I can't contact Dan, but if he contacts me, what are you offering?" Tommy asked.

"Dan has no way out. You can see that. He's got the mob after him, the NYPD and now the FBI. I'd like to try to save him."

"That's noble of you, but what do you mean by 'saving him'?" Tommy asked.

"I'd like to keep him alive first of all. Then I'd like to get him a light sentence for helping us nail some of the mob. Remember, he's killed people, even if they are mobsters."

"That doesn't sound very enticing," Doreen said.

"Maybe not, but it's the best he can hope for since he went down this road."

"I'm not sure you have the horsepower to pull off what you propose," Doreen responded.

"I have more than you know. But the key point is I'm his only hope to get out of this alive and with some life left beyond jail."

"If it's Dan who's doing this," Tommy interjected.

Mike looked at Tommy and then turned his gaze to Doreen. "You can keep up the charade, but be sure to let Dan know about my offer. I'm his best option. We can do this on his timing and on his conditions, but he needs to talk to me." He paused to sip his coffee. "I don't know how long you're planning to staying down here, but the mob is going to find out where you are at some point. If you come back, get in touch with me, and I'll make sure you're protected from them. It's part of the deal."

After Mike left, Tommy and Doreen continued to talk about his offer.

"We should call Dan," Tommy said.

"Maybe," she replied. "But I don't trust this guy. I don't think he can get Dan out of the mess he's in."

"Still, he may be right that he's his only hope."

"Maybe."

Chapter 35

Dan lay in a ditch five hundred yards from Vincent's driveway in a large cleared area that would soon have new houses going up on it. He was covered with a camouflage net, blending him in with the bare dirt. His Remington 700 lay nestled in a notch on the rim of the ditch. The rifle's magazine was loaded with sub-sonic rounds. It was Sunday morning. He had been there since before dawn. His car was parked two hundred yards away along a street with partially completed houses. Innocuous and beat up, it looked like it had been left there by a construction worker over the weekend.

He had his escape route planned. He would crawl back along the ditch for fifty yards. Then, using the cover of some piles of dirt, he would dash back to another ditch leading to a culvert running under a road. After crawling through the culvert, he would emerge, now shielded from Vincent's house, to the road where his car was parked and slowly drive away. This new subdivision did not connect to Vincent's street, so he had a clear exit once reaching the car.

Now he waited. By 10:30 he began to wonder if anyone was coming out, but then the garage door opened and a Cadillac Escalade backed out of the garage and down the driveway towards the gate which was opening. When the SUV reached the road, Dan fired a round into the back tire and, quickly working the bolt action, fired another into the other rear tire. With the suppressor and using sub-sonic rounds, you couldn't hear the shots. The SUV stopped. The driver could tell something was wrong but didn't know what had happened.

Sheila opened the driver's door. Dan smiled at this opportunity. As she went around to the back to look at the tires, he sent a round into the driver's side window. When the window shattered, Sheila looked up and screamed. Then she turned and ran back up the driveway. Dan ejected the magazine and inserted another one loaded with incendiary rounds. He fired three shots into the back of the Escalade. The rounds exploded with intense heat—five thousand degrees upon impact. By the third round the gas tank exploded in fire, engulfing the rear end of the SUV. Satisfied, Dan gathered his spent shells and started crawling back to his car.

Hearing his wife's screams, Vincent came to the front door. He stared in shock as the Escalade erupted in flames. "What the hell?" he shouted as she came running up the driveway. He grabbed his wife, pulled her back inside and closed the door.

"Someone's trying to kill me!" she shouted. "They're shooting at me, I almost got killed! We're all going to get killed!" She kept shouting and sobbing hysterically. Vincent held her with one arm and tried to calm her down while he called Tony with his free hand.

"Get yourself and some of the guys out to my house immediately. Sheila's Cadillac just got shot up."

Just then another car came down the road and slowed as it went by the burning Escalade. The driver pulled out his cell phone, probably to call 9-1-1. Within five minutes sirens could be heard.

"Shit. This is not what I need," Vincent growled. He knew the fire truck would lead to the cops when they saw bullet holes in the car.

"Not what you need," Sheila screamed at her husband. "What about me? I nearly got killed. Who is shooting at us? First the dead animal, then shooting up the house, and now this? What's going on?" She pounded on Vincent's chest with each question. By then Tiffany and Amber had come downstairs.

"What's wrong? Mom, why are you crying?" Tiffany asked.

"Someone tried to kill me. In our driveway!" She started crying again.

"Oh, Mom!" Amber grabbed her mother. Both girls began to cry. Soon Vincent was surrounded by a cacophony of sobbing females.

Marty and Jimmy got to Vincent's house after the fire was put out but before Mike Warner arrived.

"Did anyone order a copter to search the area?" Mike asked Marty when he arrived.

"Yeah. The firemen found the bullet holes and showed them to the patrolman when he arrived. He called it in. The copter probably came too late. They didn't see anything suspicious."

Mike went over to the burned Escalade; two shots to the tires, one to the driver's side window and two or more to the rear to ignite the gas tank. "The ones in the rear must have been incendiary rounds."

"Yeah," Marty responded. "The wife says she didn't hear anything except the window shattering. Then she ran to the house. She could hear some loud cracks when she got to the front door."

"Shots? Why didn't she hear anything before that?" Jimmy asked.

"Maybe the guy had a suppressed rifle and sub-sonic rounds. The last ones, if they were incendiary rounds, wouldn't be subsonic," Mike said.

"He seems to be well equipped, and he knows what he's doing," Marty replied.

"You think this is Dan's work?" Jimmy asked.

"Who else could it be?" Mike replied. "Let's talk with Mrs. Vincent. You start."

"Her name's Sheila," Marty offered.

The two entered the house. Sheila was sitting in the living room, now calmer. The daughters were off to one side of the room. Vincent was there on the couch with his wife, and two of his lieutenants were standing nearby.

"Mrs. Salvatore, I'm Detective Singleton. I need to ask you some questions about this shooting."

"We've already given statements to the police," Vincent said. "We need all of you to get out. My wife has been traumatized enough today."

"I'm sure," Marty replied. "Unfortunately it doesn't work that way. You know that. I've got to ask the questions for myself." He proceeded to have Sheila go over the morning's incident again. There was some confusion about how many shots she heard, but she had the basic details straight.

Vincent scowled. "Now can you get the hell out of my house?"

"Mr. Salvatore, do you know why anyone would be trying to kill you?" Mike now jumped into the conversation.

Sheila looked over at Vincent with panic in her eyes.

"You again?" Vincent asked. "Why're you here? This's got nothing to do with the FBI."

"We think it's connected to the other incidents. As I said before, you're lives are at risk."

"Vincent, what's he talking about?" Sheila turned to her husband.

"Don't start trying to panic my wife." He glared at Mike, and then looked back to Sheila. "No one's at risk. This is just scare tactics. Don't listen to this scumbag. He's just another cop trying to make our lives miserable."

"So someone hangs a dead animal on your gate, shoots up the front of your house and shoots up your car, almost killing your wife, and then, maybe in frustration when he misses, he ignites the gas tank and burns it up. That happens for nothing? Maybe he was just trying to scare you but from where I'm standing it looks like your family may be in serious danger."

Tiffany and Amber now began to cry again over in the corner; Sheila looked to her husband with panic in her eyes. "Vincent? Tell me what's happening?"

"Nothing." Then turning to Warner, "You shut the fuck up. We're done talking to you. Get the fuck out, now!"

Mike just shook his head as Marty looked at him nervously. "We'll be going, but I feel it's my duty to express my concerns." He looked directly to Sheila. "Call me if you feel you want some protection. We don't want this killer to get to you or your daughters."

"Get out!" shouted Vincent.

Back outside, Marty spoke to Mike as they walked down the driveway. "You laid it on pretty thick. Holy shit, I thought Vincent was going to come over and slug you. What the hell are you trying to do? You scared her shitless."

"Exactly."

That same day a courier dropped off a box at Carmine Gianelli's office. The box contained a phone with a note that said he would receive a call at 4 p.m. The phone rang promptly at four. Carmine had one of his men take the phone outside to answer it.

"Yeah?" the capo asked.

"Now that you know the phone isn't a bomb, get Carmine. I need to talk to him."

The man came back in from the street and handed the phone to Carmine.

"Who is this?"

"I'm a guy that Vincent ambushed last week. He and I made a deal and he didn't follow through with it, so I'm calling you."

"I don't have anything to do with Vincent."

"Don't be coy. I know you're Vincent's boss. You're the underboss for Silvio Palma. He runs this section of

Brooklyn. Now Vincent's been having trouble, and he
missed a chance to end it. Maybe you want to do what he
didn't."

"You the guy who's been robbing people in Vincent's
neighborhood?" Carmine's voice, normally smooth and
rich, grew harsh.

Dan ignored the question. "I've got a proposition for
you. Vincent's operations are a mess and Mr. Palma must
be getting impatient for the trouble to go away. I'm the
trouble, so your chance to end this is to pay me off."

"You want me to pay you to go away?"

"Think of it as a protection payment, just like you
collect from the local businesses. Only you pay me not to
disturb your business."

"You got a lot of balls coming to me with that."

"I think I've made my point about how disruptive
things can be."

"So what do you want to stop all of this?"

"Five hundred grand a year."

Carmine snorted, almost a laugh. "You gotta be
kidding. You must be high on something. You're a punk.
We don't pay off punks, we eliminate them."

"Carmine, that hasn't happened yet. I keep hearing
that, but no one can find me. I can strike from a distance
or up close. Your guys are amateurs compared to me."

Carmine didn't say anything for a moment. "If I'm
willing to pay you off, I may need you to do some work for
me."

"That's not part of the deal. I don't work for you. You
pay me to leave you alone, that's all you pay for."

"So I pay you and you stop now?"

"No, I called you to let you think about it. There's two
more things I got to do before I stop. Then we can do a
deal."

"What two things?"

"I've got some business to finish. Some of it fixes a problem for you, some of it's personal. Keep the phone, I'll call you when I'm done."

Later that night, Frank Varsa sat in his car behind the empty warehouse. He had pulled up near the loading docks. It was eleven p.m. He drummed his fingers on the steering wheel, his eyes searched the dark around him. Getting a call to meet with Carmine made him nervous. Throughout the troubles Dan was causing, Frank made sure he was not the target of Vincent's blame. Finding this guy was hard and now with the cops crawling all over the area, he had to move more carefully. His plan to stop everyone who looked like one of Dan's disguises had to be put on hold; the cops were doing that for him. Carmine surely couldn't be pinning this crap on him?

After ten minutes Carmine's S500 Mercedes drove up and stopped twenty yards from his car, facing him. The lights went out. Frank couldn't tell if the engine was still running. Then the headlights flashed once. Frank got out and walked towards the car. He felt exposed in the open, not being able to see inside the vehicle.

As he approached, someone got out of the front passenger door and stood facing him. When he got to the car, the man, without a word, opened the rear door for him to get in.

"You're Frank, Vincent's enforcer, right?" Carmine asked without any introduction. He was smoking an expensive cigar. The car was filled with an almost overpowering aroma even though Carmine's window was cracked open.

"Yeah," Frank replied.

Carmine flipped on the overhead light and turned to look directly at him. "You doing much enforcing lately?"

Frank knew he was being checked out. He needed to act carefully around the man. "Not really. That guy, Dan, has the crew all screwed up."

Carmine studied him. "I need to get this problem stopped. It's bad for business and it's drawing too much attention to us."

Frank didn't say anything, just waited.

"I need to know what's going on and what's being done. You're going to work directly for me from now on. You stay where you are, but you let me know what's going on down there to get this under control. I want you to report to me every day." Carmine handed Frank a slip of paper and a cell phone. "You call this number with this phone and tell whoever answers what's going on. Understand?"

"Yes sir." This was a good sign. Frank was now on the safe side of the mess. He was going to be Carmine's eyes and ears.

"And you don't tell Vincent. Understand?"

"Understand."

Chapter 36

Tommy and Doreen arrived back in New York. It had been five weeks since they had left, but Mike had informed them that Dan was still on a tear, disrupting the mob's activities. He advised them to stay in Doreen's apartment in Queens. Mike considered it safer.

Jane Tanner was alerted when Tommy and Doreen returned. She boarded a flight from DC the next day. Upon arriving, she was met by Gilbert Short, an agent assigned to the city. The agency was not allowed to spy on U.S. citizens, but after 9/11, they kept some personnel in New York to follow up any possible terrorist leads. If they found anything of interest, they were to notify the FBI and turn any investigation over to them. Jane told Gilbert to help her make contact with Tommy and Doreen. He made the arrangements over the phone and that same evening Jane arrived at Doreen's door.

After being let in, she followed them into the kitchen.

"Now, who are you, how did you find out about us, and what do you want?" Doreen asked as they sat down.

Jane smiled. "First, I'm here to help. I know about the situation and your position in it. I can't say how, but I'm in possession of all the important information. I want to help Dan out of the situation he's in."

"You and the FBI. Everyone wants to help Dan out," Tommy said.

"Perhaps you should tell us about yourself and why you're interested in us." Doreen said.

Jane could tell she wanted—no, needed—some answers. Why all of a sudden everyone was interested in Dan. Apparently Mike Warner's answers didn't satisfy her, so Jane assumed Doreen would try to get more information from her.

"My name is not important at this point, but hear me out." Tommy and Doreen waited for Jane to continue. "I need to get in touch with Dan. There is not much time before he will have no way out of the situation he's in."

"We've heard it before. Everybody wants to get in touch with Dan," Tommy said. "First the mob, and they almost killed me because of it. Then the cops, the FBI, and now you, whoever you are. Dan's really popular since he went on his crime spree, and we keep being pulled into it." His voice rose in anger. "I got a business to run. I've closed it down because my life was threatened. Who the hell's going to repay me my lost customers? Dan isn't. The FBI certainly isn't. Are you?"

Doreen put her hand on Tommy's arm. "It's been pretty hard on us these past five weeks. Our lives have been completely disrupted."

Jane nodded. They were playing a round of "good cop, bad cop" whether they knew it or not. These were not stupid people. She sensed a measure of stubbornness in both of them. It might help her if they thought she was an outsider, not part of the system that was closing in on Dan. "I know that a Mike Warner from the FBI talked with you recently. I'm here to tell you that I am not working for his team—the FBI. He has an agenda that he probably hasn't disclosed to you".

"Just what would that be?" Doreen asked.

"Can you just level with us?" Tommy interjected. "We're caught in the middle. If you want any help from us, you're going to have to give up some information. I'm not...we're not buying all this 'secret' crap. Explain what you're up to—what you're after—and why we shouldn't trust this Mike Warner."

Jane thought about what Tommy said. He was right in a way. She was asking for them to give her access to Dan, if they could. Her instincts told her they did have access to him, but now they wanted some information from her, something to give them assurance that they were not getting Dan and themselves deeper in trouble.

"I'll tell you what I can. I won't tell you who I work for. What I can tell you is that it is part of the U.S. government, but not the police or the FBI."

Doreen nodded. "That leaves some interesting alternatives."

"Please, let me continue. Don't get too hung up on my employer. I'm not with a foreign entity, or organized crime." She paused. "Dan has seriously disrupted a segment of a major Mafia mob family. Vincent Salvatore is a Capo for Silvio Palma, the family boss. One of five in New York. The underboss is named Carmine Gianelli."

"If Dan is the one doing all of this," Doreen said.

"I'm not here to be coy or play games. I'm operating under the assumption that all of this disruption is Dan's work...so are the mob, the local police and the FBI. What I'm going to tell you now is very speculative, but sometimes it's all I have to work with in my business. It'll do you no good to pass this on to anyone, least of all Mike Warner. That will only be detrimental to Dan. Can you keep this to yourselves?"

Tommy and Doreen nodded.

"Good. Now the reason the FBI is interested is that the disruptions are putting enormous pressure on Vincent.

"Right now he's a well regarded Capo of Silvio's family. But the FBI is trying to get the mob to lose confidence in Vincent. If Dan continues to disrupt operations, the mob will begin to worry about Vincent's abilities. If they decide to replace him there is only one way out for Vincent—you don't get to retire from the mob, especially when you know as much as Vincent. He knows this, so we think Mike is hoping to use Dan's attacks to create a wedge between

Silvio and Vincent. His only way out then will be to go into the witness protection program."

"So Dan's doing some of the FBI's work for them," Tommy said.

"That's correct. The carrot Mike will hold out is that he can get Dan a reduced sentence for helping bring Vincent around."

"That's what Mike suggested," Tommy said.

"I wouldn't put much faith in that," Jane said. "It would only add to Mike's victory if he brought Dan in along with Vincent. My guess is that Mike will readily burn Dan when he has no use for him anymore."

"But he still needs Dan right now," Doreen said.

"Yes, but Mike can't control the mob, and he can't fully control the local police, although he's commandeered their investigation. That allows him to try to control the pace of it. When he hooks Vincent, he'll unleash all his force on netting Dan."

"So why does he want to talk with Dan?" Tommy asked.

"Probably to get closer to him, make Dan think he can help him. It would make it easier for Mike to bring him in."

"That's pretty cold." Tommy got up and grabbed a beer from the refrigerator. "Can I get you something to drink?"

Jane smiled and shook her head.

"So where do you come in?" Doreen asked.

"I've got a way out for Dan—"

"That's what Mike said," Tommy remarked from the fridge.

"That may be so, but I'm not someone who could or would arrest him, and I don't really care about getting Vincent into the witness protection program—"

"But you have an agenda as well," Doreen said.

"I can help Dan disappear, so he can have a life beyond this mayhem. A life where no one will find him."

"Why would you do that, Miss 'Mystery Woman'?" Tommy asked as he sat back down.

Again, Jane smiled. This was not easy, especially since she couldn't divulge certain things. "Yeah, I know it's mysterious and sounds too good to be believable. Let's just say Dan seems to have some unique skills which can be useful to my employers...for the benefit of his country. I'm interested in exploring whether or not he would be willing to use them in a positive way. That is why I need to talk to him...before it's too late."

"Useful skills. It seems all Dan has done is rob and kill people," Tommy said.

Doreen stood up suddenly and pointed her finger at Jane. "You...you're the CIA!"

Tommy's mouth dropped open. He looked from Doreen to Jane and back.

"I can't, of course, either affirm or deny your statement. There are many agencies where Dan's skills would be useful. Which one of them is interested will not be divulged here, at this time." Jane was firm in her statement. "But know this. I can extract Dan from the trap that's closing in on him."

Tommy kept staring at Jane, digesting Doreen's declaration. "We'll need some time to think this over. Not saying we can help or not," he finally said.

Jane stood up and smiled at him for keeping up the charade. She handed him a piece of paper with a number on it. "I understand. Talk it over and call this number if you decide to help. You should call it by tomorrow. It will take time to set things up and we don't know how close the FBI is to Vincent. I can see myself out. Thank you for taking time to see me." With that, she turned to go.

After Jane left, Tommy and Doreen talked late into the night.

"She's with the CIA," Doreen said, "even though she denied it."

"It doesn't really matter in the end," Tommy replied. "Either she or Mike Warner represent the only possible help for Dan to get out of this situation."

"And get this nightmare over for us as well."

Tommy nodded. "I'd like to think I could go back to my shop and take up where I left off, get Emilio back and even bring on another mechanic. So it's either Mike Warner or Mystery Woman."

Doreen smiled. "What a choice."

"He really dug a hole for himself. It's like he's in self-destruction mode. That's the same way he was thinking when he left town. I guess he didn't heal from losing Rita and the baby. I don't know if I could get over that either, but it seems a shame for him to lose what future he could have. The whole family is going to get wiped out from that senseless fire."

Doreen went over to Tommy and hugged him. "You're a good friend, even after he's brought all of this down on us. That's one of the things I love about you, your loyalty." She kissed him long and hard. "When we get done helping Dan's future, let's plan our own."

Tommy kissed her back and smiled. "I'm looking forward to that. I don't understand how I got so lucky, but I'm not knocking it."

"Just keep enjoying it," Doreen said.

Chapter 37

Things were getting complicated. Tommy had called Dan and had outlined the options presented by Mike and Jane. Dan sat in his apartment and thought about what had happened in the six weeks since he had returned. He never expected the FBI and some secret agency would be trying to get in touch with him. In addition, he had noticed that not only old men with beards were being stopped on the streets, but other people who resembled some of the disguises he used. Were the cops on to his disguises? He would have to make changes; it was going to get harder to be on the street and a simple traffic stop or accident could finish it for him even with his fake IDs. He was beginning to feel hemmed in. He paced back and forth in his dreary apartment.

He hadn't thought about a future up to this point. It had all been about getting revenge—making those responsible pay for Rita's death. Thinking about it now, the prospect of decades in jail, or worse, weighed on him.

Is there any way out at the end?

Tommy's call gave him more to think about. The options Tommy presented caused him to review the consequences of his actions, and he realized that he didn't like what he was coming up with.

Finish things with Joey and then get out of here. But where? Can't go to Lisa and Rob's, the feds will already have them marked for surveillance.

A life on the run, alone; how long could he hold up? Dan had no idea. His prospects didn't look promising.

He agreed with Tommy about the FBI agent. That man certainly had his own agenda and Dan guessed he would just be his tool. He had no idea what this woman would offer. It was hard to think she could improve his options, but it seemed worth a call.

This would have to be done carefully. If she was from some spy agency—Tommy thought it was the CIA—she would have the ability to track his cell phone if he stayed on a call too long. He dug out his collection of phones. He had three prepaid phones yet unused. He would have to talk to her in multiple bursts using a different phone each time. Dan didn't know if that would help; he had no way of knowing what she was capable of and how he could counter it.

I'm out of my league here. Got to be careful.

He went over to New Jersey to retrieve his car. He decided it was better to call her on the move. It might make it harder to track him.

"Hello," Jane said picking up her phone.

"Tommy said I should call you," Dan said.

"Dan?"

"What do you want to talk to me about?" He ignored her question.

"I'd like to meet with you. I can help you out of your situation."

"Meeting would be dangerous for me. I don't know who you are or what your agenda is. I'm not walking into some trap or ambush."

"I understand your caution, but I can assure you, I am not interested in trapping you," Jane replied.

"So you say. Talk is cheap and lies come easy. You're going to have to tell me all about yourself before we meet."

There was silence for a moment. "I can only say so much over the phone. If you like I can send you a secure phone and we can talk more freely."

"Do you think I'm stupid? Or are you stupid?"

"Sorry. I understand that my offer might seem to have too many pitfalls. Here's what I can say. I'm with a government agency. We're not associated with law enforcement as much as defense. We need people with your skills. I don't think I have to go into them over the phone. I can offer you a positive way to use those skills and provide a way out of the situation you're in. You know how difficult it's getting. It is only going to get worse."

"Things may get worse but that doesn't mean I'm desperate. I might be interested in what you're offering, but I need to know more." He pulled over to the curb. "Give me an address where I can send you something. I've got to hang up now. I don't want you tracking this call. I'll figure out how we can meet...on my terms, if you're interested in that."

"I'm not tracking your call, but here's my address." She gave him Gilbert's office address. "I'll meet with you on your terms, but we shouldn't wait too long."

"I'll be in touch. I still have a couple of things to finish."

"Don't take too long," Jane said. "Things are going to close down around you and it could be soon."

With Jane's warning ringing in his ears, he hung up.

Dan sat on his cheap couch long into the night thinking about the phone call. He could guess that this woman was with any number of agencies, NSA, CIA, DHS, DIA or others he was probably not even aware of. In the end it didn't matter. She made it clear the FBI was closing in. They were using him to put pressure on Vincent to get him to turn. He had never thought that would be a consequence of his war with the mob. Could he trust this woman any more than the FBI? She had made it clear that this Mike Warner would try to bring him in after he used him to snare Vincent. Dan didn't mind helping to turn Vincent. His life would be hell in a protection program. But would Dan be able to fade away? In the end he concluded the FBI would do what they had to do; they were a law enforcement agency. Maybe this woman was the only way out...if there even was a way.

Dan now tried to look beyond that "wall" that had clouded his view of the future. Was there a future for him? With a beer in his hand, he gazed out of the window at a gritty landscape of rundown buildings. Was this his life from now on? He had found no healing from what he had done so far. No release. At this point he was beginning to think killing Joey would not bring any closure. Maybe Lisa had been right all along. Maybe there was none to be had in the end. He got up and went into the kitchen to grab another beer. *What a life*. He sighed.

With or without healing or closure, he needed a future. He wasn't suicidal. Rita wouldn't approve. With a pang he had to admit she wouldn't approve of what he had been doing these past weeks either. She would want him to get on with life, do something productive.

A decision made, he wrote out a note then headed off to New Jersey to have his delivery van modified for the meeting. The work would take a couple of days to complete.

Chapter 38

Four days later Gilbert handed Jane an envelope with her name on it. There was no return address. She tore it open.

If you want to meet, you must come alone.

What followed were detailed instructions for Jane to take different subway routes that eventually brought her out in northern Queens. She got out at 69th station on the 7 line. When she emerged from the station, as the note instructed, she went to a pay phone and called a number he had given her. Dan instructed her to go to a large planter in front of an office building. Behind the planter, under a low bush, she was to retrieve a small, dirt-colored box that held a cell phone. She was to exchange phones and put the box back under the bush. After changing phones, she turned the new one on and punched the number on the speed dial.

"Walk to the corner, turn right and walk half a block. Then hail a cab and have him continue in the same direction. I'll give you directions after you're in the cab," Dan said.

The phone went dead. She looked around, realizing she was being watched. After getting into the cab as instructed, the phone rang again. "Direct the cab to the Grand Avenue/Newtown station. It's on the M line. Get out and catch the next train heading into Manhattan. Go two stops and get off at the Steinway Street station. I'll give you further instructions when you get on the street."

"I'm not being followed. This is quite unnecessary," Jane said.

"Just do as I say," came the reply and the call disconnected.

When Jane emerged from the subway, her phone rang again. "Walk north on Steinway Street for two blocks. I'll contact you."

In the middle of the second block, a man stepped out from a delivery van parked on the side of the road. He caught her eye and could see she recognized him. He scanned the area. The block looked clear. He had followed her walk and saw no evidence of any close surveillance when he pulled ahead to park in the next block.

He opened the side door of the van and motioned for her to get in. The van had no rear or side windows. Inside was a single bench seat. A metal wire screen with a door in it separated the back area from the driver's area.

"You want me to get into that cage?" Jane asked.

"It's up to you. I'll get in with you, but I'm not legally parked and I think it would be best to drive somewhere else where we can talk."

Jane gave him a long look. She had a tiny transmitter on her so Gilbert could track her from his office, but no one was on the street following her. Whether she got in the back or the front, she was going to be at Dan's mercy to some extent.

"The door can be opened from the inside and you can get out anytime you want."

"Let's not leave town. I don't want to go on any long drive out on the Island," Jane said as she stepped into the back of the van.

"Agreed." Dan went around to the driver's side and jumped in. Without a word, he moved into traffic.

"Where are you going?" Jane asked.

Dan only shook his head and put his finger to his lips. After twenty blocks of left and right turns, he pulled into an alleyway that lead to a quiet street under some elevated tracks. There were few cars using the side road and it could not be easily closed off from both sides. After parking, he opened the wire mesh door and entered the back of the van.

"It's a Faraday cage." He motioned to the woven wire frame. If I'm right, cell phones and tracking devices won't work, so we'll be blind to any tracking you have set up. I suppose you have a tracking device on you? They'll have lost your signal miles away from here."

"Very clever of you." Jane smiled in spite of herself. "You're pretty resourceful."

"Just being careful. I learned that some time ago."

"In Iraq?"

Dan studied her. She was not glamorous, but not unattractive, with an athletic look. He didn't know what to expect, but someone in a clandestine organization probably had to be pretty fit. He guessed she was about his age. He had expected to meet someone older. "I guess you've done all your homework and know all about me. So maybe you should start by telling all about you, your organization and what you want from me."

"I'm with a clandestine organization—"

"Don't be coy. I think that's what you said to Tommy when you talked to him and Doreen."

Jane smiled. "Touché. I'm with the CIA, but a part that is very covert."

"So the CIA has secrets it keeps from itself?"

"We're full of secrets and, yes, we have quite a system of compartmentalization."

"So what do you want with me?"

"I'll get to that, but first a little background." Jane needed to take her time. Dan needed to hear enough of the story to feel he had an honorable part to play in what she was proposing. Her review of his file gave her the sense that Dan was not a killer. Not in the same way a mob hit man was. He operated from a moral sense—in this case a sense of retribution or payback—however misplaced that might be. He would need to square what she proposed with his own code of conduct.

"Politics has become a larger factor in the CIA than ever before. Our director is very focused on making sure the agency does not run afoul of public opinion and the administration. In the midst of this, terrorism has not decreased.

"We're fighting an enemy that doesn't have an army or navy or air force. This is asymmetrical warfare. It requires unconventional methods. And we've got an administration that doesn't want to own up to the full extent of the dangers. They just want to keep things from blowing up so the next administration can deal with it. Global trade, multi-national corporations are more important than defeating the enemy. Security is more about security for business and trade. But we get blamed when things go sideways.

"With terrorists, you've got a dangerous, shifting landscape of alliances and operations. Yet in spite of this reality we have cut back our HUMINT, human intelligence. Field operatives take time to develop and sometimes create embarrassing situations. Local operatives and contacts are often messy and unreliable. It's especially hard to find ones capable of penetrating terror networks.

"Because they're messy, informants are politically incorrect and have become a liability. They're generally not very moral or motivated by high minded ideals. It's often about grudges or the money. So it's become less politically acceptable to have hundreds of informants trying to get us the information we need."

"I get it. You've got problems. How does that affect me?" Dan said.

"We're relying on satellite and drone surveillance and electronic communications intercepts more and more, and when we get actionable intelligence, we often send in a drone. Now that is becoming controversial...and we can't use them in Europe. We're finding ourselves more and more de-clawed."

"Again, what do I have to do with that problem? Or do you just want to cry on my shoulder?"

Jane smiled. "I think I would pick an easier shoulder to cry on if I needed to. I'll get to the point. The CIA is not just involved in gathering intelligence. We don't just need information—stealing secrets. We need to act on the information. These terrorists are not other government's spies, they are sworn enemies of the U.S. We need to take out these characters before they act, not after.

"We're in a new era. You did two tours in Iraq. You know what I'm talking about. That war has now gone stateless to a large extent. The Islamic fundamentalists are waging war against the West and the U.S. is one of its main targets. We can't just send in troops like in a conventional battle. So we need operatives that can walk the streets of a city or stalk desert hills and who can take out these terrorists.

"In an attempt to adjust to this reality, and to get past the political correctness that has infected the agency, I have been given an assignment that's under very deep cover. It's well below the Directorate level. The Director probably is probably happy to have deniability on this one. I'm charged with setting up a small group of operatives that can function anywhere in the world."

Dan stared at her as she finished her point. Finally he said, "You want me to kill terrorists?"

She stared back at him. "Yes, and those that help them. That's what this boils down to." She let that sink in for a moment. "You have the skills. You used them in Iraq and again in attacking Vincent's crew. In fact that's how you came to our attention. I'm giving you a chance to use these skills for a good purpose."

"As opposed to how I'm using them now?"

"I'm not here to judge what you're doing. Lord knows you have motivation enough, more than I can fathom."

She turned in her seat to face him. "I'm offering a way out. Not only can I give you a positive purpose for what you're good at, but I can get you out of the trap that's being set for you. I can make you disappear...to the mob and to the Feds."

"This is not what I expected. I'm not sure what I expected, but not this." He paused. "So you're offering me a job as an assassin, is that right?"

"I'm offering you a job to use your sniper skills to take out the enemies of the U.S. It's like Iraq, only it's not conventional warfare. We haven't declared war on any country, and there's no appetite for sending in the military, and some of us in the spy business recognize that drones can't do it all, especially when they are becoming more controversial. You could think of it as being a substitute for a drone strike."

"A human drone..." Dan turned that image over in his mind. "Why don't you use special forces guys? They're good at this and trained up."

"Those guys don't fit well into civilian society. It's hard for them to walk down the streets, especially in Europe, and blend in."

"I wouldn't know what to do, how to find targets. In Iraq it was easy to find the bad guys. And we had planners setting up our operations."

"We'll teach you. You'll go to a training site. There are updates to your skills that you need to master."

"But Europe? Why there? I thought the fight was in the mid-East."

"It's spreading. Europe has cells of terrorists waiting to activate. Some jump out and shoot up a kosher bakery or other Jewish business. Others are waiting, plotting, looking for larger targets. We need to find and eliminate them. We also want to take out the people supporting the terrorists, the ones who never get into the fight but help through recruiting, logistics and money. There's no shortage of targets."

"So what training do I go through?"

"You'll get an advanced course in disguises." Dan raised his eyebrows. "Yes, I know you've used them in keeping the mob off balance. We'll make you much more effective in their use."

"Then I just sit around waiting for you to send me off to shoot someone?"

"You'll travel widely, and under cover. You'll get all the information you need about your targets. Resources will be made available to you, weapons, identities, money. None of it will be able to be traced back to any official government agency, but you will be well supplied."

"What happens if I fail, if I don't kill the target, or if I get caught?"

Jane paused for a moment then looked him in the eye. "I promised myself to be completely truthful with you, within the limits of what I can reveal. You'll be on your own. Your operations, your missions, are going to be so deep under cover that it will be very difficult to extract you from any problems you encounter. The people who will support you will not know who you are or what your mission is."

Dan frowned. "That's some recruiting pitch. So you want me to sign up for a life of being a solo killer, under cover, with no back up. And no one can know about it. How does that sound to you?"

"You're an orphan right now, except for your sister out west. And you can't reveal what you're doing to anyone now, can you? What you should realize is that I understand your situation and I understand what I'm asking...or offering."

"What would you know about my situation?" Dan asked.

"Think about it," Jane replied, "I can't tell my family what I do for a living. They think I'm some network administrator in management consulting company. And I gave up having a husband and family some years ago. I was a field operative for six years until I was called back to DC. So I know about surveillance and counter surveillance, about dead drops and live contacts. And I've given up a normal life to do what I do."

"Why? You had a choice."

"So did you, remember that. Maybe it was for the adventure or because I wanted to strike back at the bad guys...kind of like you did in the Army, only I'm doing it undercover. Now I'm offering you similar work."

Dan digested her words for a few moments, letting silence fill the van. Finally he asked, "How much does the job pay?"

Jane raised her eyebrows. She was not expecting that question. "I'm not looking for someone who just wants to do this for a big payoff. Those loyalties shift too easily."

"That's a fair point," Dan responded. "But frankly, I'm finding out its pretty lucrative ripping off the mob, dangerous, but lucrative. And since I'm going to be totally on my own with no safety net, I have to ask."

"I'm just pointing out that in our profile for this job we determined that we couldn't work with pure mercenaries. But since you asked, we can pay you well. I expect that you can become quite comfortable in a couple of years, if you don't spend it all."

"And if I live that long." Dan shifted uncomfortably in the seat. "I appreciate all this info and the sales pitch, but why should I take you up on what is a very dangerous job versus making a deal with Mike, the FBI guy?"

"That deal is less dangerous in one way, but more in another. You won't be going out to fight terrorists in a clandestine war, but you might end up in prison with multiple murder convictions hanging over your head."

"Maybe I can make a deal with him. You told Tommy he needed my help to take Vincent down."

"Yeah, he needs your help right now. But when Vincent turns, all bets are off. What guarantees you get from Mike Warner can be overridden by the AG on the case. Do you really think they will just let you walk clear of all those killings? You're going to do some time."

"I was fighting for my life. They were trying to kill me."

"Some of them, but if you're honest, not all. And that may not matter to the courts. They have to respond in some manner to public opinion and you may not be portrayed as a Robin Hood." Jane paused for a moment. "And if I'm correct, you have one more score to settle which will be a straight assassination."

"You don't sugar coat things, do you?" Dan said.

"I know what's at stake and I want to hit the enemy. You're the guy that can do it. I'm betting that you have the skills and the motivation to be very effective at this work— a soldier on the front lines of the war on terror."

"One no one knows about," he replied.

"You didn't do two tours in Iraq for the accolades. I'm betting you did it to protect your fellow soldiers. This will be a similar mission, only more secret. It's better than a life on the run, hiding underground, never getting to excel at anything for fear of being found, either by the FBI or the mob."

"You should've been in sales."

Jane smiled at him. "I believe in what I'm doing. I've sacrificed a normal life to do this. I'm good at selling what I believe in. Look, on the run, you have to stay in the shadows. It can cost a lot to stay hidden. It's a pretty grim existence and it will wear you down. You may even turn to killing for hire and that will take your soul away."

"You don't know that." Dan's voice now took on a hard edge. She had touched a nerve. He glared at her. "And that's just what you're asking me to do."

"But I'm asking you to do it for a good cause. Kill the bad guys, kill the enemy. And you will get well paid for it."

Dan changed the direction of the conversation. "Will I be just given an assignment and thrown out there?"

"No. I'll be your contact. I'll work with you while you're in the field, arrange support and resources for you and help you return after completing a mission. We'll be getting to know one another very well. My job will be to protect you up to the point it will compromise the agency."

"Then I'm toast, is that it?"

"My job is to keep you alive, and, unlike most of the desk agents, I know the streets so I'm better at it. I'll do everything I can to be successful. If I lose you, it sets us back and maybe ends the program. You see, you're going to be the prototype. If it works with you, we can add more soldiers to this battle. You fail, we all fail."

"I've got to think all this over."

"Don't wait too long. Mike will turn up the heat, and I can't protect you from that, I can only make you disappear."

"Like you said, Mike needs me for now, so there's time to think about things. I can control the pace to some extent." He got up. "You stay in the back seat while I drive you close to where I picked you up. I'll drop you about six blocks from that point. Once you're out of the van, I suspect your support team will pick up your signal and come for you. You can drive back to retrieve your phone. The one you have now will no longer be used. I'll call you at the number you gave me. If we're going to work together, it would be helpful if you didn't wear a tracker next time. Maybe we can do this without all the elaborate routine."

"I'll expect to hear from you soon. And yes, we can do this more directly. But I was impressed by your counter measures, even though this cage doesn't affect my tracking device." She smiled at him. "You're untrained but your instincts are good."

Chapter 39

Dan looked around in his apartment: unmade bed, unwashed dishes in the kitchen sink, cheap and uncomfortable furniture, worn out tan carpet, the walls painted an institutional yellow.

Is this any way to live? With the possibility of a future after this war on the mob, he caught himself looking more critically at his life and surroundings. *Is she offering anything better? Same crappy rooms, only in foreign countries?* His thoughts shuttled back and forth between hope and despair. *Man up. You chose this path. You got only yourself to blame. You weren't going to be stopped.*

He grabbed a beer from the fridge and sat on his couch. What would Rita want him to do? She would want him to go on with life, as sad as that made him feel. Rita would want him to have a wife and kids—a family—something that was denied her. Would she approve of him becoming a soldier again, a soldier without a uniform, fighting an enemy who declared war on the U.S.? Confusion reigned in his mind. Part of him wanted to call a truce, end his war, and try to find a normal life. Another part of him figured that was improbable at best; he had gone too far, and all that was left was to pick one of two bad options—life on the run, or life as a clandestine killer.

He picked up his phone.

"Jane," he said when she answered, "if I come on board with you, can you set it up to have the Feds stop looking for me? I don't want the worst of both options here. If I go to work for you, I've got to know I don't have to worry about getting pinched back here in the states. If I'm going to be a fugitive anyway, why should I work for you?"

Jane was silent.

"I don't want to be traced. Can't stay on this line much longer."

"I'll set up a meeting with Mike Warner. It will be tricky. We're not supposed to be involved in domestic surveillance, so I'm on the edge here. Sit tight, don't do anything else and I'll try to work this out for you."

Dan clicked off the phone and sat back with a sigh. So many issues to sort through. With a shrug he took a long pull from his beer. It looked like he was going to take a few days off.

Chapter 40

Two days later, Dan drove to Vincent's neighborhood. He stopped at a cross street a block away from the house to check it out. Vincent had set some of his crew out in front of the gate, two of them in a car, just sitting there. Dan wondered if Vincent really thought that would keep him safe.

He left, but later in the day, he drove back. He had mounted the shotgun in the trunk of the car with the barrel positioned at a hole cut in the rear of the trunk. For his drive to the house, the hole was covered with a round magnetic bumper sticker with the letters OBX on it. The gun had a lanyard attached to the trigger which ran to the driver's seat so he could fire it with a pull of his hand. Nearing Vincent's street, Dan stopped and removed the magnetic sticker. Then with his right hand holding the TEC-9 automatic pistol, he casually drove down the street. At first his car would draw no attention from the two men sitting in front of Vincent's driveway. It was afternoon and they were bored and tired, not paying much attention.

As he approached, he stuck the TEC-9 out of the window and opened up with a full burst at the car. His first burst took out the tires on the left side. The men dove for cover as he continued firing through the windows, high enough to miss them. As he sped away, he pulled the lanyard, and the shotgun roared repeatedly until he rounded the corner at the far end of the street. The shotgun had suppressed any return fire. The guards stayed crouched on the floor of the car. There would be no pursuit from them. Dan headed for the freeway with its anonymity and drove back to his garage in New Jersey. The car would now not be usable as any one of the neighbors might have a good description of it. The driver, if he had been seen, would be described as a long-haired man with protruding brows, a long, hooked nose and a full beard.

When the call came into the station, Mike joined Marty as they drove out to Vincent's house. Upon arrival, they found a tearful Sheila sitting in her living room.

"Mrs. Salvatore, I'm sorry about these repeated attacks." Marty said when they were let into the house. "I think we should post a police guard out in front of your home."

"Vincent had some of his employees parked out front to guard us. And look at their car, this maniac shot it up. They could have been killed," she said between sobs.

"Where are the men now?" Marty asked.

"They drove off with some others. I guess they went to talk to Vincent. He should be on his way here now. I just don't know what to do." Her eyes darted around the room. "How can this man just keep coming by and shooting up everything...and no one can stop him? It's like we live in a war zone. The neighbors probably hate us and want us to move. I don't blame them."

"Again, I'm sorry. This has been so stressful for you," Marty responded.

"Can't you stop it?" Sheila asked. "This kind of thing isn't supposed to happen in neighborhoods like this."

"Mrs. Salvatore," Mike jumped into the conversation, "I'd like to help. You remember me? I want to help keep you and your family safe. Whoever is doing this is going to escalate and strike your family one day. It could be you, your husband, or God forbid, one of your daughters."

Sheila started to cry again and looked fearfully at the men. Marty gave Mike a dirty look.

Mike put out his hand, gesturing for him to keep quiet. "Mrs. Salvatore, may I talk to you in private for a moment?"

Sheila nodded and headed for the kitchen with Mike following. Marty stared after them as they disappeared from view.

"What do you want, Mr. Warner? I probably shouldn't be talking to you, my husband doesn't like you."

"Your husband is under a lot of pressure and doesn't realize how I can help your family—"

"So, can you make this stop? Do you know who's causing this?"

"I'm not exactly sure who's causing this, but I can make it stop. Let me explain. I'm with the FBI, as you saw on my card. Right now, we think Vincent's in a very bad position. His organization is coming apart, and Carmine Gianelli and Silvio Palma are getting nervous about him."

"Vincent hasn't done anything wrong. He runs a legitimate business, the restaurant and the trucking business."

"We know about those as well as the trash business that he's part owner of. Carmine and Silvio have ownership stakes in those businesses. But, Mrs. Salvatore, may I call you Sheila?" She nodded. "Thank you, call me Mike. It's easier for our conversation...not being so formal. Anyway, we all know that these companies are covers for various crime enterprises. Enterprises that Vincent is directly involved in—"

Sheila gave him a suspicious look. "You don't know that. You can't prove that."

"I can't right now, but that's not my point. If Silvio loses confidence in Vincent's ability to control his crew, he will have to replace him. Sheila, I don't think I have to spell out for you what that means. Vincent can't just retire from this business. It doesn't work like that."

Now Sheila started crying again. Mike got up and grabbed a box of tissues from the counter and handed them to her.

"Vincent hasn't done anything wrong. Carmine's wife and I are good friends. He would never do anything to hurt Vincent and me," she said between sobs.

"Sheila, I don't want to upset you, but I have to be honest. Carmine's wife will have no influence on what happens. When the organization decides someone has to go, they make it happen. It's always that way. It could be Carmine's people, or one of Vincent's crew. It's just business to them."

"What can we do?" Her voice rose in panic.

"I can take you and your family away from here. Give you protection from anyone trying to kill Vincent."

"You can?"

"Yes. I just need Vincent's cooperation...before it's too late."

Just then Vincent charged into the kitchen.

"What are you doing here? I thought I told you to stay out of my house," he yelled at Mike.

Sheila jumped up and ran to her husband. "Oh Vincent, it was terrible, so much shooting. Did you see the car? That could have been me in my car. Why can't you make this stop? One of us is going to get killed."

Vincent put his arms around his wife as he glared at Mike. "You. Get out now. Don't talk to my wife."

Mike stood up. "Vincent, I'm in charge of this investigation, like I told you before, so I'm not leaving the house. This is a crime scene. I'm trying to help you stay alive—help your family stay alive."

"We don't need your help—"

"Vincent, maybe you should listen to him? He says he can protect us," Sheila said.

"What are you talking about?"

"Mike says he can protect our whole family. He says that Carmine or Silvio might want to kill us. Is that true?"

Vincent glared at Mike. "Stop lying to my wife and trying to panic her, you piece of shit." His voice held a tone of growing rage.

"Vincent, you know it's true. They're getting nervous because things are unraveling. And you know what happens when Silvio gets nervous."

"You don't know a fucking thing about what's going on." Vincent's face turned a bright crimson.

"I may not know the details, but someone is coming for your crew, you, and your whole family. If Carmine or Silvio see this as you losing control, they lose confidence in you. So far no one has been able to stop what's going on and it's only a matter of time before someone in this family gets killed."

"Vincent, listen to him. This has to stop," Sheila shouted.

"Be quiet. He's not telling the truth. He just wants to panic you. I'll take care of this."

"Well you haven't so far." She stomped out of the kitchen.

"You know I'm right," Mike said after Sheila left. "They'll come for you if this doesn't end, and you and the police haven't been able to stop whoever is doing this so far."

"I can take care of myself and my family without your help."

"Well I'm going to post a twenty-four hour police guard outside of your home. I don't want to see your family harmed."

"I don't want a guard. I told you to get out and leave me alone!" Vincent was shouting now.

"You don't have a choice. The neighborhood needs to be protected. Marty will go along with my suggestion. Now I'd like make you an offer of protection, for you and your family."

"I'm not going into some protection program. I don't need that."

"I think you do need that. I'll stay in touch."

"Don't bother." Vincent walked out to find Sheila. Mike looked around. The kitchen was elaborate, much like the rest of the house. A fancy pseudo-estate, overly decorated with a grand entrance hall and stairway, an example of suburban excess. It was a poor interpretation of a European mansion set in the middle of a collection of one acre lots with each house trying for the same effect. As overdone as it was, it would take a lot of pressure to pry them loose from all of it.

Chapter 41

Carmine sat down with Silvio in his office near the docks in Brooklyn. They were alone. Silvio's constant bodyguards were just outside the door. The older man was dressed in an expensive suit and tie, with a colorful handkerchief tucked into his chest pocket. Except for the tone being on the flamboyant side, he would be considered expensively well-dressed by any fashion critic. His gray hair was slicked straight back, accentuating his thin, angular face. The effect was that of an aging European aristocrat.

"What is going on with Vincent and his crew? It doesn't look like he's gotten things under control." Silvio's voice was raspy, cracked with age. It carried no warmth, nor did he intend for it to do so.

"No. We're losing money and the Feds are now involved. They've turned up at his house a couple of times now."

"Why the Feds?" Silvio asked. "What's this got to do with them?"

"The word is that they consider some of what happened extortion, so they're jumping in."

"We don't need that." Silvio's age and slight build masked how dangerous he was. He was not physically imposing but his manner expressed an absolute sense of being in command. He was known to be ruthless when dealing with competitors and threats. Even Carmine, his underboss, charged with enforcing his edicts, felt ill at ease when Silvio was upset. "What're you doing about this?"

Carmine paused; his answer had to be correct. Whatever he proposed, Silvio would hang on him.

"No one has been able to get to this guy, Dan. But we gotta stop this. We're losing money and control is slipping—"

"We know that. What the hell are you going to do? And the Feds are involved? I don't like that."

"I'm wondering why they can't find this guy. You'd think between the Feds and the local cops, they'd have flushed him out by now."

"What are you thinking?" Silvio asked.

"Maybe they want pressure on Vincent...not find this guy too soon. Maybe they want him to disrupt the crew. Mess things up until we have to act."

"So then they can get to us?"

Carmine nodded. "And if they can convince Vincent we've lost confidence in him he might think we'll take him out."

"You give Vincent any ideas like that?"

"No. But I've kept the pressure on him to get this under control. He ain't getting it done."

"This guy Dan, what's he want?" Silvio asked.

"Revenge. One of Vincent's crew torched his restaurant last year and killed his wife."

"That's not good. You talk to this guy?"

"Once. He's after Joey Batone, the guy who torched the restaurant. But now he has bigger plans. He wants to be paid to leave us alone."

"What?" Silvio almost smiled in surprise. "That's bold. What'd you tell him?"

"That I'd think about it. I said we might consider if he did work for us. He's good at what he does."

"And?"

"No deal. He just wants to be paid to leave us alone. If the cops, or the Feds, or us can't find him, it might make sense."

Silvio stared at Carmine who began to worry whether he'd said too much. "Still, it would be your call."

"Hmmm. So let's give him Joey and get him out of our hair."

"Not that easy, with all due respect. He thinks he can get Joey on his own and then he just wants to be paid to go away. I think he likes stealing our money."

"How much does he want?"

"Five hundred grand a year."

Silvio thought for a moment. He didn't like making rash decisions, but this was a real crisis and he needed to get it shut down and under control quickly. "We'll pay him for now. We got to shut this down. Whether or not we continue will depend on whether or not we can find him later."

Silvio shifted in his chair, leaning forward towards Carmine. "And I want you to watch Vincent closely. If he gets cozy with the Feds, we have to do something."

"Are you giving me the go-ahead on him?"

Silvio raised his hand. "No. Just watch him closely. And since the guy wants Joey, let's give him Joey. Send him out to the lodge in the Berkshires. This guy Dan will probably follow him if we let slip where he's hiding out." Silvio leaned back. The conversation was over.

Carmine rose to leave. Silvio stood and gave him a hug. He held his shoulders and looked into his eyes. "One more thing. Make sure Joey doesn't leave the lodge alive."

Carmine nodded and Silvio released him.

Chapter 42

J ane called Mike the next day. All she told Mike was that she had information about Dan and wanted to talk to him privately. She arranged to meet him on the promenade along the waterfront near the Verrazano Narrows Bridge. When Mike showed up, Gilbert quickly wanded him to make sure he wasn't wearing a wire.

"What the hell are you doing?"

"It's just a precaution," Jane replied. "We need to talk off the record, so no recordings allowed. My assistant is just ensuring we are having a private conversation."

Gilbert nodded to Jane and then withdrew to a discreet distance so they could talk.

"So who are you?" Mike asked. "Most people don't have access to wire detection equipment."

"True enough," she replied. I'm not a civilian."

"Again, who are you with and how do you know Dan?"

"I'm with another government agency. It's not important which one. All these robberies and killings happening to Vincent's crew are unusual to say the least, especially for those who understand these things, as I know you do. This isn't a turf war or gang vendetta. It's something else."

"We've figured that out already. You said you had information about Dan. What it is."

"First of all, you know there is no evidence to link Dan to these incidents. Not one eye witness, not one scrap of hard evidence."

"How do you know what evidence I've got?"

"If you had what you needed, you wouldn't be asking Tommy and Doreen to get you in touch with Dan."

"What do you know about that?" Mike was getting visibly angry. Jane could see his displeasure at talking to a woman who wouldn't identify herself, but seemed to know what was going on. "If you don't tell me who you are, I can't waste my time with you."

"Yes, you can. Let's be frank, you use confidential information all the time."

"So what do you have to help me? Just get to the point."

"I know your end game is to put enough pressure on Vincent and get Silvio Palma to decide he's a liability. Then you plan to turn him and whisk him away into the witness protection program. You're out to take down Silvio's whole operation, not just Vincent's crew. If Dan is the source of all this action, you want to slow down your investigation to let him keep up the pressure on Vincent. It must be getting tough for his wife and daughters, and you're betting Dan can make it tougher."

Mike scowled at her. "You have a nice theory about what is going on, but I'm wondering where you gathered all your data. Or did you just dream it up? And, furthermore, why are you interested? Are you with some spy agency?"

"There are lots of agencies I might be with, but I assure you we are on the same side. I can also assure you that I am not interfering with your investigation—nor will I."

"So how do you help me?"

"I've been in touch with Dan."

Now Mike stepped up close to Jane. "That could be viewed as interfering with my investigation. You need to explain yourself."

"I know you talked with Tommy and Doreen. Apparently Dan decided not to call you. However, he did call me—"

"And how did he know to call you?"

"I talked with Tommy and Doreen after they met with you. They're very concerned about Dan's future, even if no hard evidence points to him."

"Cut the crap. We all know Dan's behind this."

"Knowing it and proving it are two different things. But for the sake of our conversation, we'll assume Dan has some connection to events that could help your cause."

"Bottom line. What can you give me? I don't have all day to spar with you."

"Dan may not be involved and he may just leave the area and disappear. I told him how helpful these events were to you in your plan to turn Vincent."

"You what? I'll see you in jail!" Mike was almost shouting now. "If that gets back to Vincent or Carmine, the plan won't work." His face turned red. Jane wondered if he was going to put his hands on her. His body tensed.

"Stay calm," she said. "Dan doesn't want to help Vincent. In fact he thought it was quite a nice side effect. But it requires Dan, if he's the cause of these disruptions, to continue what he's doing."

Mike took a couple of deep breaths, and then stepped back. Jane could see his mind turning over how to neutralize her. She was on dangerous ground. All Mike had to do was to start making phone calls up his ladder and at some point she would get a call asking her if she was in New York and if she was, why. It could even result in being wired up to testify that she was not involved in any domestic operation. She would need some strong sweetener to get Mike to go along with her plan.

"Here's the deal," she said. "I have a job offer for Dan. He's committed no crime that I am aware of. There is nothing to link him to what you are investigating. But if he takes my job offer, he'll leave the area. What that will do to the pressure on Vincent, I don't know. It may not change anything. But you and I both know that Dan's disappearing will make your task harder."

"So you're going to snatch him away, right out from under my nose? I'll have your job if you do."

"Mike, I can make him disappear... and I will. You may have my job, but you don't get Vincent."

Mike looked away across the harbor, and then up to the massive bridge. Jane sensed he was evaluating his options. She turned her gaze to the bridge. It was amazing how being near such a large structure tended to make one feel a little smaller, less important. It helped a person to think outside of themselves. *Maybe in the greater scheme of things we weren't all that important. We certainly wouldn't be around for as long as this bridge.*

"What are you offering?" he finally asked.

"I'm offering to have Dan stay around until you can nab Vincent. What I want, what Dan wants, in return, is that you don't go after him when this is over. You have him disappear from any active investigation."

"Just walk away from all this mayhem he's caused?"

"First, you may not be able to prove he caused it. Second, you'll have your victory with Vincent. That's the plum for your career."

"I'm not sure I can just close that part of the investigation out."

"Sure you can. The killings could be written off to a disgruntled mob member—pick one, there's a lot of them to go around. You could have just been feeding info to this disgruntled mobster so he would put the pressure on Vincent, exactly how it's developed. You just switch an unnamed mobster for Dan."

"There's the local police—"

"Yes. And you've taken over their investigation. They'll go along when you point out that they helped cover up the fire in Dan's restaurant over a year ago. That crime was never solved and two innocent people died. In this situation, no innocent people are dying."

"Two people died? I thought it was just Dan's wife?"

"She was pregnant. We women think about that."

"I can't just sit by and let Dan kill more people."

"That's what you're doing now by slow-walking this investigation. Let's be honest, you need a couple of more incidents before Vincent or his wife will crack. Carmine and Silvio have to think Vincent's lost control and is cozying up to you for protection. Then you have to whisk him away before they get to him. I won't be involved. I'm not going to compromise you. Events will unfold without my interference. You just need to be ready to collect Vincent at the end."

"And then let Dan go free. How do I know I can trust you?"

"I'm the one that has to trust you. I need you to do your part of the deal after you get what you want."

"That's true." A slight smile appeared on Mike's face.

Jane noticed it. "Then we have a deal?"

"Yeah. If I can nab Vincent, we got a deal."

"Great. And just so I know you'll complete your part, I'll hold on to this ledger of your expense vouchers." She handed him a spreadsheet from his home computer that Gilbert had hacked into after Jane had first arrived in New York.

"What the fuck? Where did you get this?"

"Relax, Mike. It's just insurance between partners in an agreement. When the investigation goes away, this disappears, no record kept on my end. Frankly I'm not interested. It's not that bad. You seem to be a good agent, but this would be embarrassing and probably stall your career. But I'd be careful going forward. You're doing good work and you don't want any padding of your expense account to undermine it." She smiled and held out her hand to him.

Mike looked at her and slowly reached out to shake. "Who are you with, CIA, NSA?"

"Like I said, it's not important, and I'm not really interested in other things you're doing with the mob. You fight the battles on your front and I fight them on my front.

We're both battling our country's enemies. I just need Dan to help me. You putting him behind bars would be a waste of a good resource in that fight. When you get Vincent turned, we'll be in touch. You can contact Tommy if you need to get in touch with me." With that she turned and walked off to join Gilbert, leaving Mike to ponder the strange web of events he found himself in.

Chapter 43

Gino came into Vincent's office in the back of the restaurant. "Boss, you got to get Joey out of my apartment. It's been a week and a half and he's driving me crazy. He don't clean up after himself and he just complains...about everything, the food, the bed, being cooped up. I told him if he don't stop complaining I'm going to whack him. He won't have to worry about Dan doing it."

Vincent was working on one of his cigars. "I told you guys to stay away from the street. You tell him to shut up and stay there." All of this mess wouldn't have happened if Joey had done things the right way. And now he was complaining while being protected.

"Boss, with all due respect, Joey don't listen. He's driving me nuts. You got to stash him somewhere else."

"I don't have to do nothing. You want back out on the street?"

"Yeah. Better than being cooped up with Joey. Besides, no one's targeting me."

Vincent thought about what Carmine had told him. Now was the time to get Joey out of town and get Dan to follow him. "Tell Joey to come down to the restaurant right away. I'll work something out." He then called Frank and told him his plan.

Later when Joey showed up, Vincent told him he was sending him out of town. "You go up to the lodge in the Berkshires. I want you to hole up there until I tell you to come back."

"That's a long way out of town," Joey said. He looked doubtful, even nervous about the order.

"Yeah. I want you outta here. This crap's got to stop. You're a target, so you need to leave town. I'm sending Frank with you. He'll make sure nothing happens to you out there."

"Are you sure? I don't have any clothes packed from my apartment—"

"Don't question me. Go buy some fucking clothes. You and Frank are leaving tonight." He stood and walked up to Joey, whose eyes grew larger as Vincent got up in his face. "Call me when you get in. Get some groceries in town and stay at the lodge. Don't go around town making a scene. You're supposed to be out of sight. Got it?" Vincent put his finger in Joey's chest and blew cigar smoke at his face.

"I got it." Joey backed up to go.

"Tonight. I want you on the road and out of town," Vincent yelled as Joey beat a hasty retreat from the room.

After Joey left, Vincent talked to Frank. It was time to act on Carmine's instructions. "I'm putting the word out on the street where Joey is hiding out. I want Dan to get the word."

Frank looked at Vincent. "You want Dan to find us?"

"I want to get Dan out of town, Joey's the bait. If Dan shows up at the lodge, you take him out."

Frank nodded. "You get Dan out of your hair, and I can take him out while he's focused on Joey."

"That's it." Vincent paused for a moment. "And I want you to make sure no one comes back from the lodge but you. Understand me? Only you."

Frank looked at Vincent. "I'll take care of it." His dark eyes remained unreadable. Vincent knew Frank would do his job. He was a professional. He nodded as he stared back at Vincent for a moment, calm and cool.

That night Dan lay in the same ditch from where he had shot up Sheila's SUV. He waited until the downstairs light went out and the bedroom lights came on. A police squad car sat at the driveway entrance. Dan had hidden the muzzle of his rifle with brush, since the muzzle flash could give him away at night. He wasn't worried about the sound. He was using sub-sonic rounds again coupled with his suppressor. At five hundred yards the cops in their cruiser would not hear the shots. With his spotting scope, he could make out the two patrolmen in the car. One seemed to be asleep; the other was smoking a cigarette. No one was paying attention.

He knew that after his first shot, the cops would be looking around frantically for the source. He only had a time for a couple of rounds if he hoped to remain concealed. Then he would have to make a rapid retreat as he had done before. The dark would help him in exiting the area. He only had to drive a couple of blocks in the van before he could blend into local traffic and within a mile he would be on the Long Island Expressway and completely anonymous.

A light came on upstairs. Dan saw someone walk past the window. The figure was too large to be one of the girls. *The master bedroom.* In the family room he could see the blue light from the TV. Whoever was watching was hidden from his angle of view. Then he saw a second figure in the bedroom. *Vincent and Sheila. They've gone upstairs. One or both of the girls must be still in the family room.* It was time to act.

Dan aimed at the master bedroom window and sent a round through it. The glass shattering startled the cop who was awake. He shook his partner as they both tried to figure out what just had happened. Someone, probably Sheila, started screaming upstairs. Then the family room window shattered. Two figures ran past the now broken window and disappeared upstairs. The bedroom light went out. The cops jumped out of their car with guns drawn, looking around with no idea of where the shots came from.

Dan slid back from his shooting position into the ditch, grabbed the two spent casings and began his fast crawl to the culvert. He needed to be gone before the cops figured out the general direction of the shots and headed towards him. They would have to go a couple of blocks out of their way to get to his position, but it wouldn't take them long. He needed at least to be on the local road, out of the neighborhood, before they arrived.

Emerging from the culvert, he sprinted the two blocks to his van. He jumped in and headed away from Vincent's house to the feeder road for the expressway. As he drove down the road he could see the flashing lights of a vehicle from around a curve, coming towards him. He killed his lights, pulled to the curb, and shut off his engine. He slumped down in the seat as the cruiser came flying past all lit up. After it turned another corner, Dan started the van and drove out of the area.

Later that night, Dan pulled up to a side street parking space two blocks from the Sicilian Gardens. He was dressed in a hoodie with black jeans and running shoes. He had his .22 pistol with its suppressor in his sweatshirt. Even with a disguise, he kept to the shadows, aware of all the security cameras that could capture a picture of him. Turning the corner to the restaurant, he hung in the shadows on the other side of the street, listening. At three in the morning no one was out on the sidewalks and few cars on the streets. After a lone car drove past, he pulled his pistol and shot out the security camera on the corner that could record anyone going in, out, or past the restaurant.

Then he strode across the street and took a brick from his pocket. The brick was wrapped in a note which read, "You're next." He heaved it through the back room window and turned to walk back to his van as the alarm went off. An hour later he had the van parked in New Jersey and was on his way back to his apartment.

The harassment was becoming a task to perform. Dangerous, and one for which he was losing his passion. Maybe the offer of a future, however strange, was causing him to move on in his mind.

Better keep your focus, or there won't be any future. You've still got something to complete. Don't get careless. The idea of getting this close and getting caught or killed caused his stomach to tighten. *Don't think like that, just get this done.* He knew this was good advice, but his mind kept teasing him back to thinking about his future. That woman, Jane, didn't offer much detail, but what she said teased his imagination. *She probably meant it that way. Get me to imagine something more attractive than what the reality might be.* Still, he'd never get to find out if he wasn't careful up to the end. *Have I decided already?* He was beginning to think he knew the answer to that question.

Chapter 44

After the shots, Vincent turned out the bedroom light. The girls ran upstairs screaming. He met them in the hall and told them to go to one of their bedrooms and lie down on the floor. Sheila was in the hall, hysterical. Try as he could, he was not able to get her to calm down. Outside the cop car lit up and raced out of the neighborhood, probably hoping to intercept a vehicle leaving the area.

"I can't take this anymore," Sheila cried. "I can't live like this, never knowing when someone is going to shoot up our house. I can't go near a window now. The police outside don't help, your men outside don't help. What are we going to do?" She looked at her husband in despair.

"No one is gonna kill us. This is just intimidation." Vincent knew that was the wrong thing to say as soon as the words were out of his mouth.

"What do you mean, 'no one is going to kill us'? I could have been killed by that bullet, and they shot through the family room. Vincent, the girls were in the room! How can you say, 'no one's going to kill us'?"

"Calm down, let me call Tony and have some of the boys come over."

"Fat lot of good that'll do. Last time they were here they got themselves shot up." She paced back and forth as the girls came out of the bedroom to stand in the hallway. "What are the neighbors thinking about us right now? We get our house shot up repeatedly, in the middle of the night?"

Amber chimed in, "Yeah, the kids don't want to talk to us at school, like we got a disease or something." She began to cry.

"Everyone just shut up," Vincent shouted. He turned to call Tony.

"Boss," Tony said after answering the phone, "we got a break in down at the restaurant. The alarm went off. I'm on my way there now."

"Send someone else over there and get your ass up here to my place. I just got my windows shot out."

Vincent disconnected. Sheila and the girls were all looking at him with panic in their eyes. "Tony's on his way and the cops will be here soon. I don't want any of you talking to them. I just want to get those guys out of the house as quickly as I can.

Sheila looked at him with a piercing gaze. "Vincent, come downstairs, I want to talk to you privately." Her voice was suddenly serious and firm. She headed for the kitchen, grabbed the coffee pot and poured two cups and put them in the microwave. "Sit down, we have to talk," she said as the coffee heated. When it was done, she brought the cups to the table along with the cream.

"This has gone on long enough. Last week Gina was asking me what is going on. She's worried about us. She says Carmine is very worried about what's happening. He apparently doesn't want the FBI hanging around. The attention is getting him...and Silvio uncomfortable. Now, you know I don't pry into what goes on day to day, but even I know this isn't good."

Vincent sighed. "No it's not good. I'm trying to stop it but nothing's worked so far. Having that FBI agent prying around isn't helping things at all."

"But what will happen to us if Carmine or Silvio get too upset? Are we in danger from them? It seemed like Gina was trying to get information out of me...to give to Carmine."

"What'd you tell her? Of course she'll take anything you say back to Carmine, she's his wife for God's sake. I told you that before."

"I didn't tell her anything. I told her you were going to get to the bottom of it all. She gave me a look like she didn't believe what I said. Then she said, 'I hope so'." She looked down at her coffee cup for a moment then continued. "I talked to Mike Warner two days ago—"

Vincent jerked his head up, "You what?"

"I just wanted to know more about what he was offering, you know, in case things go bad with Carmine or Silvio."

"Oh Jesus!" Vincent exclaimed. "That's just what he wants." His face was red. He stood up, leaned over and pounded his fist on the table, emphasizing each word. "He wants Carmine or Silvio to think I'm up to something. Then they'll come after me. How could you be so stupid? You talked to the Feds? What did you say to him?"

Sheila shrank back. "I didn't tell him anything, I asked him what he could do for us. Vincent, I'm scared. This hasn't stopped and now Gina is asking me questions. I don't know what to do." She started to sob.

"You don't talk to the Feds, that's the first thing you do."

"Well, he said he could protect us from anyone coming after us. He can give us whole new identities. We could start over without all this shooting, without all this stress. It's killing me and the girls are terrorized. They're afraid to go to school."

"You know what that means, a whole new identity?" He leaned further over the table and stuck his face up close to Sheila's. "I'll tell you. It means we relocate to some new city, somewhere out in the boonies. And I have to get a regular job. You like the way we live?" He swept his arm around to encompass the whole house. "You like spending the money I give you, driving your new Escalade? Well, you can kiss all that good-bye if we go into the witness protection program. We'll have just enough to live on. Say good-bye to all that easy spending money. You want to live like that?" He was almost shouting again.

Sheila shrank back from Vincent's tirade but she wasn't quitting. "What good is all of this if you get killed? What will happen to me, the girls? We need you, Vincent. I hope we mean something to you as well."

He sighed. "You do mean something to me. I know I spend a lot of time at work—"

"And I never ask about what is going on. I know you have to do some things that aren't always legal, and I know we don't talk to cops, but this has got me panicked. I don't see a way out."

"I told you I'd handle it."

"Yeah, but it hasn't been handled. And now Carmine's getting his wife to grill me. I can't take that pressure. How do you make it stop?"

That last question stumped Vincent. He hoped getting Joey out of town and using him as bait would take the pressure off him. But if Sheila cracked, things could go bad in a hurry.

"Give me a little more time. Don't say anything else to Warner. Don't meet with him. I'm working a plan. One that Carmine suggested, so he hasn't given up on me yet." He tried to smile but couldn't pull it off. Sheila just looked at him.

When he turned the girls were standing in the doorway. "So, you been listening to our conversation?"

Tiffany replied, "It's our problem too. We're like freaks at school. No one wants to talk to us. Some say you're a gangster and we all ought to be in jail. Others are afraid to be near us in case someone tries to shoot us. How do you fix that?"

"You just shut your mouth. I give you whatever you want. To hell with your friends if they turn on you. Who needs them?" His voice rose again.

"Vincent! Don't yell at her like that. She hasn't done anything wrong. How many teenagers get their house shot up, their mother's car burned in the driveway? This is what I'm telling you. We can't go on like this." Sheila was angry now.

"Just go back upstairs." Vincent tried to regain his calm. "Your mother and I are working this out."

"I hope you do," Tiffany said as the two girls headed for the stairs.

"Vincent," Sheila said in a calm voice when they were gone, "just agree to talk with Mike Warner...just once...to keep our options open. I won't ask you again."

He looked at his wife. She was a pain sometimes, he thought. Well, most of the time, but when he was being honest, he wasn't the easiest person to live with. Not with the violence he needed to apply at times, the secrecy, and the mistresses which came and went. He wondered how much she knew about all of that. Yet here she was, hysterical for sure, but looking for a way out of the dilemma they were in.

"Yeah, I'll talk to him, but only to get you off my back. I'm going to put a stop to all of this and I don't need the cops to help."

The doorbell rang and Tony popped his head in.

Vincent got up to meet him. "Look, the cops are going to be here soon, what's going on at the club?"

Sheila stayed in the kitchen to make more coffee. It was four-thirty in the morning, but she thought no one was going back to sleep.

"Boss, a brick was thrown through the back room window. I think you know who did it." Tony followed him to the kitchen.

"Is that all?"

"It had a note wrapped around it...here." He handed Vincent the note.

Vincent stared at it for some time, and then tore it up and threw it in the trash can. Tony went into the kitchen to talk with Sheila and try to calm her down some more. Vincent paced around the living room. There seemed to be no stopping Dan, but now he had a plan, one he hoped would take care of his problem.

Chapter 45

L ater that same day, Mike called Sheila.

"Mrs. Salvatore, I heard you had your windows shot out last night. Have you talked to Vincent about coming to see me? I want to help anyway I can."

"I did, and he was mad that I talked to you. I shouldn't be talking to you right now."

"I understand. But did Vincent agree to talk with me?"

"Yeah. He finally agreed, but I don't know when he'll do it. And I don't want to bother him. He promised to call you."

"I know you don't want to bother him, but maybe you could tell him that I called, you didn't talk with me, but I called just to tell you that things are heating up and he and I should talk right away. Can you just tell him that for me? I don't want him to wait until it's too late."

Sheila sighed. "All right, but that's it. I can't talk with you anymore. You have to talk to Vincent." With that she hung up. Talking to Vincent again about Warner was not going to be easy, but it sounded like things were getting more dangerous. And what was worse was that she had a lunch date scheduled with Gina later in the week. Gina would be pumping her for more information about Vincent and what he was doing about the shootings.

Sheila needed someone to unburden herself with, someone she could trust. The stress was too heavy for her. All she wanted to do was live a nice, quiet, affluent life with time for her friends and family. She liked some of

Vincent's crew, but there were some she didn't want around her house. Thankfully, Vincent didn't bring most of the guys out. Now Tony was someone Sheila felt good about. Along with being good looking, he was well mannered. He was a good listener and always respectful. When Sheila was distressed, Vincent would have Tony come by to visit. He always made her feel better; he was so attentive. Maybe she could talk to him about her fears? It couldn't hurt; he was one of Vincent's trusted lieutenants, always around to calm things down, giving Vincent good advice. She trusted him. He had a calming effect on her and she appreciated his comments.

Vincent met with his crew later that day. He explained that they were going to lure Dan out of town to find Joey, so they had to put the word out on the street that Joey had gone to the Berkshires to hide out. Frank would be there to ambush Dan when he tried to get to Joey.

"Ain't that risky for Joey?" one of them asked.

Vincent gave him a look that indicated it would have been smarter to keep his mouth shut. "Yeah, it's risky for Joey, but his fuck-up started this whole mess, so he gets to be the bait in the trap. Don't worry about Joey, worry about yourself and why you couldn't find this guy so Joey had to be the bait. He may not like to hear about that when he gets back." He ran his hands through his hair, "We got to make this not look like a set up, so you got to be casual about letting this slip out. Get the info out to Tommy. I'm betting he'll get the word to Dan."

He sent the men out of his office. Vincent was now beginning to feel better. He had a plan and it looked like it would work. If he got Dan out of town, things would calm down. He figured Frank was capable of making sure Dan didn't come back.

His phone rang. "Who's this?" Vincent asked.

"It's me," Sheila said. "That guy Mike called me—"

"I thought I told you not to talk to him."

"I didn't call him, he called me. And I didn't talk to him. I only told him you would talk to him. Then he said to not wait too long. He said things were getting hot and he wanted to talk with you before it was too late."

"For god's sake, he's playing you. Don't you see that?"

"The thing I see is that my life is turned upside down, and I don't know what to do about it. Look, you said you were going to talk to him, just, just do it sooner than later...please?"

"Okay. I'll do it sooner. But if that bastard calls you again, you hang up, you hear me? I told you to not talk to him anymore and that means not taking his calls. Got it?"

"Yeah, I got it, Vincent, but you don't need to be so mean about it."

Vincent sighed and hung up the phone.

Tony drove down to the warehouse district near the docks and into the rear parking lot of a warehouse used by Silvio's gang. They stashed contraband from truck hijackings and thefts from the docks. In the rear was the Merc S500 belonging to Carmine. Tony turned off the engine and walked over to the Mercedes. The rear door opened and he got in.

"What do you want to see me about?" Carmine asked as Tony settled into his seat.

"I wouldn't bother you, but something came up and I don't know what to do about it. I can't go to Vincent...it's something his wife said. So I figured I should let you know." Tony hesitated. Carmine could see he was nervous. He guessed Tony didn't want to be seen as a snitch. It must be something important for him to ask for a meeting.

Carmine frowned. "So what did Sheila say?"

"She likes to confide in me...you know, talk to me. When things upset her, Vincent doesn't take time to listen. So he asks me to talk with her...to calm her down—"

"I get the picture, what the fuck did she say?"

"She's been talking to Mike Warner. He's the FBI agent that's snooping around. He's been out to Vincent's house a number of times. He's working on Sheila. She's worried that Vincent is in trouble with you and Mr. Palma, and she doesn't know what to do."

"You telling me Sheila talked with this guy? Do you know what she said to him?"

"Not exactly." Tony began to sweat as Carmine intensified his focus on him. "I think he was explaining to her that Vincent and her family could be in danger if you, or Mr. Palma, decided you couldn't trust him anymore. She said he was talking to her about protecting her and her family."

"Christ almighty," Carmine said almost under his breath. He couldn't believe how stupid the woman was. He suspected something was up when he asked Gina to sound her out to try to find out what was going on. Gina said that Sheila was very coy, like she was hiding something. Yeah, that's what she had said, "like Sheila was hiding something." Carmine continued, "She didn't say anything about Vincent's operation...about what we do?" His voice was now hard and cold.

"No. I got the impression he was just getting her to think he was going to help her."

"So what did you say to her...when you heard all this?"

"I told her that things were good between Vincent and you, and she definitely should not talk to that guy anymore."

"And she said...?"

"I'm not sure she believed what I said." Tony paused for a moment. "After all, this harassment has been going on for some time now. I get the picture that she and her daughters are really freaked out at this point."

Carmine looked at Tony closely. "You did the right thing to come and talk to me. Don't talk to Vincent about this meeting. If Sheila talks to you again, if you hear anything else important, let me know...got it?" He reached over and opened the car door.

"I got it." Tony got out of the car.

Carmine's Mercedes drove out of the lot, and Tony wheeled out just behind him. Neither of them saw another lieutenant of Vincent's crew driving down the street. He took note of both cars coming out from the warehouse. Later that day he mentioned it to Vincent.

Vincent sat for a moment with no emotion showing. "You sure it was Carmine and Tony coming out from the warehouse lot?"

"Yeah, I'm sure. I know both cars and could see Tony."

"Did he notice you?"

"Nah. He wasn't paying much attention.

"Stupid fuck. That's a good way to get knocked off by Dan. We got a war going on. You can't be careless. What time did this happen?"

"Around two in the afternoon."

"Okay, that's about right. I had Tony fill Carmine in on our plan to ambush Dan." Vincent pretended the meeting was arranged with his knowledge. "Only don't mention to Tony you saw him. He'll think I don't trust him and was sending you to spy on him. I don't need him to get all worked up. I want everyone focused on getting Dan out of my hair."

When the man left, Vincent poured himself a strong drink and sat down at his desk. Things were getting complicated. Who could he trust? What was going on that Tony would talk to Carmine without talking to him first? *You never see it coming when you get whacked. It will be someone you completely trust.* Was that what was starting to happen? *That fucking Joey got everything all screwed up.* Vincent could feel his anger grow, his heart began to pound in his chest even as his worry deepened. *I've got to get Dan and put an end to this or I'll be fucked.* He was beginning to feel he was living on borrowed time.

Chapter 46

As Vincent had ordered, the information about Joey leaving town had been leaked around the neighborhood so Tommy would pick it up. As soon as Tommy heard, he called Dan.

"I got some information you should know," he said when Dan answered. "Unless you still want me to go fuck myself."

Dan ignored the barb. "What's up?"

"So you want to talk to me now?"

"Tommy, please, what the hell is up that you need to call me. Something you shouldn't be doing."

"The word is that Joey has left town. He's hiding out in the Berkshires, up in Massachusetts."

"That makes sense. He hasn't been back to his apartment for a week."

"There's just one thing. If Joey is hiding out, how did this get out on the street? Seems odd to me."

"You think it's not for real?"

"It's not that. I just figured the mob would be better at keeping a secret."

"How'd you hear about it?"

"Some guy I know, I service his car. He was in Sally's, the bar on Utrecht Avenue. Seems some of the mob associates were there drinking and talking loud, you know how that goes. Well, they mentioned Joey getting sent out of town. Vincent wants him out of town so you can't get to him."

"They say where this lodge is?"

"Somewhere near a little town called Charlemont, in the northwest corner of the state."

"Well that's helpful at least."

"Yeah, but if Joey is hiding out, Vincent's guys were pretty careless about keeping it a secret."

"If it was some associates, they aren't so smart and not that careful." Dan paused for a moment. "I could see that happening."

"Or maybe it's a way to get you out of town."

"So, it could be a wild goose chase and he's not there."

"I don't know. He may be there, but you have to figure they didn't keep things secret for very long."

"Maybe he's the bait. Maybe they're setting a trap for me."

"Maybe, so what are you gonna do?"

"I think I'll have to check it out."

"So you go out there? How are you gonna find the place?"

"If I go, I'll figure something out. I've got something to finish."

"This...stuff, it's almost over, isn't it?"

"Yeah. It's almost over. I'm glad you and Doreen made it through all of this. I owe you a lot, maybe more than you know."

"You mean that woman? She get in touch with you?"

"I'll tell you more, later...when all of this is over."

"Just be careful. It'd be a shame for any of us to get killed this late in the game."

"That's not going to happen. And who said anything about a game? You got to stop assuming things."

"Yeah, right," Tommy replied with a harsh laugh.

Later that night, Dan called Jane. He told her about the lodge and asked her if she could find its exact location.

An hour later Jane called back. "It's at the end of West Hill Road, off route 8A, just south of Charlemont. We have to meet. Just a short one, before you head out. Meet me tomorrow at the usual place," she said, referring to the parking place under the elevated tracks where they first conversed. "Say, ten a.m.?"

The next morning Dan was sitting in his van and watched Jane drive up at the appointed hour. Earlier he had driven around the area, looking for any backup spotters and had been scanning the block while parked for the past half hour. She got out and walked directly to the van. They sat in the back, as before.

"Tommy called and talked to me. He's more and more worried it's a set up, a trap."

"Tommy?" Dan said.

"Yeah. He's your friend. He still cares about you."

Dan grunted. "He complicates things."

"You have people who care about you and want the best for you. Tommy is one of them...so is Doreen. In spite of what you've put them through. You have to know you can trust these people. You're not as alone in this world as you think you are."

"And do you care about me? Can I count on you? Can I trust you?"

"You can count on me and you can trust me."

"I'm useful to you, so you take an interest in my well being."

"I'm offering you a future. If it fits my agenda, so what? Does that make it less valuable? Was I supposed to discover you and bail you out of the hole you're falling into out of the kindness of my heart? There are lots of charity cases closer to home and less complicated. You're not a rescue project. You're to be a part of my operation, which is part of our country's war against its enemies."

"Nice speech." Dan smiled at her. "I guess you don't owe me anything. But what do you want? You didn't set up this meeting just to tell me how much I should admire Tommy and Doreen...or how grateful I should be for you offering me a way out of my dilemma."

"No, I came to give you this." She took a cell phone out of her purse. "It's got a scrambled circuit. No one can listen in on it, even if they intercept the call."

"You know I can't take that. You can track me with it."

"I thought we had gotten past that. I haven't tried to track you since our meeting. Don't you realize I'm for real? I'm not some elaborate scam to trap you. If I were, you'd be surrounded by dozens of agents right now. They would have just followed me here."

Dan thought for a moment. "I guess you're right, I did agree that we didn't have to go through that elaborate routine to throw off any tails. Okay, what do I need the phone for?"

"I don't care what you're going to Massachusetts to do. I'm not interested in some minor hood. I'm interested in you wrapping up whatever you're doing and joining me...before it's too late. This phone will allow me to help you when you finish whatever you're going to do. You're going to be in a rural, remote area. That could be a good thing with your skills, but there are some significant downsides to it. If the local police get called, it won't be hard for them to bring in the state police and seal off any area around the lodge. With so few roads, you would be stopped trying to get out of the area. And I don't think whatever disguise you're going to use will withstand close scrutiny."

"So how can you help?"

"I can be your transport out of the area. You call me, I pick you up and I get you out of the area, through any roadblocks."

"How do you do that?"

"I've got access to a vehicle with a hiding place. It's not foolproof, but will get us through a roadblock inspection."

She took out a detailed map of the area. "The lodge is here, at the end of West Hill Road. It bumps up against the Mohawk Trail State Forest. When you're done, you call me on this secure phone. Then you start hiking north." She showed Dan the route through the forest. "I'll be in an SUV and meet you here." She pointed to a dirt road that dead ended at the forest boundary. "I'll hide you and then drive out on Route 2. If we're stopped, I've just come from hiking in the forest. We won't be near the area, so there should be little surveillance, if any this far away."

"It'll just be you...alone?"

"Just me. I can't afford anyone else getting further into this. The New York office staffer only knows that I am interested in you and getting you away from a mess in Brooklyn, but he doesn't know any more. Don't worry, I've been involved in much worse. You'll be in good hands."

"And you think all this is necessary?"

"I'm hoping you'll be coming on board, so I'll take this chance to make sure nothing derails the plan."

"You go to jail for this, couldn't you?"

Jane looked up from the map. "Joey's a mob punk. He's involved in killings and robberies." She paused as if thinking about events in the past. "I've seen better men and women, innocent people, get killed in an operation. Sometimes without having anything to do with it. So I don't worry about someone like Joey.

"I have a mission and it's to eliminate bad people—people who want to harm the U.S. My mandate is to use unconventional means to get the job done. Like I said, I've seen innocents die, so if something happens to a known mobster in the process of me getting my job done, I'm not conflicted about that."

"But it is illegal."

"Much of what we do is illegal, either in the country in which we're operating, or by our own laws. That is why we don't have a mandate to operate domestically, because we operate outside of the law. What you're doing is not my operation. I'm just protecting my asset."

"That sounds more like a rationalization than a good defense."

Jane smiled. "It may be, but that's how I read it. Now take this phone and let me help you get out of there when you're done."

"What do I do with my car?"

"You know the answer to that. You leave it. An out-of-town car is the first thing the police will focus on. I suppose you'll park it near Charlemont, but you're not going back there, you're going north, through the woods."

"All right. I'll take the phone. But it seems to me that you're taking quite a chance yourself."

"Maybe now you'll trust me more, since I've got some skin in the game. By the way, we can only talk briefly on the phone. If things get hot, all cell calls will be monitored. They can pick up this call but will only hear static. If it goes on too long, or if we use the phone repeatedly, someone will get suspicious and figure out this is a scrambled call. That will raise the stakes. A single call to let me know you're on your way to the vehicle, and then one when you get close is all we can risk."

"Got it." Dan's military training was kicking in. Jane had an operational plan, for the back end of whatever Dan was planning and his instinct was to coordinate his plan with hers. He now figured he had better work out his part of the plan to the same level of professionalism.

"And we can talk about the finer points of the ethics of what I'm about later, when you are safely away from this mad adventure of yours." Dan looked at her sharply. "Yes, I do think it's mad. You have friends you put in danger and kept at arm's length and a growing paranoia that could keep you isolated forever. I hope you'll achieve whatever closure you're looking for with this last act."

Chapter 47

Vincent was growing more and more nervous about Carmine. Sheila reported that Gina kept asking probing questions about her, about him, and how they were handling the police scrutiny. It was bringing Sheila to near panic, which didn't help his peace of mind. He tried to set up a meeting with Carmine, but found him hard to get a hold of. That fact did nothing to alleviate his anxiety.

When he finally did get to sit down with him, it was not in Carmine's office near the docks. They met at a modest safe house on a quiet Brooklyn street. It was used as a place to lay low when things got too hot. There hadn't been much need for it in the last few years with things being quiet. Now things were very much not quiet.

When Vincent asked about the location, Carmine explained that with all the focus on him, Carmine had to keep him at arm's length, just until things settled down. They shouldn't be seen together. Carmine's explanation only fed Vincent's growing worries.

"Carmine, are we okay? I mean, are things straight between us?" he asked when they sat down in the kitchen. Vincent had on his usual knit pullover shirt and slacks. Carmine was well-dressed as always in an expensive suit, silk shirt and bold tie.

"Yeah, sure. Things are fine. You just need to get this mess with Dan under control." He leaned forward over the table. "Look, Silvio is getting on my back, and so I gotta put the pressure on you. And this guy, Warner, you gotta make sure no one is talking to him."

"I'm trying, but he keeps coming around, even when I tell him not to. I sent Joey out of town, like you told me. And I made sure that Dan heard about it. I figure he'll be out of town and things will settle down. Frank went with him and he understands no one comes back...just like you said. What else can I do?"

Carmine studied Vincent. He looked stressed out. Not like the calm, in control Vincent who ran his crew in a steady manner, always making money and keeping things calm. Now his territory was out of control. The drug gangs were starting to take advantage of the turmoil and skip their payments. The violence in the streets had gone up as they fought one another for an advantage. Was Vincent over his head with this crisis?

"How's Sheila holding up?" he asked.

"She's doing all right," Vincent answered.

"It's just that Gina feels she's very upset. That she may be getting panicked by the pressure...you know, the shootings at the house, the cops, this FBI guy..." Carmine kept staring at Vincent as he spoke.

"Sheila's okay, like I said. She wouldn't say anything to anyone, certainly not the FBI."

"I didn't say she would," Carmine replied, still staring at Vincent. "But I'm glad to hear that she can keep her mouth shut in times like this." Carmine could see Vincent flinch, like he regretted what he'd just said.

"Maybe I can send her away, to visit her parents. They're down in Florida. Get her away from the pressure till this is over."

Carmine thought a moment, considering the value of Vincent's suggestion. "That might help."

Finally he stood up and walked around to Vincent who also stood. He grabbed him in a big hug. "You get this under control. You finish it. And you get this guy Warner out of your life. If I hear of you or any of your family talking with him, I can't protect you from what Silvio might do."

Carmine held him tightly as he whispered in his ear. "You got it?"

"I got it," Vincent said and Carmine released him.

"Take care of business," he said as Vincent walked to the front door.

Vincent felt shaky as he headed back to the restaurant. The brick with the note on it that said he was next and now Carmine's clear threat were beginning to unnerve him. This mess that Joey created was going to get them killed.

When he got back to the restaurant, he threw everyone out of the back room and sat down at his desk for some time without moving, trying to focus his mind on the swirl of possibilities. How much did Carmine know? Had Silvio already decided he had to go? Would Dan finish off Joey? Would Frank be able to kill Dan or would Dan make good on his threat that he was next? His world was coming unstuck. Things were shifting fast, too fast for him to control. His head ached. Finally he picked up the phone and called the FBI agent.

"Warner here," Mike said.

"Sheila begged me to call you, so I'm doing it. But I want you to know that you better not call her anymore."

"Vincent, I'm glad you finally called. No, I won't call Sheila, but I'm glad she talked you into calling."

"So whadda you want to tell me?"

"I'm concerned that Carmine and Silvio are losing patience with you about this Dan thing. They're worried about you losing control and you know what that means."

"How do you know this?"

"Well, we get scraps of information, some phone intercepts. We have ways to get pieces of information, pieces we can put together to give us a picture of what's going on. I'm afraid they're losing confidence in you."

"You expect me to believe that? Just 'cause you say it?"

"Vincent, you must have your own suspicion. You gotta know I'm not making all this up."

Vincent didn't answer. Mike continued. "Look, if things get too hot, you know what happens next. You've seen it. You know it can happen to you. It would be a shame for you and your family, but it doesn't have to happen. I can provide protection for all of you. A new start, a new life away from this danger."

"Yeah, all I have to do is become a rat. That's something I won't do. You'll help me, but only if I spill my guts, tell you everything I know, rat out my friends—people I've known my whole life."

"People who will kill you without a second thought," Mike responded. "It will come from someone you'd never expect. You know I'm right. What do you owe those people who'll kill you as soon as they lose confidence in you?" Mike now raised his voice. "What do you owe people who will kill you and leave your family destitute? Tell me, Vincent? You're going to be loyal to your executioners?"

"All right, enough!" Vincent shouted back. "I gotta think about this. I can't talk any more right now. I gotta go."

"Don't think too long. Remember, you'll never see it coming."

Tony quickly stepped back from the door after he heard Vincent hang up. The scraps of conversation he'd heard didn't sound good for Vincent, but Carmine told him to let him know if he heard anything important.

Chapter 48

Joey and Frank drove west on the Mass. Turnpike. Neither of them liked being out of the city. This was Hicksville. Now Joey had to hide out for who knows how long? Still, it was better than getting shot by Dan. *Somebody needs to find that bastard and kill him.*

But how? Joey didn't have a clue. Dan seemed to live a life devoted to robbing and shooting up the crew. He didn't believe for a moment that it was anyone else but Dan. He scowled as he thought about his situation. That smart-ass broke his leg in front of his restaurant and now was back in town robbing the crew, shooting up cars and Vincent's house. It was like he had no normal life—something they could tap into—something that could link to him and help them track him down. As it was now, Dan simply appeared out of nowhere and then disappeared.

Joey didn't feel bad about Rita getting killed. What the hell was she doing there so late that night anyway, especially if she was pregnant? It was a shame, but Joey didn't feel any remorse, only anger that her death triggered this revenge campaign. It would have been better if she had lived. Dan would have gotten the message and come around. Still, both he and Rita were stubborn. It might not have come out different in the end. A surge of satisfaction coursed through Joey as he thought about Dan's loss. He could exact all the revenge he wanted, it wouldn't bring Rita back to life.

"To hell with him," Joey said aloud as they drove down the highway. Frank looked over at him. Joey frowned.

"Now maybe Dan will be taking more chances since he can't find me. He might make a mistake and the guys can find him and finish him off." He could only hope this enforced retreat to the mountains would be rewarded with Dan getting taken out of the picture. Then things could get back to normal and he could enjoy life again. Frank didn't say a thing, simply turned to look out the window.

Frank didn't talk much, didn't show any emotion. It made Joey nervous. It was going to be uncomfortable to have him around for...who knew how long.

They drove up I-95 into Connecticut and turned north at New Haven on I-91. They passed through Hartford into Massachusetts and stopped in Greenfield for supplies. After getting some groceries the two turned west on Route 2. Nearing the end, at Frank's insistence, they stopped in Charlemont to fill up the tank. After pumping the gas, Joey went inside to pay.

"What brings you out to our small town?" the cashier said, trying to be friendly. He seemed bored and probably looking to break up the monotony of the day.

"None of your business," Joey replied without thinking. He didn't like talking to strangers and didn't like people asking him questions.

"No need to get upset, I just noticed your New York plates." He reached out his hand. "My name's Fred by the way, what's yours?" Joey didn't answer, but took the clerk's hand. "We don't get many strangers to this little town, although it's a nice place. Most people are just driving through. They don't stop. They're headed for the state forests. We got the Mohawk Trail and Sandy Mountain State Forests right near here. They're great for hiking and camping. You planning to do some camping? It's a bit early in the season for that, but you're ahead of the bugs, if you're going out now. Later the mosquitoes come out and you better be prepared for them."

Joey just stared at this guy rattling off information—a regular travel guide. He was about to say something smart, put him in his place and shut him up, when he remembered Vincent telling him to not make a scene in the local town.

"That's interesting," he finally said, interrupting the cashier's monologue. "I'm staying at my boss's lodge. Got some R and R time off and figured I'd get out in the boonies. What do people do for excitement around here?"

The cashier looked at him, surprised by the response. "Well, we don't do much. If you want to see a movie, you got to drive to Greenfield. Most times the wife and I make it dinner and a movie, since we're going to drive that far. There's a Golden Corral there with an all-you-can-eat buffet. Definitely get your money's worth."

Joey's smile was thin. This was worse than the dentist.

"Where are you staying?" the cashier continued. "I'll bet I know the place. I help take care of some of the summer places people have near the forests. It's good work. There's always some interesting challenges— something to fix that you never thought would break. After a while, you think you've seen it all. Makes fixing things at the house a lot easier. I told my wife, Mary, nothing she shows me around the house can throw me off my game, since I've been doing caretaking work." He smiled, seeming to Joey to be proud of his mastery of home repairs.

"I'll bet you're a regular whiz around the house," Joey replied. The cashier didn't catch the sarcasm in Joey's response.

"So where is it you're staying?"

"You probably haven't heard of it. It's a private place, doesn't have a name."

"Most don't and I bet I have heard of it. Matter of fact, I bet I've worked at it. Go ahead, try me." He finished up with a grin.

"It's a private lodge at the end of West Hill Road."

The cashier paused for a moment. "Yeah! I know the one. Fellow from New York City owns it. Two years ago I worked on the place with Dennis here in town. He got the job to repair the roof. Seems a tree fell down in the winter and broke through the roof. That was a tricky job. And the interior was damaged from snow and rain getting in. Dennis didn't get to the camp for a few days. That was a bad storm. We couldn't get out for two days. After the storm, Dennis went around checking on the properties he kept an eye on. A lot of them were damaged. You should've seen it—"

"I'm sure it was bad." Joey didn't want to let this guy get wound up into a story. "Look, I've got to get going. Don't want to let my groceries spoil."

"Oh yeah. I carry on." The cashier rang up Joey's gas. "You sure the lodge is open?"

"Yeah, I'm sure. I wouldn't have driven all this way if it wasn't. Do I look stupid to you?" Now Joey was getting an edge in his voice. Couldn't this guy just shut up and give him his change? Now everyone in town would know where he was staying.

"Sorry. Since you came so far, I wanted to be sure you could turn on the gas when you get there. It still gets chilly at night."

"That's nice of you, but don't worry about us. Just give me my change and I'll be on my way. Matter of fact, keep the change. I appreciate the conversation," he said without conviction and turned to the door.

"Don't miss the left onto Route 8A, it's just one block up. Go over the bridge. Can't miss West Hill Road, just eight miles or so down the road."

Joey went through the door without answering. He hoped he that guy wouldn't feel the need to come out to see how he was doing. Maybe he should have said something about needing to be left alone? *Oh, well. Better not say more. This could be a long stay.*

Back in New Jersey, Dan loaded up his old car with some food, camping gear, his Remington 700 rifle and

9mm pistol. He also packed a sniper's ghillie suit. With the addition of local vegetation, it would make him almost invisible in the woods. In his backpack he had multiple loaded magazines for both weapons.

He headed out of town towards Boston. Five hours later he drove into a long term parking lot at Logan Airport. There he picked out two cars at random and removed the front plate from each. He then drove off and, in a downtown parking garage, replaced his New York plates with Massachusetts plates. They didn't match, but Dan was counting on no one comparing both front and rear plates at the same time. Seeing their rear plates, the drivers would probably not notice their missing front ones for some days. He hoped the extra few days would be enough to complete what he was planning to do.

After changing out his plates, Dan drove northwest out of Boston and picked up Route 2, which would take him west across the northern tier of the state. He avoided the faster Mass. Turnpike with its toll booths and cameras. In Greenfield, he stopped early to spend the night in a cheap motel along I-91 which ran through the edge of town. He used one of his disguises when he registered.

He wanted an early start so he could find a good place to stash his car. It would be found but Dan didn't care about that. He just needed for it to be found well after his mission was completed and he was on his way out of the area. Before leaving New York he had spent four hours wiping the car down and wore gloves on this last drive so there would be little the police would learn from it.

Early the next morning, Dan drove west out of Greenfield on Route 2 to the town of Charlemont. There he turned south on 8A following the path of the Chicksley River which flowed north joining the Deerfield River at Charlemont. He would hide the car somewhere off Route 8A before he came to West Hill Road and from there, hike into the forest to set up his sniper position.

About a mile before West Hill Road, Dan came upon an abandoned side spur. It had been used as a local dump for old refrigerators and other trash. Now, with everyone being more environmentally conscious, the spur was not used, even though the trash remained. The important point was that at least half of the loop was shielded from the road. He drove his old car up the rutted track and forced it forward until it was hidden from the road. In a final thrust, he rammed the car partly into the brush

With the car partially buried, he spent the next three hours going over it, taking off the license plates and packing them away along with the correct plates, removing the VIN plate and giving it a final wipe down. Eventually it would be identified and shown to be registered to one of his aliases. But that could take weeks. After cleaning the car, Dan invested a couple of more hours collecting brush and placing it on top and around the car to hide it. When he was done the car looked like it had been left there a long time ago and one would only see it if they drove up the spur. Looking up the spur from 8A, one would see nothing.

After a last look around, he shouldered his backpack and with his rifle slung over his shoulder, headed off through the woods. As the crow flew it was only a couple of miles to the lodge, but Dan would take a circuitous route to avoid the few farm buildings thrust up into the forest.

The forest this time of the year was still damp. The spring moisture, fed by the rains and melting snow had not yet dried up. He hiked around the boggy sections in the woods, sticking to the firmer ground. Even there the ground was soft and wet. The walking was quiet; no leaves crunched under foot. Dan felt good to be out in the remote forest. The plants were budding and coming alive with the warmer weather, showing the promise of summer richness. The trees were only partially leafed out, still allowing a substantial amount of sunlight in. Later the light would have difficulty penetrating the dense canopy. Despite the cool air, Dan could feel the strength of the sun when he came to the clearings.

He felt no need to hurry. If this was all a trap, they would wait for him. He figured, as before, the mob would not properly estimate his ability or his preparation. There was little likelihood they would guess that he would hike miles through the forest to come at the lodge from an unexpected direction. They would expect him to drive up the road, stop before the last bend and walk the rest of the way, approaching from the front. That's how they would do it. Their lack of imagination would play into his hands.

His sniper training made it easy for him to navigate the forest and endure days, if necessary, of waiting in a hide to take out his target. He could move quietly, he knew how to set up a sniper's hide, and he could maneuver in the deep woods without getting lost or turned around. The Army hadn't abandoned this basic element in its training even though the combat field had shifted to more urban action. Dan had packed enough gear to wait, days if necessary. He liked being in the forest; he was a city boy, but always enjoyed his training time in the woods. With the lodge out in the country, Dan knew he was more in his element than the mob. When he got near, he would set up his sniper position and collect brush and leaves to thread into the mesh of his ghillie suit.

Chapter 49

Vincent and Sheila sat in their kitchen the night after he spoke with Mike Warner. "Have you talked any more to Gina?"

"She called me today. Just wanted to check in. She's checking up on me, fishing for information. I don't get any warm feelings from her conversation."

"You gotta be careful talking with Gina. I told you she's taking everything back to Carmine."

"Are you sure? Did Carmine say anything? Because I've been careful about what I say."

"Carmine's fishing with me as well. He's nervous. You just keep telling Gina everything's fine."

"But they aren't. And now we have to worry about Carmine as well?" She got up, took an open bottle of Chardonnay from the fridge and poured herself a second large glass.

Vincent didn't answer. Finally he told Sheila that he had talked with Mike.

"I'm so glad. What did he say?"

"He didn't say anything specific. Those guys never do."

"Well he promised to protect us, how's he going to do that? Did you ask him?

"I know how he'll do it: the Witness Protection Program. I spill my guts to him, rat out everyone I know, and he takes us out of Long Island and sets us up in a new life. That's what he's offering."

"That seems like a lot to pay to get some protection," she said after a moment.

"Everything costs. There's no free ride."

Sheila stared at her glass, now half empty. "Will it come to that? Our whole life changing like that? I guess we got enough money to make it work—"

"It don't work like that. We don't get to keep our money. You'd have to give up this lifestyle, all the things you like." He waved his arms around to encompass the room and the house. "We'd be nothing special. I'd be a working stiff trying to make ends meet and you'd be a housewife, having to scrimp and save. And the girls? They wouldn't be able to buy new clothes every season and spend lots of money on themselves and their friends." Vincent tapped on the table. "How's that sound to you?"

Sheila sat there with a growing look of pain on her face. Vincent could see she was trying hard not to lose control. "Is it that bad? Why does it have to come to that? We haven't done anything wrong."

Vincent leaned across the table towards his wife. "Look, if things don't settle down, Carmine may be forced to take action. He's not going to buck Silvio. I know too much, don't you see? I'm in a trap, and it don't look good if this guy Dan can't be stopped. The Feds don't have anything on me, but they know I can implicate Carmine and Silvio, along with other Capos, in a lot of stuff. That's why they want me to turn. Maybe that's why they can't find this guy, Dan."

Vincent found himself drawn to Sheila in their shared stress. Maybe it was their history. They had been through a lot, and he had had the fire for her at one time. Now with his world coming apart, he found himself thinking more of her, even with her hysteria. Somehow he'd get them through this mess. He just didn't know how. The key was Frank making sure no one came back from the lodge.

Frank brought quite an arsenal with him. He had two .45 caliber Model 1911s, one with a suppressor, one without; a semi-automatic shotgun that held seven rounds, and an

AK47 which shot a 7.62 round, equivalent to the .308 rounds Dan used in his sniper rifle. The AK could fire in semi- and full automatic mode, giving Frank a rate-of-fire advantage if he got into a gun battle with Dan. He figured Dan's sniper rifle was a traditional bolt action which would limit his ability to put shots downrange, while Frank could smother any position with a dense burst of rounds.

After unloading the car and bringing their gear inside, Frank went into the kitchen and made some coffee. He explained to Joey that if Dan showed up and there was a gun battle, the cops would arrive at some point. They would have to move fast to get out of there. It would be a disaster for them to be caught with all those weapons.

Dan arrived at the lodge late in the day. Joey and Frank had been there for two days. He had approached it from the northwest, which was opposite the direction of the road. He had carefully skirted the lodge to take up a position to the north. From his position on a ridge, he overlooked a cleared area around the lodge. The distance was about three hundred yards. He was about fifty feet above the lodge. There were thickets below him, but he had a direct line of sight over the growth to the building. He had an area of fire sweeping from the driveway across the front of the lodge. The windows at the front of the building offered a possible, but more difficult shot.

No one appeared out front during the rest of the day. He could see figures flitting past the windows, just brief shadows. That night he saw the splash of light as someone went out the back door, but no clear shot presented itself. Dan watched the whole next day. It was now going into the second night, and he hadn't got a good view of either man outside the building. Frank's presence complicated matters, but didn't deter Dan from his plan. Either both, or just Joey. It didn't matter to him. Joey was not leaving alive.

The occasional glimpses of a figure moving past a window, just a silhouette as the curtains were all drawn, didn't offer a clear shot. They had to come out sometime. Now that he was there, he would wait patiently. Time didn't matter. Finishing this job did.

He was calm. There was no elation. This was the culmination of his mission, yet he felt no release. Would it come after the shot? He doubted it. A debt would be paid. He was the debt collector.

It's for you, Rita. He repeated those words like a mantra as he waited. Somehow the repetition didn't help, but he kept at it. He thought about how he should take Joey out. Dan knew it was best to take the shot and leave. One shot, one kill and slip away, silent and unseen. That was what his training called for. But he couldn't suppress a need to confront Joey. Killing him with one shot seemed too easy on him. Part of him wanted Joey to face his execution. Did he want Joey to plead for his life? Dan shuddered at that thought. As much as he hated Joey, he didn't relish him collapsing in a pathetic heap. It would be easier to exact his "justice" on an unrepentant Joey, not a sniveling Joey. Still the urge to show himself to the guy, even for a moment before his execution grew in him, against all his better judgment.

What could go wrong? He snorted. *Famous last words. Don't be a fool.*

The second night was cold like the first. Dan huddled under his survivor blanket; sleep came only fitfully. He was slowly burning his energy reserves. He had a couple of days to go with water and high energy snacks, but he would need more sleep to keep refreshed and alert. Dawn arrived. It was a chilly, late spring day, but at least the sun would be out.

Dan slipped back from his hide, stretched and relieved himself. He crept back into the nest he had made, drank some water, and ate an energy bar. Then settled down for more waiting and watching. His Remington 700 was loaded and ready to fire with the flip of the safety. He was using full load, super-sonic rounds with the suppressor. He wanted maximum velocity and accuracy. Out here in the woods, he was not worried about the gunshot. It would be heard some distance away but would be dismissed as someone doing target practice out in the woods. Short of a multiple-round fire fight, Dan's shot wouldn't attract any serious attention. He squirmed to find a comfortable position and studied the lodge through his scope.

He had already computed the distance for his shot and now adjusted his calculations for the light morning breeze from the west. He was ready. How many hours had he spent looking through his scope in Iraq? It was part of the job. He was used to it. Only out here, there was no one to relieve him. He would have to be on watch again, for a full ten hours.

Frank woke up with a stiff neck. He had not slept well. He never slept well in strange surroundings. He faced another day of waiting. Would there be any action? His preference was to let Dan take Joey out and then he would go after Dan. How long would it be before he showed up? Frank didn't doubt that he would show. Dan would take the bait; he wanted Joey that badly. He went down the hall to the bathroom to pee, and then headed to the kitchen to make coffee.

Frank wondered if he would be a target. Dan wanted Joey, but would he settle for Frank? He concluded that might be a target as well. The only question was would he be before or after Joey? With his cup in hand he stood well back from the front windows and tried to scan the woods, especially the ridge beyond the clearing. Then he went to check out the rear of the lodge. Dan was most likely to be somewhere on the ridge in the front; it had the best sight line across the cleared field, so the rear presented a possible exit route.

Up on the ridge Dan waited.

Chapter 50

Vincent's paranoia was growing. He was sure he wasn't just imagining things. Some of Carmine's guys were coming around to the Gardens more frequently. Sometimes they would act like it was no big deal; other times, they asked him questions that Carmine himself could ask if he would only call.

"Carmine don't want to call you while things are so hot with the Feds," was the standard reply. It made some sense, but it also increased Vincent's discomfort.

No one had experienced a run-in with Dan since Joey left town. The cops were still hanging out at Vincent's house, but only at night now. By retracing the path of the bullets from the holes in the wall, they had discovered the spot where they thought the shots had been taken, but found nothing that could connect the place to anyone, let alone Dan. With that discovery, Vincent figured his house was now free from any more assaults, but he still had to go to work. The restaurant was still vulnerable and he didn't want the cops staking it out. Carmine would be furious.

He still felt threatened—by Dan, and now by his growing worry about Carmine and Silvio. While he was close to the other Capos, they would not shed a tear, except for show, if he got whacked. They would figure he had to accept the consequences if he lost control. That night he talked with Sheila some more about the offer.

"If things get too hot, his offer might be our only way out," he said.

"But we don't get to take our money? That's what you said. Are you sure?"

"What do you think? I'm an expert on this? No, I'm not sure. I stayed away from this kind of thing all my life. Now you expect me to be an expert?"

Sheila looked at her husband. They had grown closer during this time although he still yelled at her. It seemed as if Vincent needed her more with this stress. She wasn't sure why now, but that part felt nice. Over the years they had grown distant and complacent. She filled her time and interests with shopping, the girls and the few friends she could maintain—most of them mob wives. Vincent seemed to fill his time with his work, and mistresses, which Sheila suspected but didn't want to know about.

"Don't get angry," she said. "We need to talk about this. Would it be helpful to ask Mike some questions? Maybe we can take our money and some possessions. If you don't know, maybe we should ask?"

Vincent looked back at his wife. She still didn't get how dangerous it was. "If I'm caught talking to this guy, I'm signing my death warrant. Do you get that? It's dangerous to talk to him. Nobody in my business does that." He didn't want to get her hysterical. Lord knows she'd been that way often enough this past month, but she had to understand.

"Okay, it's dangerous. But how else will we know about this? If, like you say, things get worse."

Vincent sat back and thought for a moment. Maybe phoning from home would be safe enough. The cops were outside and two of his guys were also parked down the road a bit. Carmine hadn't sent any of his men out to the house...yet.

"All right. If it will make you feel better, I'll call him." He picked up his cell phone and punched Mike's number.

When the agent answered, Vincent asked him what they could take with them if they decided to go into the protection program. "I'm not saying we're going to do anything. I just want to know what my options are."

"I understand," Mike replied.

"How much cash can we take with us? I get paid a lot in my work, between the restaurant and the trucking company."

"I'll bet you do."

"So, can I take that with me? I earned it and don't want to lose it. That ain't right."

"Vincent, if its legal money, not from drugs or crime, and you can prove it, you can take those funds out and re-deposit them when we relocate you."

"I earned it and paid taxes on it, so what else do you need to know about it?"

"If it's declared income that you paid taxes on, then I don't have a problem with it. If you got a million dollars in cash stashed in your attic, that's another issue and I can't help you with it."

"You're all heart," Vincent replied.

"So, you ready to get out of the game? Get your family to safety?"

"I didn't say anything about that. I told you I'm just asking so I know what the options are. What about cars, jewelry, clothes?"

"Cars can be traced. We'll help you get new cars. Clothes and jewelry you can take, but remember, we're not bringing in a moving van. This will be moving out light."

"We'll be leaving behind all our furniture, all we've accumulated here in the house. We'll need to replace that."

"We can help you. The house and furnishings will be sold. That money will go to re-supply you in your new home. So when do we do this?"

"I told you, I'm just asking for information. I got no plans to 'do this', as you call it, right now."

"Just don't wait too long. Carmine and Silvio aren't getting any calmer."

"Well, things may be settling down and getting back to normal and maybe we won't need your offer. I get the feeling this Dan guy has left the area. Maybe all this is over and you can go back to wiretapping investment bankers—you know those Wall Street guys. They're worse crooks than we are." Vincent was looking forward to hearing from Frank that this nightmare was all over. That would square him with Silvio and Carmine.

"I appreciate your career advice, but I'm not kidding you about Carmine and Silvio."

"Yeah, yeah. Thanks for the info." And with that Vincent hung up. "That dumb fucker thinks he can panic me like he did you."

"What'd you find out?"

"We can take the money we have in the bank and clothes and jewelry. We would have to pack light if we do this." He went on to explain the rest of the program. "I'll make some deposits, just in case, to get some of the cash here into the bank." Vincent was thinking ahead. He also planned to pack up some of it, if they had to leave. What were they going to do, inspect his suitcases?

Down the street, Tony listened on his scanner as the cell phone call went through to Mike. He had ear phones on so the others in the car wouldn't know he was intercepting a call from their boss. They thought Tony was monitoring the cops.

Chapter 51

Joey was bored. He had been at the lodge for three days now. He watched TV, watched the front windows, listened to the faint sounds of traffic on Route 8A, and paced around the rooms. He was beginning to talk to himself. Frank was lousy company. He just sat and looked at the old magazines left at the lodge. Joey wasn't sure how long he could stand it. He wasn't one for being quiet and reflective. If he had someone he could talk to, or who would play cards with him, it would be easier. The two of them had a few beers each day, but not much conversation.

Joey went into the kitchen. The sink was full of dirty dishes. Frank would clean his own dishes but didn't touch Joey's, which were piling up. He rinsed out a cup and poured himself some coffee. It was left over from yesterday, so he heated it in the microwave. His face twisted; it wasn't a good cup of coffee. He decided that he should have gone into hiding with a whore to keep him company. Joey smiled at the thought. He should have taken one of the girls that the mob ran. He could afford to pay her for the week. That just might be the perfect wife, he thought. Of course, she'd have to clean as well, and that was the problem; the girls he knew didn't know how to cook and certainly didn't wash dishes.

Joey thought about going back into town. They didn't need supplies. It hadn't been that long but he needed a diversion. Even that motor mouth at the gas station would be a relief from the silence. He had mentioned it to Frank who nixed the idea. Frank didn't want anyone in town thinking about them.

"How long we got to stay out here? This is driving me crazy."

Frank gave Joey a long, disdainful look. Joey didn't care.

"We stay here until I say it's time to go back."

"So when is that, since you're calling the shots."

"It's when I say it is. You got a problem with that?" Frank stared straight at Joey, challenging him.

Joey looked away. "Nah. But it'd be nice to have some idea how long we're gonna be stuck here. This ain't much fun, even you gotta agree with that."

"We get a call from Vincent, we go back. That's how it works."

Joey changed the subject. "You think Dan found out where we're hiding out?" He wondered if Dan was out there, waiting. Frank never went outside during the day, so Joey followed his example, but it made the waiting all the more confining. Frank only left the lodge after dark and then he kept to the shadows of the building. Could Dan have tracked them this far? The thought had been growing and made Joey uneasy. He took note of the fact that Frank spent considerable time carefully watching from the front windows—carefully—searching the area around the house. Why would he be doing that?

Frank shrugged. "No, how could Dan know?"

Fred, the clerk from the store in Charlemont, was talking to Dennis the day after Joey and Frank came through.

"I met someone going to the lodge just off 8A, the one owned by that guy in New York." Dennis gave him a confused look. "You know the one where the tree busted in the roof. I helped you fix it."

"Oh, yeah. What about it?"

"Well these two guys were going there, city guys. Weren't too polite, but I guess that's the way it is in the city."

"The lodge open? I didn't open it up."

"They said it was, but who knows?"

"Maybe I ought to go up there and see if they need any help."

"I wouldn't. The guy I talked to didn't want any company. Acted like they wanted to be alone."

"Still, don't want them blowing the place up."

Joey was still concerned about whether or not Dan could have found out where they had gone. "Well, someone could have let the word out on the street. It could have been picked up by Tommy. That fucker would tell Dan right away. He claims he can't reach him, but I don't believe it."

"Why would anyone do that, let slip where you are?"

"Why do you keep peeking through the windows? You take your binoculars, pull back the curtains for a moment, and study the woods outside. And I don't see you walking around out there. We've been out of this lodge only at night. And that's just to walk around in the shadows. You know something I don't know?"

"Just trying to be careful."

"I think you figure Dan's out there, playing sniper again."

"He don't play at it. He's pretty good at it."

"So you don't take any chances."

Frank didn't answer but took his binoculars out to scan the woods on the ridge to the north and west of the lodge. The sun had come out.

After a minute, Joey spoke, "So you see anything, with all that looking?"

Frank didn't answer. He closed the curtain and stepped back from the window. He had caught a glint of something on the ridge to the northwest of the house. Was it a reflection from the glass of a scope trained on the lodge?

If Dan were up there, that would make it easy. He just had to get Joey to go outside, hang around the front porch. Dan would take him out and Frank would exit out the back with the AK47 to intercept him on the ridge.

"Looks clear to me."

Joey looked at him for moment. He noticed that Frank had moved himself a bit further back from the window, but kept looking at it, as if trying to see through the curtains. He had never made a comment before. Frank had spent long periods checking the area with his binoculars, but never pronounced it clear.

Something didn't feel right to Joey. He'd always trusted his instincts. They were well honed from the streets. Now they told him something was up.

"Go ahead and take a walk while the sun's out, since you're complaining about being stuck inside. It looks all clear," Frank repeated.

"Yeah, maybe I'll do that." Joey grabbed his .45 and stuffed it in his waistband. If this was a set up, he had one advantage—he knew about it. There was a stack of wood on the porch. He would duck behind it for cover.

Joey opened the front door and stepped out. He pretended to stretch for one full second, and then dropped to the floor, and scrambled around the wood. He heard the shot just as he dropped. The bullet smashed into the stack of wood above Joey. Before another round could be fired, he was behind its protection.

"You son of a bitch!" Joey yelled out. He shattered a window next to him with his .45 and fired at Frank inside. "You set me up, mother fucker! I'll kill you!"

Frank bolted from the room. In the hallway, he grabbed his AK47 and a couple of clips, ran out the back door, and sprinted for the cover of the woods.

Dan cursed as his shot went over Joey's head. Joey must have known he was targeted and had presented himself for a second to draw the shot. *Gutsy.* Now Joey seemed to be shooting at Frank inside. A moment later he saw Frank dash out back and head for the cover of the woods. Dan got a shot off but missed. Now Joey was back in the house, having gone through the broken window.

As Frank disappeared into the cover of the trees, Joey grabbed his gear and the car keys. He ran to the back door to see what was going on. If Frank had gone into the woods to kill Dan, Joey may have been wrong about him. It didn't matter though. Joey was leaving. *Fuck him. He set me up.*

The shot had come from the northwest side, from up on the ridge. The car was partially shielded, parked on the east side of the house. Thankfully the gravel drive had led them to that side, where a larger parking area had been laid out. If he could get into the car, he could turn it around and race out of there. *Let Frank take care of Dan. Who gives a shit?* Joey sprinted across the gravel to the car.

Frank looked back when he heard the car start. From the cover of the woods he watched as Joey spun the car around and accelerated out of the yard. Anger surged up inside him. *That little punk.* Now how would he get back to New York? And would Dan leave now and nothing would be accomplished? He cursed himself for using Joey as bait. *Shoulda just killed him myself.*

After a moment he put Joey aside; he'd deal with that little fuck later and he'd make it painful. This time he'd really die in his own grave; there'd be no fake run-through. But right now he had to deal with Dan.

Frank turned to orient himself. He knew Dan was to his right, west and north of him, on higher ground. He was protected from Dan in his current position, but he needed to close the distance so he could bring the AK's superior fire power into play. Dan's sniper rifle was a long range weapon. Frank couldn't match it with his iron sights. But if he could close the distance, he'd have the advantage.

Frank started up the slope. He wasn't dressed for the woods. He was wearing street shoes with smooth soles, a tan jacket, and black slacks that didn't blend well into the foliage. He felt out of place and sensed he stood out.

As he climbed, Frank worked to calm his rage over Joey's leaving. Rage wouldn't help against a trained sniper. Frank knew he had to be cool and methodical. Once he killed Dan, he would find a way out of the place; there were lots of ways to make that happen. He assumed Dan had a car somewhere, if he could find it. Or maybe there was a car or truck in the barn that he could hot wire. If the cops came around, he'd have to wait in the woods until they left, but, in the end, he'd get back to the city and take care of Joey. That anger settled solidly into his gut, fueling him and leaving his mind clear to finish the fight in front of him.

Climbing the slope was not easy in his street shoes. Part of the way up the hill, he slipped on a rock outcropping, falling forward, smashing his knee against the granite. Cursing under his breath, Frank rolled over and clutched his knee. His pants were torn and, along with the bruising, he was bleeding from a gash across his knee cap. He lay there for several minutes before he could get up and test his leg. He could walk, gingerly, but the knee was going to swell, making it more difficult to move. Dark thoughts about how the day might end flickered in his head. He suppressed them. Not imagining things was an old habit with Frank. It helped to compartmentalize what he did, the killing, the injuring, the intimidation. It was just what he did, what he was good at. It was always better not to ruminate on those things or how dangerous situations would work out. Just focus on making them work out.

Chapter 52

Dan saw Joey drive away. He had no clear shot and didn't want to further expose his position with a wasted round. He turned back to the woods, watching. Frank had disappeared into the trees at the rear of the lodge. Dan assumed he was coming. As Frank moved up the slope, he would have to expose himself. He would be coming up to his right and he had to have some idea of where Dan was, so Dan would have to keep him guessing. He moved back from his sniping hide and headed to his right to find a new spot to wait as Frank came up the slope. Settled into his new position, he slowed his breathing, calmed his heart rate. He needed to be cool, calm, and precise. Frank might be out of his element in the woods, but he was no fool; he was a killer.

Patience wins out. He repeated the mantra over and over as he lay in a prone position, his upper body and rifle stuck out from behind the trunk of a tree. He scanned down the slope, back and forth, not looking for specific figure, just movement. Movement gives one away. Prey freezes when they think they're spotted, hoping the predator will not focus on them and move on. Now Dan remained still and watched. Dan also knew Frank was not dressed to blend into the forest. That would be another disadvantage which would work in his favor with his ghillie suit. Long minutes passed. The dappled sunlight that filtered through the trees, shifted and moved with the breeze.

Suddenly the silence was shattered by a burst of automatic gunfire. Clods of dirt erupted in front of him, flying towards his face, showering him and his rifle. Dan shrank back and squirmed backwards along the ground, keeping the tree between himself and the direction of fire. *What happened?* Something had given his position away. He heard twigs snap as the shooter rushed forward, firing in short, rapid bursts.

Can't let him get near me!

Dan frantically crawled backwards as fast as he could go. He couldn't defend against the AK's rate of fire and needed get to a defensible position before Frank got to the top of the ridge. He slid into a drainage depression which ran at ninety degrees to his backwards path. Immediately, he scrambled along it to his right, on his belly, bruising his elbows and knees on the rocks that protruded up from the soil, while keeping his rifle protected, cradled in his arms. The undergrowth tore at his face, but he pushed through frantically, trying to put some lateral distance between him and the approaching Frank.

The shallow gully was only a couple of feet deep and ran slightly downhill. Dan didn't relish giving up the high ground but he had to retreat from the automatic rifle. His bolt action sniper rifle was no match for it in a close-quarters shootout. He stopped at the base of a large oak tree. It was three feet across and gave him excellent cover. He crawled out of the ditch and around to one side. He needed to get a clear shot when Frank reached the top of the slope. Dan was in the shadows, but as the breeze flowed through the forest, the leaves moved and a burst of sunlight broke out, hitting his rifle like a spotlight. Dan lowered his rifle until the light passed.

That's how he spotted me. The sun reflected off the scope lens.

There was another short burst of automatic fire from Frank. But he was blindly shooting forward to where Dan had been, hoping to keep him pinned down.

I'm going to get one shot. I'll lose if this becomes a close-in firefight.

Dan took a deep breath. Should he just run away? He had a moment yet to decide. Frank hadn't reached the ridge top. He could probably move through the forest faster than Frank, yet the thought of being chased with the AK firing at him every time Frank caught a glimpse of him didn't appeal to Dan.

Let's finish this. With that decision his resolve grew and steadied him. He was not where Frank expected to find him. He had recovered the advantage of surprise.

Frank reached the tree where Dan had been hiding. He stopped and peered ahead, looking for him retreating. Seeing nothing, he began to scan to both sides. He stepped behind the tree just as Dan fired. The shot hit the AK, shattering the stock and sending it spinning out of Frank's hands. Frank dropped to the ground behind the tree. Suddenly he reached around the tree and fired several rounds with his .45 semi-automatic in the direction of Dan's shot.

Dan slid back into the shallow ditch and crawled back up the depression. Frank would be to his right and forward, now farther up the slope. He stopped at a thick bush to scan the area but saw nothing. He began to crawl again. He worked as quietly as he could, but crawling was not as silent as walking. Changing positions would keep Frank off guard. Although Dan didn't want to close the distance between him and Frank, he wanted to get to higher ground so Frank would not be shooting down on him. Frank's elevated position could take away his cover in the depression.

Part of the way back up the ditch, he stopped and risked a glance through some brush. Immediately two shots rang out. One hit a boulder sticking out of the ground. The chipped stone smacked into him, just above his eye. He reached up and fired a shot in Frank's general direction, and then cursed himself quietly for resorting to such amateur tactics. *Take a shot when you can see your target.* It was something hunters learn and snipers abide by. Blood from the gash in his forehead ran into his eye, blinding him.

Dan quickly wiped his eye with his sleeve, smearing the blood over his face. *No time for a bandage. Have to work around it.* He lay still and listened. Frank was about fifty yards away. From the sound of the shots, Dan figured Frank had a .45. At this distance, it was not going to be all that accurate unless he was an exceptional shot. *Gonna bet your life on that?* Dan knew the answer to his question.

He backed up in the ditch until he reached another large tree, this one on the slope of the depression away from Frank's position. He rolled up and around the tree as a bullet slammed into the trunk. *How many was that?* Counting would help, but only if Frank had one magazine. He crawled backwards away from the ditch and Frank's position, keeping the tree between the two of them. When he put some extra distance between them, he took off running in a crouch back up the slope, across Frank's field of fire. Two more shots rang out, but he was a difficult target with his ghillie suit, moving quickly with the trees and brush between the two of them.

When he thought he was out of sight, he dropped to the ground and crawled forward another twenty yards, stopping behind a boulder. Dan slid his rifle forward and looked through the scope. The range was now about sixty yards, not a hard shot, if he got a clear sight line. He wiped his face again with his left arm to clear his vision and waited. His scope would not reflect the sun from this new angle. All he needed now was to have Frank get antsy and come forward. He was beyond the point where Frank saw him last. He hoped that Frank would not realize how far he had moved to his right, and would think Dan was positioned more to his front.

Dan's adrenalin flow slowed and his breathing grew calm. The realization hit him. This was what he was good at, what he enjoyed. It was a deadly game of hide and seek, cat and mouse. In the army he had never made this connection; neither in training nor in combat. It was his job, a deadly one to be sure, but what he had trained to do and what he needed to do to protect the other guys in the field. Now stripped of other reasons, it was just him and his opponent in a deadly duel and only one of them was coming out alive. He wiped his forehead again as the blood kept dripping into his eye. He pushed the extraneous thoughts out of his mind. He could ponder this new revelation later. Now he had to kill someone.

Chapter 53

Frank's left hand was swelling and going numb even as he reached around the tree and fired two rounds from his .45. Then he stopped, realizing that he had only one magazine in the pistol. Cursing under his breath, he realized his advantage was now gone. The AK47 was lying on the ground about ten yards from him. The front stock was shattered. Would it still fire? It gave him such an advantage, he had to retrieve it. Dan still had his sniper rifle and probably a pistol. Frank studied the rifle and planned out his move. He would run, grab it, and roll forward. That would be quickest, but the trees were less substantial in that direction. But stopping to pick up the rifle and turning back to where he started would expose him for far too long. He couldn't give Dan that extra time. He was too good a shot.

Frank slowly got to his feet, back against the large oak tree. He pocketed his .45, took a deep breath and, ignoring the pain in his knee, lunged out towards the fallen rifle. In five strides, he bent down, grabbed the rifle and dove for the cover of some smaller oaks. A shot rang out. Frank felt a searing pain tear across his left thigh and twisted as he hit the ground behind the cover of the trees. The shot had torn through his left leg, gouging a channel out of the back of his thigh, damaging his hamstring. He grimaced in pain. This had to be dealt with right away. Taking a folding knife out of his pocket he reached down, cut open his pants, and examined the wound. Blood was flowing, but not pumping; an artery hadn't been hit. Still, it was serious; along with a bruised right knee he now had a damaged left leg.

He tied his belt around his left leg to support it and stem the blood flow. Could he walk? The dark thoughts gathered again, this time stronger. His options were becoming limited. Frank steeled himself to not think about how this was going to end. The game had to be played. You didn't think about the outcome, you just played it—played your hand until it was over. Later you thought about it if you were a reflective person, which Frank was not. He always felt in control in these deadly encounters. Now that sense of control was slipping away. Would he survive this fight? Could he get back to New York? He suppressed those thoughts. *Got to take Dan out.* He'd think about the rest later...if he survived.

Frank rolled over and brought the AK up to his shoulder. His left hand gripped what was left of the splintered stock. He couldn't feel the jagged edges digging into his hand which was still numb and now swollen. With his right hand he fished a fresh thirty-round magazine from his coat pocket and inserted it into the rifle. Time was not on his side; he was bleeding and losing strength. If he was going to win this game, he knew he had to finish it soon. He lurched forward, stumbling. His left leg would not work properly. His right leg with his injured knee had to do all the work to propel him forward. He moved in jerks, firing short bursts in Dan's general direction, still not sure of his position. Suddenly he saw him and loosed a longer round from the Kalashnikov and then fell forward as his knee gave out. He heard a rustling sound ahead of him. From his knees, he looked up and saw Dan's bloody face about thirty yards away. Dan raised his rifle. The dark thoughts flooded over Frank. Through the leaves only Dan's face, streaked with blood, like a demon from hell, stood out clearly. Frank started to swing the AK forward to fire. Dan's rifle was pointed at him. He saw a flash and the world disappeared.

As Frank stumbled forward shooting, a bullet from his volley sliced across Dan's right side. He staggered back. When Frank fell, he saw his chance. Ignoring the searing pain in his side, he stepped forward to get a clear shot. As Frank looked up and moved to bring his AK into play, Dan, looking through a bloody haze, squeezed off one round. The round hit Frank high on the forehead, the bullet tumbled through his brain, tearing an increasingly large channel and burst out the back of his skull after destroying his brain stem.

Dan leaned back against a tree. His knees gave way. His breath came in shallow pants, the pain in his side growing. For a long time he just sat there, leaning against the tree, panting and looking out at the forest without focus. The sound of a siren in the distance brought him back to the moment. *Can't be found here. Got to move.*

He examined his side. The flesh was torn and bleeding, but the bullet hadn't lodged in his body. He had bruised, maybe broken ribs. He would be sore, but he was not critically injured. He took out his knife and cut off a sleeve of his shirt, making a bandanna that he wrapped around his forehead to staunch the flow of blood. Now he could see better. After some thought, he decided to leave the battlefield untouched. The only thing that could connect him to the fight would be the bullet, which he didn't have time to find and dig out of the ground. If it was crosschecked, it would only confirm what everyone would already suspect and believed that whoever shot up the gang in Brooklyn, had killed Frank in the Massachusetts woods. He turned back to his hide to collect his backpack and head north.

Fred heard the rapid shots as he was driving to work. That wasn't hunters. It sounded to him like a machine gun firing. Was it connected to those guys from New York? He didn't know and he didn't want to go to the lodge to find out. He picked up his cell phone and called the local police.

The crunch of gravel announced the arrival of a car at the lodge. Dan crept to the edge of his sniper nest. In the yard at the front of the house was a county cruiser. No one had gotten out yet. He was probably radioing back to indicate that the place looked empty. Dan crawled back from the edge and turned to go. If the cop looked carefully, he would see the broken window and evidence of shots being fired; a bullet from his rifle could be found in the wood pile, shell casings from Joey's .45 somewhere on the porch, and the rounds inside, embedded in the walls. Pretty soon the place would be swarming with inspectors and a helicopter might be called in. Dan didn't relish trying to navigate the woods and stay hidden from a chopper.

When he was well clear of the ridge, he made a quick call on the scrambled phone. "I'm on my way; had some trouble, parts of me are not working quite right, so it'll take a bit longer to reach you."

"It's a scrambled line, you don't have to speak in code," Jane responded. "Are you injured?"

"Yeah. I've got a wound in my side, maybe a broken rib. Hurts like hell, but I'll get there. The cops are at the scene now. A chopper may be brought in, so I'm hurrying as best I can. May be hard to get out of the area."

"Just get here as quickly as you can and keep under cover if the copter shows up. I can take care of the rest."

In spite of his pain, he pushed his pace. He hoped Jane was right about handling everything once he got to the car. He wasn't at all sure his cover, or Jane's, would survive close scrutiny. Two hours into his trek, Dan heard the helicopter in the distance behind him.

They must have found the body. They'll start a circular search pattern, expanding from the lodge.

He called Jane again. "You hear the chopper?"

"Yeah, the vehicle is covered. I'm under some trees. I'll be fine. How are you doing?"

"Okay. Sore, but still moving. I'm not taking the easiest path, got to stay under cover."

"What's your ETA?"

"Not half way there yet. We won't get past the checkpoints before they're set up."

Four hours later Dan reached the rendezvous point. Jane ran to meet him. She reached up to him and took his pack.

"You are a mess," she exclaimed.

"Sorry. I didn't have time to clean up before arriving."

She guided him back under the trees. There, under camouflage netting was a Chevy Suburban SUV. Jane retrieved a first aid kit from the back of the vehicle and helped Dan take off his jacket and shirt. She gave him some water to drink and a couple of energy capsules. The side wound was ugly—the skin gashed and torn in a deep channel. It would leave a big scar. Jane poured disinfectant on the gash and then applied a clotting bandage to stop the bleeding. Next she removed the bandanna. The cut above Dan's eye was small but deep. After disinfecting the wound, Jane pinched the edges together and applied another clotting bandage.

"You look worse than you are," she remarked.

"Thanks."

They could hear the helicopter in the distance.

"Where do I sit?" Dan asked.

"That special place that I told you about before. It's not too comfortable, but should work." She opened the rear passenger door, unlatched the rear seat and folded it forward. Inside was a small cavity that Dan could curl up in.

"Good thing I don't get claustrophobic," he said. "What about the rifle?"

"There is a compartment in the front part of the gas tank. It's actually a sub section of the tank, so nothing can be seen from the outside. I'll put your rifle in there."

"Okay, what about explaining your presence in the area?"

"Look in the back. Remember, I've been camping. That's what I actually do with my vacation days so it's an easy ruse. I've got all the right gear. You didn't know I was such an outdoor girl, did you?" She smiled at Dan.

He shrugged as he struggled into the seat compartment.

"When we're past the checkpoints, I'll get you out. You won't have to ride all the way to New York in there." Jane closed the seat down over him. Then she pulled off the netting, packed it away, climbed into the driver's seat and drove down the trail to the road.

Chapter 54

Jane drove east on Route 2 and ran into a checkpoint where the road joined the Deerfield River. Her story was accepted without question as the state police searched the SUV. There was another checkpoint just before they entered Charlemont.

A look through the SUV showed nothing unusual. The police passed her through with an admonition to not pick up any hitchhikers as there had been a shooting recently in the area. Duly admonished, she drove off. Before reaching Greenfield, Jane pulled off at a secluded spot to let Dan out of his hiding place. It was a slow process. Dan had stiffened up and could hardly unwind from his cramped position. When they reached Greenfield they got on I-91 and headed south.

They stayed on I-91 all the way down through Connecticut to I-95. Jane sought the anonymity of the interstate, and every mile they put between them and the shootout reduced their chance of being discovered. Dan drifted in and out of sleep during the drive.

After a long silence, Jane said, "I don't want to know anything about today. That's your business and I don't want to get into it any more than I have."

"Deniability?"

"Exactly. I'm on pretty shaky ground already if everything came to light. My career would probably be over and I might be facing jail time. But if my plan works out, I'll...we'll be able to do some good and all this crap will be forgotten."

"And remain a mystery?"

"Yeah. That's what I'm banking on."

As evening set in, Jane stopped at a rest area on I-95 to check Dan's wounds. She parked away from other cars and checked him out with a small flashlight, avoiding the SUV's interior lights. Satisfied, she set out again. The SUV had an extra large capacity tank so they would not have to stop for gas.

"Where are we going?" Dan finally asked. "Are you going to drop me off in Brooklyn?"

"Not on your life," Jane replied. "We're going to a safe house in New Jersey. It's north of the city. We'll take the Tappan Zee Bridge. I want you to stay there while you recover from your injuries."

They arrived at the house at midnight. Jane pulled into the garage and lowered the door before getting out of the SUV. They entered the house. The drapes were all drawn. Jane went to the bar in the kitchen, took out a bottle of Knob Creek Limited Edition whiskey and poured two glasses, handing one to Dan.

Dan took a sip of the expensive bourbon. "You guys live quite well. This is good whiskey."

"We try. Nothing but the best for our agents. Now let's take that shirt off so I can see what we've got." She reached over to help Dan who now could hardly raise his arm above his head.

"You a doctor as well as a spy?" Dan asked.

"This isn't my first field op. I've got some experience." She opened a bottle of pills. "Here, take two of these."

Dan shook his head. "Don't want to be drugged. I'd rather have the pain."

"These aren't for the pain, they're for the swelling." She thrust the pills into his hands.

"Now we'll stay here for a few days to get you in better shape. I also don't want you around Brooklyn for a while."

"You're beginning to sound like a boss."

Jane just looked at him without responding.

"I've still got something to finish. It didn't get done back there at the lodge."

"Joey?"

Dan nodded.

"I don't want to know any more." Jane put up her hand. "But this is getting to be dangerous...for both of us. You can't keep dragging this out much longer." She turned to go into the kitchen. "Look, I'm going to heat up some pasta; the house comes stocked with supplies so no one has to go out. Sit. You must be hungry. We can talk while I make something to eat."

"Hungry and tired. It's been a hard three days."

"But you're up to it, right?"

"I got through it. You deal with whatever happens and complete the mission. But I'm near the end. Tell me more about the job. What happens after I accept your offer?"

"Like I said in our first conversation, I'll take you to a training facility. They do all the training for field agents. They won't have any idea of exactly what you're involved in. They aren't expected to know and don't want to know. They just train you. I'll warn you it isn't easy, but you made it through sniper school so you should be all right. I made it through the training if that's any encouragement."

Dan eyed her critically. He figured her to be in good shape, but didn't connect her mention of field work with what he expected was some hard training. For the first time he noticed that her eyes had a green tint to them. They almost shone as she stared calmly back at him. She was, he concluded, quite an attractive woman but she probably put off a lot of men with her strong, confident demeanor. Jane looked back at him steadily. He could tell she knew he was re-evaluating her.

"After the basic training, you'll get advanced training in disguises. We'll work out multiple identities for you, complete with background cover and all the documents to go anywhere you need to go. We'll have identities set up with disguises and without disguises. You'll be a shadow figure—a figure with many different looks. That will take some practice and training. It can be confusing to manage multiple identities. I'm afraid that may be the most grueling part of the training. It's class work and memorization with exacting teachers."

"How long before you would send me out?"

"Six months at least. Remember we've never done this to the extent we're going to now. We hope six months, but if it takes longer, I'll buy us time."

"Us...?"

She turned from the stove and reached out and put her hand on his arm. "Yes, it's us from now on. We'll be partners. I'll trust your insights and decisions from the field and you'll have to learn to trust me to provide support and cover for you when and where I can."

Dan felt a sharp wave of electricity surge up his arm. *Where did that come from?* "I thought you said I'd be on my own."

"I did. But I can and will provide field support where possible. The people helping you won't know who you are or what your mission is. That's standard practice. They'll just do what they're called to do."

"Unless there is a screw up." They were now looking directly at each other, the world outside fading away as they conversed.

"If you get caught, I can't help you. I can't acknowledge your existence or connection to the U.S. Nothing in your identities will prove that connection. Others will suspect, due to the quality of your documents, but nothing, including the funds you will use, will track back to the agency. Of course, I will do everything I can to keep you out of that situation."

"You're all heart."

Jane gave him a wry smile. "This is a tough world. It's sometimes brutal and unforgiving. I don't sugar coat it and I don't gloss over its dangers. If I let my guard down, you could die. If you let your guard down, you could die. But you'd have to live like that anyway, on the run, as I've said before."

"What about the FBI? You take care of them?"

"I did. Here is where you need to trust me. I can't get into the conversation, but Mike Warner will bury your part of all this action as a figment he created to mislead the mob. Yes, someone shot up the mob, shot up Vincent's house, but Mike will say he encouraged the story that it was you in order to create pressure on Vincent. He will theorize it was a disgruntled associate and he just used the events to his advantage. He'll have his victory when he turns Vincent and you can disappear."

"And you trust him?"

"I have some insurance in place that lets me trust him to do his part. I don't take anything for granted."

Dan thought for a moment. "I'll bet he didn't like that."

"No, but he saw what was going to be good for him—for his career. He'll do his part."

"Looks like things are getting near the end," Dan said finally.

"I hope so...for both our sakes."

Dan barely got some food in him before he began to nod off. Jane helped him into a bed and went back to the kitchen and poured herself another whiskey. She sat late into the night thinking about what she had just done and what she had committed to. It was part of the plan, but she couldn't shake some other feelings that arose in her.

Chapter 55

When Joey got back to Brooklyn, he went to the Gardens to talk to Vincent. Joey could hardly contain his rage. He didn't know exactly what was going on but his instincts told him he had been set up.

"Joey, what are you doing back?" Vincent eyes widened, seeing Joey enter his back room. "Where's Frank? I told him to stay out of town until I called."

"Yeah, well things got uncomfortable at the lodge, so I decided to leave," Joey snarled.

"So where's Frank?"

"I left him there."

"You left him there, why the fuck did you do that? How's he supposed to get back?"

Joey walked up to the table, put his hands on it, and leaned forward. "Vincent, what's going on? Was I set up?"

"What the fuck are you talking about? Set up?" Joey struggled to control himself. Vincent stayed seated. He looked a bit nervous at Joey's aggressive attitude. "What happened at the lodge?"

"Dan was there, he tried to kill me, but he missed. I swear Frank set me up. Now what's going on?" Joey pressed closer to Vincent. "I've worked hard for you, been a good earner. I've been loyal. I may have fucked up with Dan's restaurant, but I made up for that. Didn't I get in line? Didn't I increase my earnings? Now tell me what's going on."

Vincent stared back at Joey. "Calm down, Joey. Nobody set you up. I don't know how Dan found you. Most of the crew knew where you were, maybe someone said something out on the street, and it got back to Tommy. You know he's talking to Dan. Sit down and tell me what happened. Is Frank still out there?"

"I don't know where Frank is and I don't give a crap. He may be dead, Dan may be dead. They both may be dead. I only know Dan found out where we were, and I don't like it."

"It's probably Tommy. How he knew I don't know."

Joey stared back at Vincent. He didn't know who to trust. Was it further up? Was Carmine arranging for him to get whacked? Was Carmine telling Vincent to arrange it? Who exactly was Frank taking orders from? He felt unsteady not knowing who to trust, like the world was tipping to one side.

"I got to take care of some shit. I'll check back with you when I'm done."

"Don't go blow things up. I've got enough pressure on me right now, I don't need any more."

"You don't?" Joey straightened. "And I don't have any? Dan's trying to kill me, and I don't know who's got my back."

"I've got your back," Vincent said, but Joey had already turned to leave the room.

When he was gone, Vincent stepped out into the restaurant and grabbed two of his men. "Follow Joey. Don't let him do anything stupid."

But Joey had already disappeared.

An hour after Joey left the restaurant Vincent was sitting in Carmine's car in the back parking lot of one of Carmine's warehouse.

"So Joey's back and you don't know what happened to Frank or Dan?" Carmine asked.

"That's right. Joey stormed out before I could get any details. Apparently Dan ambushed him. I'm guessing Joey took off when he got the opportunity and left Frank to deal with Dan."

"This is not good. You were supposed to take care of both Dan and Joey. Now Joey's back and we don't know about Frank or Dan. This is not good, Vincent. Things are getting more fucked up by the minute." Carmine looked at Vincent with cold eyes. There was no compassion or allowance in his gaze.

"I set it up, just like we talked about. Frank must have screwed things up. How else would Joey think Frank set him up?"

"Is that what he said? That Frank set him up?"

"Yeah. Frank did something out there that made Joey think he'd been set up. If that happened, it makes sense he would get the hell out and leave Frank. He figured there were two people trying to kill him."

"So where's Joey now?"

"He said he had something to take care of and left. I sent two guys to make sure he doesn't do anything crazy."

"You get him. Get Joey and bring him in. I don't want him out there. He's dangerous to us. Get this right, Vincent. There's been enough fuck ups." The threat was clear in Carmine's voice.

"What about Frank and Dan?" Vincent asked.

"Frank can take care of himself. Either he's dead or Dan's dead. If we don't hear from Frank we can assume Dan is alive and coming back. You better hope that isn't the case."

Vincent understood the threat in Carmine's words. His problems were not over; in fact, they seemed to be getting worse. Vincent headed back to his house. After he arrived, a quick call to Mike resulted in a meeting at a small restaurant in Manhattan.

Sheila insisted on coming along. It was quickly arranged. What they didn't realize was that Tony was monitoring Vincent's calls and followed Vincent and

Sheila as they traveled to the restaurant. He took some pictures of them going in and some of Mike following them a few minutes later.

He waited. He wondered how long he should hang out in his car. The risk of being exposed would increase the longer he parked there. At some point a cop would make him move on. Finally, with nothing more to gain, Tony headed off to meet with Carmine.

They were seated in a back corner of the restaurant. Mike sensed he was close to getting the deal done. Dan had not shown himself for some days, so he was anxious to get Vincent to make a decision. If the pressure eased, he would lose his leverage.

"So, what else can I tell you about the program?"

"Where will you send us?" Sheila asked.

"Within reason, you can re-locate anywhere you want to go. We can even arrange to send you abroad, although there's less protection with that arrangement."

"What about Miami?" Sheila asked.

"I wouldn't recommend it. There are too many mob connections there. Your chances of being discovered would be pretty high."

"Forget that for now," Vincent interrupted, "Tell me how this works. And, remember, we're not making a commitment, just getting information."

"I understand, but at some point, you got to decide. When you make your decision, we move you out that same day. You'll need to be packed and ready to go. We bring a team in to give you protection and get you out of there quickly. Then we'll come back to pick up anything that might have been left. You know about the house and furnishings—how we'll handle those."

"I've got some guys helping to watch the house. What about them?"

"Best if you cancel that—"

"That might arouse suspicion," Vincent said.

"Then get rid of them just before we make the move. Before anyone can react, we'll get you out of there."

"What about our girls?" Sheila asked.

"We'll pick them up from school the same time we get you. They'll be safe and you will all meet up in a hotel."

"So exactly what do you want from me? You want me to rat on everyone, right?" This was still the sticking point for Vincent. He was having a hard time coming to terms with it. He hated those guys, guys who sold out, violated their oath of silence.

Sheila put her hand on Vincent's arm. "Honey, you said yourself that Carmine would come after you if he lost confidence in you. You told me not to talk to Gina. Now you want to protect them?"

"Sheila's right. You know that. Of course we want to get your story. That's the point. It may take a few days. That's what you'll be doing while we're hiding you in the hotel. When that's done, we get you out of town."

"So the mob can reach me or my family while I'm giving you testimony." He scowled at Mike from across the table.

Mike thought for a moment. "We've done this before. You'll have plenty of protection—for you and your family. We can take your statement at the hotel if that makes you feel better. But your safety comes from the fact that no one but me and two other agents will know where you are. The NYPD will not know your whereabouts. You'll be guarded by the FBI, not the local police."

Vincent stared at him. "I'm not so sure you can pull that off, knowing what I know from the other side."

"I can. And that's your value to us...what you know from the other side. This is an expensive program and we only use it when someone has significant information to trade."

When Tony drove off, an agent watching the streets outside took notice. He realized the car had been sitting for some time a half-block away. No one had gotten out or in. It didn't look right. He snapped a picture as Tony drove past and called Mike.

Mike picked up the call. After hearing the news, he turned to Vincent. "Someone may have followed you to the restaurant. How did anyone know you were coming here?"

Sheila sucked in her breath. "Oh, God," she whispered.

"No one followed us. How could they?"

"Vincent, the girls...what if they go after the girls?" She looked fierce, her protective instincts fully aroused.

"The girls are all right. Calm down and don't get hysterical," he said. Turning back to Mike, "If this is another pressure tactic, you can go to hell. I won't be pushed around like that."

"It's not a tactic, Vincent." Mike picked up his phone, punched in a number and told the lookout to come inside. "My guy took a picture. Let's see what it shows."

Inside, Vincent stared at the picture in the camera's view screen. It was small and hard to see. But what he could see was enough to identify Tony as he drove past the lookout.

"Fuck. It's Tony. He's spying on me. How did he know to follow us?"

Sheila just stared at her husband, her anger now turning to fear.

"It doesn't matter," Mike replied. "He may have photographed us. When Carmine and Silvio see this, they'll act. You got to make a decision now."

Chapter 56

Joey waited in the parking garage near the exit door. Two other men were hiding with him. He was taking no chances. He knew she wouldn't be docile, even in the face of a weapon. Better to just grab her, keep her from screaming, stuff her into a car, and go before anyone could notice what was going on. Speed helped in these matters. The odds against someone coming upon them as they were grabbing her were slight. If someone did, they would just deal with that in whatever way was necessary. Joey wasn't worried about keeping things neat. First Dan set out to get him and now Frank. Did the mob want him dead? He didn't know, but he'd get Dan, or get back at him by using Doreen. Joey was not going down without a fight.

Tommy and Doreen had been back for two weeks. The FBI had arranged with the police department to maintain a watch on Tommy's business and check on his apartment occasionally. Doreen refused the protection. She didn't want cops hanging out at her apartment complex. With her work being in Manhattan, and the connections she had, along with living up in Queens, she guessed the mob wouldn't mess with her.

It was late when she pulled into the garage, already getting dark. She was tired. Work had been intense ever since she had gotten back. Working hard, though, took her mind off the tangle of events being played out in Brooklyn. She and Tommy hadn't seen much of each other since their return from Atlanta. Tommy had relayed the reports he'd heard of the shootings at Vincent's house. The tension had been mounting and then everything had gone quiet. So much the better, she figured. She needed to concentrate on her work and not the deadly drama Dan had triggered.

As she approached the garage exit a man jumped out of the shadows and grabbed her from behind. One arm went around her waist, the other hand clamped down on her mouth, stifling the scream that rose up. She began to wrestle and kick to free herself when another figure stepped in front and punched her in her solar plexus. The wind whooshed out of her. Quickly her hands were tied behind her back as she struggled to catch her breath. With the fight taken out of her, duct tape was stretched across her mouth, and a hood thrown over her head. She struggled to get air back into her lungs through her nose. She was half carried, half dragged to a nearby car and thrown into the trunk. Before shutting the lid, someone taped her ankles together.

Doreen slowly regained her breath. She could hardly move in the trunk. A rising panic engulfed her. Her stomach began to heave. She fought down the waves of nausea. If she threw up with her mouth taped she could drown in her vomit. She bent her head down and tightened her stomach to suppress the impending spasm.

She tried to process what had happened. She was in a trunk, headed somewhere unknown and for what she did not know. This had to be Joey. The mob was now desperate about Dan and desperation led to bad things happening—bad things for her.

Tommy would be expecting her call tonight. He would worry when he couldn't reach her. He had not been happy about her refusal to have police security hanging around her apartment, and now she realized that he had been right. Had they grabbed Tommy as well?

As her initial panic abated, she thought through her dilemma. If Tommy hadn't been picked up, he would soon raise the alarm and probably try to reach Dan. Neither she nor Tommy trusted Mike and the FBI. Would Dan know where to find her?

Would they kill her? They probably wanted to use her as bait or a bargaining chip against Dan. Maybe negotiate a truce, an end to Dan's vendetta. Or did they want to lure Dan into a trap and kill him?

The car drove on. Finally it slowed and turned off a street. She heard a sliding overhead door screech open and the car moved again. The door closed behind them. The car doors opened; she heard footsteps, and then the trunk lid was raised. Doreen couldn't see anything with the hood over her head. Rough hands rudely jerked her out of the trunk and the tape around her ankles was cut.

Without a word, she was led stumbling through the building. She had a sense of it being a large space. The footfalls echoed around her. They climbed some stairs and entered what seemed to be a smaller room and hands shoved her down into a chair. Her ankles were taped to the legs of the chair and her arms taped around the back. Someone pulled the hood off.

She shook the hair out of her eyes as best she could and looked around. One light bulb in the ceiling cast a thin glow around the center of the room. The edges remained in shadows. The only person she recognized was Joey.

They all stared at her in a way that chilled Doreen. Her shirt and skirt were ripped, exposing her thighs and bra. She shuddered. She hadn't thought about being raped. She had concluded she was going to be a hostage in negotiations and that they wouldn't damage the hostage. Now she wasn't so sure.

Joey stepped forward, his eyes lit with a strange fire and with a wild look about him she hadn't seen before. He went over to her and ripped the tape off of her mouth. She yelped as it tore at her skin. A cold dread spread through her. This was a different Joey. She sensed she should keep quiet and not challenge him. She tried to look back at him, to stand up to his scrutiny, but she knew her eyes betrayed her, showing fear of him for the first time.

"You know why you're here?" His voice was low and dangerous. Without waiting for a reply, he continued, "We trade you for Dan stopping his attacks. No more crap, no more tough talk from you. It's simple. Dan goes away or you go away. Do your part and you'll get out of this alive. Try to screw this up and you're dead."

She shivered. The others stared at her partially exposed body. Doreen turned her eyes away from Joey. She forced her mind to function. She had to try to regain some control over the situation. Would they let her go after she got a look at all of them? The thought raised the real possibility that they would kill her. If that were so, she might be more bait than a negotiating chip.

Anger towards Dan surged up in her. He had gotten them involved with his crazy vendetta. It had torn up both hers and Tommy's lives. Now here she was, helpless with Joey and his thugs, a more dangerous Joey than before. If they were going to kill her, what would keep them from hurting her, from raping her right now? Fear grew like a cold, dark lump in her stomach, spreading through her body.

She forced herself to turn back to Joey. "If I'm a hostage, you better keep these guys off of me." She nodded at the others. "I'm guessing damaged goods would be reason enough for Dan to resume his attacks."

He turned to the others. "You can look, but don't touch. I want her unharmed. Understand?" They nodded.

"Here's how this will work. Dan will get the word about you. We'll negotiate. While that's going on, you'll be released from the chair but locked in this room. You make noise, you bang on walls, you scream, yell, we tie you to the chair and gag you. You'll wait, tied to the chair if you're a problem. Want to move around? Be quiet. Got it?"

Doreen nodded and looked around the room. It was about ten feet by fourteen, larger than a regular sized office. It had probably held a group of cube workers at one time. She guessed she was on the mezzanine level of a warehouse.

Joey then told the men to leave. When they were out of the room, he leaned close and grabbed her hair. "You got a smart mouth, Doreen. You think you're untouchable, acting all high and mighty, but look at you now. I don't give a fuck what happens to you. Those others would like to rape you. I don't let 'em. It ain't 'cause I'm a nice guy. It's 'cause it don't serve my purpose. And if you don't serve my purpose, I'll kill you. You mean nothing to me. My only interest in you is getting to Dan. You better hope he does the right thing."

As Doreen listened, she realized Joey might never let her leave here alive. There was a manic look in his eyes. She sensed more was going on than she understood. Joey looked like a cornered animal that now had become dangerous. He seemed ready to lash out at anyone, kill anyone. Something must have happened that had made him dangerous in a way she had never experienced. She had to keep forcing her panic down. He was like a live grenade now, and she wasn't sure what would trigger it.

That evening, Vincent and Sheila went over the plans for leaving. He would dismiss Tony in the morning, the Feds would arrive and they would all leave for the hotel. No one knew which hotel at that point. The girls wouldn't go to school that day, or the next. They would not get back to school until they were resettled. When asked where they were going, neither Vincent nor Sheila could answer. Since Tony had discovered their meeting they had to make the move right away. There would be time later to decide where to go.

A full day of rest did wonders for Dan. Jane had a doctor come by and suture the gash over his eye. Both wounds were still raw, but not bleeding. His ribs did not seem to be broken, although they were bruised and sore.

The morning of the second day Dan awoke to the smell of bacon cooking downstairs. His stomach rumbled. Slowly he got up from the bed, checking his body to see how well he could move. He went into the bathroom and stared at himself. Fatigue and pain lines still etched his face. His hair was flattened on one side, indicating he hadn't turned in his sleep. He had shaved yesterday, so his five day growth of beard was gone. He washed his face and rinsed water through his hair; then he put on a tee shirt and some sweats Jane had provided and went downstairs.

Jane looked up as he entered the kitchen. She stared at him, admiring his fit body, even with the stress of his wounds showing. He was attractive, tough, but not overly macho like so many of the Special Forces operatives she had met. His movements were graceful and there was still a youthful look in his eye, in spite of the terrible business he had taken upon himself.

"I figured you couldn't resist the lure of bacon," she said.

"It never fails with me." He grinned.

Jane smiled back as her green eyes roamed over him.

"You checking me out?" His voice held a light tone.

"Just professionally."

"Checking to see how quickly I can recover from a fire fight and injuries? Is this a requirement of the new job?"

"It doesn't hurt. There's fresh coffee in the pot. Pour yourself a cup and sit down. I'll cook you some eggs." She turned back to the stove.

"Not that I don't like your company," Dan poured himself a cup and sat at the kitchen table, "or you cooking me breakfast, but how long do we plan to stay here?"

"I'm glad you appreciate my culinary skills, however limited they are. You probably noticed that I'm better at breakfast than dinner. From the looks of you, I figure one more day should be enough."

Jane's phone on the counter rattled with an incoming call. "Jane, they've taken Doreen," Tommy yelled as she picked up.

"Don't shout," Jane said, "just slow down and tell me what happened."

"Doreen didn't call last night when she got home from work. She was supposed to call me, we set it up."

"Maybe she just forgot or she got home too late—"

"No. She wouldn't have forgotten. This is what we agreed to. She didn't want any protection, so she promised to call every night. I called her this morning and she didn't answer. She would have answered. Someone's taken her. Joey probably, or someone else. Maybe that Frank guy, the scary one."

"And no one has called you about this?"

"No. I've got to get in touch with Dan. He started this and he needs to take care of it. Christ, Doreen could get beat up or worse, just so Dan can have his revenge? How do I get in touch with him?"

Dan looked up from his breakfast. "What's up?"

"It's Tommy." Jane covered the phone. "He thinks someone has kidnapped Doreen."

"Shit!" Dan put down his fork and got up. "Let me talk to him."

Jane handed him the phone.

"Tommy, tell me what happened."

"I'll tell you what's happened, the shit's hit the fan. Joey or somebody's taken Doreen. You and your vendetta. It's gotten Doreen kidnapped! You gotta do something about it." Tommy was shouting again.

"Just tell me what happened—"

"I don't know what happened, only that Doreen didn't call last night like we arranged and she's not answering her phone this morning."

"Did you call her work number?"

"Yeah, she didn't show up there."

Dan stood there. His worst fear was coming true. "I'll make this right. I'm heading into town now. See if you can ask around and find out where she might be then meet me at your shop at one."

"Nothing better happen to her, that's all I got to say."

"Just see what you can find out and meet me. With your help, we'll get her back."

Dan hung up and turned to Jane. "I got to go."

"You want some help?"

"You can't help, remember, you're already way out on a limb. Besides this is my fight. I'm going to finish this now and get Doreen back."

Chapter 57

Early the next morning, Vincent went down to the end of the driveway to pick up the paper and walked over to Tony's car. Tony had arrived with another crew member a half hour earlier. He seemed so helpful, but now Vincent knew he was there to watch him.

He leaned into the car window. "How you doing?"

"Doin' all right. You sleep well last night?" Tony replied.

"Yeah." Vincent paused. "Look, I'll be going in to the restaurant this morning and Sheila is taking the girls to the art museum today. A mother-daughter field trip. Why don't you head on downtown and I'll meet you there later. Things seem to have calmed down. We haven't had anything happen for a while." Vincent smiled and patted the door of the car.

Tony looked at him for a moment. Vincent could tell he was evaluating what Vincent had said. Then he smiled. "Sounds like a good idea. Not that I don't like being out at your place, but just sitting in the car ain't much fun."

With a final glance Tony started the car. "See you later at the restaurant. I'll have a cup of Irish coffee for you when you get there."

"I'm not Irish, you dumb fuck," Vincent said smiling. As Tony drove off, he pulled out his cell phone and called Mike.

Tony's car turned the corner at the end of the street. Halfway down the street, he stopped. Something was wrong. Something didn't feel right to him. He sat there for a moment, thinking.

"Whaddaya you doing?" the other man asked.

"Shut up, I'm thinking." Then it came to him. Could Vincent be leaving today? Was he going to disappear right now while he was supposed to be watching him?

"You drive down the street. Wait for me at the next corner. I gotta talk to Vincent before he leaves. I'll walk back."

The man looked at Vincent quizzically.

"Just do like I say. Don't leave until I get back or call you."

The man drove off, and Tony headed through the back yards towards Vincent's house. He knew the house had video security, but he was betting no one was watching it. If he was right, they were busy packing. The Feds would arrive soon. What he had to do had to be done now.

Tony figured he could get in, do the job, and get out through the back yards. He'd get to the car and be gone before anyone found out. Whacking Vincent didn't bother him at all, he had crossed the line, broken the code. And taking out that emotional wreck, Sheila wouldn't bother him either. So many hours he had spent listening to her complain about the stupidest things. But the two girls— even though they were spoiled brats—he hoped he wouldn't have to whack them as well. They had never bothered him.

He got to the back wall of the yard. It was still early. People were still mostly asleep. With the large, wooded back yards in the development, he was sure he hadn't been seen by any neighbors. He took out his weapon, a .45 semi-automatic, and screwed a suppressor to the barrel. He just needed to get in, get off a couple of shots, and get out. The cops outside were down at the street. They would never hear the shots. Tony smiled as he imagined the agent, Mike, showing up and finding a couple of corpses instead of witnesses.

Tony pushed the pistol back into his coat and clambered over the wall. He dropped down on the other side and stepped behind a tree. From there he was shielded from the house cameras. Someone would have had to be looking right at the monitor for that brief moment when he was on the wall to see him. Now there was nothing to see. At the back of the house a sliding door led from the basement out to the patio. Farther along the back wall was a service door.

Tony sprinted across the yard and hugged the wall of the house as he moved down to the service door. He slipped a credit card into the latch, quietly opened the door, and stepped inside. He stood there listening.

The master bedroom was on the second floor on the east side of the house. The girls had rooms on the west side, at the end of a long hallway that looked over the entrance foyer. There was a good chance of not running into them. He hoped for their sake that he didn't.

Tony tiptoed up the basement stairs. At the top he listened before opening the door. Someone was in the kitchen, probably Sheila. The living room and den were empty. Now he needed to get around the corner and up the stairs without whoever was in the kitchen seeing him.

Vincent's probably up in the bedroom. The stairs were carpeted and would silence his steps. Slowly, carefully, he stepped along the hardwood floor until he came to the stairs. Once he got to the landing halfway up and around the corner, no one would see him from below. He started up the steps without a sound. He reached the landing and when he stepped on it, the floor gave out a sharp squeak. He froze. Move! He sucked in his breath and hurried up the last steps to the second floor.

In the hallway he was shielded from the kitchen and foyer. He stood still and listened. There were no unusual sounds. He couldn't hear anything from the kitchen any more. Someone was in the bedroom. It sounded like Vincent packing. There was no sign of the girls.

Tony slipped his .45 out of his jacket, flicked off the safety, and stepped forward. At the bedroom door he risked a peak. There, as he expected, was Vincent bent over the bed, putting clothes in a suitcase.

Tony stepped into the room with his .45 leveled at Vincent. "Going somewhere?"

Vincent spun around. "What are you doing here?"

"Something didn't seem right, so I came back to see what you were up to. So where you going?"

"None of your fucking business. And put that gun away," Vincent growled.

"I don't think so. You're going to turn witness on us, going to squeal to the Feds, aren't you?"

"You're crazy. You don't know what you're talking about."

"I saw you meeting with somebody yesterday. He looked like an FBI agent. Now I can't let you do that."

"Carmine send you?" Vincent asked. There was no use trying to bluff. As soon as he saw Tony with the gun, he knew it was over. He sat down on the bed.

"You could say that. He wanted me to keep an eye on you. I think he would have sent Frank, but he's out of town. You figured out we knew what you were up to didn't you?" Tony said.

"Yeah. But they always send the ones they trust, and I didn't trust Frank. I trusted you."

"Well, you were going to rat everyone out, so I gotta do this." Tony stepped forward.

"Tony," Vincent said, "Don't kill my family. They can't do anything. There's nothing they can testify about."

"The girls'll be all right, but I don't know about Sheila. That fat fuck of a wife of yours really pisses me off. You always had me come out here. I was the one that had to sit and listen to her talk, talk, complain, complain. Frankly it'll be a pleasure to whack her. She's an irritating, fat bitch. No wonder you shoved that job off to me."

As Vincent was digesting what Tony had just said, three things happened quickly. Sheila stepped into the doorway with a gun in her hand. "So I'm a fat bitch, am I? I thought you were my friend. You bastard."

Tony spun around and Sheila pulled the trigger. The gun roared, the bullet hitting Tony in the shoulder. Vincent jumped up from the bed and crashed into Tony before he could bring his .45 to bear on Sheila. He pushed it up as it went off with its muffled pop. The two men wrested for control of the weapon. Though he was older, Vincent was the larger, stronger man. Tony was at a disadvantage. His left shoulder was wounded, making his arm useless. They strained against each other, struggling for the gun.

Vincent grunted with exertion. The two men fell back against the bed. Vincent leveraged his weight against Tony. He focused all his strength on the gun, slowly twisting it and pressing it against Tony. "You shouldn't have insulted my wife. Don't you know how emotional she is?" Tony's eyes widened as he struggled to keep his weapon from being jammed into his chest. "And you don't talk to the guy you're going to whack. You just do it and leave. Now you gotta pay, dumbass."

He pulled the trigger. Another muffled pop and blood flew back at Vincent. Tony slid to the floor, a wet stain seeping out from underneath him.

"Did I kill him? Oh, Christ! I'm going to hell. I killed someone." Sheila's voice rose to a shriek. She dropped the gun. Vincent stood up and went over to her. He put his arms around her. A moment later Tiffany and Amber came running to the bedroom door. Vincent backed all of them into the hallway and closed the door. An FBI agent stationed at the street came running up the stairs with his pistol drawn. Vincent nodded to the bedroom.

"Call Mike and tell him to hurry. We almost didn't make it." He turned to Sheila. "No, you didn't kill him."

She shook with sobs and the girls started crying; Vincent tried to calm his family down.

Her arms around Vincent, returning his hug, Sheila began to calm down. "I thought I heard something on the stairs. When I came out of the kitchen I saw someone disappear up the steps. I knew you were upstairs, and no one else was supposed to be in the house, so I went into the study and got your gun, the one you keep in the desk drawer. I heard him talking to you. He said I was fat. He called me a complaining bitch. Is that what he thinks of me? I thought he was my friend." Her words tumbled out as Vincent held her.

He smiled for the first time in a long time. "He shouldn't have insulted you like that."

"Do you think I'm fat?" Sheila looked up at him, tears glistening in her eyes.

"No, I don't think you're fat," he said with the smile still on his face.

Chapter 58

Jane and Dan drove in silence, heading to Dan's apartment. Dan went over his options. They were limited unless Tommy could get some idea of where they had taken Doreen. At this point, he didn't worry whether Jane knew where he lived. Dan figured he would not be there much longer. In his apartment, he checked his rifle and loaded a magazine with sub-sonic .308 caliber rounds. Next he grabbed his .223 carbine, his 9mm, a .45, and the 12 gauge semi-auto shotgun along with extra magazines and ammunition. He broke down the weapons and loaded them into a large gym bag. Then he changed his clothes, putting on a pair of black jeans and black sweater. After completing these tasks he turned to Jane who had simply watched his preparations with interest.

"You mind taking the rest of my clothes and gear with you in the truck? I don't think I'll be coming back here."

"Of course. I'll save them for you. Give me your phone number before we separate. You've got mine. Call me when this is over. I'll pull you out."

Dan nodded. "It's a deal."

When he was done, they got into the Suburban and drove down to Tommy's garage.

Jane grabbed his arm as Dan opened the door. He turned to look at her. "Be careful. You made it this far, don't be foolish at the end. You're smarter than any of them, use that."

"Is that professional or personal advice?"

Jane looked straight back at him. He had begun to have a surprising effect on her. Suddenly she didn't want him to have to take this last risk, to enter into this last encounter which was in all likelihood an ambush. "Maybe a bit of both," she finally said and turned away as Dan stepped out of the car.

Dan dropped his gear in the office as Tommy rushed in.

"You son of a bitch." He charged Dan.

Dan ducked to one side as Tommy swung wildly at him. "Stop! This won't help."

"I was your friend when Rita was killed. I stood by you and now you bring this...this shit down on me. How could you?" Tommy stood with his fists clenched and tears in his eyes.

"I didn't know Doreen would get involved, Tommy. Who knew she would show up? How was I to know you two would become a couple? Jesus, I'm sick about this, but we'll get her back, I swear to you."

"If we don't, you'll have to kill me, because that's what I'll be trying to do to you."

"Okay, but truce." He grabbed Tommy by the shoulders. "We need to work together. I'm gonna need your help. We can do this, but you have to work with me." Tommy just glared at him. "Now what did you find out?"

Tommy took a deep breath. "Seems like everything's hit the shit fan. Word is Frank's missing, maybe dead, and Joey's disappeared after giving Vincent a hard time. He thinks Vincent set him up. There's no telling what he may be up to. Carmine is worried. He's got someone watching Vincent, and now you're back. The whole place is about to erupt. Vincent's crew is worried. They could be caught in the middle if Carmine decides Vincent is turning. No one knows who to trust."

"But no word on where Joey is?"

"No one's saying. Or no one knows. If Joey thinks Vincent set him up, he's not going to trust Vincent or Carmine. He's on his own."

"Why would he want Doreen? What does it get him? He should be bugging out at this point," Dan said.

"Maybe he thinks he'll lure you into a trap, finish you off and get back in with Carmine. If Vincent doesn't turn, Joey fixes the last thorn in his side." Tommy paused. "Or he could just want revenge on you or me. That's how Joey would think."

"Maybe. Self preservation is more his style. Paybacks are icing on the cake. If he wants to set a trap, we should be able to find out where he is. If we can't find the trap, we can't enter it. He has to get the word out."

"You're going to walk into his trap?"

"I'm going to go to where he is and kill him, if that's what you mean."

"And Doreen?"

"The best way to save Doreen's life is to kill Joey, the sooner the better. If he kills me, do you think he'll let Doreen go? She'll just disappear, you too."

Tommy looked down at the floor and through gritted teeth said, "All thanks to you."

Dan started to respond, but just shook his head. "I deserve that. But help me make this right."

Tommy looked hard at his one-time friend. Now he was not so sure how he felt. "I'll help, but that doesn't make it right...what you did."

Tony's stakeout partner waited at the end of the side street for Tony to return. After half an hour, he turned around and drove back to Vincent's house. At the house were four black Suburbans and multiple armed men standing outside of Vincent's home. They were not local cops. He drove past the house and when out of sight, called Carmine.

"Carmine, there's a bunch of armed guys around Vincent's house. They're not cops."

"Where's Tony, put him on," Carmine said.

"Tony went back to the house to talk to Vincent about something. Said he had some business to finish with him. I waited but he didn't come back. Now I drive around to the house and it's crawling with guys looking like FBI."

"Christ!" Carmine exclaimed. "Don't leave the area. When the cars leave, follow them. I want to know where they go. Got it? Don't lose them!"

"Got it, boss. How far should I follow? I mean, if they go a long way—"

"Follow them till they stop somewhere, idiot. Check in with me, but don't lose them." Carmine shut his phone off. It was probably tapped, but at this point he didn't care. Vincent was going to turn. Now he was sure. They probably had Tony in custody...or worse. His only hope was to find out where they were taking Vincent and get to him. He took a deep breath and opened a drawer in his desk. He pulled out a new cell phone to call Silvio. Then he would call the other capos. He was sure Silvio would put out a hit on Vincent. Carmine should have done it earlier, as he should have taken Joey out earlier. Hell, Vincent should have whacked Joey instead of just frightening him. Yeah, he had become a good soldier, but he was the magnet that drew this guy Dan, and he was the shit storm that fouled up everything.

Chapter 59

Later that day, all the Capos from the Palma family met in Carmine's warehouse. Silvio let Carmine speak.

"Vincent has gone over to the feds. We've tracked him to a hotel in Manhattan, the Ambassador. I don't have to tell you that he can bring all of us down. I'm putting a hit out on him. I'll arrange to test the security, to find out where he is in the hotel. They probably got a whole floor rented and secured. Silvio and me want him taken down. We'll blow up the fucking building if we have to. Once we know where he is in the building, we meet again and figure out how we do this."

Everyone nodded. They all knew that Vincent could put them all behind bars.

Silvio now spoke in his hoarse voice. "This is important. This is for the survival of the family. Vincent broke his oath. Now he needs to be eliminated." His thin frame bristled with authority and anger.

The meeting broke up. Silvio turned to Carmine. "Where's Joey? He started this mess? Somebody take care of him?"

Carmine hoped that question wouldn't come up. "Joey's back in town. The plan to get him out of town and set up an ambush for Dan didn't work."

"What the hell happened? Can't anyone do anything right?" Silvio asked.

"Apparently Frank, you know, Frank Varsa...we sent him with Joey. He was to make sure neither came back, and—"

"And Frank is the only one who didn't come back. Am I right?" Silvio's voice was filled with disgust.

"Yeah," Carmine said.

"Carmine," Silvio said. Carmine looked at the old man, frail but still commanding power of life and death over the family. "We are in a dangerous position. You got to get Vincent, even if it's after he puts his story on tape. He can't be allowed to produce that testimony in a court room or we're all done. Don't let this get fucked up. Don't be clever, be brutal, be effective. Got it?"

Carmine nodded.

"And find Joey. I want him and this Dan guy dead. They should have been done months ago. This has gone on too long and now we need to finish it. We can lay low and weather the heat and the headlines. Our problems will be gone and when things settle down we can go back to business as usual. If you don't get this done, there's no business as usual. Understand?"

Carmine nodded.

"Good. Now get the fuck out of here and get this done." Silvio turned and walked out of the room, no handshake, no embrace. Carmine understood. His position in the family, his life was on the line. That's the way it was. The price for failure was severe.

Joey left the men to watch Doreen and headed back to the Gardens to find Vincent. He had to play both sides of the game, and he figured setting up an ambush for Dan would show Vincent that he could be relied on. Joey didn't know how that would play out but it was better to be seen helping than to isolate himself on the outside. When he reached the restaurant Vincent wasn't there.

"You know where he is?" Joey asked the manager.

"No, he was supposed to come in today but he didn't show and hasn't called."

"You call him?"

"What am I, his boss? I don't call Vincent to check up on him. I do what he tells me to do. If he don't come in, that's his business, not mine."

Joey called Vincent's cell number. No answer. Next he called the home number. Someone he didn't recognize answered.

"Let me talk to Vincent," Joey said.

"He can't come to the phone right now."

"Who's this?" Joey asked.

"Who are you?" came the reply.

"I fucking work for Vincent and I need to talk to him about business, now who the fuck are you?" Joey yelled.

"And I'm telling you he can't come to the phone right now, so leave me your name and I'll let him know you called." The reply came through firm and officious.

Joey hung up. Something was wrong, something bigger than his situation, which was bad enough. Just then two of Vincent's crew came into the restaurant.

"Joey, what're you doing back in town? I thought you were hiding out," one said.

"Yeah, well, that didn't work out so well, so I came back. I'm going to take care of Dan myself and put an end to this bullshit." His mood was getting darker as the situation got more confused.

"Vincent know about that?"

"I told him yesterday. Now no one can get in touch with him. You talked to him today?"

"No."

"I'll bet no one has. Who else was out at the house?" Joey asked.

"Tony Tattaglia."

"He out there consoling Sheila again?"

"Hell if I know."

"You talk to him lately?" Joey asked.

"No."

"You got his number? Try to call him. Something's going on. I called the house and a stranger answered and wouldn't let me talk to Vincent."

The man called Tony's number. There was no answer.

"So Vincent doesn't answer his cell, Tony doesn't answer his cell, there's a stranger in Vincent's house taking his calls and won't let me talk to him, something's fucked up for sure." Joey looked around everyone in the bar. The other soldiers agreed.

Joey took the men into the back room. "Look, I went out to the woods to hide out so Dan wouldn't have a target. Frank came with me. But Dan found us out there. There was a shootout, I'm guessing Frank got killed, and I barely escaped with my life. Someone let Dan know where we were. Now Dan's going to come back here, if he isn't already here. You know this shit's gotta stop and I'm the one to stop it. I've got the bait to draw Dan into a trap but I need your help. Something's up with Vincent and it don't look good."

"Whaddaya think's going on?" one of them asked.

"I got no idea, but if the feds have Vincent, what's going to happen to us? If Silvio or Carmine think we're part of the problem, we'll get whacked. Help me nail Dan and we'll settle things down. You know Vincent would want us to take care of this."

The soldiers looked doubtful. One said, "I don't know...without Vincent's go ahead, you could be getting into some real shit. What about going up the ladder...to Carmine?"

"I'm already in some shit. Dan's targeted me and I've got to take care of him or he'll take me out. And what does Carmine know about all of this? Christ, by the time we get him up to speed Dan may have whacked me and half of you guys. You think I'm the only one he's after?"

Some of the crew still looked doubtful. Finally two of them offered to help. Joey took what he could get and then went out to round up his own associates. He headed back to the warehouse with six more men to add to the two already there. Now he had to set up the trap. When he got back to the warehouse, he sent one of the men to get the word out where Doreen was being held and that Joey wanted to talk to Dan and make a trade. Then he began to arrange his men.

Chapter 60

While they were at the repair shop, Tommy got a call from one of Joey's associates. Joey had Doreen at one of the abandoned warehouses, near where Dan had been ambushed. Joey wanted to talk to Dan about a trade.

Tommy told Dan about the call. "You're going to make a trade, right?"

"It's a set up. Do you think Joey will really make a trade with me? Do you think he'll be satisfied if I just promise to go away in exchange for Doreen? Of if I gave myself up for Doreen, do you think he'd let her go?"

"You're playing with Doreen's life. You can't do that," Tommy said in a low voice.

"Look, the only way to get Doreen back is to kill Joey and his gang. I don't know who's giving him permission to act, but I'll take him out...with your help."

"And they'll kill Doreen in the meantime. Just how do you plan to keep that from happening?"

"Giving myself up won't get her free, I know that." Maybe he was being too cold, but emotion wouldn't get the job done. Cold, calculated killing would. Dan needed to be precise, thorough and quick if he was to save Doreen. Tommy had to understand that.

"We're going to strike quick and hard. The key is to kill them and get to Doreen before they understand we have the upper hand. If Joey hears shooting he's not going to shoot Doreen right away. He'll figure his guys are taking us out. What we have to do is get through them to Doreen and Joey, and finish it."

"Sounds like a pretty loose plan with a lot to go wrong. We don't even know where in the warehouse she's being kept."

"There's always a lot to go wrong. You have to start and then improvise along the way. But speed is critical to keep them off balance."

Finally Tommy asked, "All right, what's the first step?"

"Call him back and ask him where to make the swap. Tell him you're trying to get in touch with me. That will make them wait while we work up our plan."

After the call they took out a map of the city and reviewed the warehouse and its surroundings.

"They're going to have guards at the front, under some cover. They'll probably have shooters on the roof. That's where Joey will expect to be able to knock me off. You're going to spot for me. We'll set up a couple of blocks away. The rifle I'm using has a suppressor and I'm using subsonic rounds—"

"What the hell does that mean?"

"That means if I can locate the rooftop shooters, I can take them out without anyone on the ground knowing about it. How many guys do you think Joey has, six, eight, ten? I doubt it's more than that. So we start off by reducing his numbers by two or three. Next, I take out the street level guards. They may be harder to get a clear shot at, but it's got to be done. After that, we have to get into the warehouse."

Tommy grimaced. "And that's where things break down."

"Look, Tommy. You can hate me and shut me out of your life, but do it later. Right now your best chance, our best chance, at getting Doreen out of there alive is to work my plan, however imperfect it is."

Tommy glared at him. His life had made a sudden turn to the good with Doreen showing up and deciding she wanted to be with him. And now his best friend was the reason her life was in danger and he was the one who could save her. Tommy stood a chance to lose all the good that had happened over the past months. But was there any other way? Joey wouldn't surrender to the cops. That wouldn't make him safe from Dan. He'd seen Dan kill from a distance. No one would know where the shot came from and Joey's head would explode. Besides, the police weren't looking to arrest him and they certainly weren't going to protect him. No, Joey was on his own. And if he was going down, he would go down fighting, taking anyone he could with him, including Doreen.

Joey sent two men with rifles up to the roof of the warehouse to watch for Dan. Dan had to get through the gates, whether in the front or back and that's where he'd be vulnerable. In addition, Joey positioned two men at ground level in front and three at the back. The remaining man was stationed in the room where Doreen was held. Joey placed himself in a room on the mezzanine with a clear sight line down the corridor leading to the room. If he got past his guards, Dan had to come down this corridor to get to Doreen. Joey would have a clear shot at him.

Dan took the Remington 700 with its suppressor from his bag and assembled it. It was early afternoon. "Here's what we do," Dan said. "There'll probably be lookouts on the roof. I'll take them out. Those shots have to count. We can't have Joey know we've started our assault that soon. So the rooftop shooters have to be taken out before anyone knows we're here.

"They won't hear the shots?" Dan asked.

"Not with the suppressor and sub-sonic rounds...and I'm going to shoot from two blocks away. They won't be the easiest shots I've taken, but they won't be the hardest This is what I did in Iraq."

"But that was a just a job and Doreen wasn't involved." Tommy's voice was compressed with the anger he was holding in.

Dan looked at him. "No, but soldier's lives were at stake. There's always a life at stake and not just the target's."

"So how do we get into the building?"

"These warehouses are connected with a steam and utility tunnel. We break into the warehouse next to where they're holding Doreen and go through the tunnel."

"And just step out at the right place?"

"For God's sake, Tommy, help me out." Dan held his hands out, palms up. "I don't have a fool proof plan, but I do have a plan. Yes, we measure the distance and pace it off in the tunnel. Can we get out of the tunnel undetected? I sure as hell don't know. But it's the best option. For one thing they won't be looking for us to come from the inside, which is an advantage for us. If we move fast we can take them by surprise."

"All right, but what about just going around back and busting a window? Seems less complicated to me."

"That's what they'll be looking for. It might work, but I don't like doing the expected. We don't know how many they have inside watching the windows and doors, but I'm betting they aren't watching the floors."

"And if the opening is locked?"

"It wasn't in the last building. I'm thinking these aren't meant to lock. There's a latch to open from the inside. Look, if we find we can't open the cover, we go back and try your way. We lose fifteen minutes, but we don't lose the surprise factor."

Dan turned back to the weapons. "You take the 9mm and the 12 gauge automatic. After we've taken out the guys on the roof, I'll use the carbine and the .45. You shot a pistol before?"

Tommy nodded.

"Shotgun?"

Tommy shook his head.

"If you have to use it, hold it tight to your shoulder, it kicks hard. It holds eight shells. If you have to fire multiple times, load shells in between shots so the gun doesn't run dry. Got it?"

Tommy nodded again and looked closely as Dan showed him how to load, set the safety, and fire both weapons.

"No time for practice. Think of the pistol as an extension of your finger. If you point your finger at something, you'll probably point pretty accurately. Just do that with the pistol if there's no time to aim. Here, fill your pockets with shells and take two extra magazines for the 9mm."

They grabbed their gear and headed out for the warehouse.

Doreen sat, still tied to the chair. The man left in the room just stared at her. He was young and had a street punk look, like he had a chip on his shoulder. He was not bad looking in a greaser sort of way, kind of like a caricature of the New York street hood.

"So...you going to untie me?" she asked.

The guy looked at her without moving.

"Joey said I could be untied. I won't cause any trouble. I just want to get this over."

"You stay in the chair, I'll untie you."

"Thanks. My hands are going numb." He walked over and, taking out a knife, cut the tape around her wrists and ankles. "Wow that helps a lot." Doreen rubbed her wrists. "What's your name?"

"Ray," came the reply.

"Well, Ray, I'm Doreen."

Ray nodded as he stepped back to the table and sat on it. He had a .45 tucked in his belt. He wore dress slacks, a silk shirt and dress shoes. Not dressed for combat, but for the street, to look cool and command attention.

"Look, I don't know you or what you know about me, but I'm not on Dan's side," Doreen said. "Dan's got some vendetta with Joey and I just got caught up in it. I know Joey from high school. I came back to town and now look...I'm a fucking hostage. How the hell does that happen? Shit, I don't know what Joey's been up to since high school, and I don't want to know. You know what I mean?"

Ray looked at her.

"You know I'm not part of this deal...this fight between Joey and Dan?"

"You are, or Joey wouldn't a brought you here."

"Ray, I'm the bait, that's all. I got no love for Dan. He's the reason I'm the bait...because I happen to know him and Joey thinks Dan'll try to rescue me. I'd rather he just went away, which is what Joey probably wants."

"Why doesn't he?"

"Damned if I know. But you got to know, I'm not going to help Dan one bit. I just want this finished and to go about my life. Joey and you guys can go back to what you do."

"It may not be that easy," Ray replied.

"There's going to be shooting, right?" Doreen asked.

Ray nodded.

"You going to shoot me when it starts?"

"Not unless you make me."

"I won't be any trouble. Like I said, Dan got me involved. He can go fuck himself for all I care."

Ray smiled.

Doreen now tried a new tact. "Ray, you got a girlfriend?"

"No one steady."

"I would bet you got a couple of girls trying to get their hooks into you."

Ray smiled. "A few, but I ain't interested. First thing is you get a steady girl, then she wants you to settle down, gets jealous if you're out with the boys, you know, havin' fun. Then she gets pregnant and everyone says you gotta marry her. Then the fun is over. I seen it happen more than once."

Doreen smiled at Ray. He was opening up. It might make him hesitate to pull the trigger on her. "Well, from a girl's point of view, we like the security of a having a man we can rely on. You know someone who provides, is a good earner and doesn't mess around...at least not too much."

Ray shrugged. "Yeah, I get that, but it comes with too many restrictions."

"You'll get there. There'll be a time when you'll like coming home to a nice, home-cooked meal and someone who knows just how to turn you on in bed. Yeah, the fast girls are fun, but the steady ones, the ones who know you, are also fun. They get to know how to please their man."

She smiled at him. Ray appeared about ten years younger than Doreen, but his look told her he liked what he was looking at. It was similar to the young lawyers just out of school that she navigated around at work. She knew how to play this scene out.

"Can I get up and stretch a bit? I'll be quiet," Doreen asked.

Ray nodded. She stood up and stretched voluptuously. Ray took it all in with interest. Then Doreen walked around the room as Ray's eyes followed her. She looked over at him as she smiled and tried to button her torn blouse. Ray smiled back.

"I like you, Ray. You're nice. When this is over, maybe we can go out to dinner sometime. It'd be fun." Doreen guessed he was thinking he was a real lady killer.

"So now you want me to spend money on you, take you to some fancy place? You figure that makes up for tying you up?" Ray asked.

"It would help. And I know how to show my appreciation for being treated nice." She winked at him.

Ray now was leering back at her. "You sound adventurous. I thought you was Tommy's girl."

"I like Tommy but he didn't protect me. A girl likes someone who can protect her as well as show her a good time."

"So you like having a good time?"

"With the right guy, I can get pretty adventurous. All this," she waved her hand around the room, "would be exciting, except that I'm the hostage. And that pisses me off."

Ray walked over to her. "Maybe we can make that happen, when this is over."

"Make what happen?" she asked, looking inviting.

"Dinner and some time in bed. I like a girl who's adventurous." He bent down to kiss her and Doreen met him with a long, full kiss.

"Mmmm, I like that," she said.

Ray started to slide his hands over her breasts.

"Not now, not here," she said breathlessly. "Let's wait until this shit is over." She stepped back, still smiling as Ray stopped, obviously frustrated.

Chapter 61

Dan and Tommy drove down to the warehouse district. The street was full of abandoned buildings. They pulled into an ally four blocks away and worked their way towards the warehouse where Joey waited. Two blocks away, they broke into an abandoned building on the other side of the street and found their way to the roof. They crept to the parapet and took position behind a cracked section where Dan could place his rifle. He helped Tommy set up the spotting scope with the range finder. After carefully measuring the distance, they looked for clues to tell them the wind direction and strength. Dan worked the numbers in his head and calculated the sight adjustments. Satisfied he had the rifle properly sighted in; they watched and waited for a clear shot.

They could see the two men staked out in front, behind two cars, watching the front entrance to the parking lot. Finally, two men emerged on the roof and split up, one going to the far side of the building, the other towards them. The men kept low while moving. The one nearest them had cover from the parapet when he sat down.

"Damn!" Tommy cursed, partly under his breath. "How you going to see him?"

"Patience," Dan said. "He has to look out to keep watch, that's how I'll get him. The other one has no cover from this angle."

"So who's first?" Tommy asked.

"The nearest one. The one on the far side can't duck if he sees the other one go down. I'll have a chance to get him, but he'll probably be a moving target."

"You can hit a moving target that far away?"

"If I have to." Dan settled down with his rifle. He had it propped up and steadied in the crack, giving him a solid shooting foundation. "Here we go. Remember, after this, we move fast into the neighboring warehouse, break a window, and get to the tunnel. We'll drop the sniper gear in the alley before we cross the street and get it on the way back."

Tommy didn't respond. He was worried whether there would be a way back and would it include Doreen. He kept silent, not wanting to disturb Dan's concentration.

His surroundings faded away, the familiar tunnel emerged between Dan and his target until they were locked together in their own private universe, defining the ends of a path on which the bullet would travel as if guided by a wire from muzzle to the target. His breathing slowed, his heart rate slowed. He waited. When the head appeared he would have two or three seconds before the man would drop down again. That was enough.

The head came up and the man scanned the block looking towards Dan but not seeing him. Even from a distance, Dan could tell he was nervous, he knew danger was out there, somewhere. He looked down the street, searching for something out of the ordinary. Dan's rifle moved slightly to the right and centered on the man's forehead. He let out half a breath and stopped. The connection was there, from his barrel to the man's head. His finger gently squeezed back and the rifle let out a muffled pop as it jumped. Tommy, looking through the spotting scope, saw the man's head fly backwards as he dropped out of sight. Dan shifted immediately to the other man.

The second rooftop lookout heard the sound of his partner falling back but thought it was just him shifting to a more comfortable position. He understood. It was damned uncomfortable to crouch behind the roof edge for cover. He wasn't even sure the raised edge would stop a bullet. What he didn't realize was that those few thoughts before he turned to look back were going to be fatal for him, depriving him of the slim chance he had to run for cover. As he turned, the .308 round smashed through his left temple, blowing out the right side of his brain. He crumpled to the roof in a tangled heap. There was no sound except for the muffled pop two blocks away. The men watching the entrance didn't know death had visited the roof of the building.

Dan thought about taking out the street lookouts, but they were just sitting behind the cars, not moving, not presenting good targets. He turned to Tommy who was still looking through the spotting scope. "Let's go, keep low." He gathered up the casings and quickly disassembled the rifle, putting it in the gear bag. "Tommy, the scope. Put it in the bag and let's go."

Tommy turned to him, his eyes wide, his mouth open. He put the scope in the bag and followed Dan across the roof to the stairway door.

They ran down the stairs from the roof and then went back out to the fire escape to complete their exit. In the alley, Dan took out the shotgun and 9 mm and handed them to Tommy. Then he grabbed his .223 carbine and .45.

"Okay, we gotta cross the street without being seen."

They waited, studying the cars in the parking area three blocks away where the lookouts were hiding. Not seeing them, Dan concluded they wouldn't be seen and dashed across the street. They began working their way towards the building where Joey waited, moving carefully from lot to lot. When they were one block away, they broke a window in a warehouse two buildings away from their target and entered. It was abandoned like all the warehouses in the three block area. Racing through the main floor, Dan finally found the cover that lead to the tunnel. The latch was rusty.

"Find a bar to give me some leverage," he told Tommy. Tommy scrounged around and came back with a steel bar used to lever up pallets. Dan inserted it and the latch finally sprang open. They quickly went down and began a crouched run towards the warehouse. Dan had measured his stride and counted off the paces. After a couple of minutes they stopped; running bent over was not so easy, especially with Dan's side still hurting from Frank's shot.

"Are we close?" Tommy asked.

"About half way. When I think we're close we walk and look for the hatch. There'll be a ladder for climbing up."

"How do we get out without getting shot?"

"I don't know. Let's see what we got when we get to the ladder and hatch."

After another few minutes, they slowed to a walk and then Dan pointed to the ladder ahead. "That's it." Tommy nodded. When they got to the bottom of the ladder, Dan whispered, "They won't be expecting us to come up from the floor. They had guys on the roof, guys out front, and probably guys out back. I'll bet Doreen's not on the main floor. Did you notice the warehouse we entered? It had a mezzanine floor with offices. That's a pretty standard layout. She's probably in an office on the mezzanine and Joey's up there as well."

"So there won't be anyone watching the floor?" Tommy whispered back.

"No. They'll all be watching the outside."

"We're going to make some noise getting the hatch open."

"Can't be helped. We need to do it quickly and get out. Then we're on even ground and not sitting ducks."

"So what's the plan?" Tommy asked.

"We get out. You take up a position where you can cover the front entrance and, if possible, the rear. I'll go up on the mezzanine and take care of Joey."

"Simple as that. Sounds too easy."

"Nothing's easy, but that's the plan we'll use. How it works out depends on a lot of things. Mostly how we react to what happens. The guys from the front will come in at some point. Be ready. You can't hesitate and you can't miss. If you get shot or the outside guys get past you, they can come at me from behind."

Tommy stared hard at Dan, and nodded he understood.

"The shotgun is loaded with double aught shot. It'll stop a man fifty yards out. Just aim at the chest, center mass, the largest part and let fly. The gun re-chambers a round automatically, so you just keep it aimed and keep pulling the trigger. Remember to load additional shells as soon as you stop shooting. You don't want to get caught empty. Got it?"

"I got it the first time," Tommy whispered back.

"Okay, here we go." Dan put the bar in the latch lever and turned it.

Chapter 62

The latch creaked as it scraped over metal for the first time in years. The creak grew to a screech as Dan swung the door open. Both men jumped up and quickly ran for cover. Dan pointed out the front door to Tommy and then located a set of stairs leading to the mezzanine. Tommy pointed to the rear with a questioning look. Dan shrugged. There were multiple doors at the rear of the building.

Joey shouted from above, "Benny, Louie, that you down there? What're you doing inside?"

His voice came from the far end of the warehouse, at the end of the mezzanine. Dan gave Tommy the thumbs up and quietly headed for the stair opposite from where they heard Joey.

The mezzanine was not uniform. Where Dan went up it consisted of a single row of offices jutting out over the main floor. Half way down the length of the warehouse, it stepped forward with another row of offices. The corridor ran in front of the offices along the narrower part and then split in two where the mezzanine jutted further out. One corridor went straight and became an enclosed hallway servicing the rear offices. The other jogged left and went around to the front of the expanded mezzanine to access the front offices. There the corridor was enclosed with glass in a vain attempt to keep the dust and dirt from the warehouse out of the offices.

When Joey heard no reply, he took out his phone and called Benny. "Where the hell are you?" he yelled into the phone.

"Out front."

"Anyone come in?" Joey asked.

"No, we're both out here. Haven't seen a thing."

"Shit. Get in here quick. He's inside."

"How could he be?" Benny asked.

"How the fuck do I know? Someone's on the main floor. I heard him. Get in here." And he hung up.

Dan was about half way down the first part of the walkway when the front door opened. He dropped to the floor. When Joey's men were through the door and looking around, Tommy's shotgun roared. One of the men went down, his chest torn open with a large red stain spreading on his shirt. The other started to run and was knocked to the ground by the second blast from the shotgun. The shot hit him in the groin and hips. He turned to fire as Tommy loosed another blast that hit him in the head and torso. He twisted on the floor for a moment and then stopped moving. The first man was moaning and gasping, barely alive.

Joey, hearing the shotgun blasts, stayed hidden in the doorway of the last office. He had a clear shot down the corridor. He waited. If his guys didn't get Dan, Joey would when he came around the corner, there was no other approach. Recognizing the sounds, he wondered why Dan would use a shotgun. He expected an AR15 or Kalashnikov type carbine, not a shotgun.

Before the shotgun blast, Doreen had begun to pace again. Walking kept Ray from getting ahead of himself in the romance department. She gave him plenty of enticing looks indicating she wanted this to be over so they could get on to more fun things.

When the shotgun fired, Ray headed to the door. He turned his back on Doreen, his attention now on what was going on outside the room. Before he reached the door, Doreen grabbed the back of the metal chair and swung it over her head with her arms fully extended. She brought it down across Ray's shoulders and head with all the force she could generate. The gun dropped from his hand as he grunted and fell to his knees. Without hesitation, Doreen swung the chair again and brought it down on him. He slumped to the ground. Then she grabbed Ray's gun and retreated to the corner of the room farthest from the door.

With more strength than Doreen could imagine, Ray got to his knees, grunting. He turned his head back to Doreen and looked at her like he didn't know who she was. "F-f-fuckin' bitch," he stammered as he tried to get to his feet.

"Stay there. I don't want to shoot you," Doreen yelled. She held Ray's pistol, a .45 semi-automatic, in both hands. Her whole body was shaking; the gun wavered and shook as she tried to keep it trained in Ray.

Ray didn't make it to his feet. He crawled forward towards Doreen and tried to stand again. "F-fuckin' bitch," he said again, this time a little more clearly.

"Stay back!" Doreen shouted now. "Don't come any closer."

Ray stopped moving forward and grasping the edge of the table, he slowly levered himself upright. He swayed and would have fallen if not for the table. "You gonna pay for that. Why the fuck'd you do that?"

Doreen didn't answer. She just kept the gun pointed as best she could at Ray's chest.

Then Ray lurched forward. "Gimme the gun, you bitch," he mumbled, his eyes wavering, rolling. He looked like he couldn't keep Doreen in focus. He took another step, and then another.

"Stop!" Doreen screamed now. But Ray kept shuffling, forward, slow and unsteady, his eyes now beginning to focus on her with a dark intensity. She closed her eyes and squeezed the trigger. Nothing happened. She squeezed harder, pulling it with all her strength. Nothing happened. *Oh God. It won't fire!*

Ray took another unsteady step. Doreen's mind raced. She had to think. The gun had to work. What was stopping it? Suddenly she remembered; guns have safety switches. Where was this one? Frantically her fingers felt around the weapon hunting for a switch of some sort. She couldn't take her eyes off Ray. He had murder in his look now as his head got clearer. He took another step, this time more steady. Another step. Doreen's fingers found a lever. She tried to move it up; it would not go. She pushed down and it flicked into a new position. Ray stepped forward. The gun fired, almost jumping out of Doreen's hand. The bullet hit him high on his right chest almost at his shoulder. Ray fell sideways and reached out towards Doreen, trying to grab her ankles. She squirmed sideways and backed herself along the wall out of his reach.

"Fuckin' bitch," Ray said again. He struggled to move.

Tommy turned to the rear after taking down the two at the front door. There had to be men stationed out back, at the loading docks. They would be coming in one of the back doors. He scanned them frantically, not wanting to get surprised. Suddenly a door creaked open. He turned to it and without hesitation, brought the shotgun around and let off two blasts at a man coming through. The man backed out of the door with only a few buckshot pellets hitting him in the chest and arms.

"There's a shotgun inside and no cover," he shouted to the other two. "Jesus, I almost got killed just opening the door."

They looked at each other. "How do we get in?" one of them asked.

"No way I'm going in there. I'm not getting killed for Joey. That guy Dan's a killer and he's got a big ass shotgun.

Let Joey take care of him." He turned and hurriedly limped towards his car holding his wounded arm. The other two hesitated for a moment and then ran after him.

Joey heard the .45 go off in the next room. Then he heard the shotgun fire again from downstairs. He took a deep breath and moved out from his hiding place. He stepped to the door where Doreen was held.

"Ray, what the fuck you doing shooting?" He opened the door. When he started into the room, Doreen fired off two rounds from Ray's pistol. Joey backed out and shut the door. His mind reeled. What had just happened in there? As he was getting ready to open the door and storm in, someone called his name.

Joey spun around. Dan shot him in his right shoulder. He staggered back. "What you doing up here?"

"Thought I was downstairs? That's Tommy. He's got my back."

"How'd you get in?"

"Through the tunnels."

"What the fuck?" Joey said, not understanding. Then he pointed with his left hand. "Doreen's in the room. She's not hurt. I was going to trade her for you leaving town. You can have her if we can make a deal." Joey was trying to get his right arm to work. If he could get his lower arm muscles to work without engaging his shoulder, he could bring his pistol up and shoot Dan who was walking towards him. Dan didn't have his carbine shouldered.

"I'll get her. It's you I want now."

"Didn't mean to hurt Rita, you know that," Joey offered.

"Don't plead, Joey. It's not like you. You enjoy being the tough guy, knocking others around, especially when you have help. You've killed your share and beat up your share, so don't start trying to sound innocent. I know how you worked Tommy over. I could let him shoot you with the shotgun, but this is my mission."

"Fuck you, Dan. Fuck you and fuck Rita and fuck your kid. Your life's ruined no matter what you do to me." Joey lurched and swung his arm forward. In a moment he would have a bullet in Dan's chest.

The .223 rounds came quickly, one after another. Joey heard and felt the first two, but not the last two. He crumpled against the wall at the end of the corridor. His pistol lay in a pool of blood at his side.

Tommy shouted up from the main floor, "What's going on up there?"

Dan shouted back. "Everything's okay up here. You okay?"

"Yeah, the guys from the back started in and then backed out after I shot at them. I think I heard a car drive off."

"Keep watch. I'm gonna get Doreen and come down."

"She all right?"

"Yes, I am," Doreen shouted from the room.

Dan opened the door and Doreen ran into him. "You son of a bitch!" she shouted as she tried to hug and slug him at the same time with Ray's gun waving wildly.

"Give me that before you shoot me." Dan backed up from her onslaught. "Tommy's waiting for you at the end of the hallway, down the stairs." Doreen turned to run to where Dan pointed.

"Doreen's coming down," Dan shouted down to Tommy who went over to the stairs, still keeping his eyes on the back doors.

Dan entered the room and found Ray lying on the floor, crawling to the table in an attempt to get to his feet again. He looked as Dan walked up to him. Dan stood over him for a moment with Ray's gun in his hand. Then, without a word, he brought it up and shot him through the forehead, and then through the heart. He stuck the gun into his belt, turned and walked out of the room.

After checking Joey, he headed to the stairs and came down to find Doreen and Tommy in a tight embrace. "Stay here." He checked the two guys Tommy had shot. The second man was dead, but the first man was still hanging on. He wouldn't make it, and Dan made sure with a shot through the head with Ray's gun. Next he went back to the rear and opened one of the doors. The rear lot was empty. Nothing moved.

Going back to Tommy and Doreen, he said, "Let's get out of here." They both nodded and all three climbed down into the tunnel.

Chapter 63

When they got to the car Dan called Carmine. "I finished what I had to do, but you have a mess at your warehouse. You better send some boys over to clean it up." He gave him the address.

"What do you mean, 'mess'?" Carmine answered

"You'll see when you get there. I wouldn't leave it. One of your problems just got solved as well. I'll be in touch about my bill." And he hung up.

His next call was to Jane. "We're done. I've got some friends with me, where can we meet?"

"Meet me where we first spoke," Jane replied. Dan acknowledged and disconnected. They drove in silence to the underpass where Dan and Jane had their first conversation in the van. They were there only a couple of minutes when Jane drove up in the Suburban. She had two men with her. They got out and watched the perimeter. Jane handed Dan and the others plastic Tyvek overalls and told them to put them on over their clothes.

"Get in the SUV. One of my men will drive your car, Tommy."

"Where we going?" Tommy asked.

"Somewhere safe to lie low," Jane replied, looking at Dan.

"Where we were before?" he asked. She nodded.

They quickly drove off. When they reached the safe house and unloaded in the garage, Jane directed them to the main bathroom. She spread a plastic cloth on the floor and instructed Doreen and Tommy to strip everything off on the plastic and get immediately into the shower.

"We'll dispose of your clothes. I've got new ones for you."

"Why?" Doreen asked.

"You have gunpowder residue all over you and your clothes, like a fingerprint. They have to disappear."

"There is a .45 that has to disappear as well," said Dan.

"All the weapons have to disappear," Jane replied.

"Even my Remington?"

"Especially your Remington."

"Damn, that's a good rifle." He wanted to be angry, but couldn't raise the emotion. He was drained.

"What about my car?" Tommy asked. "We sat in it. The gun bag was in it."

"We're going to treat your car to a wash and detailing like it's never had before. It'll seem like a new car when it's done. It's on the house." She smiled at the two of them. "I'll leave you two alone, get stripped, and don't step off the plastic until you step into the shower." They left them alone and went downstairs. In the back was another bathroom where Jane had Dan go through the same procedure.

"The clothes and guns will disappear like I said. Get cleaned up and we'll talk."

"What about Tommy and Doreen?" Dan asked.

"I've got some food and drinks laid out for them in the bedroom. They'll be fine, but they're going to have a deep, restful sleep."

"You're going to drug them?" Dan asked in surprise.

"Just a sedative in their drinks. It will calm them down and nature will take over. I imagine this has been an exhausting day for everyone, but especially for them. They need to sleep, and we need to talk."

Later Dan and Jane sat down in the kitchen. She poured each of them a snifter of bourbon, neat.

"No ice?" He took the glass.

"Just hold it, inhale it, savor it. Remember this is the good stuff," she said.

Dan bent over the glass and inhaled deeply. He coughed, and then more gently breathed the aroma of the whiskey. "This smells so smooth and rich."

"Now you can sip, but slowly. The mission is completed. It's time to think slowly, decide slowly, and be sure of what you choose. Just relax and enjoy the present. The battle is over and there's nothing for you to do at the moment. Savor it, like you savor the bourbon."

Dan took a sip and rolled it around his mouth. "It's not thick, but the taste is thick. That's odd. No harsh or sharp edges."

Jane smiled as she watched him.

He concentrated on the bourbon for some time, staring at the glass, focusing on it, driving all other thoughts out of his mind. They scattered but kept creeping back in like wolves surrounding him, closing in on him. He focused harder now, not sure what would happen if they overran him. He had reached the end, but where was he? He didn't know. He had not thought about this moment, not planned for it. It was always something out there, the completion of the mission, his retribution for a terrible wrong done. He had often imagined righting that wrong, but now that he had completed his task, what had he righted? Dan felt a hollowness creep in, an emptiness. He was drained. What would fill that now? The thoughts circled closer, dark images, flashes of Rita flitting around the edges, no recovery for her; no redemption for him.

His body slumped lower in the chair. He grasped the glass tightly with both hands. Jane watched. She knew his mind was going places she couldn't go, places she shouldn't intrude. She waited.

Dan began to quietly sob, drawing harsh breaths, trying to keep it down, keep the emptiness at bay. But it came, like a tide, inexorably flowing into and over him. The shadows closed in.

"I took my revenge. Joey's dead. But nothing's changed. Rita is still gone, the baby gone. What good did it do them? It seems like it didn't do me any good either. Where am I now? I almost killed two of the few people who care for me. Now I wouldn't blame them if they came downstairs to announce they were leaving and never want to see me again. I didn't know what it would be like to get my revenge, but now that I've exacted the retribution, it doesn't feel like anything. I'm still where I was, without Rita."

Jane took a sip from her glass. "You took apart a bad crew. You brought justice to Rita's killer. No, none of that brings her back and none of that dissolves grief. It isn't meant to. But it balances the scales."

"How?"

"I don't know, but somehow. The people who do evil have to pay. They must not get away clean. I don't know why, but I just know it doesn't seem right. If the universe is just, they must reap what they sow."

"Then why don't I feel better? Feel some satisfaction?"

"There may be no satisfaction in retribution, in making the bad guys pay the price. Maybe we shouldn't look for it there...in that act. But I do think the act is necessary."

"Which is why you do what you do?"

"I'm not sure. I know that I want to strike the enemy. We seem to be getting softer, the agency is becoming politically correct, and people are operating more and more under the CYA principle than working to be effective against the bad guys. So I've carved out a subset of the mission where I don't have to be PC, where I can bring action to the issues and take the fight to those who want to take down our country."

"And they let you do that?"

"So far. I'll take it as far as I can go. The higher ups may not think much of my group. They may not want to think of us at all. They may just think we're a safety valve, letting off some pressure that allows them to continue to play politics, to play around at the edges while not ruffling feathers in DC.

Dan's interest dissolved as a fresh onslaught of grief came over him. "I don't think I'm your man. I feel empty, drained. My reason for doing is over. There's nothing left to do. I've delivered my payback. Delivered it to the ones who deserved it and now I'm done...and done in." He bowed his head, staring at the floor.

"No you're not," Jane said in a sharp voice. Dan looked up at her. "Don't you fall for that melancholy crap. I know your demons are closing in, telling you it's all over. I know you still grieve and, now, finding your revenge didn't provide closure for that grief, you're getting all weepy and thinking it's all over. That's crap. You didn't do this for healing. You did it for retribution, to balance the scales. You know that in your heart. I think, from what you've told me about Rita, she would agree."

Dan continued to stare at her.

"I don't know if Rita would have wanted you to pursue this path you took, but I damn sure know she wouldn't want you to give up on life, on doing something useful, something to make a difference. You're better than that."

Jane sat back, her face flushed. She hadn't expected that outburst. She had hoped to remain under control, calm and cool.

"For a moment you sounded like her," he said, finally. "My sister said this path wouldn't heal the hole in my heart. I heard her, but said I had to do it anyway. Maybe I didn't believe her. Now I know she was right." He sat up straighter in the chair. "I did what I set out to do and now I guess I've got to suck it up and move on." Dan seemed to have made a decision. "Tell me more about this private mission of yours."

Chapter 64

In the morning, after a huge breakfast, Tommy and Doreen were briefed on what they were to do next. Jane told them they had gone camping in the Poconos. She had arranged two people to stand in for them. They were seen on surveillance cameras, but wore hats that always partially hid their faces. Size, hair color and length were a match. Tommy and Doreen would meet up with them and collect their receipts, continue the camp experience and return in two days. When questioned by the police or FBI, they would state that when they heard that Joey had returned to town, they decided they had to leave for their own safety and a camping trip seemed the best way to hide out.

Their car was delivered, fully cleaned, and they departed. The goodbyes were cool. Tommy and Doreen had mixed emotions. Dan had involved them, put them in danger, but had saved them in the end.

While putting his story on tape in the hotel, Vincent became violently ill. Food poising was suspected and later confirmed; possibly by a sou chef who had subsequently disappeared from the kitchen. Vincent was near death for weeks and his throat was so damaged that he couldn't speak afterward; probably because the cops forced him to vomit up the poisoned food, which may have saved his life, but damaged his vocal cords.

Mike Warner put together the testimony as best he could and went to work attacking the mob. Everyone had lain low, a few of the capos did some time, but Silvio was never prosecuted. Carmine endured a lengthy trial which resulted in a hung jury.

Vincent, Sheila and the girls relocated to Dayton, Ohio. Sheila opened a beauty salon called the Brooklyn Hair Palace. She brought in some genuine New York beauticians to lend it an air of authenticity. She had found her calling as an entrepreneur and enjoyed spending her days running the shop, chatting up her customers. She specialized in stories about life in Brooklyn that everyone thought were fanciful and made up. The women loved the exciting east coast flavor she brought. Sheila instinctively understood that the ladies came for more than haircuts and beauty treatments; they came for the pizzazz and spice Sheila provided.

Tiffany and Amber spent a difficult year adjusting to being regular teenagers. But by the second year they had made some good friends. They were survivors, like their mother and father.

Dan slept most of the way during the drive. He and Jane left the day after Tommy and Doreen had departed the safe house. A heavy layer of fatigue flowed over him and he didn't resist. There was nothing left to do, so he let himself slide under its surface. He was vaguely aware that they were not driving to Camp Peary. The camp was located near Williamsburg in the tidewater region of Virginia. It was a 9,000 acre military reservation officially known as the Armed Forces Experimental Activity center. Within the camp was a facility affectionately referred to as "The Farm", a covert CIA training center. It was here that Dan would hone the skills needed to enter into his new role.

Near evening they stopped at a quaint mountain log cabin nestled in the Monongahela National Forest. When the forest was set aside, a number of the houses that were taken over were renovated and now rented out to guests who wanted to get away to the quiet of the backwoods but enjoy the benefits of a roof over their heads.

"What are we doing here? You abducting me?"

Jane smiled at him. "The thought may have crossed my mind, but business before pleasure." She grabbed her bag and headed to the cabin. "Get your pack and bring in the food," she called back over her shoulder.

The cabin was made of logs; one story. It had a living room with a stone fireplace at one end. On the other side was a kitchen. In back were two bedrooms and a bathroom. It was small but comfortable. Outside was a front porch overhung by an extension of the roof. A wooden rail traced across the front edge of the porch. On one side was a rack of firewood stacked alongside of the cabin; the other side held four Adirondack style wooden chairs. It was nestled into the hillside and looked like a natural part of the landscape

"So, really, what's up?" Dan asked as he came inside lugging the bags.

"Some R-and-R is what's up. You've just come off of a period of intensity that few have experienced. You need to rest before you start your training."

"I won't argue about that. You have a preference for bedrooms?"

"Take whichever one you want. I've never been here before."

After dropping his gear in one of the rooms, Dan came out to find Jane with two glasses of bourbon in her hands. She handed one to Dan.

"To a mission accomplished." She raised her glass.

Dan nodded and took a sip of his drink. "You're going to corrupt me with this high quality whiskey. I won't be able to drink the cheap stuff if this goes on too long."

"Enjoy it while you can." She gave him a bright smile. Her eyes flashed and her whole face lit up. Dan couldn't help but smile back. She was a thoroughly good looking woman. Not glamorous and immediately eye catching, but someone who pulled you in. Maybe you had to combine her looks with her sharp personality. She knew who she was and you suspected she knew what she wanted.

He watched her move about the cabin—athletic, nimble. Her attractiveness, even her sexuality, was embedded in her movements. Observing her, Dan could see depths beneath the surface that she kept under control. They didn't show unless you looked close, but they were there. A bit like Rita he thought. He could feel his face cloud over for a brief moment as Rita's image came to him mind.

They did very little most of the week. Dan hiked in the forest every day. Sometimes Jane would accompany him. He liked the way she could effortlessly keep up. When he walked alone, he thought of Rita. Thinking of her was still painful, but moments of pleasure—the good memories— began to creep in. *Maybe this is how we heal. We remember the good parts and hold on to them. Let them fill the spaces.*

In the evening they would sit by a fire and talk; the weather was cool at night in the mountains. There were long moments of silence. Jane would sit, not interrupting the quiet, not knowing, but instinctively guessing that Dan needed the silence but also needed the company in the silence. She was doing her part by just sitting there. She was happy to do that.

This man was different than others she had known. She had experienced the climbers, the manipulators who worked the system. They seemed to her to not be of much use except to move up in position. They would figure out what was needed and perform, not for success as much as for recognition. Thankfully the two would combine often enough.

Then there were the adventurers, in it for the adrenalin rush. They were the risk takers. She found herself attracted to them, but quickly learned they were not stable partners. She found herself just another challenge for them on their endless journey of thrills. Jane learned to keep them at bay.

And there were the mercenaries, the killers. They seemed to enjoy the thrills of a dangerous life, but were driven by other things; their demons, or money, or both. She avoided entanglements with such men. It was dangerous and generally sabotaged a mission.

Dan was different from them all. He had taken on the mob, single-handedly. Not for gain, although he admitted to her he had found it lucrative, but for revenge—payback. When that was accomplished he had ended his mission. From what she could discern, the killing (and he was good at it) had not destroyed his soul. He retained his own sense of morality through it all. She liked that.

Jane smiled. He did have a boyish charm. She could see it in his eyes, just as she had seen the darkness in his eyes before he set out on his killing spree. He was a mixture of youthful charm and deadly killer. She found herself drawn to him. *Careful, girl.* She could not afford to risk the larger mission by falling for her hired assassin. *Remember, that's what he will be.* Still she could not put aside those feelings.

Dan's energy returned. He began to grow restless as the week came to a close. "Maybe it's time to get on with this new mission," he said one night.

"You rested? Ready?"

He nodded. "Don't think I'm going to get more ready. I'll only start thinking about the past months if I sit around too much longer. Time to get on with it."

Jane studied him closely. "How do you feel now that it's over? Any demons haunting you?"

Dan gazed away, into the distance of the room. "No. I think I've got a certain ability to compartmentalize. It's over so I shut that off. I know that's probably not healthy, but that's a habit I developed in Iraq."

"But will that come back to haunt you? Most people can't do what you did. And if they did, they would be emotionally scarred."

Dan shook his head. "I don't feel it." He turned to her. "You think I'm a freak?"

"No." She looked into his face, now youthful, filled with his question. "You're very special. I haven't figured it all out, but you're different from others I've worked with."

Dan leaned forward, towards her. "Look, you've given me a new lease on life, a life after death, so to speak. I know what I'm setting out on is not normal, but it's a chance for me to have a life, to do something beyond what I just completed. I'll never let go of Rita...or the loss the fire brought...family, normalcy, or as much of it as we could create. But now I can have purpose in my life, even if it's not a normal one." He smiled. "I'll take that."

They left the next morning. Jane fought off urges to go into Dan's bedroom on that last night. *Can't jeopardize the mission.* Little did she know Dan had spent much of the night wrestling with his own urges to join her. In the morning, after a quick coffee and something to eat, the two of them loaded the car and drove down the gravel drive.

The cabin sat alone again, tucked into the mountains. The two who left it were off on a new adventure. Where it would end up neither of them knew.

The End

Afterword

Payback is the first of a new thriller series I am writing. You can follow Dan's adventures along with Jane and some other memorable and surprising characters in subsequent books.

If you enjoyed this story, please consider writing a review on Amazon. Reviews do not have to be lengthy and are extremely helpful in getting a book noticed. I very much appreciate your support.

In *The Shaman*, Dan heads to Mexico on his first assignment. Things don't go according to plan as you will read.

Other novels published by David Nees:

The Shaman; Book 2 in the *Dan Stone Assassin* series
The Captive Girl; Book 3 in the *Dan Stone Assassin* series

After the Fall: Jason's Tale; Book 1
Uprising; Book 2 in the *After the Fall* series
Rescue; Book 3 in the *After the Fall* series

For information about upcoming novels, please visit my website at *https://www.davidnees.com*. You can sign up for my reader list to get new information. Scroll down to the bottom of the landing page to click on the "follow" button. I never sell my list and you can opt out at any time.

You can also find me on Facebook;
www.facebook.com/neesauthor

Thank you for reading my book. Your reading pleasure is why I write my stories.

Made in the USA
Coppell, TX
06 February 2021

49615053R00207